THE LIE
OF THE LAND

First Published in Great Britain 2014 by Mirador Publishing

First edition: 2014

ISBN : 978-1-910104-54-5

Mirador Publishing
Mirador, Wearne Lane
Langport, Somerset
TA10 9HB

THE LIE OF THE LAND

Patrick Gooch

WHEN FORMER JOURNALIST, DANIEL KINDRED, IS PLUCKED FROM THE RANKS IN THE AUTUMN OF 1914 to work for the War Propaganda Bureau, the horrors of the battlefield are exchanged for something far more deadly.

Kindred enters a world that feasts on the excesses of Germany and its warring partners, publicising their acts of aggression and ruthless oppression.

Success invites reprisal. Saboteurs set out to halt the work of the Bureau.

When Daniel takes on responsibility for propaganda in the United States, he is seen as a prime target; and narrowly escapes several attempts on his life. The dangers increase when he befriends Clare Johnson, European correspondent of the New York Herald.

With the spectre of revolution looming over Russia, seriously weakening its resistance in Eastern Europe, Great Britain and France desperately seek another partner in the conflict. The pressure mounts on changing the mindset of the United States: a country that remains stubbornly neutral.

However, an elaborate scheme, carefully laid by Kindred, might just prompt a reversal of their stance. But it entails working within Berlin, the very heart of the German war effort..

Time is running out. If Russia succumbs to revolution, its military machine will collapse, allowing Germany to redeploy its battalions in the west. If that occurs the British and French lines will be overrun - all would be lost. . .

CHAPTER ONE

London, 1914

'Kindred! Get in here. . .now!'

I rose from my seat in the corner and walked slowly towards his office. It was a typical Monday. Everyone at their desk, the hub-bub of loud conversation, the furious ringing of telephones, the clacking of typewriters, and intermittent cries of "copyboy". Yet, for the briefest moment, the room stilled when the editor's door was wrenched open and he bellowed my name.

All eyes followed my progress. I reached the threshold and hesitated.

'I said, get in here. . .and shut the door!'

I sidled into the room.

'Sit down!'

I perched on a chair.

Geoffrey Robinson stood the other side of the desk. His clenched fists squarely placed on its leather-covered surface. Outrage suffused his features.

This is it, I thought. Six years hard work about to go up in smoke. Why on earth did I join the others Friday lunchtime when the piece was unfinished.

'I've just received a phone call from Bourne's office. I presume you know to whom I'm referring?'

I nodded.

'Do you know the reason why?'

'I think so.'

Robinson was not a tall man, but he seemed to rear over the desk at me.

'You think so! You think so! How, in all that's holy, could you write something like that? It's unthinkable that a newspaper such as The Times could be associated with such idiotic prose! When I took you on to do page nine, I regarded you as someone who knew the boundaries. Who would work to the prescribed formula Not go off on flights of fancy!'

I sank low into the chair.

Robinson grabbed a copy of the Saturday newspaper, feverishly skipped through the edition, and held up the offending page.

'Look! Look at it! Our many readers have! God knows what they will think. The people in Bourne's office are furious. Do you know what proportion of our readers are Catholics? More than half... and you write stuff like this!'

His finger ran down the column beside the photographs.

'Here it is. . ."Giuseppe Sarto was fond of cooking. He was especially creative with his rigatoni and linguini. But his favourites were ossobucco and risotto dishes, learned from his mother in their Lombardy home of Riese."

He threw the pages to the floor.

"What the bloody hell were you thinking? The man has just died, and instead of listing his achievements, you write about him being a first-class cook! Then you tell readers that, being a poor family, Giuseppe would often go with his brothers and sisters to catch freshwater trout and whitefish to supplement the family meals! This was supposed to be the obituary of a pope, not some village postman!'

'That was his father.'

'What?'

'The village postman. . .that was his father.'

'Listen, you were employed to write obituaries. The obit for Pope Pius the Tenth was prepared long ago, ready for the moment his death was announced. All you had to do was ensure his passing was listed in Births, Deaths and Marriages on the front page, and insert the appropriate dates in the obit for page nine. Who agreed you should change it?'

'Well. . .no one. But the copyboy showed you and the sub-editor what was written.'

'I don't need to read obits. They're standard fare. All I expect from you is to update existing records. No embellishments, no personal interpretations, nothing fancy or questionable. Now I've got Archbishop Bourne, the Primate of England, baying for my blood!'

He was working himself into a lather. Any minute now he is going to throw me out on my ear. What newspaper could I work for next, I wondered briefly.

There was a perfunctory knock on the glass-panelled door, and Wickham Steed walked in. He, too, had a copy of the Saturday edition under his arm. Wickham Steed was Lord Northcliffe's right-hand man. I have never fully understood the relationship between the titled owner and this bearded, ascetic-looking individual who had just walked through the door. Though, one thing I did know. Wickham Steed was often employed as the newspaper's "lord high executioner". If Northcliffe wanted some distasteful act performed, he called upon the services of WS.

Robinson's gaze fell upon the folded paper.

'Hello, Henry. If you have come about the obituary of Pope Pius the Tenth, I have the culprit right here. Has Cardinal Bourne's people been in touch with you as well?'

Steed glanced sharply in Robinson's direction.

'No. Why, should they?'

'I was telling young Kindred he should have stuck to our way of doing things. No fancy add-ons,. Obits are too serious for whimsical comment. He should have given the Pope's death due deference. Praised his lifetime's work as priest, prince, then Supreme Head of the Catholic Church,' declared Robinson forthrightly.

'All he had to do was insert the date and time of his demise. But no, he

4

had to tinker with a perfectly sound, well-researched summary of his life. The result, we are being lambasted at every turn, and made to look a laughing stock in the Street!'

Robinson's face was now a mottled red.

Any moment now the axe was about to fall.

'Actually, Geoffrey,' murmured Wickham Steed, 'I rather like the human touch brought to the piece. Have you read what the others have written about Pope Pius? Most of them have produced a catalogue of righteousness and selfless acts. Where was the man behind it?' He stared questioningly at the editor.

Robinson's eyebrows twitched. A look of puzzlement was added to his bright pink complexion.

Wickham Steed continued. 'More importantly, the old man likes it. And that's what I came to tell you. Perhaps we should liven up the obits with more personal revelations in the future. It portrays the man, or woman, in a far more accessible light. Not of marble on a pedestal, but as a real person.'

He glanced at Kindred, nodded and turned on his heel.

At the door Wickham Steed turned and said. 'Obviously you approved Kindred's piece before it went to press, Geoffrey. So well-done both of you.'

The silence lasted for a full minute after the door closed.

Eventually, Robinson's features assumed their normal bucolic hue, and he found his voice.

'I would say you came within a hairs-breadth of being fired, Kindred. Go back to your desk. In future I want to see every scrap you produce. One step out of line and out you go!'

I walked back through the press room. Again all eyes followed me. The grin on my face told its own story. The editor's voice, when raised to the level when everyone is party to what was said, was invariably the precursor to some hapless reporter being demoted, moved to another Northcliffe newspaper, or sacked.

Here I was, jauntily returning to my desk having braved the editor's wrath.

That day, my standing rose among my fellow journalists. Secretly, I realised I should never have drunk so much before finishing the Pope's obituary. In the afternoon it seemed right to tell the world of his life-long passion for cooking pasta dishes. In the cold light of the Saturday morning, when I read what I had written, that mellow glow had been replaced by the gut-wrenching feeling that come Monday morning I would be looking for another job.

It had been a close-run thing.

CHAPTER TWO

Thereafter, whenever he walked into the press room I felt Geoffrey Robinson's gaze upon me. With the approval from on high, he allowed me the occasional deviation from the factual, no-nonsense obit; but now, each submission was carefully scrutinised before being passed to the sub-editor.

When notables of rank were featured on page nine, the rules were strictly applied. There was no leeway for those likely to pass on in the near future: whose life's work had been meticulously compiled and filed.

I was twenty-six, and had been with The Times for two years, having first acquired a grounding in press journalism on a provincial newspaper. My parents owned two grocery stores in Worthing, and it was expected I would join them in the business. However, my Italian mother clearly saw the benefits of a good education, and encouraged me to apply for a scholarship to nearby Lancing College. I sat the entrance exam, and to my surprise, was awarded a place at the school. Tuition was free, but there were any number of additional charges, which my mother and father had to meet.

It was a strain on their resources; and later, attending university was out of the question. Particularly, as they also had to provide for my sister and brother's schooling. So, I began working in the store in South Street close by Worthing Town Hall.

I tried to disguise my lack of enthusiasm. After several years learning the art of trading in comestibles, I was quite despondent. Journalism was what I really wanted to do. At Lancing, I had been praised for my writing, and won several prizes: even picking up a national award. Weighing foodstuffs, wrapping them in brown or blue bags, marking and adding up the prices on scraps of paper was not how I envisaged the future.

My father saw through the façade. Unlike, Peter, my brother, who looked forward to donning a boater, a long apron, and attending upon customers, he came to realise my interests lay elsewhere.

It was he who introduced me to John Ashby, the assistant editor of a local newspaper. This led to an interview, and the offer of a job as copyboy, tea-maker and messenger at the paper's offices in Arundel. Within a week I had acquired lodgings in the town in Maltravers Street, a mere two hundred yards from the gabled and timbered building housing the West Sussex Gazette.

I delighted in my new job. I was a junior learning the ropes; but I could foresee this was my destiny. I had long yearned to become a newspaper reporter; and at last, I had been set upon the right path.

I worked at the Gazette for six years. By 1912, I had made my way from general dogsbody to chief reporter. Being a provincial paper, one covered every sort of news story - flower shows and village fêtes to criminal cases and personality interviews. It was a good grounding for the move that came from a totally unexpected quarter.

Someone happened upon two of the editorial features I had written that year. One was about Charles Dawson, the solicitor who came across the skull known as "Piltdown Man". The other covered the exploits of José Weiss, the gifted artist and aeronautical genius who developed and flew gliders and powered aircraft on the South Downs. Weiss had an infectious, likeable personality, and this, with his achievements, came over in the lengthy piece about the aviator.

It would appear they caught the eye of a reporter working for the prestigious London Times. He showed my work to Geoffrey Robinson, and I was invited to London for a brief word with the editor. A week later I was offered a job working on obits. Another major rung on the ladder beckoned.

All went well, until that fateful Friday, when a surfeit of alcohol had so nearly triggered an untimely return to the provinces. I had escaped being fired, but Robinson had a long memory. It would be hard for him to accept Wickham Steed's intercession when on the point of administering the *coup de grâce*.

'Are you going then?'

Walton's head appeared over a filing cabinet.

'Sorry, Ian?'

'I said, are you going to Mr X's bash at his place in Kent? We are all invited, apparently. Even you.' Walton grinned. 'You can then thank our Mr Steed in person for saving your bacon.'

I was puzzled. 'Who's Mr X?'

'Mr X, my friend, was the sobriquet of our esteemed proprietor, Baron Northcliffe. When he bought The Times in 1908, he didn't want anyone to know, and suggested he be referred to as Mr X. Not really necessary, we discovered his identity within the first week. Still, we went along with his supposed anonymity.'

'Where's his place in Kent?'

Giles, one of the sub-editors was passing.

'It's in the village of St Peter's, near Broadstairs. We are all going by train, as we do each year. It's a two hour journey, but you'll find it's worth it. Plenty of food and drink. We always have a splendid time.'

That June morning there must have been about sixty people who took the train from Victoria to Broadstairs. Thereafter, we walked the two miles along the North Forelands Road to Elmwood, Lord Northcliffe's residence. They were not only from The Times, but The Daily Mail, The Mirror, The Evening News, and several other journals owned by his lordship.

We were greeted by the masters of our respective papers, and led to tables

7

laden with refreshments. Over coffee and biscuits, Geoffrey Robinson nominated the teams for the archery competition, the tug-of-war, and the likely individuals for a tennis tournament. I was selected for the team events.

I soon discovered that I had little talent as a toxophilite, sending my first arrow off into the countryside. I fared little better with the second. The third, by dint of luck and a helpful crosswind, hit the straw target, landing in the red zone.

'Good shot, Kindred,' declared Walton, as he stepped up to loose his arrow.

By a slice of good fortune we managed to beat our opponents and won through to the next round.

As the morning progressed, the refreshment took the form of wine, beer and cider. I was enjoying myself. The competitions, though lighthearted, became more intense as people strove to win.

Called for the second round of the tug-war, I could see we would be little match for those representing The Evening News. We were only The Times' 'B' team.

We lost the first pull quite convincingly. Taking the strain for the second, I tried to anchor my feet by stamping into the ground. But our efforts were futile. Suddenly, I was skidding along the grass and it was all over.

As losers we were given a hearty cheer. But I was more concerned about the grass stain I had acquired. I went to the tent to refresh my glass of wine, and attempt to rub away the stain.

Whilst occupied, a voice boomed. 'Aggravating things, grass stains. What you need to do is treat it with a mixture of water, white vinegar and alcohol. Go up to the house, cook will sort it out for you.'

I looked up to see my adviser turn back to the group he was with, which I suddenly realised included the editors of the various newspapers.

'It's Kindred, isn't it?'

At my shoulder was Wickham Steed.

'Yes, Mr Steed.'

Remembering Walton's comment, I steeled myself and added.

'I must thank you for your intervention a few weeks ago.'

'Really. . .what was that?'

'I was in Geoffrey's office when you came in and mentioned the Pope's obituary. You found the reference to his cooking skills lightened a sombre portrayal of the man.'

'Right. . .so?'

'I believe Geoffrey was on the point of firing me for its inclusion.'

Wickam Steed burst out laughing, and slapped me on the back.

'I didn't know that. Well. . .well. . .well. Lord Northcliffe, can I interrupt you for a moment. Let me introduce,' he turned round to me. 'What's your Christian name?'

'Daniel.'

'Let me introduce you to Daniel Kindred. He does the obits in The Times. He's the one who wrote about Pius the Tenth's abilities in the kitchen.'

'Are you now?' murmured Northcliffe. 'I enjoyed your touch. It struck just the right note. Not unkindly, just showing the other side of someone who had attained high office, who lived an exalted life. What are you drinking? Is that red wine? Henry, could you organise a glass for our young friend?'

He drew me by his side, saying to the coterie of senior executives around him. 'This is Daniel. . .Daniel Kindred. He works for Geoffrey doing the obits.

`What I like about this fellow is his notion to bring a more personal approach to the pieces we feature in The Times. Not just recording the status and achievements of individuals, but touching upon the more down-to-earth aspects of their lives. Making them appear more human. That obit on our late, venerable Pope cast him in just the right light.'

I noticed Geoffrey Robinson was peering introspectively into his glass.

Before I could excuse myself, informing the host I was wanted for the next round at the butts, he began expounding about the military build-up in Europe. The way he spoke strongly suggested he had been warming to the theme before my introduction.

I stood there hesitantly, looking for an opportunity to slip away.

Someone thrust a glass of wine into my hand.

Northcliffe was a forceful speaker. Even if you did not agree with him, it would be easy to be swept along by his oratory. His editors were. The barrage of editorial in all their newspapers railed against Asquith's government over its failure to prepare for war.

It would be thought impolite to move away whilst he was in full flow, so I drank my wine and listened. Unconsciously, my glass was taken from my hand and I was given a replacement.

It was evident Northcliffe was on his current hobby-horse.

'In his articles for The Clarion, Blatchford wrote of the dangers Germany posed for Britain. In one piece he stated, "I believe that Germany is deliberately preparing to destroy the British Empire", and warned that Britain needed to spend more money in defending itself against attack. Don't forget, he went to see for himself what was going on. Blatchford travelled extensively around Germany. He had ample opportunity to gauge attitudes, to see what the Kaiser was up to.'

I drank my wine and quietly considered what he was saying. The heads of the editors were nodding in agreement. I noticed several others in the party seemed to be inwardly questioning his words.

'We have to mobilise our forces now. Give them the arms and ammunition to act as the bulwark against the inevitable. Mark what I say. Germany will ally itself to Austria against Russia and France. We shall support France, then the balloon will go up. It's going to happen. Let's be prepared for it.'

He glanced in my direction.

'What do you think, young Kindred? After all, you'll likely be in the front line.'

I put down my empty glass on a nearby table.

'Like you, I believe war is inevitable, sir.' I paused. I had missed breakfast to get to the station early, and the intake of alcohol was easing the brake on my tongue.

'Quite a few nations are standing by, waiting for the Austro-Hungary Empire to fall. It has reached the end of the road. For some, it will be a blessed relief, for others it signals an uncertain future. Who knows who will give it that final nudge. When it crumbles, that's when the in-fighting will begin. Thereafter, internal squabbles will quickly escalate to suck in other combatants. And they are waiting in the wings. The blood-lust is up. Let's have a scrap. But the reality is... '

By now I had turned to face Northcliffe. Everyone else seemed to have retreated into the background.

'The reality is, what happens afterwards? What do you think the outcome will be? I'll tell you. Despair - because no one is ever an ultimate victor. The vanquished will lick their wounds, and make reparation. The winners will go home and count the costs. But no payment they receive will bring back the many dead, the bread-winners of bereaved families.

'Take the Franco-Prussian War in 1870 as an example. The French lost, and were made to pay five billion gold francs, and part with Alsace Lorraine. They also deposed Napoleon the Third, who led them into the fray. The war lasted less than a year. I believe the total number of dead, on both sides, was around two hundred thousand.

'Go further back to the early eighteen hundreds, to the Napoleonic Wars. They lasted twelve long years, and the number who died in battle was well over two and a half million. In both instances, one can broadly say the cost was around a quarter of a million lives lost each year. How do you make good those sorts of human losses? Assuage the suffering, overcome the pain and likely destitution of being without a loved one. Now, with today's sophisticated weaponry, just imagine what the carnage will amount to when we wage war.'

I suddenly became aware of the others. In particular, Geoffrey Robinson, whose look was thunderous.

'Kindred, you've said enough,' he murmured fiercely.

'Are you a conscientious objector, young man?' Northcliffe enquired in a low voice.

'No, sir. When the call comes, I shall be one of the first to enlist. All I'm saying... '

'Enough, Kindred!' declared Robinson angrily.

Northcliffe glanced at him. 'Just a minute, Geoffrey, let him finish.'

'All I'm saying, sir, for all the tub-thumping and rallying to arms, will the outcome be yet another military exercise in futility. Nothing gained, nothing lost. . .except those who gave up their lives for an imperfect cause. Perhaps, Asquith's softly, softly approach is right. Perhaps he foresees the consequences of a blood-bath.'

We lost the next round in the archery competition. In fact, The Times' sporting prowess was woefully lacking in all the events. Not that I was concerned about the results. What occupied my mind more was the parting remark Robinson made late in the afternoon, when we were leaving for the railway station: "See me, in my office, first thing Monday!"

'What have you been up to, Daniel?' Walton enquired as we strode towards Broadstairs.

'I rather fear that I have well and truly blotted my copybook this time, Ian. I had too many drinks on an empty stomach, and intimated to our lord of the realm he was war-mongering.'

CHAPTER THREE

'What do I do with you, Kindred? You're a loose cannon. What on earth possessed you to tell our proprietor he was far too bellicose. . .misguidedly itching for the country to go to war?'

'I didn't say that.'

'Not in as many words, maybe. But the inference was plain enough.'

He leaned back in his chair, and stared fixedly at the ceiling.

'I may have to let you go, Kindred. You don't fit in here. You'll infect the others if you persist with your conduct. I can't have that. It would be bad for morale.'

He swung forward suddenly, and placing his elbows on the desk, rested his chin on steepled fingers.

'I'll tell you what I'm going to do. Go home, go anywhere, for the next week and think earnestly about your future. Take yourself in hand, then come in and tell me to my face that you will adhere strictly to the conventions of this office. In addition, during your absence from the press room, you will write a letter to Lord Northcliffe, apologising for your unwarranted comments at his garden party. It is only on that basis that I shall allow you to return to the newspaper. Do you understand?'

I left the building, ignored the omnibus and tram, and strode out along Fleet Street, down the Strand in the direction of Victoria Station. At the booking office I bought a ticket to Worthing.

My parents have a large Victorian house overlooking the sea in West Worthing. I walked the mile or so from the station along West Parade to what I still regarded as home. In this instance, as sanctuary.

'Hmm... I can understand Mr Robinson's dilemma. From time to time I've come across similar situations with the staff in our stores. By the way, did I mention that Peter has his eye on premises in Littlehampton, which could become out third outlet. What do you think of that?'

He paced up and down the sitting room.

'Never mind. . .that can wait. Let's deal with the immediate problem. As I said, Daniel, I have encountered something of the sort at work. One individual contrives to do something not in keeping, and even if it does not upset trade, you can't afford to let such things pass. Someone has to set procedures, and everyone must abide by them. If not, and people do what they think, it's the quickest road to a collapse of business.'

He stopped mid-stride.

'In the second incident, from what you've told me, it could be seen as undermining authority. It stands to reason one doesn't openly air a entirely different viewpoint from your boss when in his company and those of your peers. In their eyes it might be thought diminishing. You must see that, surely?'

'I. . .I suppose so, father. But he did ask my opinion.'

'I thought by now you were wise to the ways of the world. He wasn't asking your opinion. He was asking you to agree with him.'

I pondered on his remark.

'No, I don't think so. My belief is he's not that sort of man.'

'So, are you going to take Robinson's advice? Are you going to toe his line?'

'I will do what he requires of me in the press room. But I shall not be writing to apologise to Northcliffe. I felt he wanted a true opinion, not a sycophantic reaction to his utterances. I leave that to his editors.'

CHAPTER FOUR

'What's this? Your apology?'

'No, it's my letter of resignation.'

He stood to look me in the eye.

'If I accept this, you won't work for The Times again while I'm in charge. You realise that, don't you?'

'Mr Robinson, the conflict draws ever closer. When it does I shall volunteer. We are only talking about weeks, not even months. When I return. . . .if I return, I shall go to work for a provincial paper, where I am involved in all that goes on. Here, I'm just a cog in a huge enterprise. I'd probably have to wait years for the opportunity to make my name as a journalist. So, on reflection, it will not be too much of a disappointment.'

He nodded thoughtfully. 'Do you know, I was going to bring you out of obits in a few months time, and start you on reporting. Now, do you want to change your mind?'

'I don't think so. You see, I couldn't fulfil the second part of your demands. I gave it a lot of thought, and came to the conclusion that when Lord Northcliffe asked for my assessment, I would have been false to myself to give him anything other than my firm beliefs.'

Geoffrey Robinson leaned over his desk and shook my hand. As I was shutting the door, he suddenly said. 'I am not going to accept this, Kindred. It will remain here, in my drawer, until you come back from the war. If, as you say, you come back from the war.'

I was working in my parents' store in South Street on the fourth of August, when Great Britain joined Russia and France in declaring war on Germany and its allies.

CHAPTER FIVE

They were mostly local lads, drawn from the towns and villages between Brighton and Bognor. It seemed, even before the ink was dry on the recruiting posters, they had begun arriving at Shoreham. The town was the enlistment centre for the 24th Division, part of Kitchener's Third Army. K3 as it became known.

I signed on in September 1914.

After the perfunctory health check, I was one of the few issued with a thick woollen tunic, dyed khaki. A stiffened peak cap of the same material, puttees for wearing round the ankles, and ammunition boots with hobnail soles. They also had steel toe-caps, and a steel plate on the heel, making them uncomfortable to wear and hard on the feet when walking any distance.

I realised why I had acquired a uniform when directed to a tented encampment in a field on the outskirts of the town. The unseasonably, cool September weather was not ideal for living under canvas; and though provided with a field kitchen and latrines, my introduction to military service was far from what I had envisaged.

Initially, there were no instructors to train recruits, few uniforms and no small arms. Regular servicemen returning from abroad found themselves posted to Shoreham to pass on their military skills.

Rifle practice, without the use of ammunition, was conducted in the community hall. Parades and marching drills were conducted on the concreted yard of a local farm.

This early training, we were informed, was to instil discipline, the ability to take orders, bodily exercise and an "early to bed/early to rise" routine.

When it came to washing and changing our clothes, the army inserted a notice in the local paper displaying a tariff of charges, and asking for laundering services from the housewives of Shoreham.

Perhaps Northcliffe had been right in questioning our preparedness to engage with the enemy.

I had been in the army a fortnight; and following yet another parade, a number of us were marched to the hall for a bout of rifle practice. We had yet to shoot a bullet, but I could clean and dismantle the moving parts, point, and squeeze the trigger at a target.

'Bang!' I said forthrightly. 'Another Hun consigned to his maker.'

'No jokes, Kindred!' shouted Sergeant Rogers, our instructor. 'You just wait until you have the real enemy in your sights. Then you'll find out if you can kill another human being.'

He was an experienced soldier, having served in India for some years.

'You could be right, Sergeant. When confronted, when it's kill, or be killed, I wouldn't question my instinct. But to take the life of some unsuspecting soul from a distance. . .that's all-together different.'

He stared at me for a moment. Then walked over to where I was standing.

He came close, and looked up into my face. He was a short man, with a bustling air and a manner of self-importance. I am six foot, and he had to crane his neck.

'If I ordered you to, Private Kindred, you would do so, and no mistake.'

'Do you know, Sergeant. . .I'm not sure I would.'

'Private, I could have you for insubordination! You would do as you're ordered! Do you understand?'

A door opened. Out the corner of my eye I was aware someone had stepped into the hall.

'I understand perfectly, Sergeant. What I'm saying, and at the moment it is purely hypothetical, is could I kill someone so dispassionately. That has yet to be discovered.'

'You impudent upstart! You would do as you're bloody well told! Even if you were in a firing squad and ordered to shoot a British soldier! Do I make myself clear?'

'You do. . .and I wouldn't Sergeant. Not even if it meant me standing alongside the victim.'

'That's it, Kindred! The charge is insubordination! '

He turned to the others. 'You four. . .step out. Escort the prisoner to the command post!'

As we made our way to the officers' hut, whoever had come into the hall followed in our footsteps.

Sergeant Rogers went into the adjutant's room. They exchanged a brief word. The commanding officer was notified, and we were beckoned forward. My escort stopped at the door, and Rogers and I marched in to stand at attention before his desk

'Right, Sergeant, what's the charge?'

'Insubordination, sir.'

'Give me the circumstances.'

'Well, sir, we were performing rifle drill and Private Kindred declared he would not shoot at the enemy. He openly refused to obey an order. I had no choice but to issue the charge.'

'What do you have to say to that, Kindred?'

Before I could reply, there was a sharp rap on the door, and the adjutant eased into the room. There was a whispered conversation, which ended with the commanding office saying. 'Show him in. . .show him in.'

A moment later the adjutant opened the door, and stepped aside to let Wickham Steed enter.

'Still getting yourself into hot water, I see, Kindred,' he said, a smile touching his lips.

I sat in the passenger seat of the Austin Vitesse. Not only was I surprised by his sudden appearance, but at the colour of his vehicle. Invariably, Wickham Steed's manner was distant, almost withdrawn: his style of dress, ultra-conservative. Yet here we were, bowling along in a twenty horsepower, bright red motor car.

'I'm bewildered. You say you want me to meet someone, and so you come all the way from London to find me. By the way, how did you discover where I was?'

'From the Times' records I learned where your family resided, and that they had a grocery business. It was a simple matter to come upon Kindred & Sons in Worthing. I spoke with your father. He told me you had enlisted and were stationed at Shoreham. It was quite straightforward.'

I thought about his explanation for a few miles.

'So, what was in the letter you handed to Colonel Bryant? And who is this person who wants to see me?'

'I can't tell you his name. Not yet anyway. But the letter was written by Lord Northcliffe, and stated that you had an important task to perform. It was a military matter of the greatest urgency, and as a serving soldier your duty was to return with me to London immediately.'

'But I no longer work for Lord Northcliffe or The Times.'

'Daniel, you are still on our books as an employee. So don't ask me any more questions, I shan't answer them. Northcliffe simply told me to find you and bring you back to London.'

'OK, just one more. . .where in London?'

'The War Office in Whitehall, of course.'

CHAPTER SIX

I was still dressed in my private's uniform. An insignificant figure between two high-ranking betters who led Wickham Steed and I along tiled corridors in the cavernous building.

We came to a tall, mahogany double-door. One of our escorts knocked, and one side was promptly opened. We were ushered through.

Seated at a large ornate desk, I instantly recognised Lord Kitchener, The Secretary of State for War. This side of the desk sat three gentlemen. One of whom I knew - Lord Northcliffe.

'Do I see a member of my regiment?' Kitchener boomed, staring at the patch on my uniform 'You are most welcome, sir. Come, take a chair. You too, Henry. Tell me, young man, why we have your presence here today?'

Fortunately, Northcliffe responded. I could not have said why.

'Herbert, Private Kindred worked for me on The Times before he enlisted. As a journalist his writing embraces a personal touch that reaches out to the common man. Moreover, in his role as a soldier, he has acquired a wider appreciation of what they can endure, what one might expect of them. I have brought him along, for if the need arises, he can give us what could be lacking, a deeper understanding of the public and our forces' needs.'

'Right. You are most welcome, Private Kindred.'

My immediate thought was that my erstwhile employer had over-stretched my contribution to the war effort. Two weeks training in an ill-fitting uniform hardly qualified me as someone with a comprehensive knowledge of British soldiery.

'Now we are all here, shall we get on?' asked Kitchener.

An aide said to him in a low voice. 'We are still waiting for Colonel Swinton and Mr Tomlinson, sir.'

I was still perplexed. Why had I, an inexperienced recruit, yet to witness battle, been picked from obscurity and plunged into the very heart of British military power. But the thought quickly left me when there was a knock at the door, and a tall military figure and a civilian came into the room.

Upon their arrival, Kitchener rose from behind the desk and led us to a large conference table, where I found myself seated between Northcliffe and Wickham Steed. Kitchener sat at its head. There was a brief silence while he scanned each of our faces, before turning to his aide.

'Michael, I want you to take notes of this discussion.'

Then, with both hands gripping the table edge, he opened proceedings.

'Now the object of this meeting is to consider the need, or otherwise, of a unit to produce and circulate propaganda material in countries not engaged in the current conflict. I believe you all know, or at least, know of each other.'

He paused briefly, and turned towards the two men last to arrive.

'F. E. Smith could not join us today, but he sent Colonel Swinton to represent the War Office Press Bureau. As you are aware, Swinton is responsible for producing the reports of the British Army's endeavours on the Western Front. In this regard he is soon to be aided by Mr Tomlinson here, a journalist presently with the Daily News. As I understand it, the Bureau is not in favour of a propaganda unit, and believes that, with a minor extension of its role, it could encompass such duties. I won't say more at this stage. I'll leave it to Swinton to elaborate on their line of thinking.

'On the other hand, Lord Northcliffe and his people are fully in favour of the notion that a separate office, devoted to circulating news about the legitimacy of British military action, telling the people of other nations why they should support this initiative, should be established with all speed. Thus, we have two conflicting opinions.'

Kitchener half turned in Northcliffe's direction.

'Frankly, Alfred, I'm not convinced either that we need this additional press service. But I'm prepared to listen to what you have to say. So, would you like to give me your reasoning behind such a proposal?'

'Thank you, Herbert, I'll begin by asking Charles Masterman to tell what the Germans are about. Charles, as you know, following stints in the House, is currently with the Treasury. He also enjoys fame as an author, and importantly, as a journalist. Charles.'

Masterman was sitting the other side of Northcliffe. For some reason I took careful note of this fresh-faced, individual who rose from his chair.

'Thank you, Lord Northcliffe. Gentlemen, I'll stand if you don't mind. Then I can see you all the better.'

He was older than I thought. I put him in his early forties.

'I have little doubt F.E. Smith's team, headed by Colonel Swinton, would do a sound job within the limits of their organisation. More especially with the guidance brought to the War Office Press Bureau by Mr Tomlinson. But would it stand up to the professionalism being brought into play by our opponents?'

He looked around the table.

'I think not. . .for several reasons. We are well acquainted, I'm sure, with the name, Matthias Erzberger. But are you aware he has created the *Zentralstelle für Auslandsdienst*. This translates as the Central Office for Foreign Services. An innocuous title for a well-organised propaganda unit funded by the Foreign Affairs Department of the German Government.

'It deals principally with printed matter, collecting and studying works from all perspectives for its information. However, its main task is to distribute German outpourings abroad – purchasing suitable material from publishers and encouraging or commissioning propaganda. The majority of their work is in the form of pamphlets, books, official documents, speeches, fiction. . .even anthologies of war poetry and children's books.

'Make no mistake, it is a highly-efficient machine employing over a hundred writers, journalists and photographers. Moreover, they have groups of people devoting their efforts to specific countries. USA, naturally, but they are also targeting all the neutrals in Europe including Turkey.

'Frankly, I doubt Colonel Swinton and his team could match their productivity or the scope of their activities. We have to fight fire with fire. We need to get across our message forcefully, and with the same degree of coverage. Gentlemen, although at the moment, there are only five principal combatants. However, there are at least a dozen neutral powers that, if they were to join in the conflict, could tilt the balance in favour of either the Entente: Great Britain, France and Russia, or the Central Powers: Germany and Austro-Hungary.

'Each side is seeking allies to their cause. In this case, use of the media could well decide the outcome. We cannot, I stress, we cannot be caught napping. To ignore such a profound weapon as good propaganda, which could be used to highlight the merits of our cause would be courting disaster.

'As I said at the beginning, the War Office Press Bureau might do a sound job, if the right structure were in place. But run as a military operation, we would lose the propaganda war. Let me make it clear,' Masterman paused deliberately, to give emphasis to his submission. 'Victory will only be achieved by devoting money and trained personnel to do an effective job. Because, at the end of the day, that is what this contest will come down to. . . a war of words.'

There was silence around the table when Masterman sat down.

Eventually, Kitchener said. 'Thank you, Charles. Colonel Swinton, he thinks you are not up to the task. How do you respond to that?'

Swinton rose to his feet.

'Of course we are up to matching what this.' He peered at his notes. 'What this Central Office for Foreign Services can do. Though, obviously, it would take a little time to bring people on board. The right sort of people. Those who understand the concept of warfare, and can justify why this nation has taken up arms against other countries set on territorial expansion.'

'It's not the concept of warfare, it's the effect of warfare on the man in the street.'

'Sorry, Private Kindred, I didn't catch that,' said Lord Kitchener.

I had muttered the remark under my breath. At least, I thought I had. I looked up startled. All eyes were upon me. I saw Northcliffe's eyes twinkle.

'I'm not sure I wanted you to, my Lord.'

'Come, come Kindred. You interrupted Colonel Swinton, so you have a point to make. This is an open discussion.'

I did not stand. My legs would not have taken the weight.

I cleared my throat as eleven heads swivelled in my direction.

'The Colonel declared that his bureau would employ people with the knowledge of warfare. Presumably, to convey a militarist point-of-view. In my opinion, no neutral country's population is likely to take much note of armies going to war in distant lands. To get their interest it would have to have direct, potential impact. To disrupt their lives or their livelihood.

'I totally support Mr Masterman's vision of the use of efficient, well-directed propaganda. But let me add, in this instance whatever the politicians, strategists and military types may feel is an appropriate course of action, in this instance, in democratically-run nations, it will be the people, the ordinary men and women in the street, who will decide whether their country should join in the fray.'

'Are you saying, Private Kindred, that people in high office, in command of a country's welfare and its economy, would have little say in the matter?' asked Swinton aggressively.

'In this particular instance. . .yes.'

'Absolutely preposterous! On what basis can you possibly declare such nonsensical reasoning?'

'Personal experience, Colonel. When you've been raised to work behind a counter in a family grocery business, you come to appreciate what governs people's outlook on many issues. You also learn how to bend them to your way of thinking. Believe me, if you want to influence national governments, first get the country's residents to be sympathetic to your cause. An overwhelming groundswell of public opinion could over-ride the earnest intentions of any head of state.'

'Rubbish!'

I shrugged. It was not my place to argue tactics.

'I think young Kindred has a point, Colonel,' remarked Tomlinson quietly. 'I've found some evidence to justify what he is saying at the Daily News, when we've conducted straw polls among our readers.'

'You can't tell me, Tomlinson, that the president or prime minister of a country, when about to pursue a course of action, can be deflected from carrying out his objective because a few inhabitants don't agree. I refuse to believe it!'

'I didn't think it would take you long to make comment about the military's attitude to propaganda.'

I twisted round.

Seated once more in the red Austin, I was next to the chauffeur. Northcliffe and Wickham Steed were in the rear seats.

'I didn't think anyone could hear my remark. I mumbled it without thinking.'

'How do you think he managed to stay alive in such spots as Egypt and the Sudan. Staying alert, and sharp hearing. It hasn't deserted him,'said Northcliffe over the noise of the engine. 'Anyway, I'm pleased you said what you did. Now we can move forward with the War Propaganda Bureau.'

'Really? How do you know?'

Northcliffe grinned, and rubbed his hands together.

'The Secretary of State for War took me to one side after the meeting and told me so.'

'Right. . .so how will it work?'

'Lloyd George, the Chancellor of the Exchequer, will have to confirm the appointment. But it's already agreed, Charles Masterman will run it.'

They were en route to Lord Northcliffe's London home in Belgravia.

As we drove down Victoria Street, I said to the driver. 'Can you drop me at the railway station, I can take a train back to Shoreham.'

Northcliffe's arm came over the top of the seat and clasped my shoulder.

'Didn't WS mention it? You're not going back. You've been seconded to a new post. You're the War Propaganda Bureau's first recruit!'

CHAPTER SEVEN

I did go back to Shoreham; but it was a brief visit. I collected my things and returned the uniform. Sergeant Rogers ignored me, and the adjutant said nothing while I signed for the pay that was due.

Then, I took an omnibus along the coast to West Worthing and stayed with my parents for several weeks. During that time I had several long telephone conversations with Charles Masterman, my new boss.

I had to explain to my parents why I was no longer a serving soldier, and what had occurred after Wickham Steed appeared at the army encampment. At first, there were looks of disbelief, which gradually changed to incredulity.

"You actually met Lord Kitchener? You shook his hand? You are going to work for the National Insurance Commission? What on earth will you do there?"

When the War Propaganda Bureau came into being, on Masterman's suggestion, I took rooms in a lodging house in Ebury Street. One room was a sitting room and a small kitchen. A door led through to a spacious bedroom. They were on the first floor at the front, overlooking the road. The bathroom was at the end of the corridor, which was shared with someone who occupied a room further along the landing.

The propaganda unit was established in Wellington House, situated on the corner of Buckingham Gate and Petty France. Masterman had been working on a project for the National Insurance Commission which occupied the building. With the need for anonymity, he decided to house the unit within the confines of the organisation. The flow of personnel in and out of the Commission would be the ideal cover for its activities.

On that first morning, Masterman and a half dozen of us, gathered in one corner of an uncluttered expanse, which would eventually be converted to our needs.

'Before we get down to business, gentlemen, I want to make a couple of things patently clear. This is a clandestine operation. No one must know what sort of work we are doing. If asked, tell them you are attached to the NIC at Wellington House.

'The second point. We are the nucleus of the War Propaganda Bureau,' declared Masterman. 'Our initial efforts will be the spur, the catalyst, from which the Bureau will develop. So, I am relying on you to do a first-class job. Our future depends on it.

'Now what I want is for each of you to take responsibility for the neutral countries. Everything connected to those powers uncommitted to the war must been directed through you. So that you have your finger on the pulse, you are aware precisely what is happening in your allotted territories. It would be ideal if you spoke the local language. So, let's go round the group. You can each tell me if you speak anything other than our native tongue.'

Surprisingly, most of us were fluent in German.

'Excellent,' said Masterman, 'that will certainly give us an edge when dealing with the competition.'

A few spoke French, and one of the group had a smattering of Russian.

'What about you, Daniel. Anything else besides English?'

'German, of course, adequate French, conversational Spanish, and colloquial Italian, Charles.'

'Really? Not many people show an aptitude for the romance languages. Where did you learn Italian?'

'At my mother's knee. She is Italian.'

'Well, that makes my task easier.'

There were eight neutral countries which could have an influence on the outcome of the war: Denmark, Italy, Netherlands, Norway, Portugal, Spain, Sweden and America.

Predictably, I got Portugal, Spain and Italy.

Two countries, of course, were critical in the propaganda battle – Germany and Austria. Alex Brewer, a journalist formerly with Reuters, was appointed to this critical desk.

Over the next weeks the offices gradually took shape. Partitions were erected; desks appeared; telephones, typewriters and filing cabinets were installed. Progressively, the once empty space was filled with researchers, secretaries. clerks and, importantly, the tea lady. Every member of the staff signed the 1911 Official Secrets Act.

As the months passed, we carefully studied what the Germans were doing. It was immediately obvious that although Great Britain was a nation with a strong literary tradition, it lacked an epic cultural mythology. German mythology, in the Nordic tradition, was perfectly suited to its militarist aims. Many German war posters contained images of dragons, Valkyries, and sword-wielding, Wagnerian style heroes. Portions of the Hindenburg Line were even given such names as Siegfried and Wotan.

Since the German government had effectively portrayed their struggle as defensive, they placed less emphasis upon recruitment. Not that they needed to. The German military machine had been slowly building its numbers for years.

Our immediate aim was to encourage young men to join up. Pointing the finger at those reluctant to do their "duty".

Meanwhile, besides writing articles for worldwide circulation to newspapers and magazines on the brave efforts of the British troops, I was getting to grips with the Southern Europe desk.

'Got a minute, Daniel?'

Masterman put his head round my door.

'Of course, Charles. I was just finishing a lengthy piece on the Battle of Ypres that I want to get out today. I must say our chaps did a first-class job repulsing the Germans, halting their advance to the Channel.'

'Yes, I heard about that,' he remarked. 'A month-long battle against superior odds. That will make an excellent story in the neutral countries' press.'

He slumped into a chair. 'Daniel, I want to know your reaction to something.'

'Right. . .'

'I've been thinking. We've got some excellent authors and writers in this country. People like Arthur Conan Doyle, Arnold Bennett, John Galsworthy, Thomas Hardy. What if we got a group of them to write short stories, books, pamphlets to aid our efforts. What do you think? I'm sure I could prevail upon some publishing companies to produce them for us.'

'A brilliant idea, Charles. They are well-known abroad, and would be a subtle, yet effective string to our bow. I wouldn't bother discussing it with our masters at the Foreign Office, I'd just do it.'

He rubbed his hands together.

'You're right. I'll get on to it straight away.'

While you're here, Charles, I think it would be practical to visit the capital cities in my purview. To gauge the strength of feeling about the war firsthand. I'll go through our embassies initially, then seek out likely officials who might provide a more incisive view of where they stand, and whether they are likely to side with us, or the enemy.'

Masterman did not hesitate. 'Sensible idea, Daniel. I'll speak to the Foreign Office and get them to pave the way. When are you thinking of going?'

'In a couple of weeks time. I've got a fair amount on at the moment, but I could clear it by then.'

'By the way, you do know that Sir Edward Grey, the Foreign Office Minister, had several discussions with the Italian ambassador and people from Rome not so long ago?'

'Yes, I want to find out what the reaction has been to Grey's offers. As I understand, he put part of Austria, Albania and even some of the Greek islands on the table. Overdid it a bit, I think.'

I was fortunate to get a passage on the Royal Mail Steam Packet Company's ship, *Arlanza*. It had docked in Southampton, having crossed the Atlantic from Buenos Aires. The next leg of its journey was to Lisbon.

I was shown to a cabin, and was unpacking my things when a knock came at the door.

'Come in.'

25

It was one of the officers.

'The commander sends his compliments, sir, and asks if you would care to dine with him this evening?'

Commander Down was an affable host.

It was a pleasant meal in his boardroom, and coffee had been served before he put the expected question.

'So, Mr Kindred, I'm intrigued. Why would the Foreign Office contact the company and request I include you on the manifest for the voyage to Lisbon? Is it some sort of covert operation?'

'Good Lord, no. I have to discuss a matter with our ambassador in Portugal. It concerns a possible move to other premises in the city. Housework. Of little account, Commander.'

He nodded, not fully convinced by my explanation.

'You see, sir, if we are stopped again by enemy ships, I do not want to be thought I am carrying a spy on this vessel.'

'Stopped again? How do you mean?'

He peered at me long and hard.

'We left Buenos Aires, and made our way up the coast towards Brazil. We were just about to take a different heading, turning north-east to cross the Atlantic, when a German cruiser, the Kaiser Wilhelm der Grosse, ordered us to heave to. Obviously, we did as they suggested. We could have been blown out the water.

'We were boarded and questioned. However, once the Germans realised we had women and children on board, they let us continue on our way. However, we had to do without our radio equipment, which was thrown over the side. I didn't enjoy the encounter, Mr Kindred, and neither did my passengers. The enemy could take a much harsher line if I were thought to be harbouring someone who was out to influence the course of the war. I'm sure you understand my concerns.'

'Absolutely, Commander.'

Back in my cabin I collected together all those documents that might reveal my intentions, put them in a bag, and weighted it with a pedestal ashtray. If we were boarded, evidence of my true purpose would be dispatched through the porthole.

CHAPTER EIGHT

I had several conversations with the ambassador, though more searching enquiries were raised with the political officer. I was aware of the status of Portugal, and the British government's reasoning that the country maintain its neutrality. As a senior secretary at the Foreign Office explained to me. "I hope you are not going to upset the applecart, old chap. Our people have been working hard to stop Portugal from declaring for us in this irritating conflict."

I had asked why.

'My dear fellow. . .Africa. That's the real hotbed. Germany and Portugal have long been at odds with each other over rights to territory. If our Iberian friends became our allies in Europe, when we win the war, they'd want us to surrender some of our African possessions. Can't have that, can we?'

The political officer in the embassy interpreted the situation a little differently.

'Portugal, as a nation, is weak, yet it still regards its holdings in Africa as supremely important. Why? Because they are symbols of the country's glorious past. They will fight hard to hold onto them. In my opinion that should be encouraged. Let them wage war on Germany in Africa. It will distract the Hun, and force them to send troops to Angola and Mozambique.'

I never did get to speak to any Portugese officials, although I walked the streets of Lisbon and picked up the mood of the people in numerous coffee houses.

Five days after my arrival I took the Sud-Express to Madrid.

The Atlantico Hotel is on the Gran Via, a short distance from the Puerta del Sol, a favourite gathering point for *Madrileños*. I left my case in the room and headed north for the embassy in Calle Fernando el Santo. It was a pleasant stroll, no more than a kilometre,

'Mr Kindred, how do you do? My name is Soames, Paul Soames, the resident intelligence officer. I'm afraid his excellency is tied up for the moment, and he asked me to greet you and help in any way I can. Tea and biscuits?'

Wherever the British establish a small enclave in some foreign part, the afternoon tea ritual never deserts them.

Soames led me to an office on the first floor, and a young lady appeared with a silver tray.

'Excellent, Daphne. Thank you.'

He poured the tea and proffered a plate of shortbreads.

After a few minutes, Soames placed his cup carefully on the saucer.

'Right, Mr Kindred, tell me how I can help you.'

'I'm sure you are aware, Mr Soames, that the Chancellor, Lloyd George, has authorised the creation of the War Propaganda Bureau.'

Soames nodded.

'I am one of Charles Masterman's people. In addition to producing a regular flow of pamphlets, leaflets and material for newspapers and various journals on our war effort, I also have a responsibility for Portugal, Spain and Italy. In that regard I have to determine whether or not our country would benefit from any of these nations coming into the fray on the Entente's side.'

'I would have thought our communiqués established that position already.'

'Forgive me, I am not discounting what you've sent to the F.O. It's more what the people in the street, the academics, the military, those whose voices have influence in political circles, feel about Spain's role in the conflict.'

'Hmm. . .you think that the common man is key to Spain's attitude to this war, do you? Well, I know for a fact King Alfonso is keen to uphold the neutrality of his country, regardless of what his subjects might wish.'

'That position may well stand for the duration. But, as I said, I would still be interested to learn what others feel.'

The ambassador said much the same thing.

This time over a gin and tonic.

'Sorry I can't entertain you this evening. Important engagement, you know. But Soames will act as host in my place.'

In the event I took Soames to some haunts close to the Plaza Mayor. We visited several tapas bars, before dining in one of my favourite restaurants.

The food was superb and Soames was enchanted, frequently repeating himself as the wine flowed. Eventually, I put him in a taxicab, much the worse for wear. But not before he had written the names and contact details of academics, men of influence and two military advisers on a table napkin.

The next morning I walked to the Central University, again no more than a short stroll from the hotel. Although the university has a long history, it is currently housed in a number of government-acquired properties – mainly aristocratic mansions and grand houses from centuries past, abandoned by their owners for more contemporary quarters. Though not without charm, these ancient buildings are not ideal as educational settings. Students often find themselves attending philosophy lectures and anatomy lessons in elaborate spaces that had once served as ballrooms and salons.

I was seeking Doctor Juan Valverde, a professor of politics and philosophy. According to Soames, much-respected in government circles. I was conducted by a gaggle of enthusiastic students to a lecture room in a nondescript building on the Calle San Bernardo.

'Are you a student, Señor? I don't recall seeing you before.'

He spoke with a Catalan accent, which had a slight guttural ring. I speak Castilian Spanish, and it took a moment for my ear to adjust.

'No, Professor, I am not at the university. I am a journalist, and I was hoping you would grant me an interview.'

He looked up sharply from his notes.

'Why would you wish to interview me?'

There was little use prevaricating further. 'I want to understand Spain's attitude to the war now raging in northern Europe? I am aware of the so-called official views, but what does the government truly feel about the war? Will it participate at some stage? Or will it stand by its neutrality?'

He rose from his chair; but even standing he was not much taller than when seated. He strode towards me, and staring me intently in the face, said in a low voice.

'You're English, aren't you? Your Spanish is good. . .better than good, but there is the slight trace of an accent. Why have you really come to see me?'

I nodded. 'I am English journalist. Moreover, I know you are a government adviser. It may be that you tell your ministers to hold to the party line of "no comment". I want to write about the thinking that prevails at such meetings. Why Spain has not come out openly and declared the country will maintain its neutrality, join the Alliance, or favour the Entente.'

Valverde gave a gentle smile. 'You're bold, young man, believing you can walk in here, simply ask and be told such high-level thinking.'

He hesitated for a moment, as though coming to a decision.

'Actually, I do advise our Ministry of the Exterior to make known publicly the government's true position. It would help the people to make up their minds. At the moment there is too much uncertainty.'

'I've only been in Spain twenty four hours. But in that short time I have heard any number of opinions expressed on the street. From what I can gather, the general view is that the country should back the German military effort.'

He shrugged. 'That's because the Germans are good publicists. They are painting themselves as defending their lands against British, French and Russian aggressors. Where they have moved into other countries, photos are being circulated showing how local residents welcome them with open arms. They are capturing the minds of the people. If the authorities are not careful, the decision could be taken away from them.'

He turned back to his desk. 'Now you must go. I have a lecture to give.'

I stood there for a moment, thinking that my request for an interview had come to an abrupt end.

But then he added. 'Come back and see me at four o'clock.'

****

I knocked on the door.

'Come in, Señor Kindred.'

However, with my first step into the room, I paused, ready for instant flight.

'Come in. . .come in'

He saw my alarm, and held up a hand.

'You have no need to worry about this gentleman. He is also a member of the forces liaison group, as well as being a close friend. Let me introduce him. Colonel Diego Calabozo, allow me to present Señor Daniel Kindred.'

I took a tentative step forward, and we shook hands.

'Don't get me wrong, Señor Kindred,' remarked Valverde. 'I am not about to give away my country's secrets. That would be unforgiveable. But I . .we,' he glanced towards the colonel, 'firmly believe that providing you with certain information will help to stabilise the situation. King Alfonso wants neutrality for his kingdom. But he goes out of his way to avoid saying or doing anything which might upset the balance. We firmly believe he is wrong. If you knew the facts, and were able to write material that demonstrated the tyrannical approach of the Germans, and what the British might do for this country if it sided with the Entente, we think it would have a significant effect. It would help steady the views in the street, which, you are right, at the moment are pro-German.'

'Are you aware of what the Germans are offering us, Señor Kindred?' enquired Calabozo. 'This isn't widely known. For one thing, what is proposed one week, is often altered the next.'

I shook my head.

'Last week they offered us sovereignty over Gibraltar and Tangier if the Alliance won. This week it's more. In addition to Gibraltar and Tangier, the suggestion is we could have territorial control over Portugal and French Morocco as well.'

'And they are offering you that in exchange for becoming part of the Alliance?'

'Of course,' declared Valverde. 'But in the long run it is our fervent belief we would lose more than we gained. We would become mere puppets of Kaiser Wilhelm and the Reichstag, a German satellite like Austria is about to become.'

'It's highly confusing. Let me get this straight in my mind. Your aim is to keep Spain neutral, right?'

They nodded in unison.

'King Alfonso wants the same thing, but is burying his head in the sand. If he does so for too long, the people might think him weak, depose him and declare a Republic.'

I stopped briefly to collect my thoughts.

'Now Germany could hasten this shift from a monarchy as a result of the strong pro-German feeling they are stirring up with the people in the streets.

And where the authorities are concerned, the people you are advising, they could well be tempted to take the offer of Portugal, Tangier, Morocco, and Gibraltar and join the Alliance. Does that sum it up?

'There are a number of side issues in all this,' said Calabozo. 'But, yes, that's broadly the situation.'

'OK, I think I've got the picture. What you want to happen is for the British to counter the publicity being circulated by the Germans, which would, hopefully, re-balance the general regard given to both the Entente and the Alliance. Doing that would safeguard the status of the monarchy, and maintain this country's individuality in world politics. It's a tall order, gentlemen, for a mere journalist. But I do have one or two friends in high places. I'll do whatever I can.'

I also had several conversations with Spanish politicians. But for the most part, their comments were anodyne, and to direct questions their responses were guarded. But I had a much clearer understanding of what was needed. Something that was lacking in the official reports sent back home by the embassy.

CHAPTER NINE

They first met at the Cookery and Food Exhibition in London during 1885.

He was keen to discover new products to sell in the family business; and because Sofia spoke English, she had accompanied her father, a trader from Trastevere.

The exhibition was held at The Royal Aquarium, in the back streets of Westminster in London.

He showed considerable interest in the salami the company was offering, and enjoyed several lengthy discussions with her about introducing it in his shop. When she had a free moment, he also offered to show her some of the sights of London.

In 1886, they were married in the church of Santa Maria in Trastevere, Rome's oldest church.

The following year, I arrived – Daniel Roberto Kindred.

The ship from Barcelona docked in Civitavecchia. An hour and a half later I got off the train at the Termini Station in Rome, and a cab took me to my grandparent's home in the Via della Luce in Trastevere.

The massive front door opens directly onto the narrow street. I heard shuffling feet from within, several bolts were drawn, and the door creaked open to reveal the peering stare of Antonio, their factotum of many years.

His rheumy eyes made the connection.

'E' Daniele! E' Daniele! he cried.

My grandparents hurried down the stairs from the sitting room on the first floor. Both had tears of joy running down their cheeks as they took me in their arms.

When, the bombardment of questions finally eased, and Antonio had made coffee, we moved out to the patio within the well of the building. I had answered all the queries regarding my parents' health, and how my brother and sister were faring. Grandfather was keen to learn about the new premises he was opening.

'And so, Daniele, what brings you to Italy?'

'Unfortunately, *nonno*, it's the war. I want to find out more about Italy's intentions. Is it going to join the Alliance in the conflict, or side with the Entente?'

His face dropped. 'Are you writing about the war, Daniele?'

'I am trying to gather material to write about it, yes.'

'A bad business. Why do we have to choose one side or the other? As you know, the company sells to people in all the countries fighting this war. Why should we shun our customers, many long-standing friends, because they are now shooting each other?'

There was little I could say.

'I tell you, Daniele, no one will win. No country ever does.'

My grandmother rose from her chair. 'You are staying with us I hope, Daniele? If so, I need to prepare your room. I'll get Antonio to help me.'

When she had gone into the house, Grandfather Roselli turned to me.

'Did your mother know you were coming to see us?'

'No, *nonno*, I did not mention it.'

So. . .it's a secret trip, is it? Some kind of official visit you don't want anyone to know about?'

He noticed my eyes widen slightly. His intuition had caught me out.

'I thought so. What exactly are you doing here, Daniele?'

'I really do want to find out what the Italian position is. I can't tell you who I work for, but you're right it is a semi-official body.'

'Are you a spy of some sort?'

I could tell he was upset. He did not want to believe his own grandson was plotting against his beloved country. That he might well be on an opposite side in the conflict.

'*Nonno,* I am not spying for anyone. My mission is to gauge the authorities' standpoint; the *cognoscenti's* attitude to Italy joining in the war, what side it would support; and whether the people would really favour close ties with the Alliance.'

I could tell he was not convinced.

'And how would such information be used?'

'Look, I am only too aware of Italy's links with Germany. They go back a long way. But if I wrote some articles that pointed out to Italians the truth is about Kaiser Wilhelm's exploits. . .that he is a land-grabbing tyrant, a megalomaniac bent on taking Germany down the wrong path. Well, frankly, it would be bringing home to people that any arrangement with this man could well lead to disaster.'

'But would associating with the Entente, France, Russia and Great Britain, serve us any better?'

'*Nonno,* I sincerely believe it would.'

He was silent for a long while, thinking about what I had said.

When my grandmother came into the room, I made my excuses, saying I had a meeting in the centre of the city, and would be back around seven that evening.

The British Embassy is situated in the Via Veneto district.

A letter of introduction had been sent to the ambassador in the diplomatic bag, but it was soon obvious he did not want to be acquainted with the reason for my visit. To the one question I asked. "What has been the response to Sir Edward Grey's proposals?", he was non-commital.

'Nothing yet. When I do, my first duty will be to convey their reply to the Foreign Office.'

He added quickly.

'I feel sure, Mr Kindred, that Fielding, our resident intelligence officer, would be best able to facilitate your needs. I'll call him in.'

A few minutes later a tall, cadaverous individual appeared .

'Ah, Fielding, there you are. Mr Kindred has arrived. Take him along to your office and sort out the arrangements he needs. There's a good chap.'

It soon became apparent that Mr Fielding's grasp of the language was as wanting as his grip on local affairs. An hour later I left the embassy with the feeling I would be better off without their assistance.

When I got back to Trastevere, my uncle Emilio, who took over the business when grandfather retired, was waiting for me. We embraced, but it was perfunctory. He was clearly perturbed. Evidenced by his first words.

'Daniele, you have upset, *il papa.* I am not happy that you have come here to obtain information for the British. Don't your Italian roots count for anything?'

'Forgive me, Uncle Emilio. I would not have that for the world. Perhaps, I should explain exactly what I am doing here, besides wanting to see my family.'

'I think you should, Daniele.'

'First of all, I am not a spy, as grandfather seems to think. But I am a British citizen, and, as you would expect, that entails certain obligations. They include recognising and honouring the monarchy. Another is being prepared to defend the country against attack. And doing one's best to uphold the laws and institutions that are part of the British culture.'

I cleared my throat.

'Having been raised in Britain, the loyalty I hold to that country may be contrary, in your eyes, to where my allegiances should lie. Alas, neither of us can change circumstances. But you have to understand, I love and respect you all dearly.'

I looked intently at him, before continuing.

'I was working for a newspaper in London, before I volunteered to join the army. However, I did so to fight the Germans. If Italy had been part of the Alliance, I would not have enlisted.

'Shortly after I became a soldier, I was recruited to join a department of the Foreign Office called The War Propaganda Bureau. They have a similar organization in Berlin - The Central Office for Foreign Services. In fact, they have been at it longer than us, and have turned the hearts and minds of the Spanish people in their favour. I get the strong impression that they have also been successful in this country.

'My visit, on this occasion, is to gauge just how effective German propaganda has been, and to determine how much the authorities are committed to the cause of the Alliance. I am well aware, Uncle, that Italy has had a close association with Germany in the past. I want to know if it is still as strong.'

He sat opposite me, stroking his chin. I had spelt out some obvious truths, which he had never thought to confront.

At long last, he murmured. 'I think the government is undecided. Do they throw in their lot with Germany? If they did what is there to gain? On the other hand, I can't see what they would achieve joining the nations in the Entente. You're right, the people in the street have absorbed the stories in the newspapers and magazines, praising the Germans for the defence of their country against those who would run roughshod over their lands.'

'It's all nonsense, Uncle.'

'That may be, Daniele, but they tell convincing lies. Frankly, I hope we stay out of it. Remain neutral. However, I don't think Germany would let us remain uncommitted. If we don't support them, we must be against them. In all likelihood their aggression would turn in our direction. Either way, we could become embroiled in the conflict whether we like it or not.'

The silence lengthened.

Eventually, my Uncle Emilio murmured. 'Perhaps I might be able to help you, Daniele. If you were to create counter arguments in the press, it might just balance the views of ordinary men and women, and influence those in authority to look more closely at what the Entente could bring to the negotiating table.'

Before dinner, my uncle had a quiet word with *il nonno.*

At the table the atmosphere was lighter, much more congenial.

Uncle Emilio returned the next morning.

'Daniele, I am going to introduce you to several people I know. Interestingly, they do the same job as you. The first is the political correspondent for *Il Messagero.* As you know it's a national newspaper, the most popular in Rome and central Italy.

Signor' Luciano was a dapper individual, well-dressed, but elegant in an obvious way. He was given, even for Roman, to expressing himself in a most flamboyant manner. His arm waving adding drama to our conversation. More so when *il mio tio, Emilio,* candidly revealed my mission.

'Excellent... excellent, that's what we need! More material about the British, French and Russian triumvirate. Well, perhaps not Russia. It's too close to what we have here. Ineptitude, corruption and inefficiency are rife in both countries. We are probably too indolent, but if the Russian authorities are not careful there could be revolution.'

He removed a heavily embroidered handkerchief and mopped his brow.

'Your uncle is right. This country's government is in a cleft stick, and at odds with the Italian people who, at this moment, are championing Germany.'

We spent the next hour talking about ways and means of redressing the balance.

Towards the end of the discussion, Luciano declared. 'If I were you I would visit Milan and Turin, also our main publishing centres.'

Uncle Emilio's other contacts repeated much of what was said by Signor' Luciano, though without the same level of embellishment.

Two days later I made my farewells, bought a passage on a ship heading for Marseille, then boarded another for Liverpool. Both voyages were without incident, and I travelled down to London on a crowded, uncomfortable , over-night train which finally steamed into Euston Station as dawn was breaking over the capital.

CHAPTER TEN

'I was surprised so many turned up.'

Charles Masterman was recounting the meeting he had held with noted authors.

'I invited about two dozen of them, and would you believe, thirteen showed up. The big names too. What is more, when I explained all about the War Propaganda Bureau, they declared to a man they would be more than willing to help. What about that?'

'That's really good news, Charles. When do they start?'

'About five can start now. The others have commitments and deadlines they are obliged to fulfil. But I reckon they'll all be working for us in three months time.'

Masterman rubbed his hands together. I had come to realise it was his favourite way of displaying pleasure at achievement.

'Right, tell me about your foray to foreign parts.'

It took over two hours to relate the substance of my trips to Portugal, Spain and Italy. When I had finished, Charles immediately remarked.

'It doesn't seem as if our so-called embassy specialists have their fingers on the pulse. Good job you found out what was really going on. Well done, Daniel.'

'I've almost finished my report on the visits, which will also include my recommendations on how we go about tackling the problems in each country. I'll get it typed tomorrow, and it will be on your desk in two days time.'

'Excellent. I'm going over to the Foreign Office on Thursday, I'll take it with me. Get them to shake up their people in these overseas havens.'

He added. 'On reflection, it might be worthwhile sending the others to their respective zones of operation.'

CHAPTER ELEVEN

The three of them met in the Flying Angel Club in Victoria Dock Road.

Run by the Missions To Seamen, the club, as well as the hostel and chapel in the main building, were open to all ships' crews coming through the port of London.

The Missions was founded a half a century earlier by the Reverend John Ashley. His Christian aim being to give practical, emotional and spiritual comfort, as well as welfare and emergency support to seafarers of all ranks, nationalities and beliefs. His efforts bore fruit. Many foreign ports now boasted MTS facilities.

The Flying Angel centres, set up later, provided a "home away from home", and were hugely popular with seamen at sea for lengthy periods.

However, while the concept was laudable, the current war footing of the major powers made it open to abuse.

The steady flow of nationalities made the Flying Angel an ideal meeting place. Disguising the imperfections in their command of the language, the three men mingled easily with merchant sailors from all parts of the globe.

With just minor changes, they had even retained their first names, Erik, Karl and Ernst had become Eric, Charles and Ernest. Moreover, their forged British seamen's tickets, were all that was necessary. No one bothered with surnames, particularly as they were often difficult to pronounce.

Each one of the trio represented a cell operating in London. Most of the time the cells worked independently, unless there was an operation which warranted their joint cooperation. This was such an occasion.

Eric, the acknowledged leader, murmured. 'I have received word from our chief, Steinhauer, that the British have established their own propaganda department. It is hidden in the National Insurance Commission office building in Buckingham Gate. The brief he has given us is to reduce its effectiveness.'

'How does our friend, Gustav, suggest we do that?' asked one sneering at the order. 'Kidnap all the people or burn down their offices?'

'Close, but not close enough. Initially, Gustav Steinhauer wants us to tread carefully. Harassment of the women who work there. Small accidents happening to minor personnel. Just enough to cause worry and uncertainty. Then. . .we hit them hard by taking out a senior member of the organisation.'

'When is this operation due to start?' queried a stocky fellow in a hard-wearing, seaman's jacket and a peak cap that had seen better days.

'From today. . .now. We shall commence the softening-up process immediately.'

CHAPTER TWELVE

'Have you seen Lisa? Is she in today?'

I was in Monty Beresford's office when Charles put his head round the door. Monty looks after the Netherlands' desk, and we were discussing ways of disseminating propaganda material.

'I haven't seen her this morning,' I replied.

Monty came from behind his desk.

'Is she in the general office?'

The space allocated to the WPB in Wellington House had changed markedly since that first get-together. Now it was sub-sectioned into corridors and rooms, the floor carpeted to reduce noise, and many of the walls sound-proofed.

She was not there, or in the small kitchen used by the tea-lady. One of the girls checked the ladies' cloakroom. There was no sign of her.

'Damn,' muttered Charles. 'Pretty inconsiderate. She should have let us know if she were not coming in.'

Just then the outer door swung open and Lisa Newman limped in.

'What's happened to you?' one of the typists cried. Several rushed forward to assist her to a chair.

Normally carefully-groomed and even-tempered, the young woman who worked for Masteman was incandescent with anger.

'Some bloody idiot! I was waiting to cross the road by Victoria Station, when someone bumped me. I fell right into the path of an oncoming taxicab. Fortunately, someone else grabbed my arm and pulled me out the way. But it was bloody close! The bumper caught my leg.'

I looked down at her torn stocking. Blood seeped from a gash in her knee.

'My saviour helped me to the entrance. I've still got his handkerchief. I promised to wash and return it.'

Lisa was clearly shaken by the episode, and several of her fellow typists escorted her to the cloakroom.

'That's a bad business, and no mistake,' said Beresford, voicing my thoughts.

'Come in, Daniel. Read what Conan Doyle has written.'

He handed me a sheaf of papers. It was headed, "To Arms", a recruiting pamphlet.

'Damn good, don't you think? It's exactly the kind of material we need.'

It took a moment to read through it. As Masterman said, it would certainly arouse those with thoughts of enlisting.

'It gives just the right message, Charles. Any other offerings?'

'I'm told there are several pieces in the post from H.G.Wells, and Kipling is currently penning some material. Though he did say they were more in the way of poems than prose. Other are working on articles and stories. So, it's a good start. Frankly, I am pleasantly surprised. Writers, traditionally, take a stand against the state and warfare. It's the implications of those pistol shots in Sarajevo that has shocked them. As Samuel Ratcliffe pointed out, "They have nearly all undergone a spiritual conversion".'

I passed him Conan Doyle's material.

'Of course, there were a few who didn't go along with the idea. Shaw held fast to his beliefs, as did Bertrand Russell, and some other lesser lights.'

He rubbed his hands together in his time-honoured ritual.

'But I'm delighted to say those who count are on board. Anything to say to me?'

'It's about the report. What time are you off to the Foreign Office?'

'Not until three. Why?'

'Jill Hadfield also ran into a bit of a problem this morning, and was late in. Still, if she's got another couple of hours, it will be ready for when you leave?'

'What was the problem?'

'Apparently, in the crush of people coming to work this morning, she was knocked down the stairs in the underground.'

'Good Lord, is she OK?'

'She's shaken. But it could have been worse. But don't worry, she is coping and working on the report.'

I glanced back as I left his office. He was staring thoughtfully out the window.

CHAPTER THIRTEEN

A similar incident occurred a few days later.

Masterman recounted what had happened to the assembled staff in the general office.

'It would appear Maureen Fowler, one of our women clerks, lives in Hammersmith. She was on her way home and walking through Green Park to the London Electric Railway Company's underground station .

'As you'll recall it was a dark evening, misty rain and swirling winds. Suddenly, from bushes along the path, two men sprang upon her. She was pushed heavily to the ground. and her handbag wrenched from under her arm. For good measure, one of the assailants kicked her in the head and ribs.

She was found unconscious and taken to nearby St George's Hospital, on the corner of Hyde Park. She was kept in overnight for observation. Fortunately, no serious harm was done, and Maureen is now at home resting. We shall not see her for the next few days.'

Later in the morning Masterman stepped into my office.

'Got a moment, Daniel? I've got a first-class piece by John Buchan. Shades of *The Thirty-Nine Steps*. It's an exposé of German atrocities when they marched into Belgium. Organise its translation, will you, and get onto the steamship companies for copies to go to Spain and Italy.'

'I'll do that right away. While you're here, what's your reading of the Maureen Fowler incident? That's another of our people in just a few days.'

'It could well be the fourth, Daniel. A young woman, working for the Commission, was dragged off the street and raped last week. The police were called, but there were no clues to who did the deed. All she could say was that there were two attackers wearing masks.'

'Do you think it's a case of wrong identity? Whoever they were, mistook the woman for one of ours? Are we being targeted do you think?'

'Possibly. . .despite our efforts to keep the lid on what we are doing, it was inevitable our cover would be blown at some point. A loose word, someone inadvertently mentions what they do here, and ears are sharp. We cannot ignore the fact that German agents are in this country just waiting for tidbits of information to feed back.'

I wondered if what I had disclosed in Italy had been passed on.

'I think it's time to take precautions,' muttered Masterman, almost to himself. He looked up.

'I'll have another chat with our people this afternoon, and sort something out.'

'So you see, while they may have been random attacks, and we've just been unlucky, we can't afford to take that risk. I have been studying all your files, and most of you live close to someone else in the office. For example, Janet here has a flat in Southwark, just across the river. Paul Swithers lives no more than ten minutes walk away. In future, we'll stick to the normal office hours and Paul will escort Janet to and from her flat. As I said, it works in quite a number of cases, and I'll hand round the suggested pairings for you to discuss with the chosen partner.

'The only unfortunate ones are Bob Brady, Daniel Kindred and Alex Brewer. These gentlemen should come and see me after this meeting.'

'I don't think I need a bodyguard, Charles. I take the underground train from St. James' Park, which is close by. I get off at South Kensington, and live no more than fifty yards from the station.'

Bob Brady was in charge of the American desk. With an American father, he had lived in the United States until his early twenties, before moving back to England with his mother. Bob was a gifted journalist and mixed easily with his American compatriots, who tended to congregate around the South Kensington area.

'I don't want you to take any chances, Bob. Nor you two,' he glanced at Alex Brewer and myself. 'If you are sure it's safe to walk that short distance on your own, OK. What about you, Alex?'

Alex Brewer was responsible for Germany and Austria.

'I have a friend who works in a government office in Petty France, just round the corner. He's trying to come to grips with this new Aliens' Bill which demands foreigners register with the police. At the moment we share a flat near Finsbury Park and travel together.'

'That's all right then. Daniel?'

'I usually walk to my place in Ebury Street, Charles. But until we know for sure whether we are in somebody's sights, I'll get a taxicab to take me door to door.'

Another development to aid the Bureau's workload was the formation of the so called "Neutral Press Committee", under the leadership of the former editor of the Daily Chronicle, George Mair. The Committee agreed to promote British newspapers and journals abroad as well as the transmission of "news abroad by cable and wireless". This was a bonus for Bob Brady, for news could now be broadcast by the many small, local radio enthusiasts in the United States.

****

By the early months of 1915 the Bureau was producing and translating into a dozen languages more than two thousand items of propaganda each week. These ranged from press articles, photographs, to pamphlets, posters and short stories. The publishers, Hodder & Stoughton, Methuen, Oxford University Press, John Murray, Macmillan and Thomas Nelson, all readily provided their services.

I was working on an editorial for the Rome paper, *Il Messagero,* writing the piece in Italian so it could be sent by wire that day, when Masterman burst into the office.

'Do you realise, Charles,' I said looking up, 'that we are no longer journalists, but publicists? Instead of writing the news as it is, warts and all, we now pick out the juicy morsels and inflate their value. We are becoming very selective. . .'

'Never mind about that, Daniel. This is far more worrying. Bob Brady has disappeared!'

'Several members of staff remember him leaving the building, and one of the typists saw him catch the underground train at St James' Park. He was supposed to be meeting friends. They were waiting for him at South Kensington. It seems he never arrived.'

Charles explained the circumstances to the heads of the various desks.

'Are you saying he got off the train before it reached South Kensington? ' queried Thompson, responsible for France and Belgium.

'It looks that way, Alistair. If he had arranged to meet up with a group of people, conceivably he would not have left the train without good reason.'

'Or he was abducted,' I remarked.

'What, taken by force?'

Yes, Charles. I can't think of any other explanation.'

Masterman's face grimaced with worry.

'I don't know whether to contact the police, or not,' he said.

'I'd tell the F.O. Let them decide. In all probability they'll call in the Special Branch,' I murmured.

'Hmm. . .it only happened last night. I had an important meeting scheduled with him this morning, that's why I'm concerned. Still, he might well show up with a plausible excuse for his absence. I'll give him another twenty four hours.'

Bob Brady had vanished without trace.

Special Branch officers interviewed us all, then checked the route, and where he might have been likely to leave the train. As there were only two stations before Bob reached South Kensington, it would have been Victoria or Sloane Square.

Charles briefed us on the investigation.

'Special Branch interviewed the ticket collector on duty at Sloane Square. He seems to recall, about six thirty, three men jostling past him, one of them being pushed along by the other two. They showed him Bob's photo, but he couldn't be sure. And there the trail ends. I'll keep you posted if anything comes to light. Daniel, wait behind will you?'

When they had gone from his office, Charles shut the door and returned to his chair.

'We've got a serious problem, Daniel.'

'True. Suddenly we're all rather vulnerable.'

'Hmm. . .if Bob has been taken, it's possibly by enemy agents. There are all sorts of networks in Britain. It could be our efforts are making them sit up and take notice. Perhaps they want to stifle us by kidnapping our key people.'

He leaned back in the chair. 'I should have said two serious problems. Bob's disappearance is one. The other is that he was off to America on Friday. Like you did in Southern Europe, to check the pulse, to get a fuller picture than that coming out of the embassy over there. Now, it looks like I'll have to cancel his trip, unless I can come up with a practical solution.'

'How do you mean?'

'Unless I can find a substitute. So what about it?'

'What about what, Charles?'

'Going to America on a fact-finding mission. You've done as much as you can on your patch for the moment. The Portugese will stay out of it, despite their enthusiasm to join the Entente. Spain won't budge from its disinterest in the whole affair. And Italy, thanks largely to your efforts, are showing much greater enthusiasm for the Entente.. In fact, I've heard a delegation is coming over to London shortly to discusss the finer points of an agreement. So what about taking on the American desk, until I can sort things out?'

CHAPTER FOURTEEN

I boarded the *SS Tuscania* after enduring a seven hour train journey. Owned by the Anchor Line, a subsidiary of Cunard, the ship sailed regularly between Glasgow and New York. Although a luxury liner it now had a dual purpose, carrying fewer passengers and plenty of much needed food supplies back to our beleaguered island.

That first evening, we were rounding the coast of Northern Ireland when the steward came to my cabin to turn down the bed. I started chatting to him, casually bringing up his sailing experiences. Then I pressed him on the attitude he had to possible attack.

He seemed quite unruffled by the situation.

'Aren't any of your fellow stewards concerned about the threat of German submarines?'

'Not really. Although there's a war zone around the British Isles, our route takes us too far north to interest the U-boats. I would say we are pretty safe.'

He thought he was lessening my concerns. In truth, I was trying to find out whether, in these latitudes, ships were ever likely to engage with the enemy.

It was an uneventful journey, for which I was thankful A room had been reserved for me at the Algonquin Hotel, in midtown Manhattan, just off Sixth Avenue. Before dinner I sat in the bar drinking a whisky, without ice.

It was a slow night, and the barman was a garrulous individual given to picking topics out the air to maintain a conversation.

'So what brings you to New York?'

'Business.'

Yeah? What kind of business is that?'

'I'm a journalist.'

'Is that right? We get quite a few of those dropping by.'

'Really?' I was on the point of leaving.

'We sure do. A fellow often in here is Benchley, Robert Benchley. He writes for the New Yorker. Another is Alexander Woollcott, he's with the New York Times. Oh, and there's Franklin Adams, who stops by occasionally. Usually, he occupies the seat you're in. Adams writes a regular column in the Tribune called, "The Conning Tower." There's a young woman who also hangs around the hotel, name of Dorothy Rothschild. Apparently, she writes for Vogue magazine.'

By now I was listening intently. Had a pot of gold just fallen into my lap?

The barman continued wiping glasses and adding to the list of Algonquin regulars.

'Then there's Heywood Broun. . .funny name. He also works at the Tribune. Comes in here with his wife, Ruth Hale. She's a journalist as well.' He leaned over the bar. 'I don't know what he sees in her. She's an out-and-out feminist. Always banging on about the cause.'

The following morning I took a train to Washington D.C., and headed for the British Embassy on Connecticut Avenue, not far from Dupont Circle. My initial reaction, that I was entering a gentleman's club in Pall Mall, was quickly dispelled when introduced to the ambassador, Sir Cecil Arthur Spring-Rice.

'Come through, Mr Kindred.'

He led me into his office.

'Coffee?'

'Thank you, sir. That would be very welcome.'

He picked up the phone and made the request.

'Right, let's make a start, shall we?' he said briskly, rubbing his hands together. Shades of Masterman, I thought.

'Perhaps I ought to begin by explaining, Mr Ambassador, who I work for, and what I'm doing here.'

'No need for that, my boy. I already know. Masterman and I were at university together. At one stage we were both occupied with the university Liberal Club. We've kept in touch ever since. He went into journalism and politics, and I into the diplomatic service.'

Sir Cecil had a clipped manner of speaking, in short, staccato sentences.

'Then you'll know that, for the moment anyway, I am looking after the propaganda being directed at the United States. This visit is by way of digging a little deeper, finding out what we have to do to get this country involved with the Triple Entente in the war in Europe.'

There was a tap on the door, and an aide came in bearing a tray, which he placed on a side table.

'Thank you, Paul,' the ambassador murmured as the young man withdrew.

'Let's sit over there, Mr Kindred. We'll be more comfortable.'

We moved to sit in large, deep armchairs either side off an ornate marble fireplace. The ambassador picked up the tray and placed it on a coffee table between us.

'White or black, Mr Kindred?'

'Black, sir, please.'

He poured and passed a cup to me. When he had satisfied his own needs, he sank back into the chair.

'I'll tell you straight away, Mr Kindred, or as they say over here, "straight off the bat", it will be no easy task. The President, for one, is against it. He is vehemently opposed to entering a conflict that in no way affects this country. And his stance reflects the attitude of the people. It would take a monumental shift in their outlook for him to send American troops overseas.'

He raised his cup to his lips. Then hesitated.

'Mind you,' he added thoughtfully. 'His mindset could be altered. When he gained office in 1913, he was opposed to women having the vote. But the suffragette movement is gaining ground, getting stronger and stronger. So much so, Wilson is now beginning to acknowledge women have a point. Conceivably, their voice should be heard. Particularly, when he preaches, "just government must rest upon the consent of the governed.". More coffee?'

'Thank you.'

'So. . .Mr Kindred, what's your plan?'

'The key newspaper is the Washington Post. I would like your people to provide me with a review of the correspondents that could be most useful to us. Information such as, their areas of interest, the causes they feel deeply about, their politics, a general profile.'

'We can do that. Obviously, you realise we can't give them material ourselves. It would be seen as biased, too one-sided. But, I'm sure we can help in many other ways.'

'What about introductions. Say to the editor or chief reporter?'

'No, I wouldn't do that. I meet up with the editor from time to time, and drop bon mots in his ear. I don't want to compromise that easy relationship. You're on your own on that one.'

'Fair enough. Any other papers I should consider?'

'Well, Stars and Stripes should be on your list. That's a weekly journal written by young soldiers and veteran reporters specifically for servicemen.'

'Right. Thank you. Back to your question. . .as I see it there is an entrenched view that this country is not affected in any way, so why get involved. Understandable. Perhaps I would feel the same at this distance. So do we, the Bureau, keep pushing propaganda in this direction? Or are we just banging our heads against a brick wall?

'We write about the atrocities committed by the enemy. We release photographs to illustrate such acts. We rail against the losses of our gallant soldiers. Seen by the people living in Europe, that's enough to jolt them. They could be next. . .so get ready, join the Entente.

'Over here, none of that sort of propaganda is going to work. To get a positive reaction from the United States, we have to tell of the more direct effect it could have on this country's citizens. Aggression by the Alliance that could impinge directly upon this nation.'

Sir Cecil was nodding in agreement.

I went on. 'As I see it, signs of aggression are already apparent. There was that American schooner sunk off the coast of Brazil by a German cruiser. Even more telling was the sinking of the *RMS Falaba*, last month. It was torpedoed by a U-boat and an American, Leon Thrasher, went down with the ship. I heard that Americans were quite vocal in their concern about the incident.

'Moreover, when the British steamer *Harpalyce*, a relief ship heading for

Belgium, was torpedoed without warning that also outraged American citizens. The ship had been en route to America to collect food for the starving Belgians. A mercy trip, and the vessel was displaying clear signs of its neutrality.'

'What are you saying exactly, Mr Kindred?'

'I think that while the United States maintains friendly relations with both Great Britain and Germany, as we increasingly rely on this country supplying essential commodities, ships crossing the Atlantic will become targets for the German Navy, and that will probably include American ships. I don't want to think of major loss of life, but it is a strong possibility. That could be the catalyst, the spark that commits America to side with the Entente.'

'I'm not sure I relish that line of thinking, Mr Kindred. Unfortunately, you may well be right.'

That evening, I was invited to dine with the ambassador and a few guests.

One being the industrialist, Samuel Insull, the other the cultural attaché from the Russian Embassy, with whom the ambassador had struck up a friendship when a young diplomat in Moscow. Sergei Mitzkov spoke English with the polish of an aristocrat. He was witty, erudite, and I found him a joy to converse with.

Insull was an achiever. I discovered he had once worked for Thomas Edison before founding the General Electric Company. Now based in Chicago, he was gradually creating an empire based on the domestic and industrial provision of electricity, and all that entails.

When the ladies adjourned to another room, Insull turned to Mitzkov and said. 'Been home lately, Sergei? What's the situation on the Eastern Front?'

Mitzkov hesitated a moment before replying.

'Our forces halted an offensive in Poland, and are now pushing into Galicia, the north-east corner of Austro-Hungarian territory. But I think they are over-extending themselves, and are increasingly vulnerable to counter-attack.'

He added. 'In truth, we are not very good at war games. We have had some successes, but far more reversals of fortune. When the Duma declared the country would fight on behalf of the oppressed Serbs, the people were in total agreement. Now there are rumblings, prompted by rising food prices and fuel shortages. The economy is in disarray, and there is growing tension between the Tsar and the government.

Mitzkov lowered his voice. 'Perhaps I should not say this, but the situation at home is likely to worsen. What isn't helping is a madman called Vladimir Ilyich Lenin. He has always been a radical and a subversive. He was arrested for sedition and exiled to Siberia some years ago, but fled to Western Europe. The *Zentralstelle für Auslandsdienst* could well be providing the facilities he needs to foment unrest in my country.'

Mitzkov glanced briefly in my direction when he referred to the Central

Office for Foreign Services in Berlin. Presumably, the ambassador had mentioned my current role.

Mitzkov rubbed a hand over his face. 'Lenin is stoking the fires. I think he wants to bring about another revolution like we had in 1905. This time it could well succeed.'

'And if it succeeds, what would happen then?' asked Insull.

'I would say the Eastern Front would collapse. Germany would be able to withdraw its troops, leaving merely a token force to rub the Russian noses in the mire. They would then strengthen the Western Front, and with superior manpower run right through the British and French armies' lines.'

CHAPTER FIFTEEN

I heard the news when I returned to the embassy the following morning.

The German troops were on the offensive.

Desperate to reach the Channel, on 22nd April they began their push on the Western Front with the usual opener of a three hour artillery bombardment. They fired upon the French, Algerian and British lines which covered most of the salient around Ypres. On this occasion the British forces also included Canadian and Indian troops.

When the shelling died down, the defenders waited for the first wave of the German infantry. Instead they were thrown into panic when a gas cloud wafted across no-man's land into their trenches. The Germans targeted four miles of the front with the wind-blown poison gas, decimating the Entente's troops. The Germans, shocked by the effect of the gas, failed to take full advantage. Despite the gas clouds, the Entente's forces managed to hold their positions. However, the effect was devastating. Approximately six thousand soldiers died within minutes, primarily from asphyxiation and damage to the lungs. Many more were blinded.

A few days later there was a second gas attack against a Canadian division. In both instances, over a hundred and fifty tons of chlorine were dispersed. This incident marked a new chapter in the war.

A few minutes after the ambassador had told me, Samuel Insull was ushered into the room.

'Sam, thanks for coming over. Have you heard the news?'

'About the use of chlorine gas?'

The ambassador nodded.

'The trouble is,' remarked Insull, 'resorting to this sort of warfare will scare off the Americans even more. They don't want to hear about these sorts of atrocities. Who, in their right minds, would send soldiers three thousand miles, to an unknown country, for them to be killed, or worse, wind up not being able to breathe without effort for the rest of their days?'

I was intrigued. How was it an American was talking about Americans in the third person, as though he were an outsider.

The ambassador caught my puzzled frown.

'Mr Kindred, Mr Insull was born in London. He still has a British passport, though he emigrated to the United States when he was twenty one. Like all ex-patriots he is a staunch supporter of his homeland. As an Anglophile, he not only distributes propaganda material, he often pays for its publication.'

Insull smiled in my direction.

'I know what you do, and why you are here, son. But you've got an uphill struggle. I'm not sure America will ever alter its neutral stance. Though, the ambassador was telling me about the conversation he had with you before dinner last night. If the Germans resort to attacking shipping in the Atlantic, forgive the pun, it might well turn the tide.'

I caught a train back to New York in the late afternoon, and arrived at the Algonquin Hotel to find an interesting set of people grouped around the bar.

'Good evening, sir. What can I get you?'

'Gin and tonic, please.'

'Well, what have we here? A Brit by the sound of it.'

A fellow two stools up the bar tilted his glass in my direction.

'So, what's a Brit doing in this place, in this year, at this very hour, when others of his age are waging war in the trenches of Northern France? Not hiding away in neutral territory, are you?'

I smiled. 'I was in the army, but was pulled from the ranks to do some important work.'

'Hear that everyone. And what, pray, is more important than having a drink in a bar in an hotel in Manhattan? Come sir, let me buy you another. Johnny, pour this gentleman one of your special gin and tonics.'

He turned to those around him. 'Right, for once I'm buying, so speak up while the mood is upon me. What are you all having?'

A woman draped an arm across his shoulder.

'Heywood, darling, I'll have my usual.'

So that's Heywood Broun. She must be Ruth Hale, I surmised. But somehow she did not look the blue-stocking type.

Another woman with chiseled features and a deep voice, echoed the request. 'And so will I, Heywood.'

Broun stared at the barman bleary-eyed. 'Johnny, give everybody their usual, or we'll be here all night.'

'We've been here all night already, Heywood,' came a voice, with the sibilance of alcohol washing his words.

'Are you still here, Alex? Shouldn't you be filing copy or something?'

'Did so long ago, my friend,' came the reply.

The drinks were dispensed, and hands reached out to take the glasses.

Someone declared. 'I say we drink the health of our new friend. Great Britain is doing a grand job, sorting out its enemies.'

A tall fellow with spectacles slipping down his nose, hoisted his drink in salute.

'I agree, Franklin. Raise your glasses everyone. Now repeat after me. "The British are always on their toes, which makes them a harder target to hit, God Bless'em."'

Eight voices, trebles, tenors and and a solitary bass, intoned this obscure sentiment.

"The British are always on their toes, which makes them a harder target to hit, God Bless'em!"

'Who said that, Heywood?' someone asked.

'How should I know. Someone in the War of Independence. I don't think it was one of ours.'

He stood up suddenly, and taking the arm of the woman with the chiseled features, said. 'Right, methinks it's time to eat. Would you care to join us, my young British friend?'

Although the restaurant appeared to be closed, the manager led us to a round table large enough to accommodate nine slightly inebriated diners.

I found myself next to the dark-haired woman who had first laid a proprietary hand on Heywood Broun's shoulder.

'So what's your name, Mr Britain? Mine's Dorothy. . .Dorothy Rothschild.'

'Daniel Kindred, Dorothy.'

'So, Daniel, are you married? Don't worry, I'm not looking for a partner. I've already got one lined up. Edwin Parker, a Wall Street broker, with more money than sense if he's going to marry me.'

She gave a half-smile. Then said. 'Seriously, what was so important they removed you from the ranks? Hush, hush work, was it? Are you a spy finding out how the Germans enjoy themselves over here? No, on reflection, Germans never seem to enjoy themselves. . .even when they're enjoying themselves.'

'Would you believe, I'm a journalist for the London Times. At least, I think I'm still on their books.'

'Are you telling me they pulled you out the war so you could report on it?'

'Something like that.'

'Listen up everybody,' declared Dorothy, standing up. 'I have an announcement to make. This gentleman next to me, who proclaims to be a worthy British citizen, is no higher up the food chain than ourselves. He, too, is a member of the fourth estate, working, no less, than for The Times in London. Though, at the moment he is working undercover on something or other.'

For some reason there was a smattering of applause, and another round of drinks was ordered.

Time passed. I am not sure how, but at one stage I was leaning over, my head close to the table and talking to Alexander Woollcott of the New York Times, who was bent forward in a similar position. Between us were the chiseled features and ample bosom of Ruth Hale. She was sitting boldly upright, like the figurehead on the prow of a ship, unblinking, unaware of what was going beneath her frontage. Some people just topple over when they have drunk too much. It seemed that for Miss Hale, alcohol had the opposite effect.

I interrupted Woollcott, who was in full flow. About what I had not the slightest idea.

'Tell me, Alexander, I don't remember ordering anything. Have we eaten?'

'Ages ago. . .I think. I'll ask Heywood. By the way, Dan, when you get any nuggets of information from the front line, any tidbits about the war, why don't you wire them to me? I'll do the same from here.'

Apparently, we had eaten.

At odd moments during the evening people left their chairs and circulated. All, that is, except Ruth Hale and I. She sat rigidly upright, while I sprawled across the table. As a consequence, at one time or another, they all occupied the seat to my left – and all made the same request. Wire anything of interest in Europe to them.

When I awoke the next morning, my head was pounding, the taste in my mouth was vile, and my eyes refused to focus. Worse the sun was shining directly into my room.

I gingerly tottered across to the window and closed the curtains. In the bathroom I stood under the shower, trying desperately to recall how and when I had got to bed.

Dressing slowly, my thoughts turned to the previous evening. When I first arrived in New York, my aim had been to try to meet several noted journalists and writers, and hope they would be interested in receiving material from me.

But the situation had reversed itself. I had been welcomed into a group of people who were the cream of New York's newspaper and magazine reporters. What is more, they had asked me to send them news from the front. The headache, queasy feeling and nausea seemed a small price to pay.

CHAPTER SIXTEEN

I managed to secure a last minute cancellation for an Atlantic passage departing on the first of May. It was a shared cabin on the Shelter deck.

Arriving at Pier Fifty-Four, I was surprised to see notices pinned up at various points in the terminal building. I stopped to read one next to a Cunard poster.

"Travellers intending to embark on the Atlantic voyage are reminded that a state of war exists between Germany and her allies and Great Britain and her allies; that the zone of war includes the waters adjacent to the British Isles; that, in accordance with formal notice given by the Imperial German Government, vessels flying the flag of Great Britain, or any of her allies, are liable to destruction in those waters and that travellers sailing in the war zone on ships of Great Britain or her allies do so at their own risk."
IMPERIAL GERMAN EMBASSY WASHINGTON, D.C., APRIL 22, 1915

'Take no notice of that, my friend, it's just an idle threat,' said a fellow passenger as a steward examined out tickets.

'He's right, sir, they won't attack a passenger liner. They might fire on a merchant steamer carrying cargo, but we'll be perfectly safe. What you've got to bear in mind is the liner's speed and its watertight compartments. If it came to it, we could outrun any ship of war.'

At dinner that first evening, the people on my table dismissed entirely the notion we were in any danger. Even the waiter remarked. 'We've made quite a few trips since the war started. Haven't seen a sign of an enemy ship.'

'What about a submarine?' I asked.

He grinned. 'Well, you wouldn't see them anyway,' prompting a mild ripple of amusement.

My cabin companion was from Ayrshire. He shook my hand, even more enthusiastically when I agreed to take the top bunk.

'Name is Burns, sir,' said the elderly gentleman, in a rich Scottish accent. 'An' I ken what you're thinking. . .but he's nae kin to me. . .e'en though my first name is Robert.'

The Second Class accommodation was confined to the stern of the ship, behind the aft mast. The public rooms were situated in partitioned sections of the Boat and Promenade decks. These comprised a smoking room, a large panelled salon, a tastefully decorated ladies' room, and an ample lounge for reading and relaxation.

Occasionally, I ventured outside for a stroll, or to participate in games of deck quoits and shuffleboard. But much of the time was spent in the lounge writing up my notes on the trip, and how we might exploit the situation in the United States. My good fortune was in finding a conduit for news and judiciously placed propaganda with my Algonquin press contacts.

At mealtimes, I frequently found myself in the company of Carl Foss, an American doctor about the same age as myself. A specialist in gunshot wounds, he was travelling to Britain to offer his services to the Red Cross Association.

Seven days out from New York, and coming towards the end of the voyage, I decided on a turn on the Promenade Deck before lunch. Rounding the port side of the ship, I could see several knots of people looking towards the distant Irish coastline. A figure detached itself from one of the groups.

'Daniel, quick, come over here,' declared Carl Foss. 'Tell me what you see.'

He pointed into the middle distance. My eyes followed his arm.

'What do you make of that?'

'What am I supposed to be looking at?'

He wagged a finger. 'That. Keeping pace with us.'

I fixed on where he was gesticulating, and stared intently for a moment.

'Carl, that's a submarine! And most likely a German one!'

'That was my thought.' He rubbed his chin.

'I was told this ship could outrun any other naval vessel,' I murmured. Then added. 'I'm going to get my camera and take a photograph of it, to prove they are lurking in these waters.'

A few minutes later I returned with my American Tourist Multiple in its oilskin bag.

'Smart camera,' remarked Carl.

'It's American-made. Takes pictures on a thirty five millimeter film strip.'

Just then the liner started to swing to starboard, away from the submarine.

'It seems someone on the bridge has spotted the U-Boat as well,' said Foss. 'But why don't they increase speed?'

However, when we looked again the submarine had disappeared. Presumably it had dived beneath the surface.

At the second sitting for lunch, Carl and I discussed the sighting.

As we spoke I saw uneasiness on the faces of our fellow diners. A waiter, overhearing the conversation was at pains to play down the incident.

'Nothing to worry about, ladies and gentlemen. After all, these are international waters. If the U-Boat came to the surface it must have been to get a closer look at the ship, and confirm it was merely a passenger-carrying vessel.'

The explosion occurred as he was clearing the soup plates. The whole ship shuddered, followed by a violent trembling running fore and aft, the whole length of the ship. The effect was devastating. No one moved. Slowly, the realisation dawned - the liner had been struck a mortal blow.

A moment passed, and the ship gradually listed to starboard. Then the panic erupted. Chairs were knocked over, people were sent flying, plates, cutlery and table lamps fell to the floor. Everyone charged for the exits.

Carl shouted,' I'm going back to my cabin.'

I grabbed his arm. 'Don't be a fool! You'll never make it back to the lifeboats.'

Before he could free himself I had pulled him into the milling crowd heading for the door.

Suddenly, there was another loud explosion, and the smell of coal permeated the air.

'A torpedo must have hit us near the bunkers,' Carl shouted. 'That second blast was probably highly flammable coal dust!'

The ship lurched a second time. Voices could be heard shouting over the din. It was impossible to launch the lifeboats from the port side. Everybody rushed to starboard, and it became a free-for-all. I still had my camera with me and started taking photos of the scene. People were scrambling and fighting to secure places in the remaining boats, regardless of the cry, "Women and children first!"

While many of the ship's company were helping passengers, particularly the more elderly and infirm, other crew members were desperately trying to put together the collapsible boats and life-rafts. But at the rate at which the liner was now foundering, most were thrown over the side unassembled.

As the ship listed further, one of its huge funnels crashed down on the top deck with frightening force. It rolled ponderously over the side, injuring many on its downward path into the sea. Panic gave way to hysteria.

I leaned over the starboard rail. Almost as a disinterested onlooker, I took more photographs. The area around the vessel was littered with boats and bodies. Hundreds of heads were bobbing about in the sea. Some swimming away from the ship, others floating face down in the water. Hit, tragically, by people unavoidably jumping on them, by falling debris, or when lifeboats plummeted from the davits.

Ten minutes had passed since the explosion. The bow and forward section started to dip, and the great stern of the ship, with its propellers still turning, rose out the water.

Carl suddenly appeared at my elbow.

'Daniel! Here, I've managed to get us each a lifebelt,' he shouted. 'C'mon, it's time to leave before the undertow takes us down with the ship!'

I fell awkwardly, and hit the sea hard. The lifebelt was torn from my body as I sank into the depths. Though the strap of the oilskin bag holding my camera still hung on my wrist It seemed like an age, but eventually I started to rise, and was nearing the surface when a broken spar crashed down, catching me across the head and shoulders. A searing flash of pain went through me, everything went black, as I lost consciousness.

When I came to, Carl was holding me with one arm, the other was wrapped around a rope trailing from a life-raft.

'You OK?' he spluttered, as the sea eddied and flowed around us. 'Good thing you were still under water, otherwise you would have been decapitated.'

God, it was cold. I turned to look for the ship. It was no longer there.

'Did you pull me up?' I asked him, haltingly.

'You came up by yourself. At first I thought you were dead.'

Carl passed me the rope while he stretched out for another.

'But you started coughing. I grabbed hold of your jacket and managed to swim to this life-raft.'

I glanced up. Three women were lying on the raft, one of them whimpering softly. 'My husband. . .my husband. . .have you seen my husband?'

CHAPTER SEVENTEEN

Kapitänleutnant Walther Schwieger's orders from the German Admiralty had been clear and concise. He was to take Unterseeboot -20 to the northern tip of Great Britain, skirt Northern Ireland and head south on the Atlantic side. Then east to the Irish Channel to destroy any ships blatantly carrying supplies to Liverpool in England.

Schwieger was a loose cannon. He was known frequently to attack vessels without warning; and fire on neutral craft he suspected might be British. In an earlier voyage, he had narrowly missed hitting a hospital ship with a torpedo. His reputation was such, there was every likelihood he would destroy at least one sizeable vessel carrying a great number of civilian passengers before a break came in the hostilities.

On the seventh of May, the U-20 was travelling in a westerly direction. The captain was aware of another U-Boat operating in Irish waters closer to the coast. About noon, Schwieger and his crew sighted the *Juno*. However, the old war cruiser escaped attack by adopting a ziggag course. Its constantly changing path making it difficult for the submarine to loose its torpedo.

At 1:20pm British time, frustrated by his inability to dispatch the *Juno*, a member of Schwieger's crew sighted something of greater significance.

"Starboard ahead, four funnels and two masts of a steamer with course at right angles to us... "

He submerged the U-Boat, approached the passenger liner at nine knots, and waited. At 1:40pm, when it was seven hundred metres away, the ship turned thirty degrees, making it a plum target. The order was given to launch a single torpedo into the midships of the *Royal Mail Steamship, Lusitania.*

CHAPTER EIGHTEEN

I was sitting in the conservatory of the Kinsale Community Hospital when Carl Foss appeared.

'Daniel. Well, I must say you're looking a sight better than the last time I saw you.'

I got up slowly, and clasped him to me.

'Carl, thank you for helping me when we jumped from the ship. I am in your debt.'

'Nonsense, my friend, you would have done the same for me.'

I let him go.

'I cannot ignore the reality. But for you I would be one of the many who didn't make it.'

'Daniel, it was just bad luck that spar falling where it did. In a way, I guess you were lucky to still be under the water when it crashed into the sea. If you had been on the surface, you wouldn't have lived to tell the tale.'

He sat down on a nearby chair.

'So tell me, when were you picked up?' I asked.

'Well, after they had hauled you and those three women aboard that fishing boat from Kinsale, there was, quite literally, no more room. So, I hefted myself onto the life-raft, and waited to be rescued. About an hour later a flotilla of small craft and ships arrived and took us back to Queenstown. We've been looked after rather well. However, there's a ship coming this afternoon to take many of us, those who can walk and who suffered only minor injury, onto Liverpool. How about you. How long will you be in hospital?'

'I've been asking the same question. It could be another couple of days. Besides the bang on the head which caused concussion, there's heavy bruising and lacerations across my back, and apparently I suffered a couple of broken ribs.'

I changed the subject.

'Still intent on helping the Red Cross Association?'

'Yes, but not straight away. I managed to send a wire home, confirming I'm alive, but my wife is really concerned. She didn't want me to come to Europe in the first place. As a consequence, I'm going back to Harlem, a small out-the-way town in Montana, to prove I'm safe and well. So, I guess, we won't be seeing each other for a while.'

He rose from the chair.

'But let's keep in touch. I'll write and let you know my plans.'

CHAPTER NINETEEN

That afternoon, I eventually got through on the telephone, first to my parents and then to Charles Masterman.

'My God! You're still alive! Thank God for that!'

Then he was demanding. 'Where are you? Why didn't you contact me earlier? We all believed you were dead! Inconsiderate bugger!'

'Actually, Charles, I'm still in hospital. I should be released in a couple of days time.'

Then he was contrite.

'Sorry, Daniel. Are you badly injured? I didn't think. . .forgive me. Where are you by the way?'

'In Ireland still.'

'Queenstown?'

'No, in a hospital in Kinsale.'

'Brilliant! You won't have to go far then.'

'What on earth are you talking about?'

Masterman spelt it out in detail.

It appeared Kinsale jealousy guards its ancient privileges as an independent authority. When he discovered that five bodies had been landed in the town harbour by Kinsale boats, the local coroner, John Horgan, speedily convened an inquest. He went over to Queenstown on 8th May, the day after the tragedy, and subpoenaed the captain of the *Lusitania* and a number of survivors to appear before him.

Shrewdly suspecting that a higher authority might forestall him, he was going to open a special hearing before a coroner's jury of local merchants and fishermen.

On 10th of May, I persuaded the ward sister to let one of the nurses push me over to the Market House of Kinsale, where the hearing was taking place.

She stayed with me at the back of the courtroom when the coroner opened the proceedings. First to be called was the captain, William Thomas Turner, who appeared clad in an ill-fitting old suit. Clearly, provided by someone for the occasion. It was obvious to all he was suffering the strain of his experience. Nevertheless, Turner gave evidence in a confident manner.

To the question posed by the jury foreman; "In the face of the warnings at New York that the Lusitania could be torpedoed, did you make an application to the Admiralty for an escort?"

Turner responded: "No. I left that to them. It is their business, not mine. I simply had to carry out my orders to go – and I would do it again."

Horgan added: "I am glad to hear you say so, Captain."

It was when Horgan condoled with him and with Cunard at the loss of the ship that, clearly overwrought, Turner collapsed in tears.

Throughout the day other witnesses, members of the crew and a number of passengers, gave their evidence. The appalling memory of the last moments of the liner reducing many to tears.

When the coroner, John Horgan, began his summing up in the late afternoon, one could tell he too had been touched by the heart-rending accounts. Delivered in a sonorous tone, his words added to the emotional distress of those in the courtroom.

"Seven hundred sixty-one people were picked up by boats from Queenstown and Kinsale. They are to be commended for their swift action in setting out to rescue as many of the survivors as possible. However, one thousand one hundred ninety-eight people perished. A death toll rivalled only by that of the Titanic disaster three years ago.

"Many of the survivors suffered injury, and almost all were traumatised by this sad experience. But now, added to their misery, is an overwhelming sense of outrage at the German Imperial Command. Many claim that their notices, placed beside Cunard posters, was a deliberate declaration of intended aggression. They were planning to destroy the RMS Lusitania.

"Many survivors lost family members, and in some cases, entire families were wiped out. We feel deeply for those from the United States who lost their lives. They have no part in the conflict between Great Britain and Germany and its allies. Yet one hundred and twenty four American men, women and children perished in this tragic incident."

Horgan stared hard at the twelve jurymen.

"You now have all the facts. I sincerely hope that you come to a considered, but inevitable, conclusion - and that your verdict clearly identifies the transgressor in this barbarous act."

Twenty minutes later the jury brought in the verdict: "This appalling crime was contrary to international law – and charge the officers of the submarine and the German Emperor under whose orders they acted, of wilful and whole-scale murder."

The nurse was preparing to wheel me back to the hospital, when a naval officer burst into the courtroom waving a direct order from the Admiralty to stop the inquest and to prevent Captain Turner from giving evidence.

It was too late. The condemnation would reverberate around the world.

CHAPTER TWENTY

Sea water had ruined a number of them, but there were still nine clear images.

'Remarkable,' murmured Masterman, bending over and peering intently at the prints. 'People will sit up and take notice when they see these.'

I looked at the photographs for several minutes, reliving the cries, the terror, the sheer misery, the dreadful loss of life.

'How are you feeling now, Daniel? Are you up to working?'

I had recounted to Masterman the details of the successful trip to the States; and then, more hesitantly, about the voyage and the last moments of the *Lusitania*.

'I need to work, Charles. To blot out recurring memories.'

He nodded in understanding.

'What I must do, while they're still fresh in my mind, is to write up all my notes. They were lost when the ship went down.'

Again the nod. Though this time he chewed at his bottom lip. It was a sign he had something to impart – usually, never good news.

'OK. . .what have you got to tell me?' I asked.

At first he seemed reluctant to answer. Then it came out in a rush.

'They've found Bob Brady's body. It was in a coal truck in a railway siding. The pathology report suggests that he had been tortured before he died.'

Masterman stroked his chin.

'I suppose it will come out sooner or later, so I might as well tell you now. Hanging round Brady's neck was a placard saying, "This is what happens to filthy homosexuals". '

'I didn't know Bob was a homosexual.'

'Not many did. Especially as it's illegal. The trouble is people are highly intolerant of men and women who enjoy their own sex. Regardless of his persuasion, Bob Brady was a damned good journalist. Unfortunately, his reputation will be tarnished when this becomes public.'

'Hmm. . .this puts a different complexion on his disappearance, then. This could be the work of homophobes, not enemy agents.'

I was now looking after the American as well as the Southern Europe desk. Not that the latter was demanding too much attention. For the moment, the situation in both Portugal and Spain was stable; and following a meeting at the Foreign Office in April, I fully expected the Italians to declare for the British, French and the Russians.

A great deal of propaganda material, defining the role of Germany and its allies as barbaric aggressors, sweeping through Northern Europe and occupying vast swathes of other countries was appearing daily in the Italian press. More telling were the photographs that accompanied the printed word. In my absence, the Bureau had done a first-class job, not only maintaining a steady flow of information, but sending it to those people I had identified as strongly favouring the Entente.

Within a few hours of returning to Wellington House I had written graphic pieces about the sinking of the *Lusitania*, and together with copies of my photographs, mailed the package to Franklin Adams, care of The Algonquin Hotel, New York City. I also recommended he, and the other members of the press group, interview Dr Carl Elmer Foss of Harlem, Montana, for a first-hand account of the disaster.

Rightly, the American people were enraged by the incident, and while maintaining a pacifist stance, on 13th May, President Woodrow Wilson sent the first of four protests to Germany.

Germany tried to defend itself against the attacks and protests. It claimed that the *Lusitania* was armed and carrying munitions to be employed against German forces. Then they insisted the liner was carrying Canadian troops. There were three hundred and sixty Canadians on board on that fateful voyage. None of them were soldiers, although one was planning to enlist in the Canadian Expeditionary Force.

The Germans also tried to justify the sinking by saying that the British were using their "illegal" blockade of stopping and confiscating ships carrying cargo to Germany in order to starve their citizens, and this nationwide suffering was worse than the *Lusitania* disaster.

However, the majority view was that the U-Boat attack was a cowardly, unwarranted act against a defenceless ship, and was roundly condemned by all neutral nations.

I received a letter from the Algonquin group, thanking me for the material, also telling me that Woodrow Wilson was having a hard time containing the anger voiced in the Senate, Congress and by growing numbers of the American public.

With no let up in the denunciation being expressed in the world's media, I was surprised that Italy, having acknowledged the accord, now wanted to review the agreement.

Charles told me about the secret meeting with the Italians last year, and the draft of the "London Treaty", which was signed a few weeks ago. Now it seemed, the Italians wanted to be more precise on what was being offered. In addition to control over a large part of the Dalmatian coast; the Austrian Tyrol and littoral, including the port of Trieste; and the Dodencanese Islands, the feeling was they should also have a share of the Turkish Antalya coast.

As a consequence, yet another meeting was arranged, and Charles asked if I would attend it. It was to take place at the Foreign Office in Charles Street.

'Who will be there?' I asked.

'Sir Edward Grey, the Foreign Secretary, will head up our side. Italy will be represented by Sidney Sonnino, their Foreign Affairs Minister, and Marquis Guglielm Imperiali, the Italian Ambassador.'

'Sidney sounds very English.'

'Apparently, his father married a woman from the Welsh valleys.'

'Right. . .am I present as an onlooker, or a translator?'

'Both. You can translate what they're say for me.'

CHAPTER TWENTY ONE

They met again in the Flying Angel Club in Victoria Dock Road.

A discreet word from Erik had been passed along the chain, until it reached the ears of Karl and Ernst.

'We have another task, my friends, which requires our combined resources. I have learned from "Fritsches". . .'

'Who the hell is "Fritsches"?'

'"Fritsches, my dear Karl, is the pseudonym for Gustav Steinhauer, our beloved leader. He used the name when he came to Britain last year to rally his people on the ground. As I was saying, sources have informed him that the Italians are back in London shortly to conclude an agreement to join forces with the Triple Entente. He has set us a simple task. He wants us to spoil the occasion by killing the Italian ambassador and their Foreign Affairs Minister before any discussions can take place!'

CHAPTER TWENTY TWO

'But I look nothing like him!'

'You will do once they dye your hair, and fix a large grey moustache to your top lip,' grinned Masterman. 'Don't worry. You won't come to any harm, armed guards will be surrounding you the whole time.'

'If it's perfectly safe why do I have to impersonate Sonnino?'

'It's just a ploy, to fool anyone who might want to hinder the meeting. You know, placard-wavers, people who throw eggs and other things. I've asked Roger to dress as the Italian ambassador. All you both have to do is walk to the motor car, converse in Italian to sound convincing. That's all.'

'And the real ambassador and foreign secretary?'

'They'll be driven away from Wimborne House, behind the Ritz Hotel, without anyone knowing. Their motor car will take a different route. Really Daniel, nothing could be simpler,' declared Masterman, emphatically.

They had taken up their positions in the early hours. One marksman and an aide covering each entrance.

It had been no hardship finding the perfect location overlooking the entrance in Arlington Street. A building, earmarked for a showroom for Wolseley motor cars, was being erected directly opposite; and the skeleton of the structure, faced with scaffolding, allowed easy access. It also provided more than sufficient height to look down on those emerging from the hotel, giving a clear view of the dignitaries over the shield of security officers.

It had been more problematic gaining a suitable eyrie in a building in Piccadilly. They had had to pose as potential buyers of the sixth floor offices across the road from the main entrance to the Ritz hotel, and even paid a deposit.

Now all was in readiness. The marksmen had practiced with their weapons, fine-tuning the telescopic sights. They were both using the Swedish Mauser m/41 rifle, the sniper version, fitted with the German AJACK scope.

Erik was the primary shooter, taking up his position facing the main Piccadilly entrance. Karl was his back-up. The rifle was chambered to take 6.5x55mm cartridges. Throughout the long wait, Erik frequently loaded, unloaded and re-loaded the weapon.

It was a precision-built instrument. The mechanism silky-smooth when pulling back the bolt to chamber another round. The one drawback was its length of travel. Unlike the Lee-Enfield, drawing back the bolt, you had to move your face, and therefore your eye from the target – which meant refocussing your next shot. Perhaps, taking a second longer. Circumstances can change in a second.

He wondered if Stefan and Kurt were also thinking the same. They had been co-opted into the team because of their supposed shooting abilities. Erik's face twitched slightly with concern. He would have welcomed being satisfied by their proven abilities. He disliked making decisions on someone else's word. It was not in his nature. He had survived by being cautious, and well-prepared. It had been unfortunate they had not had longer to plan the job.

Come the moment, he sincerely hoped the Italians would come out the main doors of the hotel.

'Surely, I don't have to wear this as well?

Charles had handed me a waistcoat of overlapping steel scales fixed to a leather lining.

'If it's perfectly safe, why on earth do you want me to put this on?'

'A precaution only, Daniel. Of course, you'll be perfectly safe. I can't understand why you complain so. He's happy to wear one. Aren't you, Roger?'

Charles Masterman had turned in Roger Mann's direction. Roger was our resident accountant, in charge of the Bureau's budget. He was a precise, uncomplicated individual, with a keen eye when checking our expenses and other outgoings. He kept our books nicely poised in the black, with never a penny out of place. But, we all knew he harboured a secret envy when those in charge of the various desks went on their travels. As a consequence, he had leapt at the chance to be at the sharp end for a change. No one remarked that his short, rounded figure and slight hooked nose had put him ahead of any other contender for the role of Italian ambassador.

He strapped on the extra eleven pounds of steel vest without demur. Over that he eased the ornate three-quarter length coat, complete with medals and medallions. Finally, he donned the sash of office.

I gazed at him. 'I must say, Roger, you look more the ambassador than Il Marchese Guglielmo Imperiali di Francavilla.'

I bowed my head in obeisance.

'You look the part too, Daniel,' he smirked. 'I only hope you can keep that moustache on long enough.'

I glanced in the mirror, and wondered how anyone could go through life behind one of these.

As we came down the stairs, everyone in the reception area halted to watch our progress. So this is what celebrity status feels like, I thought. My eye fell upon a character who suddenly started forward and went out the main exit.

I turned behind me to where Charles Masterman was walking with the four rear guards.

'Signor Masterman, which entrance are we using?'

'The one onto Piccadilly. The motor cars should be there in readiness. Don't worry, Minister', he added, also playing the part, 'you'll be quite safe.'

'I wish to change it. Please get them to come to the side door.'

Charles stared at me.

'Sorry, Minister, I can't change the arrangement. It's too late.'

'You will do as I say, or the meeting is off! Do you understand?'

I turned to Roger.

' Signor Ambassador, we are not going a step further!'

Masterman stepped closer to me, and whispered fiercely. 'What the hell are you playing at?'

'Charles, just do what I ask. . . please.'

He stared into my face, then abruptly turned on his heel and walked out the main entrance.

He soon returned.

'The vehicles are going to the Arlington Street entrance, Minister. Allow a few moments, and then we can leave.'

The fellow I had seen earlier came back through the door, and stood uncertainly in the lobby with other onlookers.

A guard waved to Masterman.

'Good. Shall we proceed Minister, Mr Ambassador?'

Charles walked ahead, and we followed with four guards in front, and three at the rear.

'Where the devil are they?' he muttered fiercely for the fourth time.

Karl said nothing. He knew how tense, how on edge, Erik was.

'Felix came outside five minutes ago. They should have been right behind him!'

'A little more patience, Erik,' Kurt murmured finally. 'Any minute now.'

'Well the motor cars have moved. There must be a reason why.'

'Just take it easy, Erik. Felix's appearance means they intend to come out the main exit. Just breathe deeply, and relax.'

Stefan peered through the sight, trying to glimpse what was happening in the hotel. The motor cars had pulled up outside the Arlington Street entrance. So they were coming out the side door.

His shoulder was beginning to ache, sweat was running into his eyes. He briefly moved the rifle stock, and reached for a handkerchief to mop his brow.

Kurt was keeping close watch.

'The commissionaire is opening a side door. Get ready.'

Stefan jammed the rifle back into his shoulder, and peered through the telescopic sight. He beheld the commissionaire's face, still with a blob of shaving soap beneath his ear lobe. Stefan moved the weapon a fraction sideways. Here they come.

His heart gave a lurch, he mentally played back the route they would take when making their escape.

Out onto the top step trooped four bodyguards. They looked left and right, and behind themselves. Oddly, they never looked up. But even if they had they would not have spotted Stefan, his rifle steadied on a scaffolding cross-member.

More movement at the door. The targets were sandwiched between two sets of guards. At a signal, the front row walked down the steps, and for that brief moment, the upper torsos of the Italian Foreign Secretary and the country's Ambassador to the Court of St. James were exposed.

Stefan held his breath, and gently squeezed the trigger, sending a bullet towards the bright, third medal on Guglielmo Imperiali's chest.

Even an eleven pound armoured vest is no match for a 6.5x55mm cartridge. But the contest was not put to the test. At the moment the cartridge was despatched, Roger Mann, every inch the ambassador, turned sideways to ask something of me.

At first I wondered what could possibly have made the sharp whooshing noise followed instantly by the thud of exploding slivers of wood. Roger tumbled to the step, and I was violently knocked off my feet by the bodyguards.

Handguns appeared, and there was another loud crack of a rifle. One of the guards was felled, and immediately the front of the building opposite was hit by a fusillade of gunfire.

The comatose Roger, the injured bodyguard, and the commissionaire, who was bleeding profusely from a head wound caused by flying fragments, were pulled hurriedly back into the hotel lobby. I was jerked to my feet and shoved through the door, while three of the guards went after the marksman.

Through the half-open entrance I saw another of the guards pitch forward, and roll into the gutter.

I kicked the door shut.

Turning to Roger, I could see he had been fortunate. In pivoting sideways the bullet had dealt him a passing blow, denting the armoured vest and ruining a medal before glancing off and burying itself into the woodwork of the hotel entrance. It had, quite literally, passed through the inches-wide gap between us.

'I've been hit! I'm wounded!' he shouted when he came round. 'Look, there's blood everywhere.'

We were back in my hotel room. Roger was lying on the bed.

'Roger, you were knocked out when your head hit the step. That blood is from the doorman,' explained Masterman, 'not from you.'

'Well, I've got a splitting headache.'

He slumped back on the bed, and murmured. 'By the way, Daniel, I told you it would happen. You've lost half your moustache.'

CHAPTER TWENTY THREE

'I can accept that my role in the Bureau is a hazardous one.'

I was thinking of what happened to Bob Brady.

'But what on earth were you thinking exposing Roger to such dangers?'

We were in Charles' office in Wellington House. He was leaning forward on the desk, his hands steepled, almost in prayer, his chin resting on the pinnacle.

'Your very words to him were, "nothing to it, old boy, just play the part". Then this happens. One dead, two injured, and Roger nursing a bruised chest.'

I had been ranting for several minutes. As the anger gradually subsided I realised it was likely the aftermath, the nervous reaction to nearly being shot.

I stopped abruptly, and slumped into a chair.

'Finished?'

'For the moment.'

'Daniel, I was fooled too. Vernon Kell, who runs this new outfit, Military Intelligence, assured me everything would be safe. No one would get hurt. How wrong could he be. . .he has lost one of his own people.'

'It was stupid to get the motor cars to come to the Arlington Street entrance. In truth, I blame myself for the incident. What was I thinking?' I said disconsolately.

He stood up suddenly, came round the desk, and took a chair next to mine.

'Believe me, I would not have risked either of you if I had known what we might be facing. Kell phoned me a short while ago to tell me that, in fact, there were two sniper positions. The one in the motor car showroom on the corner of Arlington Street, and another in a building across the road from the main hotel entrance.. It was the sniper in empty offices in Piccadilly who shot that bodyguard as he raced across to the construction site.'

He stared at me, as though gauging my state of mind.

'By the way, why did you suddenly demand that the motor cars come to the side entrance?'

'I don't know. . .a small thing really. When we came down the stairs into the hotel foyer, out the corner of my eye a fellow got up from a chair and went out the main entrance.'

'So?'

'He was wearing a blue suit.'

'Right?'

'He was also wearing brown shoes. No one with a British dress sense would wear brown shoes with a dark suit.'

****

'Have you seen the new recruiting poster? Now the government has got involved a number of changes have been made.'

Charles had walked into my room with several posters rolled up under his arm.

'Oh. . .what are they? I thought it gave out just the right message. Your country does need you.'

He unfurled the latest version.

'It's headed, "BRITONS", and beneath Kitchener's image, "wants YOU".'

I peered over his shoulder. In two lines of red type was the message, "JOIN YOUR COUNTRY'S ARMY!" and "GOD SAVE THE KING".

'The final line was added by Kitchener himself,' explained Masterman. 'He insists that all advertising for the army should end with these words.'

'Hmm. . .not as compelling as the simplicity of the first one. How is recruiting going? Do you know?'

'After the rush to sign up in the first few months of the war, it seems that enlisting has started to decline. We haven't gone over to conscription, like the French and the Russians, but it might come to it if we don't get sufficient numbers.'

'I may have to go to the front after all,' I mused.

'What do you mean?'

'I was in the army, training to march and shoot at the imaginary enemy before I was told to report here, to Wellington House.'

'I never knew that. Well, you do too good a job to go to the front now.'

While I stood there looking at the poster, an idea formed in my mind.

'I don't know, Charles. Perhaps I should go.'

'What are you talking about? At this moment the Bureau is far more important. There's no way I would release you!'

'No, I don't mean as a soldier. I was thinking. . .what about taking a cameraman and filming what it's really like. We would be able to show what the enemy are up to, what the local people are suffering, and the grit and determination being shown by our British soldiers.'

He stood there staring into the distance. Then said slowly. 'How would it work? Where would you go?'

'Well the fighting is still raging in the Ypres Salient. This is the second time the Germans have tried to force their way through to the coast. They're throwing everything they can at us, including chlorine and mustard gas. Portrayed on film would be a first-class way of showing the neutral powers just how ruthless the enemy is.'

'Do you know any cameramen who would be willing to go into a war zone?'

'As a matter of fact, I do. His name is John Benett-Stamford. Went off the South Africa and filmed the skirmishes in the Boer War. He was at Belmont with Lord Methuen's force, filmed the goings-on at Orange River, and troops crossing the Modder River, as well as other military set-to's. Benett-Stamford would be the ideal choice.'

I did not mention that he was a larger-than-life character, a tearaway with the nickname, "Mad Jack".

He rubbed his hands together in that now familiar way.

'Great! Let's do it! I'll get on to the War Ministry and set it up.'

He hesitated when he reached the door.

'By the way, the other reason I came in was to tell you we are to attend a function at the American Embassy. The Ambassador, Walter Hines Page, is holding a get-together, some sort of soirée, for noted press people based in Britain, Alex Brewer, you and I have been invited. Apparently the ambassador was a journalist in his early years.'

CHAPTER TWENTY FOUR

Observing the social niceties, fifteen minutes after the given time, the three of us alighted from a taxicab, and made our way into the embassy building in Grosvenor Gardens.

Handed a glass of champagne, when Charles veered off to join a group, and Alex saw an old colleague from Reuters main office in the London Royal Exchange, I wandered through the crowd, until I caught sight of Wickham Steed. He edged away from three or four people deep in conversation, and came over.

'Well, well, young Kindred. How are you?'

Steed thrust out his hand.

Before I could reply, he added. 'I've heard good things about you, Daniel. I understand you're the War Propaganda Bureau's blue-eyed boy.'

'Indeed, so have I,' came another voice.

I half-turned. Lord Northcliffe was at my elbow.

'Good evening, sir.' I grinned at Wickham Steed. 'You shouldn't believe all you hear, it's just propaganda.'

They both smiled.

'So, Daniel, when all this has ended, can I presume you will be you coming back to us?' asked Northcliffe.

'I doubt that Mr Robinson will have me back,' I replied.

Was it my imagination? Did I see a telling glance exchanged between the proprietor of the Times and his man-Friday?

Wickham Steed changed the subject.

'By the way, someone mentioned that you were one of the survivors from the *Lusitania*. Is that true? Were you on-board when she went down?'

An involuntary shiver. It still catches me out when that question comes unexpectedly.

'Yes. . .yes, I was.'

'That's interesting. I was speaking to an American earlier who almost went down with the ship,' said Northcliffe. 'I'll see if I can find. . .' His head swivelled round, searching the salon. 'Yes, stay here, I'll be back.'

I continued chatting with Wickham Steed, who was explaining the changes that might be taking place at the newspaper, when a hand grabbed my arm.

'Daniel meet Ambassador Page,' said Northcliffe, 'and, Clare Johnson, the daughter of a friend of his. Walter, Clare, this is Daniel Kindred, who works for me. Though at the moment he is on secondment elsewhere.'

Walter Hines Page smiled as we shook hands. His hooded eyes peered at me through rimless glasses, giving the impression he knew what I was thinking, even what I might next say. What was intriguing, he wore a moustache similar in style to the Italian, Sidney Sonnino. Perhaps it was the dress diplomats and those in government were expected to adopt, much like the striped trousers and black jacket.

In comparison, it was beauty and the beast. When I shook Clare Johnson's hand, I beheld a young lady with auburn hair, green eyes and a determined chin. She was lovely. I did not know what to say next. Fortunately, Wickham Steed rescued me.

'I understand Miss Johnson that you were on the *Lusitania* as well?'

'As well?'

'Forgive me, I should explain. Mr Kindred was also on the ship that fateful day.'

She turned her gaze in my direction.

'Ambassador, would you mind if I drew Mr Kindred away for a moment? I would like to hear another survivor's views of what happened. And how he survived.'

'Not at all, my dear.'

'Then come, Mr Kindred, let us find somewhere to sit down.'

The ambassador murmured. 'Take him into the parlour, Clare. Away from the chatter.'

'Would you like another drink, Mr Kindred? Some more champagne, perhaps?'

'Please.'

She leaned over and tugged on a bell pull. A moment later she had requested two glasses, which quickly appeared. As the door was shutting on the maid, Miss Johnson said. 'Right, now tell me your version of events.'

I recounted that Carl Foss and I had witnessed one U-Boat on the port side. How the liner had turned to starboard, and while we were eating lunch the torpedo from another submarine had struck the liner midships.

'What happened then?' she pressed.

'When the ship listed heavily, we all moved to the starboard side. But it was chaos. I took some photographs. The crew was launching lifeboats, and trying to assemble collapsible boats and life-rafts. But, in truth, it was too little, too late. Carl and I eventually jumped off the ship. Unfortunately for me, I was struck by falling debris, and Carl Foss saved my life. I was picked up by a fishing boat from the village of Kinsale. Carl was rescued, and taken to Queenstown.'

'I was lucky,' she said in a low voice. 'I was in one of the lifeboats lowered early on. But we lost our oars. Then people started clambering into the boat. Mothers were in the water screaming for us to take their children. Bodies were floating by... '

Tears sprang to her eyes. She sniffed. 'I still wake up with the nightmare of it all. Do you?'

'I still find it unsettling. But I was injured and unconscious a great deal of the time. In a way, perhaps I was more fortunate.'

'Were they your photographs that appeared in the New York Times and some other papers?'

'I believe they were.'

'Hmm. . .the Herald missed out on that one.'

I did not mention the group at the Algonquin.

We were still talking about the disaster, when the ambassador's wife came into the room.

'My, do you know how long you've away from the reception? Over an hour. Perhaps you should join us now, Clare?'

'My apologies, ma'am. I kept Clare talking and didn't realise the time.'

The woman smiled. 'I have the feeling Clare was equally talkative.'

We rose from our chairs. Walking towards the door, Clare said. 'Could we finish our conversation tomorrow, Mr Kindred? You haven't told me about the inquest yet.'

'Well, yes. I'd like that. What time would you suggest?'

Early evening. . .after dinner. Shall we say, seven o'clock? We could go for a stroll in Hyde Park. '

CHAPTER TWENTY FIVE

'Actually, I work for the New York Herald. Well, almost work there. I want to be a journalist. Daddy knows the Gordon Bennetts, who own the newspaper. I just kept on pestering him to get me a job there.'

Clare Johnson and I were strolling through Hyde Park. I had asked how she came to be on the *Lusitania.*

'Mr Gordon Bennett Junior agreed to take me on, with the proviso that I prove myself. I said OK, let me be your roving European reporter. They've got a man over here already, so let me see how I stack up against him. If I do well, maybe there's a permanent job. What about you? What do you do if you haven't yet been persuaded to enlist in the army?'

'Actually, I am a journalist. I was working for the Times, that is until I was seconded to write for the war effort.'

'What does that mean?'

I was loath to reveal what I did. 'I write leaflets and things, encouraging others to join up. You know, shades of "your country needs you".'

She glanced at me quickly. What was she thinking? Did she believe I was shirking a patriotic responsibility. Telling others what I should be doing myself?

'Actually, I did enlist. . .I was taken out the ranks to do this job.'

She nodded. But I could sense her thoughts, her doubts.

'What about your comrades? The soldiers you were with?'

'The 24th Division? I heard they moved to Aldershot. It's a garrison town where soldiers do their final training.'

'Then what?'

'Then they were transported to France and Begium to join the battle.'

We walked on in silence for a while.

'While you'll still be here, in England?'

The implication was all too obvious.

Another silence.

Then I said. 'Not exactly. I'm going to the front line, among the action in a few days time.'

I hoped Masterman had managed to fix it with the War Office. Benett-Stamford had readily agreed.

'Really? Why?'

Now I was in a difficult situation. So as Clare Johnson did not think the worst, I had overplayed my hand. Male pride had over-ridden discretion.

'I'm not allowed to say.'

'Too late, my friend... too late' she grinned. 'Let me see. You are friendly with Lord Northcliffe, your erstwhile employer. Ambassador Page told me he was involved in publicising Great Britain's efforts in this war with Germany and its allies. Last night you mentioned you had taken photos of the *Lusitania* sinking. . .which appeared in some of our newspapers. They were accompanied by some trenchant words about America doing right by its people killed when the ship went down.'

She halted suddenly. I had walked on a few steps.

'You're a propagandist, aren't you? You work for that outfit Uncle Walter was talking about. Now what is it called. . .yes, the War Propaganda Bureau! Well I'll be damned!'

'Keep your voice down!' I muttered. 'You shouldn't know that. It could be dangerous,'

'How on earth could it be dangerous, for God's sake?'

She used pretty strong language for a young lady.

I took her arm and hurried her along the path.

'I'm taking you back to the embassy. It might not be too safe if you're with me.'

'Let go my arm! Who do you think you are telling me what to do!'

I halted and peered intently into her eyes.

'Because people have been killed doing the job I do! That's why!'

We walked on in silence.

As we neared the entrance, Clare said in a low voice. 'How has anyone been killed?'

I told her briefly about Bob Brady's abduction, and about the incident outside the Ritz Hotel. How we had created a diversion so the Italian Foreign Minister and the ambassador could sign the finalised London Treaty.

'It's all very hush-hush, but they are going to join the Entente and fight on our side. The declaration will be made in late May. There are still one or two details to be hammered out.'

That doesn't sound very dangerous.'

Once more I stopped. She turned to face me.

'I should explain. Brady's body was found dumped in a railway yard. When we created a diversion for the Italians, we were shot at. Several people were killed.'

'My God, I didn't realise. . .' she murmured, and squeezed my hand .A simple act of contrition. I squeezed hers back.

'Can I see you again,' I asked hesitantly.

'When did you say you were going to France?'

' Next week, I expect.'

'Right, I'm coming with you. If you're on a reporting mission, then so am I. I want to see the fighting myself, first hand. No hiding away in cosy little England.'

I did not mention anything to Charles. All I said was John Benett-Stamford was bringing an assistant to help with the equipment.

'Right, what's his name?'

'Err. . .actually he's a she.'

'Can't have that, Daniel. It's too dangerous for a woman.'

'I'm afraid he insists, Charles. She is too good to leave behind. Apparently, she knows what Benett-Stamford wants before he does. And this exercise calls for speed and alertness.'

'I don't know. . .it's too much of a risk.'

'Tell that to the young women driving the ambulances out there.'

We met at Victoria Station.

We were taking a train to Dover, then a cross-channel ship to Calais. From there we would travel by road to the British Command headquarters in Saint-Omer.

John Benett-Stamford was talking to a woman when I arrived at the station. It took a moment to realise it was Clare. She was dressed all in brown. A long skirt over dainty boots, and a three-quarter length jacket topped off by a wide-brimmed hat. When she turned towards me she was not wearing any cosmetics.

'I've been briefing my assistant, Daniel. I must say I've never had such an attractive one before. This should be an entertaining little trip, what.'

He grinned wickedly at her.

For some reason I felt put out by his easy familiarity.

'I've got the tickets and our official passes, so we might as well join the train,' I said woodenly. 'Does this stuff go in the guard's van?'

'Well, it could. But I'd feel happier if it were in the compartment with us,' John replied.

In fact, it fitted onto the luggage racks quite easily, along with our cases.

At Dover we boarded a troop ship. As the vessel cleared the harbour it was met by a flotilla of craft – a destroyer, a trawler, minesweeper, and several fishing boats.

'Are they escorting us?' I asked a rating.

'Yes sir, they're part of the Dover Patrol. They protect us from being attacked or hit by U-Boat torpedoes. Sometimes an airship flies overhead. Up there, they can spot if there are any enemy submarines lurking.'

At Calais we boarded a lorry which took us thirty miles south-east to the British Command headquarters at Saint-Omer. Here, the officers dictated the battle that was raging around Ypres. I was taken to the major in charge of operations and supplies. He studied the letter which outlined our role and sought all possible support.

'You've come at a difficult time, Mr Kindred. We are right in the thick of battle. You might get hurt, or worse, you might cause some of our men to get hurt.'

'We won't get in the way, Major. But filming the war, our troops, and what conditions are really like, will help garner a better understanding of what it's all about. Especially, for the people in neutral countries. Those whom we believe should be fighting alongside us.'

He nodded. 'That makes sense, Mr Kindred. Now, let's see how we can get you up to the front. Give me a minute.'

He disappeared briefly from the room, to return a few moments later.

'Right, it's all organised. A field ambulance has just delivered a number of injured Commonwealth soldiers to a nearby hospital. It will take you and your team to the outskirts of Ypres.'

I thanked him and we shook hands.. As we moved towards the door, he remarked. 'By the way, have you got your respirators?'

I looked at him blankly.

'Sorry?'

'Respirators. . .gas masks. You may need them. According to reports the Germans are massing for another offensive to the east of the town. If they use chlorine or mustard gas again, we all could be in trouble. Just a minute.'

He went back into his office, and came out with four or five gas masks.

'I suggest you take these, and slip them on at the first sign of an approaching gas cloud.'

At first glance the woman driver appeared to be in her thirties. She had left England six months earlier to "do her bit", was the phrase she used. John and I were in the back of the ambulance, among the rows of shelves which housed the stretchers of the injured. We were sitting by the opening to the driving section. Clare occupied the passenger seat.

In profile, Jean Hampton - that was her name – looked careworn. As she spoke about her work it was evident she was younger. The gaunt look, the dark circles around her eyes were a product of the horrors of war and exhaustion.

'What is really harrowing about this job are the cries, the bitter anguish of the wounded. Normally I have a medical orderly sitting where you are,' she nodded in Clare's direction. 'He administers morphine when they're in a bad way. But at times it's heart-rending.'

She wiped the back of her hand across her eyes. 'But its work that has to be done.'

I couldn't think of what to say. Nor could my travelling companions, and we rode for a time in silence.

Eventually Clare murmured. 'Don't you take a rest at times? Surely, you need to.'

'Two or three days a month we go back to Saint-Omer and take a train to Paris. But I'm too tired to party, all I want to do is sleep.'

'When do you next take a break,' asked John.

'In ten days time.'

Northern France has never been a tourist attraction.

The unending, flat countryside, divided by hedges, lines of trees and roadside ditches, once overflowed with fields of wheat. Now the landscape was bleak and uncultivated. The remaining inhabitants, mostly the aged and infirm, all had the same countenance – despair. Misery was etched into their features.

'Stop the ambulance!' cried John, 'I want to capture them on film!'

Clare turned towards me and rolled her eyes.

'We have to portray how it is,' I said.

John spoke adequate French, and they allowed him to set up the camera. He explained, although no one would hear what they were saying, he wanted to their comments to be made known. Dialogue cards would be interspersed with the scenes, so one was in doubt about their plight.

As we neared Ypres, Benett-Stamford recorded the devastation. On the approach to to the town it was evident the enemy was intent on reducing it to rubble. It was being progressively destroyed by an unrelenting bombardment of German artillery

Something whistled over our heads.

All of us, except Jean, ducked low.

Seconds later there was an earth-shaking thrump as a shell landed.

'That was close,' murmured Clare, slowly rising back into her seat.

'Not really,' Jean remarked. 'When you get to the front you'll find the shooting is a lot more personal.'

Instead of taking us into the town centre, Jean veered off to the north and headed for the nearby village of Vlamertinge.

'I'm taking you to the schoolhouse, which a number of us are using as a dormitory. You can sleep there tonight. In the morning, I'll drop you off in Rue Carlton before I go to the field medical centre at Bellewaarde. You're to see the acting town major, Lieutentant-Colonel Hankey.'

She grinned. 'He'll brief you on the "do's and don'ts", and issue you with passes so you don't get taken for spies.'

We were each given a sandwich, a cup of tea, two blankets and a pillow. Jean led John and I to the classrooms men were using, and took Clare further down the corridor, presumably to those occupied by women.

After an uncomfortable night's sleep I was woken by someone roughly shaking my arm. It was Benett-Stamford.

'What time is it?' I yawned.

'Just gone seven. We'll have to get our skates on. Apparently, we're to see this town major fellow at eight.'

I shaved in cold water. Seeing my discomfort, John forsook the experience. I wondered if, in future, I should do the same. A piece of toast served as breakfast. When we walked out the school gates Clare and Jean were standing by the ambulance.

'This town major, Jean,' I remarked. 'I can't recall the name you gave him.'

'Lieutenant-Colonel Hankey. Edward's a decent sort. Used to come to our garden parties when I was young. He was a friend of Hugh. . .my eldest brother.'

She tilted her head away.

'Hugh was killed in the very first engagement at Mons, last August. That's what prompted me to become a VAD.'

'A VAD?' asked Clare.

'Oh. . .it stands for Voluntary Aid Detachment.'

'You mean you risk your life for free?' John said, astonishment in his voice.

'Less than anybody else. I drive a vehicle with a red cross painted on the sides, remember. They won't shoot at me.'

John shook his head in wonder.

Lieutenant-Colonel Edward Barnard Hankey was a tall, narrow-faced individual with a flourishing moustache. He peered out from beneath a cap that appeared to be a size too small. While we were standing in his office, he frequently eased it back on his head and mopped the red weal across his brow.

'I'm not certain, Mr Kindred, I welcome the idea of civilians running around while we are conducting a war. You could get yourselves killed, or worse some of my men might when trying to protect you.'

The same comment made at the War Office in London, and the army headquarters in Saint-Omer. I was ready with my reply.

'Lieutenant-Colonel, I can understand your concerns. Given your position I might well react in the same manner. Let me explain in more detail than is stated in that letter. Our aim is to illustrate what you are doing to halt the German invasion of Europe. You are the bulwark, countering the attempts by the enemy to over-run and annex their neighbours' lands. And make no mistake, if allowed to succeed, Great Britain would be next on their list.

'I don't think the people at home fully appreciate that fact. What is going on, what is taking place elsewhere. Yes, many are horrified at what is happening, but they are remote from the actuality of killing, being killed by the enemy. The reports of the fighting, and the bloodshed, are portrayed in the newspapers – but no one has a true idea of the sacrifice and the heroic efforts our soldiers are making on their behalf.

'A film showing what warfare really means, what is being achieved, the price our armies pay to defend their country, the camaraderie in the trenches. What we are doing is to give a true picture of what we, the British nation, are up against. Surprisingly, it will also stimulate enlistment. You need more men at the front, and this would be an ideal way to encourage them.'

Hankey looked at me dubiously.

'I don't see how showing what we are up against will prompt an increase in numbers. On the contrary, it could well bring about a downturn. Leastways, that's what Colonel Swinton of the War Office Press Bureau advised.'

'That does not accord with received opinion, sir. You show a soldier fighting, even against unwelcome odds, and young men invariably want to join in the fray.'

'Hmm. . . '

Hankey tapped the War Office letter on his desk.

'All right, I'll smooth the way for you, Mr Kindred. Let me call in my people to see how we can best help.'

He bellowed out. 'Everyone in here!' Then turned to Clare.

'As for you, young lady, I would strongly suggest you remain here in the town.'

I glanced at Clare's face. Any moment now she is going to erupt, I thought.

John stepped forward.

'With respect, Lieutenant–Colonel, I need Miss Johnson by my side. She is essential. I doubt I could do justice to the project if she were excluded.'

Another "hmm" from Hankey. He then added.

'I shall allow you to go to the front line. But once Mr Benett-Stamford's equipment is set up, you leave. Understood?'

The office door opened and in trooped six men in uniform and two civilians.

'These people are key to helping me run this township.'

He pointed towards a dapper, short civilian. 'This is Monsieur Roland, he is a Belgian interpreter. Next to him is my sanitary officer from the British Army Medical Corps; the Assistant Provost Marshall; my Acting Garrison Sergeant Major; my clerk to help with the routine; and my orderly. Those two lieutenants at the end are attached to the General Headquarters' Intelligence Department. Now, gentlemen, our task is to help these people film the war in action. What would you suggest we do with them?'

A half an hour later everything had been arranged. Jean and her ambulance had been commandeered to ferry us around, and we were to head east out of the town. The intelligence officers believed the next attempt by the German forces to punch a hole in the Salient would be through Sanctuary Wood, two miles south-east of Ypres on the Menin Road. As a consequence, we would be taken to Bellewaarde, where we could experience the likely engagement at a safe distance.

'It's no longer a wood, though,' declared one of the intelligence officers. 'It's more a collection of shattered tree stumps and glutinous mud criss-crossed by our trenches. At the moment they are occupied by the 2nd Battalion, the Gloucestershire Regiment.'

Jean Hampton was called into the office, and given her instructions.

She was polite but firm about her priorities.

'Lieutenant-Colonel, if there are seriously injured at the regimental aid posts or the advance dressing stations, my first duty must be to transport them back to the hospitals.'

'Of course, Jean. I respect that. You would have no other choice.'

Mike Rawson, one of the intelligence officers, accompanied us when Jean drove to Bellewaarde.

'Have you ever been in a war zone before, Mr Kindred?'

I shook my head.

'It's no place for the squeamish.'

His gaze encompassed Clare.

'I have,' replied John Benett-Stamford.

'Then you know what to expect. It is not pretty.'

The sound of heavy artillery, initially a distant thump, grew louder. Now one could pick out the sporadic, throaty rattle of machine gun fire.

'That barrage will go on for a couple of hours,' explained Rawson. 'It's intended to soften us up, so that when, or if, their forces attack we shall offer only token resistance. We use the same tactic. It doesn't work, of course. Though the generals on both sides are convinced it's the right strategy. So, we sit it out for two or three hours, then prepare to face the hordes rushing across no-man's land. All very predictable.'

I was surprised. I was not sure it was wise to question a superior officer's decision so openly, certainly not express personal views to outsiders.

Rawson looked at me and grinned.

'You look startled. You wouldn't be if you spent as much time as I have in the trenches. And not the back, the forward trenches. Witnessing soldiers going over the top.'

From the front seat Clare looked over her shoulder. 'What's going over the top?'

'Charging over a trench parapet towards the enemy when someone blows a whistle. Running towards distant trenches occupied by the Germans and their allies. Like us, they have a wall of barbed wire in front of their dugouts. So before you can engage with the enemy you have to deal with that. Meanwhile, you are being shot at, explosives are being hurled at you. Its indiscriminate killing on a grand scale. . .and we do it to each other.'

'Do you think you should be voicing these shortcomings to us, Lieutenant? We might quote you,' I murmured.

'I'm telling you how it is, Mr Kindred. Perhaps you'll witness the folly of it all yourself.'

John and I exchanged glances.

'Lieutenant Rawson, you'd better call me Daniel. I can't keep referring to your rank and surname.'

The grin I'd seen earlier came readily to his lips.

'I'm Mike.'

I leaned through the canvas sheet separating the cab from the body of the vehicle, and watched Jean turn off the muddy track and pick her way past shell craters, discarded vehicles and the carcasses of dead horses, towards the support lines. She brought the ambulance to a halt beside a large fawn tent.

'This is as far as I can go.' She nodded in the direction of the tent. 'This is an advance dressing station. Surgeons patch up wounded soldiers there. If more extensive treatment is needed, and they can't walk, my ambulance takes them to the hospital in Ypres.'

At that moment, a tent flap lifted, and a doctor, identified by the hanging stethoscope, and a military officer strode in our direction.

'Which one of you is Kindred?' demanded the officer.

'Who wants him?' I asked.

'Major Nicholls, 12th London Regiment.'

Mike Rawson stepped forward. 'This is Daniel Kindred, Major. And these are his film crew, John Benett-Stamford and Clare Johnson.'

Rawson hesitated, then added in a rush. 'I was sorry to hear about what happened.'

He turned to me.

'Two weeks ago, the 12th London Regiment was sent to support our soldiers under attack on Frezenburg Ridge. But the shell fire was so intense almost all of them were killed. Few made it to within a hundred yards of the forward trenches. Major Nicholls was one of the survivors.'

Nicholls bowed his head when Rawson continued.

'Our artillery couldn't cope with the German bombardment. The men tried to file back through a communication trench, but they are narrow, shallow and were full of bodies. The only way was on the open ground in front of the German machine guns. Few managed to reach the support trenches in front of Wieltje.'

Nicholls' mouth had formed a thin, white line.

'I've been assigned to the 1st Monmouthshire Regiment for the time being, and given the job of sorting things out for you.'

He stepped towards me and shook my hand.

'Personally, I think what you are doing could be extremely useful. You have my full support. So, what exactly do you want to film?'

I had thought about what I wanted to achieve before we left England. In fact, I had outlined the concept and how it would be structured at some length for Masterman. But as we had neared the front, so other thoughts intruded. I wanted to portray the reality of war in a different way. That re-definition came to me as this little group stood together in this bleak, battle-scarred landscape. At first I felt my way.

'I want to capture two areas of the conflict, Major. First, the everyday life in the trenches. I want people to see how tough it is for British soldiers. But, at the same time, to convey the strength of the bond that exists among them.

85

The sharing of small comforts, of moral and physical support. I want audiences to witness the reality, and the unity that thrives when they are under attack. Even, dare I say, the preparedness, at times, to lay down their lives to save their fellows. It's a powerful message, and you and I both know that the unstated, selfless regard for one's comrades is very much a British trait.

'Another approach has come to me since I arrived. I want to have on film the tireless work performed by the support staff. In this instance, I would take a VAD, a representative of the Voluntary Aid Detachment, who give their help freely, without reward. I would like to use Jean Hampton, our driver, to give her perspective on what she and others do in this war.'

Nicholls nodded in silent agreement, then he muttered. 'Right, well we'd better get you up to the forward trenches.'

He glanced at Clare. 'Though, I'm not certain it's the place for this young lady, Mr Kindred.'

John had been expecting such a response.

'Don't worry about her, Major. She has been in with me in a great number of unpleasant locations. We are quite used to the unsavoury. . .and the dangerous.'

'I'll leave you in the capable hands of Major Nicholls, Daniel,' said Mike Rawson. 'I'm remaining here to have a word with the surgeon about the hospital arrangements in the town.'

We shook hands.

I had not appreciated how trench warfare functions.

There is a front line, or "Main Fire Trench" facing the enemy. It is not straight, but follows contours or other natural features allowing adequate defence or a view over the enemy lines. It also is dug in sections rather than a straight line, so if a shell explodes inside one of these bays, also known as "traverses", or the enemy manages to penetrate the line, only that section is affected.

Behind it is another row of trenches, called the support line. In this would be found "dugouts" cut into the trench wall. Small, confined spaces, housing the platoon or company commander and a signaler.

Communication trenches link both lines; and along these are ferried by hand all the equipment and supplies. Projecting from the front line are narrow trenches, called "saps", which run beyond the protective belts of barbed wire, terminating somewhere in "no man's land". These are listening posts manned by infantrymen.

We made our way along a communications trench accompanied by the frequent rejoinder from Nicholls to keep our heads down.

'If a sniper sees you, he will gauge your progress, and at the first opportunity blow a hole in your head.'

Difficult to do with the camera equipment all three of us were carrying. At

86

the same time trying to keep our balance on duckboards covered in mud and often submerged in water.

As we neared the front line Clare, who was leading, suddenly stopped.

'What's that awful smell?'

My nose twitched. I caught it, too.

'Unpleasant isn't it.' remarked Nicholls, bringing up the rear.

'It's something no one talks about. It's when men are confined to living cheek by jowl. It's a mixture of smells. . .the latrines, damp, soggy clothing and the odour of unwashed bodies. If I'm away from the trenches for more than twenty-four hours, it catches in my throat. I think it will stay with me for the rest of my life.'

We meandered along the trench until we came to the junction with the front line. Whereas the route we had followed had been roughly hewn from the earth, we were now confronted by a more permanent ditch-like structure. Six to seven feet deep, the side towards the enemy was faced with sandbags and wooden steps. The big problem was the waterlogged ground. Though duckboards had been laid, the pathways oozed liquid mud.

'Unfortunately, the water table is high in this area, and constantly seeps into our trenches,' Major Nicholls explained 'As you can imagine, it's even worse when there's a downpour. The German trenches are on higher ground, they don't have the problem of wet feet.'

Soldiers in this section were sitting on crude wooden benches recessed into the rear trench wall. Others were standing on boards set in the forward walls. I waded over to one group and began chatting. They were interested in the camera, and I explained what we were trying to do. It was soon obvious our presence was a relief from their discomfort, and the boredom.

One fellow, a lance-corporal judging by the stripe on his arm, said. 'Do you mean we are going to be film stars, like Charlie Chaplin?'

I grinned. 'Not exactly. I want to show life in the trenches as it is. What you have to endure. What it's really like when the fighting starts.'

There was an uncomfortable silence.

The one-striper rose from a bench and stood facing me.

'And who's going to see your little film? Generals in their grand houses far from the front? Politicians in Westminster, who couldn't care less? The public in comfortable seats in picture houses, glimpsing our misery before the main film? Who really cares what we have to endure? Go on. . .tell me, who really cares?'

I glanced at Nicholls. He had a calculating look on his face, suggesting he sympathised with the soldier.

He had not finished.

'It's easy for you to leave your comfortable office and spend a few short hours in this hellhole. You'll be gone soon. You won't suffer the deprivation, the despair, the awareness that at any moment you will be sent to your death at the command of some short-sighted officer!'

He was angry, and I was the catalyst unleashing all his pent-up frustrations. I glanced over at Clare and John. Shocked faces on a still tableau.

'So we go over the top. For what? A few hundred yards of this blighted landscape. Then the Hun attacks us, and we're back where we started. Except we have lost hundreds of men. Friends, relatives, all gone!

'Go back to Blighty, you'll be safe there. Go. . .leave us to our misery! I doubt you've ever been close to danger! Where any moment you are likely to lose your life. We are. . .night and day!'

He was shouting at me now. At first he did not catch what I said.

'What was that?'

In a voice that carried just to him.

'I said I know what you are talking about. I was on the *Lusitania* when it was torpedoed. I was one of the few survivors..'

The soldier stared at me for what seemed a lifetime. Then he tentatively thrust out his right hand, and put his left on my shoulder. We shook hands.

'Sorry,' he mumbled. 'I wasn't thinking straight.'

I held onto his hand. 'I was lucky.'

'So. . .tell me how we can help,' he said.

Lance-corporal Jim Oakley took part in a number of scenes. Over the next few days, he explained and demonstrated to the camera the demands of waging trench warfare. John filmed the morning inspections of the platoon's sleeping arrangements – which were on the benches recessed into the trench walls, over which tarpaulins were draped for protection against the weather. We captured the equipment and weapons they used; the meagre, daily rations sent up through the communication channels; the drills they undertook in the confined space. What was hard to define in words, though came over when filming, was the camaraderie Oakley and his platoon unconsciously demonstrated. By simple gestures, without the need for any statement, it was patently clear they looked out for one another.

'Why the inspection of your bedding and sleeping arrangements, Jim?'

'Rats and lice, Daniel,' he explained. 'You've probably seen the rats. We are infested with them. They are often drowned when the trenches flood. But a few days later their place is taken by a fresh lot. If a soldier is uncaring about where he sleeps, he could so easily be harbouring them. But lice are worse, you've probably seen the men scratching, often tearing at their skin for relief. They get everywhere. We could lose the war if we don't control the lice.'

Each night we returned to the school. I decided to give up shaving, it was so much easier than attempting the chore without hot water. Moreover, we were back at the Bellewaarde trenches by five o'clock each morning. Most often the mist burned off quickly and we could film shortly afterwards. On other days it was some hours before the sun shone through. When it rained, we still went up to the front line, working with the men while getting soaked to the skin.

After that first day, I came to appreciate Hankey's concerns for Clare, and she did not join us when we went into the trenches. Instead, I suggested she followed up the second part of the project by spending time with Jean Hampton. Observing the war from another perspective: from a volunteer who unselfishly gave of her services. Clare's experiences in Jean's company would provide the necessary insight when we came to this part of the film.

We got to the front earlier than usual, before the dawn light gave birth to a new day. As John was setting up his camera, there was a scuffling, and bodies started tumbling into the trench. Some alive, the greater number dead. Oakley's head appeared over the sandbags.

'You're early, Daniel,' he declared, sliding down beside me.

I looked around me at the corpses of dead servicemen.

'This is what we do at night.' He nodded towards the bodies.'We go into no-man's land and retrieve our dead. After dark, reconnaissance parties and marauding groups go through gaps in the barbed wire to catch out the enemy. It's a dangerous business, and sometimes we're the ones caught out. A star shell will suddenly light up the battlefield, and if our boys have nowhere to go, a shell hole or behind a tree stump, they're trapped, like rabbits in a motor car's headlamps. When you hear the rattle of a machine gun you know they've been spotted.'

He beckoned me away.

'We might be witnessing an assault on the line soon.' Oakley sniffed. 'One of the reconnaissance people told us the German are massing in this corner of the Salient.'

'I've heard it could be through Sanctuary Wood, south-east of here,' I remarked.

Oakley looked at me strangely. How would a civilian know that sort of information.

It started to rain, and I turned up the collar of my mackintosh.

'I know you wanted to film a battle scene,' Oakley declared. 'But if it is at Sanctuary Wood, I don't recommend you go there. Believe me, it's not a picnic. Bullets fly everywhere. If there is a battle, you'll be far safer here.'

I looked at John. For a moment I thought he was going to live up to his nickname of "Mad Jack"

He nodded. 'I think Jim is right. But I would like to go up a "saps" with one of your observers. Then I could get a marauding party on film as they go out on night patrol'.

'When do you want to do that?'

'As soon as possible.

'What about tonight?'

Jean collected John and I at the advance dressing station, promising to run us back to Bellewaarde at eleven that evening.

'According to a pilot in the Royal Flying Corps,' she remarked, when we explained the reason for our night-time visit, 'there seems to be some activity around Hill 60, which the Germans now hold, but nothing which suggests an push towards Zillebeke.'

At the school we ate a meal of bully beef, potatoes and some unknown vegetable. The same as the men in the trenches. But at least it was warm. I could not help glancing frequently at Clare. She had acquired that haunted look I first noticed about Jean.

Conversation was sporadic, and Clare went to bed soon after we had finished. My concern was noticed.

'You'll have to allow her time to come to grips with what she has seen, and what she has been doing, Daniel,' murmured Jean. 'She was with me today when we picked up some Canadians who fought at Mouse Trap Farm.'

She saw my puzzled look.

'It's between Wieltje and St Julien. The casualties were in a pretty bad way. She also witnessed the effect the chlorine gas attack when the Germans dispersed it in April. The bodies of farm animals, ordinary people and numerous French soldiers, were strewn either side of the road.'

I had read much about the gas attack. A hundred and sixty eight tons of the stuff had been released across a wide front. The gas clouds appeared to be heading for the Canadian trenches before the wind changed direction and blew it towards the French lines.

Two French divisions had seen yellowish-green clouds appear either side of the village of Langemarck at five o'clock in the evening. As they drifted closer, the two clouds merged into one, and soon the unprotected infantry was weeping and gasping as the chlorine took effect.

The German infantry, wearing masks, clambered out their trenches and followed the gas cloud as it drifted on a light breeze over the French lines. As the gas settled, so the two French divisions fled in blind panic. No one could blame them. Eyewitness accounts all conveyed the horror of watching men gasping, retching, choking and dying in their thousands. Clare had come across the aftermath. It had overwhelmed her.

What I could not accept was the blatant attempt to declare firstly that the Hague Convention of 1907 only referred to gas projectiles. It did not prohibit the use of drifting gas clouds.

The German propagandists had been at work, trying to redress widespread condemnation by implying the Entente's forces had used such a weapon earlier in the conflict. But their protests had fallen upon deaf ears.

All that had erupted a month ago. Despite their "unfair and blackguardly tactics", to quote one general, it was still being used against our troops. I had merely read the many reports. Unfortunately, Clare had been confronted with the full horror of it.

John and I were getting ready to leave when she appeared.

'I've come to see you off,' Clare said. 'When will you be back?'

I glanced at Jean.

'Whenever you are free tomorrow morning? Is that all right. We'll make it back to the clearing station by seven o'clock, and wait for you to arrive.'

'Right,' said John, 'let's go, I don't want to miss the patrols.'

Clare walked with us to the ambulance, and started to wave as we drove out the school gates.

Suddenly, Jean braked hard, and Clare appeared breathlessly at the passenger side of the vehicle.

'I was running after you. Have you got your respirators?'

I hadn't. Nor had John.

'Go and get them,' she declared forthrightly.

I shrugged. 'There's no need. We'll be all right.'

She opened the ambulance door.

'Get your respirators! Otherwise you don't go!'

I went to argue, but was stopped by the look in her eye.

'OK,' I mumbled.

'Do you know what today is?' Jim Oakley asked, as we wormed our way up the trench to the look-out post. It was difficult to answer as John and I hauled the tripod, camera, canisters of film, and of course our gas masks, up the narrow gully.

'No,' I managed.

'Whit Monday. . .twenty-fourth of May. . .a bloody bank holiday. Some bank holiday this is!'

I grinned, even in the dark.

'Cheer up, Jim,' I grunted. 'Things could be worse. . .though not much worse.'

We reached the infantryman squatting in the dug-out. I was surprised it managed to accommodate the four of us. Oakley sat forward with the look-out. Over his shoulder he remarked.

'Tell me, John, how do you expect to use your camera when there's no light?'

Benett-Stamford was busy erecting the tripod to its lowest setting.

'I'm sure your friends across no-man's land will send up the occasional star shell, Jim. Then we'll be in business.'

'Just so long as our boys are sheltered when it happens,' came the curt response.

Thirty minutes passed before there was a faint scuffling to our right, and six bodies slithered through the mud towards the enemy lines. It had been raining for the past two days, and everywhere was a sea of mud. The

91

trenches were several inches deep in water, yet I was almost inured to getting mud-splattered and wet feet. I suppose you can get used to anything after a while.

As if on cue a star shell burst above us, and we were bathed in strong, white light.

'Heads downs. . .except you, John,' Jim murmured.

I could hear the camera handle cranking behind me, then a shove in the back, followed by.'Move yourself, Daniel, so I can focus on that shell hole fifty yards away. Some of our chaps are in there.'

When the light faded, I was blinded for a few moments. When my night vision returned, it was to be confronted by one of the outward-bound team slithering into our pit.

'Quick, use the telegraph to alert Major Howard. I overheard a conversation out there, and it looks like there a barrage imminent. What is more, they'll be firing at us!'

He turned and was gone: absorbed into the darkness.

While the look-out was using the field telephone, I said to Oakley. 'That's useful, him speaking German.'

'Most of them do on these sorts of operations. It's surprising what they overhear.'

I turned to John. 'Shouldn't we be getting back?'

'What, and miss all the fun?'

Peculiar way to get enjoyment, I thought.

I think I was dozing off when the first shell screamed over our heads and exploded beyond the distant support trenches. It was starting to lighten, yet when I glanced at my watch it was only a quarter to three.

'My God, What was that?'John shouted, as yet another thundered over the lines.

'I don't think you quite understand how it works, John,' said Jim Oakley, laconically. 'He was right. It looks like they are going to launch an attack on Bellewaarde. So, for the next few hours, before they charge our trenches, the Hun will use their heavy calibre guns to soften us up. They use two hundred and ten millimetre shells, packed with high explosive. They make a lot of noise, produce a big hole, and if you're anywhere in the vicinity when the fuse detonates, we'll just find the pieces.'

'We're in a dangerous position here,' I said. 'Shall we crawl back to the fire line.'

'In fact, we are quite safe for the moment. No-man's land is only a hundred yards deep at this point,' said Oakley. 'So they won't fire too close to us.for fear of hitting their own soldiers. It's when the bombardment stops, and they come over the top. Then we could be in trouble.'

The onslaught continued for some hours. As the day brightened so the fusillade was accompanied by close-quarter machine gun and rifle fire; and our forward post was periodically under attack

After one sustained barrage, our look-out peered through the sandbags that lined the top of the dugout.

'I think we could be in trouble here' he murmured. Jim Oakley squirmed over to peer through the spyhole.

He turned quickly.

'Have you got masks?' he demanded fiercely. 'There's a gas cloud coming right at us!'

John and I scrabbled to retrieve them from among the camera equipment, feverishly pushing the tripod aside I saw them lying under the film canisters. As I lifted mine, I realised I had not worn it before, and for a moment sat there puzzling how to put it on.

Jim Oakley snatched the mask from my hand, pushed it over my face, and pulled at the elastic straps to get a tight fit. He did the same for John. It was difficult to see through the two small, perspex windows, and the sound of my breathing was claustrophobic. The breathing tube was attached a square box, which must have been the filtering system.

I could dimly perceive Jim Oakley and the look-out wearing goggles and heavy cloth pads over their nose and mouth. Then everything went misty as the chlorine gas engulfed us. We sat in the dugout for half an hour before it was considered safe to remove our masks.

The gas cloud was now some distance away, and slowly dispersing. But it was at least forty feet in height, and God knows how wide.

There was the bitter smell of chlorine, and I started coughing. But it was more a reaction to fear and being enclosed in a rubber, tight-fitting mask in which every breath was laboured.

'What's that pad you used over your mouth and nose?' I gabbled loudly.

'It's cotton waste soaked in water. Though urine is better,' he replied urbanely. 'Now, we'd better retreat to the lines before the Hun start moving in our direction.'

We scuttled back along the trench with all the equipment. In the front trench we were confronted with the bodies of dead soldiers who had fallen victim to the gas. No one living was in sight.

'We'd better keep going', growled Oakley. 'We can't do anything here.'

At the end of the communications trench, we came upon the support line. Officers and troops were removing everything portable and withdrawing to new positions. There were too few troops to defend the emplacements around Bellewaarde.

I shook Jim Oakley's hand, and thanked him. John and I owed our lives to his quick reactions.

Then we turned and walked through the carnage and devastation wrought by the continuous shelling, across ruined fields that I doubted would ever crop again.

At the medical clearing station, ambulances were in constant demand ferrying the badly-wounded to the hospital in Ypres. It was late afternoon before Jean's vehicle appeared. When it drew up beside us, Clare leapt from the passenger seat and rushed towards me. She jumped into my arms.

'I thought you were dead,' she cried, and burst into tears.

CHAPTER TWENTY SIX

We spent another week in and around Ypres.

It was apparent to all that the Entente troops had suffered a beating during the past month. The Salient – the bulge into German-occupied Belgium – had been severely reduced.

After the skirmish at Bellewaarde, the number of gas attacks diminished. Both sides replenishing their losses, re-arming for the next phase of the war.

After her outburst at the clearing station, Clare had been unforthcoming, and kept her distance. Whereas, I had been intrigued by her response, and now took a deeper interest. I had noted what an attractive young woman she was when we first met; but her manner had seemed remote, suggesting she would not welcome advances.

Conceivably, I was reading too much into the greeting. Perhaps it was just relief to find a fellow journalist alive and well after such savage action by the enemy. I was not sure how to react. While I had had girlfriends in the past, in the last year I had concentrated on the job in hand. It had left little time for amorous forays.

At mealtimes, I tried to catch her gaze, but it eluded me. When we were with Jean, filming her driving along pot-holed roads, crossing muddy tracts of land, stowing patients on stretchers in her vehicle, Clare always seemed to be engaged in helping her. There was never an opportunity for conversation.

Except that one day.

John and I were in the back of the ambulance, en route to collect another batch of patients, when a heavy shell plunged into a ditch by the roadside. Luckily the side walls of the ditch meant the blast went upwards, ripping through the side and top of the ambulance roof. As the vehicle was hurled sideways I was knocked unconscious,

I came to, lying on the verge, with Clare sobbing and wiping blood from my face.

Jean appeared in my vision, and took Clare's place.

She then proceeded to bandage the deep cut in my forehead, and help me to my feet.

'You'll probably have a headache, but I'm sure Clare will look after you.'

I glanced at the ambulance, and saw that it was still upright.

'Am I the only casualty?' I murmured.

'Yes, thank God. Are you now fit for duty?' he asked. 'I wouldn't fancy lugging all the equipment on my own with you out of action.'

It was meant as a light-hearted remark, more to ease the tension.

Clare missed the joke. Instead she rounded on John and at first I thought she was going to strike him.

'You mean-minded, selfish bugger! Can't you see he's been hurt. All you can think of is yourself. How everything affects you! For two pins. . .'

'Clare, he was only joking,' I said feebly. But as I stepped forward to come between them I wobbled, and my knees started to buckle.

John put out a hand, which was brushed aside by Clare, who immediately took my weight on her shoulder.

'Come on, I'm going to put you on a stretcher in the ambulance.'

Jean helped, and I was manhandled into the back of the vehicle. She stayed with me while Jean jumped in the driving seat and John sat with her in the front. Even when we collected three wounded soldiers, Clare remained by my side. . .holding my hand.

CHAPTER TWENTY SEVEN

A few days later we were back in London.

I had quickly recovered from the knock to the head. Aspirin and three stitches had solved the immediate problem. The doctor who examined me decided I was concussed and merely needed to rest.

Clare had fussed, and I had enjoyed her ministrations. Nothing was said, just meaningful glances and a little hand-squeezing. We parted at Victoria Station, where I helped her into a taxi and promised to be in touch very soon.

John Benett-Stamford was staying in London to process the film.

With that I walked down the quiet, well-ordered streets with my suitcase, marvelling at the fact that no more than a hundred miles to the east thousands of British soldiers were fighting for them to remain so.

The next morning I presented myself at Wellington House.

'Daniel! Have a good trip? How did it go?'

Charles Masterman's first words when I walked into his office. He gestured to a seat, and followed up with another question.

'Coffee?'

'Please.'

'By the way the Italians are finally in. They've just declared war on Austria.'

A few moments later we sat opposite each other in two comfortable chairs. Cups and saucers in our hands.

'So, tell me. . .was it successful?'

'I believe it was, Charles. The films should be ready by the end of the week. We can then assess what Benett-Stamford has got, and from the material create two worthwhile propaganda films.'

He nodded. Then peered closely into my face.

'It wasn't a picnic, was it? What were those stitches for?'

'An ambulance banged me on the head.'

Masterman frowned. I then explained how it had come about. Indeed, I spent the next two hours telling him the unpalatable truth of what was really taking place on the Western Front. I dwelt on how we had survived a gas cloud, when others had not. How the troops' morale was being sapped by the high death rate in the trenches. The unbelievable conditions they endured.

'Do you know, according to regulations, our soldiers should be in the forward trench, the front line, for four days, then four days in close reserve and finally four at rest. In reality they are kept in the forward trenches two to three weeks at a time. In close reserve, men have to be ready to reinforce the line at very short notice. They may have been in a trench system just behind the front system or in the dubious shelter of a ruined village, a shell-torn farmhouse, or what remains of a wood.'

I stared out the window: my memory all too sharp, seeing again the deprivation these men were experiencing. Many had suffered from exposure and frostbite that first winter. Nearly all had been plagued by Trench Foot - a wasting disease of the flesh caused by feet being wet and cold, and constrained in boots and puttees for days on end.

'As we suspected, the one outstanding factor to come out of this was the indomitable spirit that came to the fore whenever a fellow British soldier needed help and encouragement. They suffered the worst the Hun and the elements could throw at them, yet the camaraderie was undimmed. The readiness to support one another was there for all to witness. I sincerely hope we've captured it on the film.'

He never interrupted once. Nor did I drink my coffee, which remained untouched in the cup, clenched tightly in my fist.

He rose eventually, and walking over placed a hand on my shoulder.

I gave a wan smile, and cleared my throat.

'Right, I'd better catch up on things.'

Masterman was uncertain.

'Would a few days rest help, Daniel? We could manage until you feel up to it.'

'No, that's all right, Charles. I want something to occupy my mind.'

My desk was submerged in papers.

I had been away just over two weeks, yet the pile was threatening to topple to the floor.

One of the female clerks was passing the door.

'It looks worse than it is, Daniel. I would say the majority is propaganda material we have been churning out while you've been away. Copies of the leaflets, flyers and press articles.'

'Thanks, Veronica.' I hesitated. 'Do I really have to to go through all of it? You've got your file copies. . .I don't really think I need read every item, do I?'

'I shouldn't think so. Much of it is old hat anyway. Things have moved on. I'll get you a sack, you can dump what you don't want in that.'

I worked my way quickly through the pile. Shoving most of it in the waste sack to be burned. I had got down to the few remaining items when I came across a copy of the New York Herald. The newspaper Clare worked for.

It was not on the front page, but a banner headline announcing the Treaty was prominently displayed on page four.

I went cold. I had told Clare about Italy's change of heart; that the country would be going to war on our side. It seemed she had disregarded what I had mentioned in confidence, and sent the story to her newspaper. What an idiot I had been. She must have seen me as a naïve young man on whom she could work her charms to obtain a raft of stories to send back home.

I beat the desktop in frustration. I had thought there might be something between us. I had simply been an unknowing dupe. Those large eyes staring intently at me. Holding my hand while shedding crocodile tears - and I had fallen for it.

If Masterman saw this editorial, which came out over a week before the actual declaration of war, I could be for the high jump for giving out secrets. I steered well clear of him for the rest of the day.

In fact, I managed to avoid him for the rest of the week.

During that time I received several telephone calls from Clare, which I ignored. Once bitten, and all that.

She even wrote a letter to the flat inviting me to a party. Again I did not respond. She obviously wanted to maintain the link, to have a conduit to any worthwhile tidbits of information. Clare had told me she needed to send back home some decent stories to make her mark with the Herald's editor. Well, I certainly was not going to provide them.

There were more telephone calls to the office. These were fielded by my clerk. I had advised her that if a Miss Clare Johnson phoned, tell her I was away. Towards the end of the third week, they finally stopped.

It was late one Friday evening. I was putting the finishing touches to an article for the American press, in particular my friends at the Algonquin, on the modern day version of rape and pillage as practiced by the Hun, when Charles walked through the door.

'You're working late, Daniel.'

'I wanted to complete a piece for the American media.'

He nodded, and perched on a corner of the desk.

'I wanted to talk about the two films you made with John Benett-Stamford. They're good. . .damned good. I like the way you woven a telling story into each of them. So let's talk about how and when we launch them.'

As he said "launch them", he crossed his legs and clasped a knee. In so doing he dislodged a filing tray, sending its contents to the floor. He jumped off the desk with an apology, and I came round to retrieve the contents as he bent in the same direction.

Masterman held up the copy of the New York Herald. My heart lurched.

'Did you see the article, Daniel?'

I nodded.

'While you were away I took over the American desk for a while. Northcliffe suggested we send an editorial to the press over there about Italy forsaking the Germans and coming over to us. Would you believe, only the Herald picked it up. Where are you going?'

CHAPTER TWENTY EIGHT

I went to her address in Bayswater, to learn from the new tenant that she had vacated the flat. I took a taxi to the American Embassy in Grosvenor Gardens; but they could tell me nothing of her whereabouts.

I wandered dispiritedly towards the entrance, holding the door open for a woman coming up the steps.

'It's Mr Kindred, isn't it?'

I suddenly realised the woman was the ambassadress.

'Err. . .yes, ma'am.'

'What are you doing here, Mr Kindred?' She grinned. 'You're looking for Clare, aren't you?'

A lifeline. I brightened visibly.

'Yes, I am.'

'What a pity. Didn't you know she has gone back home?'

'We could send copies of the films to the intelligence officer at the embassy. I don't see any need for you to traipse over there,' said Masterman.

I was in his office with Northcliffe, Wickham Steed and several people from Military Intelligence.

'I'm not so sure, Charles,' remarked Everett, the senior of the two officers. 'Inevitably, there will be questions when the films are shown. These could range from, is it a spoof, a fabrication?. . .to what experience have you had of trench warfare? None of us could give authoritative answers. Who better to answer such queries than the person responsible for the films? He was on the spot.'

Everyone else agreed.

Ten days later I arrived at Pier Fifty-Four in New York City on the *Aquitania.* A liner that had become a troop carrier, and which was soon to be converted to a hospital ship.

When I walked through the terminal building I noticed the posters advising the possibility of attack by German vessels had been removed. I waited in line for a cab and told the driver, `The Algonquin Hotel`.

At six o'clock that evening I walked into the bar. If they followed their customary habit of meeting on a Thursday, by now most would have arrived. Things had not changed in my brief absence. Seven of them were already occupying the far end, noisily chatting and drinking their "usuals" served by the long-suffering Johnny.

I sidled towards them unobtrusively.

The barman came over to take my order. Frowned, pointed a long finger, then grinned. 'I didn't recognise you at first with the beard. One of my special gin and tonics, right?'

Ruth Hale saw me first. A look of puzzlement crossed her features, as though she could not immediately place where we had met. Then she remembered.

'Daniel? It is Daniel. Goddamn it, you've grown a beard! What the hell are you doing here?'

They looked at her. Then slowly turned to look at me.

There was a chorus of yells, and I was submerged under a welter of backslapping from the men, and kisses from Ruth and Dorothy. There was a face I didn't recognise. Ruth Hale saw me regard him questioningly.

'Tom, come over here and meet Daniel Kindred. Daniel works for the London Times, and from time to time, is the source of some useful information . Daniel say hello to Tom Sawyer, no jokes now, he works for the Herald.'

It was another meal at which a lot of alcohol was consumed. This time I was more wary, and later that night remembered quite clearly making my way to my room. Though it took several attempts to insert the key in the lock.

I was taking a shower when the phone rang.

Grabbing a towel I went to the bedside table and lifted the receiver.

'Hello.'

'Daniel, it'sAlexander. . .Alexander Woollcott. We're all set. I spoke to Mitchell Mark. He said if we get to the picture house just after lunch he'll arrange for a showing. So if you come over at about one thirty with the two films, we can watch them before the picture shows start. I'll phone the others, and tell them to be there at two. OK?'

'You mean the films I brought from England?'

'Of course I mean the films you brought with you. Say, are you feeling all right?'

'Yes. . .yes, I'm fine.' I hesitated. 'Where exactly is this picture house?'

'The Mark Strand Theatre is at 1579 Broadway, at the northwest corner of 47th Street and Broadway in Times Square.'

When I arrived Alexander Woollcott came out to meet me with a large-framed man sporting an equally large moustache.

'Dan, I want you to meet Samuel Rothafel, the manager of this remarkable edifice.'

'That's generous of you to making your theatre available to us,' I said as we shook hands.

'Think nothing of it. Since we opened in 1914, the Times has been really helpful in getting the Strand established. It was the least we could do.'

'You've got a lot to offer, Roxy. All we did was tell our readers.'

Roxy. . .that was an interesting abbreviation. Woollacott called me Dan, but I always called him Alexander. I hadn't heard anyone shorten his name.

Rothafel led us to the projection room, and I spent some time explaining the sequence and running time of the two films. Then, as two o'clock approached, we went down to the auditorium. Woollacott took a seat and I walked to the front, before the screen that towered above me. The Algonquin crowd and some others, about a dozen in all, looked at me expectantly.

'What are you going to show us, Dan?' called Dorothy. 'Do I need to buy some popcorn?'

What had I told them last night? Were they expecting a comedy film show? a drama maybe? or some lighthearted documentary?

'My friends, the two films you are about to see will occupy you for three quarters of an hour. I honestly cannot recall how I described them to you last night, but I have to tell you they both show the war in Europe as it is. . .warts and all. They may not suit the faint-hearted, the squeamish, those of you who are out-and-out pacifists. Unfortunately, in any conflict there are those who live through it. . .and those who die. If you decide to stay, you will witness both sides of the coin.'

I waited ten seconds. No one left their seats.

I waved to the projectionist and walked to a seat a few rows back. The better to gauge their reactions.

CHAPTER TWENTY NINE

When the lights came up I walked down the aisle and stood before them. I wanted a good look at their faces.

There was a tense, almost unreal silence. Then one of them started to clap, then another, then all dozen. They rose to their feet. It went on for several minutes before they sat down.

Alexander Woollcott came forward, and putting his hand on my shoulder said. 'My boy, I speak for everyone here, that was a damn powerful eye-opener to what is really going on. Goddamn it! I don't think any of us appreciated what people have to endure for freedom and the right to live in harmony with their neighbour. You know what was really got to me in that first film. . .the spirit, the desire, the willingess to help fellow soldiers. That sure is a most telling message.'

Franklin Adams of the New York Tribune stood up.

'Dan, I totally endorse what Alexander has said. But I also want to know who that woman ambulance driver is. I want to shake her hand. I want to embrace her. I have never seen such a selfless act in my life.'

Robert Benchley shouted. 'What's her name, Dan?'

'Who is the girl helping her?' called Dorothy Rothschild. 'The one who ran through all that mud to tend the guy hit in the head? She also changed that ambulance wheel. She really is something!'

My heart missed a beat when I heard that.

'The ambulance driver is a British woman called Jean Hampton,' I replied. 'She is what they term a VAD – short for Voluntary Aid Department. The young woman helping her is an American.'

'Well, I won't introduce her to Ed Parker, my fiancé,' declared Dorothy. 'She's not only attractive, she's a motor mechanic. . .an unbeatable combination.'

Woollcott held up a hand.

'I don't know how you feel, but what we've seen here today demands a bigger audience than us lot.'

'Too right!' exclaimed George Kaufmann. 'We should fill every seat in this theater!'

At that moment Samuel Rothafel, the manager, walked down the centre aisle.

'I agree with Mr Kaufmann,' he said, turning to face those seated. 'I watched the films from back there.' He waved an arm. 'Pretty powerful stuff. So, I have a suggestion to make.' Rothafel paused, then said. 'What would you say if we held a special event in this theater, and invited all the movers and shakers in New York City to see what we have just witnessed?'

****

When we were leaving the theatre, I had a quick aside with Tom Sawyer.

'You may or may not have recognised the ambulance driver's helpmate, Tom. It was Clare Johnson, who also works for the Herald. She was in Belgium helping to make those films. I want you to bring her along to this event we've just been discussing. But don't tell her what it's about, and certainly don't mention my name, OK?'

CHAPTER TWENTY NINE

After the Algonquin film show, I had wired Charles Masterman to inform him of the forthcoming event, and to request negative versions of the two films so prints could be made.

In the meantime I travelled down to Washington and held a private showing at the embassy on Connecticut Avenue. The response by the many staff in the embassy was similar to the Algonquin set.

'Hmm. . .thought-provoking stuff, Mr Kindred,' responded the ambassador. 'What do you think, Paul. . .Malcolm?'

Paul was one of the ambassador's aides, and Malcolm MacKenzie, his chief intelligence officer.

'I would say, Ambassador, that this is the sort of thing that will jerk the Americans out of their complacency,' responded the officer in his soft Edinburgh burr. 'The first film treads a fine line between hardship and the bulldog spirit conquering all. It's a good portrayal of what our soldiers have to endure, yet it holds onto that essential determination that, against the odds, they will win through. Damned good propaganda.'

'Paul?'

'I agree with Malcolm. That first film is the gritty reality of what warfare is about. Shocking, yes. . .but you cannot deny it is terrific box office. The second film ideally complements the first. What marvellous people are those volunteers. . .especially that ambulance driver.'

'They sum up my sentiments exactly, Mr Kindred. A first-class production. Did you use professional film-makers?'

'Actually, I took with me a cameraman who revels in filming war scenes. A character somewhat over the top, but his experience of being in the thick of action worked to our benefit. Yes, when we came back we used a well-known film production company, which edited the many rolls of film and put it all together. I think they did a fantastic job.'

He nodded. 'What I did notice is the fact there is no reference to you lot, or the War Office Press Bureau. Was that deliberate?'

'Well, sir, we don't like to feature our name. We try to keep a low profile. Only those whom we want to know are told of our role. Just the cameraman and the film company who worked on the project are featured in the credits.'

I got back to New York to discover it had become a black tie affair.

The invitation was waiting for me when I got back to New York.

This is a personal invitation to those Americans who believe what happens in other parts of the world could ultimately impinge on our lives and livelihood.

You are requested to attend an evening at the Mark Strand Theatre at 1579 Broadway, New York City at 6.30pm on June 24th, 1915.

Cocktails until 7.30pm.

Thereafter a special presentation, followed by a buffet supper.

BLACK TIE

RSVP, Mitchell Mark

A note from Alexander Woollcott accompanied it.

Dan, each invitee has received a personalised invitation, followed up by a telephone call during which we gave the briefest explanation why they should attend. With a week to go we have almost a full house, Alexander.

On the train from Washington I had begun to wonder if the Algonquin crowd realised they were party to a major lobby for the minds and hearts of those coming to the event. I felt I had to say something, and the best person to speak to was Alexander. I phoned and asked him if he were free for lunch.

'This must be serious if you are bringing me here.'

We were dining at Mouquins on Sixth Avenue. The budget might be put to the test, but I felt it right to voice my concerns somewhere appropriate - to soften the blow.

We were also drinking a particularly good wine.

The waiter served our main course before I hesitatingly raised the subject.

'The thing is, Alexander, I might be thought guilty of misleading you. Not just you. . .but your compatriots at the Algonquin. You see, I may work for the Times, but for the moment I've been transferred to another organisation.'

'Yes, I know.'

'You know? How could you possibly know?'

'You mentioned it the first time we met you. When you joined us for the late night meal we had at the hotel. Don't you remember? You stood up, or attempted to stand up, and told us, shushing us not to tell a soul, that you had been seconded to the WPB... the waste paper basket. At least, you said, it felt like a waste paper basket, with the amount of paper you were churning out. I think you eventually told us it stood for the War Propaganda Bureau. Great Britain's equivalent to the. . .well whatever it was you said in German.'

I stared at him for a moment.

'Did I really? I must have worse than I thought.'

Woollcott grinned suddenly. 'I get it. You were concerned you might be using us. Taking advantage of our friendship. That was it, wasn't it? And you wanted to break it to me gently. . .hence the lunch?'

I gave a rueful nod.

'We know what you do, Dan. . .and we're right behind you. We all agreed not to print a word about the films until after the show at the Strand Theater Now, let's enjoy this delicious food.'

I called for another bottle of wine.

CHAPTER THIRTY ONE

Tom Sawyer telephoned to confirm he would be escorting Clare Johnson to the Strand Theatre. He had not told her much about the event, nor had he mentioned my name.

When the day actually arrived I was nervous. Not about the film show, nor the audience's reaction. The real fear, the jumble of thoughts that cascaded through my mind, was that Clare would leave immediately she realised what was happening; that she might reject any plea I made to renew our friendship; that she might have another man in her life.

Uncertainties plagued me throughout the day.

At the theatre I passed the two films to "Roxy" Rothafel, and wandered into the auditorium. A microphone and stand had been placed on the staging in front of the screen.

When Rothafel returned from the projection room, strolling down the aisle, he called out. 'Do you want to test the microphone, Dan?'

I clambered up the steps and walked to the centre of the stage. When I looked out across the vast auditorium, my stomach turned. In front of me was a colossal expanse of seats. There were boxes lining the walls, a huge, sweeping balcony, and the many stalls retreated into the gloom. All to be filled by over two thousand people. I now realised what they meant by stage fright.

Rothafel saw my reaction.

'Best you stay there for a while, Dan. Get used to the view and the lighting. We'll use a following spot.'

He waved an arm. Immediately I was bathed in bright light. I couldn't see a thing. Was that good or bad? At least I wouldn't be able to see all those expectant faces waiting for me to talk about the films they were going to see. I would be in my own little world. On the other hand, I wouldn't be able to read my notes.

'Do I have to have that light, Sam?'

'It's important they see as well as hear you, Dan. If you don't, a voice coming from a dark shadow will have no impact at all, believe me.'

He then added.' By the way, I've asked our organist, Ralph Brigham, to come in. I thought some softly-played, serious music might well suit the occasion. He used to play the church organ in Northampton, Massachusetts before coming here, so he'll choose something appropriate. Is that all right with you?'

The foyer in the Strand Theatre is like an elegant ballroom. The full complement of the Algonquin set were there to receive the guests they had invited. By seven o'clock, many had moved through to another salon, and others were taking their seats in the auditorium.

There was no sign of Clare or Tom Sawyer.

At seven fifteen I went backstage, and peered through the curtains at the gathering audience.

'How long is your introduction, Dan? So the projectionist does not miss his cue,' Rothafel asked.

'Five minutes, not much more,' I said, scanning the rows of seats. Tom was supposed to be sitting five rows back, and they still had not arrived.

'Another few minutes, then I think we should begin,' Rothafel said over my shoulder. 'Everyone's in their seats. Say, are you expecting someone?'

'Well, yes. But she doesn't seem to be coming.'

'Well, I don't think we can wait much longer. The organist is standing by as well as the projection room boys. So. . .I guess this is it.'

Disappointed, I started towards my position centre stage behind the curtain, then halted.

'Roxy, the fifth row back, in the centre. If she does arrive I want you to do something for me.'

The organist began playing a piece of music I could not place; but it was exactly right as an introduction.

The curtain slowly began to rise. In those few seconds before the spotlight blinded me, and I lost sight of the audience. . .there she was, slipping into her seat. Though, Tom Sawyer, her supposed companion, was nowhere to be seen.

I took a deep breath, and momentarily closed my eyes. My wish had been granted.

The music ended, and I stepped up to the microphone.

'Ladies and gentlemen, good evening, and thank you for coming to the Mark Strand Theatre to view a picture show. However, I must point out, this picture show is like no other you have ever seen.

'My name is Daniel Kindred, and as you can immediately tell, I am a Brit. As you also know, my country, together with France and Russia, are currently at war with Germany and its allies.

'The reasons why are complicated. When we first learned of the growing unrest in Europe, it prompted the predictable reaction. . .not our problem. There's a stretch of water between Great Britain and the continent which, I must admit, allows us to be insular. We are not like the French, the Belgians, the Portugese, the Spanish. We are not excitable, we don't suffer mood swings, we don't wave our arms about when we're talking. However, we are blighted by the inclination to be sceptical, even if it is compensated by an over-riding sense of. . .fair play.

'When war was first declared, the British did not send its troops in an instant to fight in the fields of Flanders, or the hills of the Ardennes.

Scepticism abounded. Yes, we had heard reports. We'd been told what was happening. But, in typical fashion, we dismissed the idea there was a truly, full-scale war. Even if there were, once tempers cooled, it would all be over by Christmas.

'Frankly, we British were not attentive to the events unfolding just across the Channel. In the early Summer of !914 we played our national game, cricket; families went to the seaside; some of us took holidays. In other words, we carried on as normal. When the Belgians suggested we help relieve the city of Antwerp, the government grudgingly sent a handful of marines and a smattering of the British Expeditionary Force, the majority of which were of pensionable age. The all pervading feeling being, "really, aren't we making too much of this."

'They got more than they bargained for. The German army rolled over the British contingent like a knife through butter. Suddenly, we were caught up in a real war as the Reichswehr swept through Belgium heading for the French border. At home, the mood of complacency was rapidly replaced by the urgent need to stem the annexation of great swathes of Europe by Kaiser, Wilhelm the Second.

'Great Britain stepped into the fray to defend the rights of peace-loving nations. In truth it was a chaotic scramble. We were unprepared to fight another man's war. But, at the same time, we could not sit back and watch a tyrant change the face of Europe

'It has been tough on the civilians caught up in the fighting; losing their homes, their livelihood and loved ones in the destruction all this is causing.

'It has been doubly hard for the soldiers withstanding the onslaught thrown at them by the German army. Few have any real idea of what they go through. That's why you are here this evening. You will be witness, for the first time what life is like on the front line, in the heat of battle.

'Not so many years ago the saying "the pen is mightier than the sword", became a reality. This evening, you will see that "the spade is mightier than the gun". When I show you this first film, you'll see what I mean.'

I nodded to "Roxy" Rothafel as I walked off the stage

Twenty minutes later I walked back onto the stage.

Suddenly, the theatre erupted in applause.

I bowed my head for a moment before stepping to the microphone.

'Ladies and gentlemen, what you have seen is a portrayal of grim determination. The soldiers in that film illustrate the will to resist the artillery fire thrown at them; to endure the hardships of trench warfare; and now this additional hazard, the use of chlorine and mustard gas. I lived among them for a short while and discovered something else. . .a commitment to their comrades. There is an amazing bond of camaraderie, which I believe came over in the film. I found it a amazing experience.'

Rothafel signalled. The projectionist was ready.

'In this next film, that commitment to one's fellow man goes a step further. I won't say any more. But if you have any questions after you have seen it, I'll do my best to answer them.'

I left the stage as the lights dimmed.

CHAPTER THIRTY TWO

Applause rippled through the audience while the film was still showing.

When it finished, there was a hushed silence before everyone stood to clap the leading ladies - Jean Hampton, and her unknown assistant.

Once more I moved to the microphone.

'This film, more than the first, underlines the sacrifice of those who voluntarily give of their services to a cause. The heroine, whose name you saw on the text cards, is Jean Hampton. She is not with us tonight. I know for a fact, she is still driving her ambulance in the battle fields of Ypres.

'However, her unnamed assistant, the young woman you saw helping Jean in the film, is with us. Her name is Clare Johnson, an American, who went to the Western Front to witness for herself what the cause, and the effect, this war was having on the local population. As well as what the troops have to deal with, day in, day out. Ladies and gentlemen, Clare Johnson!'

As I had requested, the spotlight swung round to pick out Clare, who was sitting at the end of the fifth row.

The applause was tumultuous.

I negotiated the steps and made my way to where she was sitting. The aisle seat was empty, for Tom was absent. Clare was cowering in her seat when I stood next to her.

'Come on! Stand up! Acknowledge the applause.'

Slowly she rose to her feet and turned to face the audience.

'How dare you, Daniel,' she whispered savagely. 'You not only ignored my phone calls, you have now embarrassed me in front of everyone present.'

Someone shouted "Speech". . .suddenly there was a chorus calling for the same.

I dragged her unwillingly onto the stage, and pushed her in front of the microphone.

She glared at me in fury. But there was nothing she could do, but respond.

'Ladies and gentlemen. You have been most generous. In truth, I did no more than any of you would have done, given the same circumstances. It is difficult to be oblivious to the suffering of others. I simply went forward to help. I did not know what I was doing had been caught on camera.

'I am a journalist. I went there to do a job. But like many others I despaired for the lives so unnecessarily disrupted, brought to tears by what I witnessed. I am still writing my thoughts and experiences for the New York Herald. But it's hard to put into words. May the conflict soon be over, for all our sakes.'

The theatre erupted once more.

Clare turned to me, tears in her eyes.

'Damn you, Daniel. Now you've ruined my eyelash darkener as well!'

****

I stayed close to her at the supper which followed. Though at times I was pushed out the ring that surrounded her wherever she went.

Something else I found endearing. She vehemently denied she was anything but a helper. One that only assisted for a brief moment in time. Not like the women volunteers in Belgium running the gauntlet every day.

I found I could not take my eyes from her.

When the party began to break up, I asked if I might accompany her home.

'Why? You didn't ask me in London. As far as you were concerned, I no longer existed.'

But after a few moments. . .she said yes.

In the taxi I asked about Tom Sawyer.

'The editor told him to get himself up to Buffalo. There's been a report someone tried to explode a bomb near the Welland Canal.'

Clare turned towards me. 'Never mind that. Why didn't you want to see me? Not return my calls? I want a straight answer. No prevarication. You're good at bending the facts, it's your job. So, give it to me straight. The plain truth.'

I bit at my lip. I had thought to say I had been so busy. . .that I'd been away. But she would have seen through that in an instant.

'I didn't return your calls because I thought you had been responsible for something that appeared in the Herald that I had told you in confidence. All sorts of things went through my mind. Uppermost was the notion that you had been using me to wheedle information out of me. I was upset, deeply upset. It was only later I discovered that my boss, Charles Masterman, had circulated the news of the Italian *volte face*, and your newspaper had picked it up. I'm sorry. . .that's what it was all about.'

Hurt and fury suffused her features in equal measure.

'My God! I'm shocked you think me capable of such duplicity! You, you pompous upstart! You unfeeling pig!'

She leaned forward and shouted at the driver. 'Stop this taxi! At once!'

The vehicle skidded to a halt.

'Get out! Go on, get out! I never want to see you again!'

CHAPTER THIRTY THREE

I had not realised that Samuel Insull, the industrialist had been in last night's audience. We had first met at the British Embassy in Washington. At first, I had not appreciated he was British or for that matter, a committed patriot, who did all that was possible to publicise the efforts Great Britain was making in support of a free Europe.

He came into the dining room when I was at breakfast, and took the opposite chair at the table.

'First class, last night, Daniel. You handled it well. Though, I didn't recognise you with your beard. How long have you had that?'

'Since going up to the Western Front, Sam. I dislike shaving in cold water, and just let it grow.'

Hmm. . .suits you. I was in New York on business and got invited to the theatre. I'm pleased I went. So, what I want from you is. . . '

He stopped mid-sentence, and stared at the person standing at my shoulder. A strident woman's voice said in my ear. 'I want a word with you! Now!'

I rose to my feet to see Clare marching from the room.

'Wait here for me, Sam. This is important.'

I followed in her wake as we moved into the hotel lounge.

She did not sit, but pivoted on her heel and confronted me.

'When you said you were upset, what did you mean?'

I stared at her. Taking in the auburn hair that framed her face. Her slender frame and the tapping foot.

'Well?'

'I. . .I was upset, because I discovered you mean a lot to me. And for that reason, it hurt all the more and I over-reacted. I'm sorry.'

'What about last night? Were you trying to embarrass me?'

'Of course not. I thought you were remarkable in working alongside Jean Hampton. I wanted everyone to witness the compassion, the strength you showed on the battle field.'

Anxious eyes scanned my face.

'Oh, Daniel, I didn't know what to think when I didn't hear from you. I didn't sleep last night going over, again and again, the reason why. In a way I can understand how you felt. Not fully, but more so in the cold light of day.'

I interrupted her. 'Can't we make a fresh start? I'll never believe anything ill of you again. I promise.'

I had not appreciated we had an audience. When I kissed her, a dozen or so people in the room gave faint cheers.

With her hand in mine I led her back to the dining room.

'I recognised you from last night, my dear,' said Insull, after introductions were made: Clare still blushing from her earlier entrance.

'I thought you were very brave to work with that ambulance driver. Artillery shells are indiscriminate, they make no concessions for the red crosses painted on such vehicles.'

'I'm not sure I thought about danger, Mr Insull. Jean, the driver, had to get as close as possible to the injured, and I walked in front guiding her through the mud, trying to miss the craters, and avoid where the track would not take the weight of the ambulance.'

'But you frequently carried one end of a stretcher, and helped dress soldiers' wounds.'

'Faced with the same situation, any right-minded person would have done what I did.'

She was playing down her contribution to the overstretched field services. I was so pleased John Benett-Stamford had caught her performing such essential tasks. In that moment I was intensly proud of her, When I look back, Samuel Insull was right. Clare had been brave.

'By the way, have you seen any of the morning papers?' queried Insull.

We both shook our heads.

He passed a copy of the New York Times. Clare's face stared out at us.

'You're on most of the front pages, my dear.'

He grinned in my direction. 'Fortunately, there's no mention of you.'

She was much in demand for interviews.

Ruth Hale, a feature writer for Vanity Fair, particularly wanted to do a major piece. Ruth, a staunch feminist, wanted to show how women can cope and adapt under pressure. She saw Clare as an excellent role model.

While she was occupied, I accompanied Samuel on his return to the "windy city". During the visit I came to appreciate what Insull was achieving in the mid-west. He had a strong rapport with intellectuals, and was always advocating that the United States should join in the conflict on the side of the Entente. He personally funded numerous propaganda campaigns, and was forever striving to alter entrenched views on neutrality.

The show took place in the thousand seater Paramount Theatre, just off Logan Square. We received the same reaction as that in New York; and in the next day's newspapers the photograph of Samuel Insull, who had brought the two films to the city, was widely displayed on all the front pages.

He came to see me off at Union Station.

'We'll keep plugging away, Daniel. But the population here comprises a high proportion of German immigrants. They don't want their background called into question if the public voiced approval for this country to join in the war on the British side. So they are fiercely neutral. And work hard to maintain that standing.'

Two days later I was back in New York.

CHAPTER THIRTY FOUR

Clare was at the station to meet me.

She ran down the platform.

'Guess what! My editor has confirmed it. I'm now officially the Herald's European correspondent! What about that?'

'That's wonderful!'

'And I'll be based in London!'

I grinned, and hugged her more tightly.

'When does the appointment start?' I asked.

'Next month. There's lots to do before I go.'

Then her face took on a solemn look.

'Daniel, I've told my parents about you. They would like to meet you. Is that OK?'

The next day we took a train from Grand Central Station to Scarsdale, twenty miles north of the city. We walked the short distance from the station, and rounding a bend came upon the Johnsons' mansion.

A sweeping drive amid well-tended lawns brought us to imposing entrance set beneath a portico supported by two massive Doric pillars.

'Impressive,' I murmured.

One side of the tall, double door was opened by a man whom I saw immediately could only be Clare's father.

Clare said breathlessly. 'Hello, daddy. I want you to meet, Daniel.'

'Don't I get a kiss first, honey?' he smiled.

They kissed. We shook hands.

'Come in both of you. We're sitting out on the terrace at the moment.'

Clare's father led the way through a large, tiled hall, with a wide marble stairway curving up to the next floor.

On the terrace two women were seated at a table under the shade of a large parasol.

'Mother, Margaret, our daughter is here, and this is Daniel.'

After Clare had greeted her mother and grandmother, I stepped forward and shook their hands.

'Come, sit next to me, Daniel. I want you to tell me about what my younger daughter has been up to,' said her mother.

There was no ice to be broken. I had felt a little apprehensive at the thoughts of meeting Clare's parents; and that feeling had intensified when confronted by their lifestyle. By comparison, I had been raised in much humbler surroundings.

However, within minutes we were chatting easily, the conversation flowed without effort. Of course, talking about their daughter's exploits was a subject that came easily to me.

Perhaps, I gave too much away. For their smiles suggested my remarks had also described the depth of my feelings for Clare.

And so the day passed. We enjoyed a splendid lunch and an early dinner before leaving to catch the train back into the city.

A few days later I sailed for England. Now desperate to get back, I had enlisted the help of the embassy to obtain a passage on the *Justicia*. Intended as a liner, it had been commandeered by the government as a troop ship, and all thirty five thousand tons of her had been covered in camouflage paint.

When I entered the WPB offices the morning after disembarking at Southampton, it was like a ghost town. Several clerks and a few secretaries were about the place, but Charles and all the senior staff were missing.

'Where is everyone?' I asked.

'They're all at a meeting at the War Office in Horse Guards Avenue,' said Lisa Newman, Charles' assistant. 'Apparently, there's a bit of a flap on.'

They trooped in just before lunch

I came to my door, and Charles waved to me to follow him into his office.

'Hells Bells! What a bloody mess!'

'What's happened?

He swivelled round. It was then I noticed the haunted look to his eyes.

'Monty Beresford has hanged himself!'

'Christ! That's a shaker.'

'On the pairing roster I drew up he was supposed to come in yesterday morning with Laura Wilson. He never arrived at her flat, which is only two or three hundred yards away. Laura telephoned his landlady, who checked and told her there was no one in his flat.'

'I suppose you got in touch with Special Branch?' I said.

Masterman nodded. 'They went round there, broke down the door and found him hanging from a rope in the ceiling.'

'They're sure it was suicide? Not enemy agents making it look like self-murder.'

'That's what the meeting was about this morning. The police took one look and declared Monty had taken his own life while the balance of his mind was disturbed. What do you think? You worked with him. . .used the same typist.'

I shrugged. 'Monty didn't seem the type to take his life. Still, who knows what goes on in other people's minds?'

I left Charles' office and walked towards my room. The more I thought about it, the more implausible it became. I retraced my steps.

117

'Charles, can I go round to Monty's flat? I want to satisfy myself about something.'

He looked up questioningly. 'About what? Don't you accept the police report?'

'Did Special Branch?'

'I presume so. Leastways, they haven't raised any queries. But then they didn't know the man as we did. OK. . .I'll telephone Inspector Brightwell. He's the policeman in charge of the case. I'll get him to release the key to you.'

The next day Charles informed me that the key was available at Highgate Police Station, and would be handed to me by the duty officer when I showed proof of identity.

'You've got strict instructions not to remove anything, disturb anything, or leave anything there. Do you understand? Normally, they would send someone to accompany you, but they are up to their eyes at the moment.'

Monty Beresford's landlady was a garrulous soul in her sixties. She assumed it was an official visit, and was at pains to inform me that her neighbours and friends had been shocked by the incident, as well as the shopkeepers in the high street.

'What a thing to happen in a respectable house. And I've been told not to rent out the rooms for the moment, until the police have decided they no longer need them for further investigations. I suppose your visit is part of these further investigations?'

I had the strong impression a certain amount of pleasure was being derived from the notoriety she was attracting.

I made my way up the stairs with the landlady in close attendance. At the door to the flat, I said. 'This is as far as you're allowed to go for the moment. Though, I'm sure you will soon be free to take another lodger.'

I turned the key and stepping smartly inside, shut the door behind me.

There was a strange silence about the place. Perhaps it was one's heightened senses. A death had occurred here. A man I thought I knew well. In the stillness I could recall his bantering voice, his laughter, his ability to give measured assessment of the work we did. All that had now gone.

I forced myself to enter the sitting room, where he had been found.

The hook was still in the ceiling. Though the rope had been taken with the body. After a few minutes I wandered into the kitchen and went through the drawers of the dresser and food cupboard. From there, I wandered into the bedroom and bathroom. I peered in the medicine cabinet. Not that I knew what I was looking for. Perhaps, a prescriptive drug for depression. A bottle of pills, a cache of aspirin. Nothing, other than a razor and a toothbrush with a box of tooth powder.

I went back to the sitting room and stood looking at the hook. Accepting,

118

for the moment, that Monty had committed suicide, in my searches I had not come across any tools to open a hole in the ceiling rafter, or pliers to screw the hook firmly into the wood.

When Monty Beresford was found, the police report indicated that the victim had stood on a chair before kicking it away and choking to death.

The landlady gave me directions to the nearby shops. She had heard my footsteps on the stairs and had darted into the hallway to enquire if I were any further forward in my investigation.

'No, but you may be able to help me.'

At once she was attentive and eager.

'Is there a hardware shop close by?'

Deflated, she had told me of Skinners in the high street, then returned to her fireside, slamming the door behind her.

I bought six feet of rope. The same width and strength as that detailed in the official report.

At the flat I used a chair to reach the hook, tied a firm knot, and stood there for a moment contemplating what I was about to do. Then looping a good length of rope about my wrist, I jumped.

My arm was wrenched painfully upwards. Fortunately the spasm was brief, for the hook came out the ceiling and the rope coiled about my feet.

'What I'm saying, inspector, are you still convinced Beresford committed suicide? If the hook failed to take my weight, it certainly would not have taken his when he tumbled off the chair. The sudden weight would have pulled the hook out the ceiling. It was not man enough for the job.'

'So, are you suggesting Mr Beresford was strangled then hung from the ceiling? '

'Frankly, I cannot see any other explanation. The chair on its side was meant to deceive us. For everyone to conclude he had taken his own life.'

'The pathologist has re-examined the body, Daniel. While he won't admit to a mistake, he is amending his findings to suggest that the victim could have been dead before hung by the neck,' said Masterman, replacing the receiver.

'The time lapse before Monty was found could well have affected the morbidity. Pathological jargon for a possible way out. So, we are left with the likelihood Monty was murdered. Perhaps we ought to review our precautions.'

I had another thought.

'Charles do you think there just might be an enemy in the camp?'

'How do you mean?'

'You know, a Trojan Horse, a spy, an infiltrator, Call them what you will. What I'm saying is. . .how could outsiders get hold of information concerning

119

the pairing arrangements and timings? Especially when they are changed every few days.'

****

We had a wire from the intelligence officer at the embassy in Washington that there had been a substantial demand for the two films. Numerous picture houses wanted to include them in their shows.

'A worthwhile trip, Daniel,' commented Charles. 'In fact, I feel you should send them to Italy. To drum up fire in their belly, now we are all on the same side.'

I'll take them over myself, Charles. I'll translate the text boards and get the film production company to prepare some copies.'

'Good idea. When will you go?'

'Give me a week to organise everything. I'll check sailings and let you know.'

'I've told the others to come in early tomorrow morning. Special Branch want to discuss how better to protect ourselves,' declared Masterman.

But, in reality, they could provide nothing that was totally safe.

Their best advice was to continue the pairing system as much as possible; constantly vary the ways one travels to and from Wellington House; and for added measure, adopt several disguises.

They did not touch upon carrying a gun, and I had the feeling they would have been strongly opposed to the suggestion. Nevertheless, we desk operators all kept a firearm by our side. A point reinforced by Masterman now two of our number had been eliminated.

CHAPTER THIRTY FIVE

This time it was a tight, manly embrace.

'We are on the same side, eh?' cried Uncle Emilio. He turned and called over his shoulder. '*Papa, vengo presto, è Daniele!*'

Both my grandparents came to welcome me.

'You are staying with us, Daniele?' asked my grandmother.

'Of course he is, *cara*... of course he is,' declared my grandfather. 'Emilio, bring his case.'

'So, we are fighting alongside Great Britain, France and Russia now. The mood is changing in our country, eh?'

'Roberto, give the boy a chance to sit down and drink something. Have you eaten, Daniele?'

'Not for a few hours, *nonna.*'

'You see, he is starving and all you want to do is bombard him with questions!'

Grandmother walked out the room calling for Antonio.

Emilio went to a cupboard and retrieved a bottle of Chianti. Before pouring he had the grace to ask. 'Is this OK, papa? Shall I use this?'

Grandfather nodded, but he was only vaguely aware of what Emilio was doing.

'Now we are fighting the same fight, my boy, why have you come to Rome. Is it to meet with Signor' Luciano of *Il Messagero*?'

'Yes, and I shall also be travelling to Turin and Milan. But naturally, Rome had to be my first visit.'

I sipped the wine. It was very good.

'Talking of visits,' said Emilio, 'I had a letter from Rosa the other day. She commented that she hadn't seen you for months.'

'Uncle Emilio, I have been very busy. In fact, I've just come back from the United States.'

But I felt a little embarrassed. Aunt Rosa, Emilio's and my mother's sister, lived in London, in a well-known enclave often referred to as "Little Italy".

'She remarked the family had got together at your parents' place in Worthing recently, but you couldn't even make it to that.'

'You must go and see her, Daniele,' said grandfather reproachfully.

Aunt Rosa and Uncle Thomas, along with their five sons, lived in Clerkenwell, behind St James' Church. But, it was a protestant house of worship. Being staunch Catholics, they chose to attend St Peter's Italian Church a mile or so along the Clerkenwell Road. It was a vision I well recall: my diminutive aunt and uncle, flanked by their tall, strapping, heavily-built sons, coming home after Sunday service. The sight of them, walking as a group with aunt and uncle in their midst, prompted passers-by to edge into the roadway, or take to the opposite pavement.

The fact they looked formidable belied their nature. My cousins ran a coal business, and were gentle giants. They were well-regarded by their customers, and enjoyed a thriving trade. No doubt, humping sacks of coal all day contributed to their physiques.

'How is your work, Daniele? You say you are travelling often?' queried my uncle.

Grandmother and Antonio came into the room with a meal they had prepared for me. In truth, I was not overly hungry, but grandmother likes to make sure everyone was more than well-fed.

I rose and embraced Antonio. He is virtually one of the family, having been with my grandparents for so long.

As I ate, between mouthfuls I told them of my adventures. The sinking of the *Lusitania,* and how I awoke in Kinsale hospital; the trips to the United States; and my impersonation of Sonnino, the Italian Foreign Affairs Minister, which they found highly amusing. Until I mentioned the shooting.

'You were shot at?' questioned grandmother. 'You really are impossible, Daniele, worrying your mother and father like that.'

It pulled me up short. It may have been the wine that had loosened my tongue, for Uncle Emilio had been topping up my glass with some regularity.

'Actually, I've not mentioned any of these escapades to them. Perhaps, I should. I'm convinced somebody, it could well be a number of people, are attempting to undermine our work at the War Propaganda Bureau. Even resorting to dispatching some of the people I work with.'

It was a sobering thought, and for a moment there was silence in the room.

'What is being done to protect you?' asked Uncle Emilio quietly.

'My boss, Charles Masterman, introduced a pairing system after the first incident. Safety in numbers, people coming into work and returning home together. But it doesn't seem to have worked very well. We have lost two of our number.'

'What do you mean. . .lost?'

'I believe they were deliberately murdered.'

'This is dangerous, Daniele,' said grandfather. 'Can't the police do anything?'

'Not really, *nonno.* The police have too much to deal with. Do you know that the Germans have begun bombing London? They are using their airships, Zeppelins, to drop bombs on the city. They have bombed several coastal towns, but a few nights ago they came over London and killed thirty people, as well as damaging buildings.'

'Can't you use aeroplanes to attack them?' asked my uncle.

'They come at night when flying a plane is difficult. What is more, these airships travel at over a hundred and thirty kilometres an hour. It could become quite a threat.'

Grandmother interrupted, reverting to the previous topic when I deliberately changed the subject.

'Do you carry a gun, Daniele? In case you are attacked.'

My uncle looked at me enquiringly.

'No, *nonna,* I don't. But then a taxi collects me at the front door of a morning, and takes me back in the evening. So I don't think I'm at risk.'

'If, whoever it is, sees you as the next target, Daniele, that won't stop them. Other means of protection should be devised. You should arm yourself and seriously consider better ways of dealing with the situation. What would Sofia, your mother, do if something happened?'

I stayed in Rome for three days then took a train to Milan. Forty eight hours later, after leaving copies of the two films with contacts, I moved on to Turin. The same length of time elapsed, before I caught another train to Marseille. The route took me south initially, and then along the Riviera, which appeared to be untroubled by the war raging in the north of the country. Yet, I was aware many of the hotels had been converted into hospitals and shelters for wounded soldiers and refugees.

CHAPTER THIRTY SIX

'What do you think of this?'

Masterman thrust a poster in front of me.

It depicted a searchlight highlighting a Zeppelin airship hovering over St Paul's Cathedral. The text read :

IT IS FAR BETTER
TO FACE BULLETS
THAN TO BE KILLED
AT HOME BY A BOMB

JOIN THE ARMY AT ONCE
& HELP TO STOP AN AIR RAID

GOD SAVE THE KING

'I looked up from my desk. 'Have there been more raids?'

'Three or four so far. But they're becoming more frequent. It's not so much the damage, or the loss of life. . .it's been pretty light on the whole. It's more fear of the unknown. No one hears them coming. The next thing is an explosion, or a building struck by an incendiary, bursts into flames. These airship raids are starting to terrorise people. I thought this poster would help with recruitment. What do you think?'

'It's not very subtle is it? I think the second point, "stop an air raid", is far more telling.'

'Do you. . .hmm. Well It's printed now, I can't change it. How did it go in Italy?'

'I'll be doing a report, but briefly, the films went down very well. I gave copies to Fielding at the embassy, and this time he was more amenable, more than ready to use them. However, I didn't leave it just to him, I also passed copies to Luciano at *Il Messagero,* and my contacts at *La Repubblica* and *La Stampa* in Turin. I think we'll find the films will get wide circulation over the next few weeks.'

Charles nodded. 'Good. . .good. Well done. As you can see from the material on your desk, we've been busy here. Alex Brewer has come up with the notion of dropping propaganda items from our aeroplanes when they fly over enemy lines. It sounds a good idea. I've called a meeting of the desk operators and senior staff just after lunch, We can discuss his proposal then.'

Now why would he want everybody's attendance I wondered. It sounds a worthwhile scheme, one we should try out. What was there to discuss?

Eight of us trooped into his office. Some occupied chairs, others leaned against the wall. I sat on a wide window ledge.

'I used Alex's suggestion, to drop leaflets over the German lines, as a reason to get you all together without creating undue concern,' said Masterman solemnly. 'In fact, we are already gearing up for a test run. The War Office has sanctioned the drop, and this will take place in about a week's time, once the leaflets are printed and sent to an aerodrome close to the front. They will be at Izel-Les-Hameaux, which is forty miles south-west of Ypres. The mission will be carried out using the new Vickers T.B.5.'

'That's a pusher engined aeroplane, Charles,' said Brewer. 'Whoever is dropping the stuff will have to mind it doesn't fly back into the propeller.'

How did he know that, I wondered.

'Good point, Alex. I'll make a note of that. However, as I said, there was a more telling reason for getting you together.'

He paused and scanned our faces.

'A body was removed from the Thames last night. Special Branch has just confirmed that it was an employee of the National Insurance Commission, with whom we share the building. I have to tell you that he did not drown, it was not an accident, he was shot twice in the head before being dumped in the river. It was a professional assassination. Now, it may be that it is not related to our work here. But being realistic, it could well have been another case of mistaken identity.'

'My God,' murmured Alex Brewer. 'There was a fellow in NIC I knew. We would often walk from the underground station to Wellington House together. He was in his fifties, bald, with a pencil moustache. About my height.'

'Can you stay behind afterwards, Alex? I'll speak with Special Branch for a description.'

Brewer nodded, adding in a concerned voice. 'If it is the fellow, no one in the Bureau is safe. What are we going to do, Charles?

'What did he say to that outburst?'

I was telling Clare over supper in a local fish and chips bar not far from her flat in Bayswater.

'I've never seen Charles lost for words before. He stared at Brewer for a moment, then said regardless of what the police say about not providing protection, he would be speaking to the Home Office Minister about twenty-four hour cover for all personnel.'

'What does that mean?' Clare asked. Then she grinned. Do you mean when we're together someone will always be sitting between us? Listening to what we say?'

'I doubt it somehow. There are twenty five people in the Bureau, of which ten are the most likely targets. All-round protection would demand two, maybe three bodyguards for each of the ten. I know for a fact that no force, police or Special Branch could release that number for protective duty. I've got a feeling we'll be told we're on our own. There's a war on. I doubt Charles could even raise twenty people capable of dealing with our attackers. We'll just have to be more alive to all possible threats. Change our routines, hours, means of travel, everything.'

I could see concern growing in Clare's eyes.

CHAPTER THIRTY SEVEN

The first attempt Charles made to improve our protection failed miserably.

He called me into his office when I arrived one morning, and told me that a meeting was taking place the following day at the War Office. All the desk controllers and their assistants would be expected to attend.

'I've briefed the others. Each of you will give a brief summary of your activities to date, and your proposals for the next three months. We shall all go together in our new vehicle.'

He noted the frown on my face.

Charles grinned, and gave his customary rubbing of hands..

I raised an eyebrow.

'I'm not saying anything more. Just be ready at ten o'clock tomorrow morning to go to the meeting.'

We waited in the Wellington House foyer for Charles, who suddenly appeared through the main entrance.

'Right,' he declared. 'Everyone outside.'

We assembled on the pavement by a Leyland lorry, parked at the kerbside in front of the building.

'So, what do you think?'

'Sorry, Charles,' said Alex Brewer. 'What are we supposed to think about?'

'Well, that. . .the lorry!'

'What about the lorry, Charles?' asked someone else.

His face stiffened. 'This is it. Our new mode of transport.'

He went to the rear of the vehicle and swung open the two doors.

We gathered around him and peered over his shoulder.

Small windows had been fitted, to give a modest amount of light to the interior. What we saw were rows of seat fixed to the floor.

Masterman pulled a narrow set of steps down, remarking as he did so.

'It's great isn't it? Everyone aboard, we going to the War Office in style!'

'Err. . .I think I'd rather walk, Charles,' someone remarked

'Nonsense. This is ideal. It will ferry us about as the need arises.'

The unwilling passengers climbed the steps and took their seats.

Masterman stowed away the steps and shut the double doors. Then he went to the front of the lorry and climbed in next to the driver.

The lorry jerked forward and we were off.

The little hatch between the cab and the body of the vehicle was pushed to one side and Charles' face filled the aperture.

'I managed to get hold of this despite the Royal Flying Corps seizing Leyland's entire production. I can't for the life of me see why they would want so many of them. As I say, I commandeered this one and had it converted. In the future, it will collect you and all other personnel from your homes of a morning, and deliver you back there safely at night. What do you think of that?

Each of us wrestled with the idea. We all saw shortcomings in the scheme.

'What if we're working late to get something out?'

'Picking us up could mean taking several hours to get to work, and take the same amount of time again in the evening.'

'What happens at weekends?'

'What about when we need to travel abroad?'

'Do we call upon this vehicle when one of us needs to visit an embassy?'

The hatch door was pushed to with a thump.

The gathering was to be conducted by a brigadier. He was flanked by an array of military types, ranging from generals to captains. When we entered the meeting room, they occupied much of one side of a long, green, baize-covered table.

'Sit down, gentlemen. We shall wait for the chief secretary to the Secretary of State for War to arrive. A Mr Pemberton, I believe?'

He cast an enquiring glance at a half-colonel to his right.

'He should be here at any minute, sir,' came the reply.

At that moment the door opened and a tall, bespectacled man in his fifties hurried into the room. He was traditionally dressed: striped trousers and a stiff collar under a black jacket.

He nodded in the direction of the officer in charge, and took a seat midway along the table.

'Gentlemen,' began the brigadier, 'the purpose of this meeting is to review the general status of the war effort, and to determine how we might improve our reporting of events. Colonel Swinton, whom you all know, was appointed by Lord Kitchener to report on happenings on the front line. He has done a first class job. Moreover, he has been skillfully aided by Charles Masterman and his team at the War Propaganda Bureau. I must tell you we were quite prepared to block the issue of the two films the WPB made recently on activities at the front. Shown to the public, they could have sensationalised warfare, and cast it in an unwelcome light. A good thing we didn't. They have been instrumental in a great many people sympathising with and lauding our efforts to free Europe from the German-Austrian tyrants.

'That is why we have decided to allow certain journalists to report directly from the front. Today, for your ears only, I am announcing, that five journalists, Philip Gibbs, of the Daily Chronicle and the Daily Telegraph, Percival Philips of the Daily Express and the Morning Post, William Beach

Thomas of the Daily Mail and the Daily Mirror, Henry Perry Robinson of The Times and the Daily News, and Herbert Russell of the Reuters News Agency will be submitting stories from the front line. However, before their reports go to their respective newspapers, they will be submitted to C. E. Montague, the former leader writer of the Manchester Guardian, who will act as our official censor.

'But we need to do more. As well as persuading neutrals to come off the fence and join us in the conflict, the army desperately needs more men at the front. That is why I am informing you now that from the beginning of 1916 we are going to introduce conscription. We shall be calling up single men between the ages of eighteen and forty one for military service. Any questions?'

Ten seconds later the brigadier continued.

'Good, now I think you should know the reasons for these proposed actions. It is no secret we are not doing well in the Dardanelles campaign. The aim, to force a route to Russia by sea, to penetrate the soft underbelly of the German Axis, is being repelled by the Turks. Along the Western Front we are gradually being pushed back Moreover, although the Russians are now better equipped than when they first entered the war, there are worrying signs their resistance is faltering. They were ousted from Galicia, north of the Carpathian mountains, and now they look like losing Poland.

'One of the problems, certainly in the near future, is this Jewish radical, Alexandre Parvus. He is working for Germany to encourage a Russian revolutionary by the name of Vladimir Ilyich Lenin, to publish a manifesto with the aim of inciting unrest in Russia. His main thrust is "Get rid of the Tsar, let equality reign." And the people could well be persuaded.'

The brigadier looked round the table. 'Any question so far? Anyone want to make comment?'

The silence prompted me to say. 'I think you're right, Brigadier. I was chatting to the Russian Cultural Attaché in Washington not so long ago. He is strongly of the view this fellow Lenin could become a significant menace. Firstly, to the authorities. Lenin was a leading light in the 1905 revolution. He could well be the central figure in another attempt to overthrow the Russian hierarchy. We know for a fact he is being funded by the *Zentralstelle für Auslandsdienst* while living in Switzerland.

'As a consequence, if the Central Office for Foreign Services in Berlin is grooming him for subversion, the Western Front could be in serious trouble if, as a result, the Eastern Front were to collapse. And the likelihood is greater now the Tsar has now taken charge personally, proclaiming himself commander-in-chief of the army.'

The brigadier stared at me intently.

'You sum up the situation well, young man. Although that may not occur immediately, it is a potential threat.'

He whispered something to his ADC, before continuing.

'Right, that's where we stand militarily. I'll ask you first, Colonel Swinton, to give us a brief summary of your activities.'

'So, what do you think?'

We were back at Wellington House. Charles was at his desk, leaning back in the chair.

'I was surprised the brigadier called all of us to such a meeting.'

'No, not that. The lorry?'

'Charles, it is not one of your better ideas. The opinions voiced en route to War Office were valid remarks. What is more, given time to think about the vehicle and its usage, there will be a great many more negative comments. It just won't work, Charles.'

'Damn, I thought I'd cracked it. Well, what do we do now?'

I recalled my grandmother's observations.

'For one thing you could arrange for us all to be armed. The most likely targets at any rate. I think most of us would need some tuition in small arms, in case we have to use them. Then I would give us motorcycles, like the troops use in France and Belgium. Those accompanying women to work could have a motorcycle fitted with a sidecar. In fact, there's a company called, A.J.S, who do an eight horsepower machine that takes a sidecar or it can be unbolted to ride as a ordinary motorcycle.'

Charles nodded thoughtfully. 'The point being that they can outrun a motor vehicle, are far more manoeuvreable, and don't take up too much parking space. Hmm. . .not a bad idea.'

'So why did the brigadier really call the meeting? After all, you provide comprehensive updates every month on the output of the Bureau and it forward plans. What was the real reason behind it?'

'Actually,' confessed Masterman, 'it was at my suggestion. I often exhort you and the others to do this, to do that. I thought it would carry more weight, be more effective, if you had an honest appraisal of the war effort. If you then heard from the top brass the reasons why the continual flow of good, punchy propaganda material is so important. Why you should do all you can to further the cause.'

I nodded, but it did not quite ring true.

Each of us had given verbal summaries of our individual efforts to gain the favour of the neutral countries, if not their participation. An hour later the brigadier had up-to-the-minute reviews of the situation in the Netherlands, Denmark, Norway, Sweden, Luxembourg, Switzerland, Greece, Spain, Portugal, and the United States.

At the moment I was responsible for the last three nations. I was able to report that from being pro-German, the Italian people were now undergoing a change of heart, supporting their government's declaration of war against their old allies.

However, despite our best efforts to play down anti-Germanic feelings, the mood for war among the Portugese was growing. Joining the conflict was almost inevitable.

In the United States, public opinion was for the country to maintain its neutrality. On closer evaluation, it was evident that the influx of European migrants over the past fifty years was now a major influence on holding back any commitment to war.

One distressing piece of information I gathered at the meeting was given by John Priest, who was responsible for the minor powers of Lichtenstein and Luxembourg. He was currently looking after the Netherlands, Monty Beresford's old desk.

'Although it has not been officially confirmed, Brigadier,' declared John solemnly. 'On the grapevine I have learned that the matron of the Berkendael Medical Institute in Brussels, Edith Cavell, has been arrested by the Germans. Although the hospital tended the wounded of both sides, she and several accomplices, were helping our soldiers to cross into neutral Netherlands. It appears she has helped more than two hundred of our men be repatriated to Great Britain. I fear for her life.'

CHAPTER THIRTY EIGHT

Autumn arrived early in 1915, and with it the setbacks continued to mount. The Entente's armies were repulsed in the Battle of Scimitar Hill in Gallipoli, losing more than five thousand men.

British and Canadian regiments took Hill 70 at Loos, but lacked the reserves to exploit the breach. As a consequence, many were killed, the Canadians alone suffered nine thousand casualties.

Whitehaven, a naval base in Cumbria, was attacked by German submarines, illustrating how vulnerable our defences were.

But the tragic news was the execution of Edith Cavell by firing squad.

A ray of sunshine in the gloom was the arrival in London of Jean Hampton. Clare had kept in regular contact, and it was a most welcome sight to meet her at the station at Waterloo.

She stayed with Clare at her flat for almost a week. It was soon evident that as the weariness and heartbreak dropped away, her features brightened and her whole demeanour lightened.

We were having lunch in Soho, and she was telling Clare and I her plans for the next few months, which included a lengthy stay with her parents in Suffolk.

'The nearest town, two miles away, is Diss, in Norfolk. We are just south of the River Waveney, the border between the two counties.'

'Are you planning on going back to the front, Jean?' asked Clare.

'Yes, when I've recharged my batteries.'

After lunch we took her back to Wellington House to show her the two films. While Clare closed the curtains, I busied myself at the projector. Then we were ready.

I cranked the handle, and there on the screen appeared "The Day In The Life Of A Remarkable Ambulance Driver".

Twenty minutes later flickering white light played on the wall.

Jean sat there, silent, introspective. Finally, she said in a low voice.

'I think you have painted too worthy a picture of what I do, Daniel. It portrays me a some sort of heroine. . .which I am not. You'll have to change it.'

Clare rounded on her.

'Absolute, bloody nonsense! It does not give you anything like the regard you deserve!'

Jean stared at her. 'You were helping, too. Why don't you get some credit as well?'

'Because, I was there a matter of days. You've been at the front caring for the wounded for months. That's why!'

I fitted the next film to the projector. This time it was about life in the trenches.

Again, when it finished, she sat very still. When I opened the curtains, there were tears in her eyes.

'Those poor men. I collected some of the mortally wounded in my ambulance at the field dressing station. That fellow, the Lance-Corporal in your film, was one of them. Brought back from no-man's land after going over the top. I'm sorry to say he died on the way to the hospital. I remember him because his name was Oakley. My parents' home is in the village of Oakley.'

I was choked at the thought Lance-Corporal Jim Oakley - that earnest, forthright, young man, who had had so much to live for - was gone. Another statistic in the conflict.

'Are you all right, Daniel?' asked Clare.

I busied myself putting the films back in their cans.

'Yes. Just give me in a minute.'

A good-sized crowd had gathered outside the room. As one they started clapping when Jean appeared. It grew in volume and was accompanied by cheering. Tears sprang to Jean's eyes.

It was Clare who took charge of the situation. She took the ambulance driver by the arm.

'Daniel, can we use your office. I'm sure Jean would welcome a cup of tea.'

Five minutes later Charles Masterman put his head round the door,

'Can I come in?'

The door was left open. Gradually, the numbers increased. Overwhelmed at first by the reception, Jean Hampton was now participating in various discussions, which, for the most part, entailed answering questions. Many of the secretaries wanted to know what prompted a woman to enter a situation fraught with such danger. Conversation went on for almost an hour, until Clare decided that Jean had had enough.

That evening, I went to Clare's flat on my new A.J.S. motorcycle.

'Jean is resting, Daniel. Which gives me a chance to have a word with you.'

She drew me into the sitting room, and we sat together on the settee.

'I've got to go home, Daniel. My mother is unwell. I don't know when I shall return. Perhaps, the newspaper won't want me to come back. I thought I should mention it.'

She looked down at her hands, clasped tightly in her lap.

All I could do was stare at Clare in dismay. I had intended to ask her to come down to Worthing at the weekend. I wanted her to meet my parents.

'When are you going?'

Was that my voice asking the question? It was more a strangulated gurgle.

'As soon as I can book a passage. Probably next week some time.'

I took her hand.

'I haven't said this before... but you mean a lot to me,' I said hesitatingly.

'I was rather hoping you might feel the same, and. . . '

I did not get any further. Clare turned to face me, peered deeply into my eyes. . .then kissed me hard on the lips.

'God! You British really are slow at showing your feelings aren't you? Why haven't you said it before? All this nonsense of being the perfect gentleman, waiting for the right moment. The right moment was several months ago when we were in Belgium. I wanted you to wrap your arms round me! To protect me! Now, when I'm on the verge of disappearing from your life, you casually mention, "you mean a lot to me". Damn you, Daniel Kindred!'

She stood up abruptly. ' Now it's too late. I think you'd better leave!'

Two pink spots flared on her cheeks. She was angry. . .very angry.

I was not going to listen to this tirade.

I got hurriedly to my feet

'I'm not the type to take advantage of a vulnerable female, away from her home, in a strange country, facing dangers in times of war. What do you take me for?'

I realised I was shouting as I added. 'Go home, for all I care!'

I was frozen to the spot. Of course I cared. I didn't want her to go away.

In a low voice I murmured. 'No. . .no, I didn't mean that. I care a great deal. If you're going home, I'm coming with you. Having found you, I'll be damned if I'm going to let you go.'

With that I grabbed her by the shoulders, and kissed her long, tenderly, yet with all the passion I felt for her.

Then we clung to each other.

Jean walked sleepily into the sitting room.

'Is everything all right? I heard raised voices.'

CHAPTER THIRTY NINE

Clare sailed from Southampton a week later. I was there at the quayside to see her off, first waving frantically, then just standing there until the ship was a mere speck in the distance.

After Jean Hampton had departed, Clare came with me to Worthing. My mother and father had been enchanted by her.

There was one brief moment in the garden when just he and I were together. Clare was with my mother in the kitchen.

'Where did you find her, Daniel? She's a delightful girl. You must count your good fortune, my boy.'

'So you approve?'

'Of course your mother and I approve. I'd snap her up before someone else does.'

We went for walks along the coast. I borrowed my father's pride and joy, his Singer, two-seater motor car. He had never before allowed me to drive it. On this occasion, he actually offered the car to me, all the while beaming at Clare.

We toured the south coast, and visited many of the picturesque villages that dotted the South Downs. It was a remarkable three days.

On the train back to London, Clare took my arm and said. 'Your mom and dad are terrific people, Daniel. That was an idyllic few days.'

Then she added wistfully. 'I shall miss England.'

That brought me down with a jolt.

That night I stayed at Clare's flat.

Nothing was said until the taxi pulled up outside her building in Bayswater.

'Help me with my bag, Daniel.'

I paid the driver wondering why it should suddenly become too heavy.

She took a key from her purse and opened the door.

'A cup of tea, Daniel?'

'That would be welcome, Clare.'

As I pushed the door closed with my foot, I was standing on one leg with both hands occupied. It was the moment she chose to launch herself at me. I was helpless to respond. . .at first.

I regained my balance, dropped the cases, and swept her into my arms. We kissed. . .and kissed again. I surprised myself by the surge of feeling that welled up within me. It was an effortless manoeuvre to lift her off her feet, and carry her through to the nearest bedroom.

She was still in my arms when I sat, then rolled onto the bed.

Unaware of time, oblivious to everything except the woman beneath me. Clothes were shed, discarded to the four corners. The intensity of feeling was overwhelming. I was burning up. As I touched her body, it was hot with emotion. We were demanding of each other: locked in desire that seemed to last forever.

Afterwards we held tight to each other.

In the small hours we made love, then made love again.

I never did get that promised cup of tea. We had coffee at breakfast time.

I was late arriving at the office.

Charles appeared as I came through the door.

'Alex's motorcycle has been stolen! What do you make of that?'

'You can't afford to take any risks, Charles. Thus is definitely a matter for Special Branch. They could be getting ready to nab him.'

They recovered it in three hours. It had been taken by a drunk, who had missed the last bus home. As Alex had failed to padlock it, and left the machine where it was all too obvious, it was an embarrassment for the Bureau. Worse, it diminished the Special Branch's response to any future calls we might make upon their time.

Alex was suitably chastened. But the damage was done.

We wrote to each other every day.

Fortunately her mother was making a good recovery – she did not say from what – but felt that it would be sensible to spend the Christmas with them. Her editor at the New York Herald was quite happy for her to continue as the European correspondent, and accepted she would not be returning until the New Year.

Clearly, I was pleased for Clare's sake. But having been a carefree spirit where the opposite sex was concerned: girlfriends had come and gone without any real tug at the heart-strings. Not any more. Now I was consumed by all sorts of emotions.

Was it the infatuation of the moment. Was it because we had shared danger together that created something of a bond. One that, at such a distance, was now stretched to the full. That was sufficiently fragile it might be severed in an instant if someone else appeared on the scene. I was suffering like never before.

All previous loves had been fun, while they lasted. When they ended, usually by mutual agreement, there were no feelings of remorse or sadness. In fact, many of the women I had known remained friends.

But this was different. Never before had I been listless, off my food. I had long thought such a state of mind was dreamed up solely for women's magazines. Now I knew it to be true.

As Christmas approached, I received a card from Clare.

It was not so lovingly penned as her usual letters. I analysed each word, the import of each sentence, the overall impression of what was written under the phrase "Have a Merry Christmas".

That was it.

Again I was lucky.

I had tidy sum lodged with the Capital & Counties Bank, and with Masterman's agreement, I managed to get a berth on the SS *St. Louis*, an American Line steamship, sailing from Liverpool the next day. It was in steerage class, or "tweendecks", which meant sharing a cabin in the bowels of the ship with three other passengers. But it only cost forty one dollars, about eight pounds.

CHAPTER FORTY

Seven days later, when we docked in New York, I hurried to the nearest telephone and asked to be put through to a number in Scarsdale. After several rings it was answered by Lyons, the Johnsons' general factotum.

'The Johnson residence.'

'Mr Lyons, it's Daniel Kindred. Is Clare at home?'

'Mr Kindred, nice to hear your voice, sir. I believe she has gone into the city. I'll inform Mrs Johnson you are on the line.'

I heard the sound of the receiver being put down. Moments later the sound of voices grew louder, and Mrs Johnson said.

'Where are you, Daniel? Are you in New York?'

'Yes, I've just disembarked. I'm at the Chelsea Piers.'

Her voice took on a note of urgency. 'Daniel take a cab to nine, Broadway. Clare is there, about to buy a ticket on the next White Star Line ship bound for England!'

I hailed an electrobat.

'Number nine, Broadway, as fast as you can!'

'Someone's in a hurry,' called the driver. 'How much of a hurry?'

'A five dollar hurry!'

That was sufficient for him to drive almost recklessly down West Street. We covered the two miles from nearby Twenty Third Street to the Bowling Green at the foot of Broadway in minutes.

I jumped out and thrust the five dollar bill into his hand. Then I ran, my suitcase banging against my legs. Charging through the entrance doors, I headed for the White Star desk. And there she was, her back to me, just one person in the queue ahead of her.

I called her name. 'Clare!'

She turned towards me, her face displaying irritation. . .which gradually changed into the most beatific smile, lighting up the whole of her features. It simply took my breath away.

She took several steps from the line of people, then ran towards me. I picked her up until she was head and shoulders above me. Then I whirled her round and round, while she laughed delightedly and bent to kiss my upturned face.

People stopped what they were doing: a still tableau of onlookers frozen in time. I slowly lowered Clare to the ground, and we kissed, hugged, and kissed some more.

Suddenly the booking hall was filled with cheering and whistling. Slightly embarrassed, but elated, I waved to everyone. Then I retrieved my suitcase lying on the tiled floor, placed my arm around Clare's waist and we moved towards the entrance. They were still cheering when the doors closed behind us.

'I thought someone wanted something, just as I was coming to the head of the line.'

Clare was explaining to her mother while we sat side by side on a couch. She had not let go of my arm from Grand Central Station to her parents' sitting room.

Clare's mother smiled, and looked over at her daughter's grasp which had now moved to my hand.

'You'll have to let Daniel free for a moment, dear, while he drinks his tea.'

Clare grinned as she released me. Then her face became serious.

'How long are you here for, Daniel? You haven't said. You're not going back before Christmas, are you?'

'If you are staying over for the festivities, Daniel,' said Mrs Johnson. 'You are most welcome to join us here. Come Christmas Eve and stay on for a few days. On Boxing Day we usually invite friends and neighbours for a little celebration. I do believe you might enjoy it.'

'That's very kind of you, Mrs Johnson, but... '

I glanced at Clare, and realised she thought I was going to decline the invitation. I squeezed her hand.

'But I don't want to put you to any inconvenience.'

'I don't see it like that, Daniel.' She was amused. 'I think it might make someone's Christmas if you came.'

Part of Charles Masterman's agreement to my hasty departure was that while in the United States I should go down to Washington D.C. and meet up with the intelligence officer at the embassy. A few days later I left the Algonquin, walked the dozen or so blocks down Seventh Avenue and took a train from Penn Station. Four hours later we pulled into Washington's Union Station.

I stayed overnight at The Willard on Pennsylvania Avenue, just along from the White House, and presented myself at the embassy on Connecticut Avenue early the next morning. Malcolm MacKenzie was there to greet me.

'Mr Kindred, nice to see you again.'

We shook hands.

'Let me lead the way.'

I followed him upstairs to his office.

'So, may I ask, what is the purpose of your visit on this occasion?'

Just then the door opened and the ambassador walked in.

'Mr Kindred, I heard you were in the building.'

I rose from the chair and we shook hands.

I resumed my seat and he moved to the window. Peering out, with his back to me, he asked the same question as his intelligence officer.

'Well sir, I am seeking your thoughts on just what might edge the United States into joining the Triple Entente. Now four, with Italy joining forces with us.'

He turned and seated himself in an adjacent chair.

'I remember on one occasion I was here, we both agreed that nothing short of a direct threat to this country would jolt it into action. I presume that remark still stands?'

The ambassador nodded thoughtfully.

'So, the reason for my visit is to review with Malcolm the sorts of threat that might just do the trick.'

His eyebrows went up, and he smiled.

'I am not going to get involved in that discussion. However, as you're in Washington, there is something I'd like to talk to you about. Come and see me before you go.'

After an hour MacKenzie and I had identified two possible factors that might push the US into some form of military reaction. The growing discord between Japan and America, due to marked differences of opinion over China. Japan wanted to dominate that country's economy, while the United States urged the "Open Door" principle of free trade. The tensions this was causing could well spill over into conflict.

The trouble was Japan had an alliance with the Entente, and had seized German possessions in the Pacific and East Asia. If the United States entered the war on this premise, it might well be on the side of the Central Powers.

The other sensitive area was America's recent invasion of Haiti. US marines had installed a puppet president, dissolved the legislature at gunpoint, denied freedom of speech, and forced a new constitution on the nation.

President Woodrow Wilson feared Germany might invade Haiti and establish a military base on the island. A strategic move that would be very close to the precious Panama Canal. He had a right to worry: there were many German settlers in Haiti who had financed the rampaging terrorist bands – *cacos* – and were begging their mother country to invade and restore their form of order.

This second situation looked more promising. Perhaps we could play on that in some way? However, I felt a degree of disquiet. Was it right to encourage warfare in another quarter to safeguard one's own position? A vexing question.

The ambassador's secretary knocked on the door.

'The ambassador wondered if your meeting had finished, Mr MacKenzie? It seems he would like a word with Mr Kindred before he leaves.'

'I think we have gone as far as we can, don't you, Daniel?

I nodded. 'Thanks for your time, Malcolm. I'll keep in touch.'

I followed the young lady past the winding staircase, along the corridor to a large double door.

She knocked, turned the handle, and stood to one side allowing me to enter.

Sir Cecil Arthur Spring-Rice rose from his desk, and ushered me to a chair close to the ornate, marble fireplace. He sat opposite, and assumed the habit I had noticed on the first occasion we met – he rubbed his hands together.

'Tell me, Mr Kindred, when are you leaving for New York?'

'I had intended getting the late afternoon train today, sir.'

'Do you have any appointments for tomorrow? By that I mean, would you be free to attend a reception here in Washington, tonight?'

I was hesitant.

Sir Cecil hurriedly explained. 'The recently appointed Secretary of State, Robert Lansing, is holding a Christmas party. Ostensibly to meet the ambassadors and staff of the various nations, to get to know them on a more informal level. The German ambassador and several of his people will be there. Malcolm is coming with me, and I wondered if you would care to join us, as the third member of the British diplomatic team?

'The reason I make the suggestion is I have learned the German Embassy's intelligence officer will be bringing their press agent, an American who has been appointed to promote the kindlier face of that blighted nation. Neither Malcolm nor I speak German, and frankly, I want to gauge the stamp of this man. He's called William Bayard Hale. No one knows you in diplomatic circles. You might be able to get close enough, to come up with an opinion, to learn his strengths and weaknesses. What do you say?'

'Well, yes, thank you. That could be very useful. I'll have to make a phone call, if that's OK?

'Use my telephone.' He studied me for a moment. 'Hmm. . .you're about the same size as Paul Sutton, my aide-de-camp. I'll go and ask him to lend you his dinner jacket.'

When he left the room, I phoned Clare, and explained about the ambassador's invitation, and that I would be back in New York a day later.

'No problem, Mr Kindred, Paul will bring everything to your hotel. It's the Willard, isn't it? My driver will collect you at six o'clock and take us to the function on Massachusetts Avenue.'

I raced back to the Willard and had the barber give me a haircut and beard trim. When I returned to my room Paul's suit was hanging in the wardrobe. He had even supplied cuff links and studs for the dress shirt.

I did not know what to expect.

It was a carefully stage-managed event. As we entered the building we

141

were escorted to a welcoming line in which we were introduced to Robert Lansing, the Secretary of State. The ushers knew their job, manoeuvring the representatives of the many countries present into a formation which avoided contact with those on opposing sides of the conflict.

In the large salon there was further division. Subtle: it only became obvious when pointed out to me. Those nations which favoured the Central Powers formed one cluster; and those supporting the Entente, congregated in another.

We drank good champagne and enjoyed a variety of canapés. As the evening progressed, the wine flowed, conversations grew louder, and there was a gradual intermingling of the two groups. This was due largely to Robert Lansing. He moved first to one side then the other, talking with ambassadors and their entourages.

Malcolm leaned in my direction. 'He's doing a good job working the room, isn't he?'

I had never encountered the phrase before, but it neatly summed up the Secretary of State's efforts to convey to those present that America was a friend to all, and held an uncompromising stance on neutrality.

I spent some time chatting to the Italian contingent, and sympathised with the Portugese about their running battles with Germany over territorial sovereignty in Africa.

At one stage Malcolm drew me away from some Dutch representatives in that practiced manner diplomats acquire.

'Daniel, let me point out the fellow working with the Germans who presents their better side to the media.'

We edged our way through the throng, until close to their delegation.

'There he is. William Bayard Hale is on the left of that group. From what I gather he was once managing editor of *Cosmopolitan,* and was responsible for the publicity campaign that got Woodrow Wilson elected president. To his immediate right is Heinrich Albert, their principal intelligence man. So I'd better make myself scarce.'

I sidled a little closer, and over the rim of my flute appraised Mr Hale. Of average height, he had a narrow frame topped by a naturally-smiling face. From this vantage point I was able to overhear the conversation.

He was an erudite speaker in English, commentating on a variety of topics with ready facility. Clearly intelligent, with a good grasp of foreign affairs. However, when it came to conversing in German, it was stilted as he searched for words, suggesting it had been learned from a textbook.

Eventually, I moved away, and rejoined the British party which was now easing towards the exit. We made our farewells to the Secretary of State, and waited briefly for the ambassador's motor car.

Fifteen minutes later I was deposited at the entrance to the Willard.

CHAPTER FORTY ONE

The following morning I sat in the ambassador's room, Malcolm MacKenzie alongside me.

'So, as I understand it, Mr Kindred,' mused Sir Cecil, 'Mr Hale knows his stuff on foreign policy, He is on the ball where his client's dubious ambitions are concerned, and he professes to hold the same ideals. Moreover, he reckons he has the contacts to achieve coverage of their good intentions in the press. Hmm. . .could be a thorn in our side.'

'The one factor, Mr Ambassador, where he lets himself down is his command of the language.'

'Is that important?'

'I believe it is when talking about the subtleties of communicating the right message. Their embassy staff speak English, but a lot of visiting Germans will not. He could have a problem there.'

I arrived back at Penn Station in New York City, and phoned Clare at her office. It was only a short distance, so I walked to the Herald building at the top of Broadway and Thirty-Fourth Street. I waited outside the ornate structure, close by the elevated train track along Sixth Avenue. A huge statue of Minerva graced its pediment, with numerous owls arrayed along the roof line.

Periodically, I peered through the ground floor windows, watching the great presses printing the next day's edition. Above me the hour bell was struck by two of Minerva's acolytes. Was it my imagination? Did the eyes of the owls dotted along the top of the building briefly glow green?

Clare came through the main door.

'Am I seeing things, or was it my imagination? I could have sworn those owls' eyes lit up when the bell was struck.'

She laughed and grabbed my arm.

'You're not seeing things. Gordon Bennett Junior, the founder's son, was obsessed with owls. When he had this place built in 1895, he decorated the roof with twenty six of them. Their eyes actually do light up when the two blacksmiths strike the hour bell.'

I took her out to dinner, and recounted why I was delayed and what happened in Washington.

'At times, you wouldn't believe we are at war with some of these people. Diplomatic niceties, everyone smiling, never quite meeting when walking the room; and all done with style. I suppose they teach that sort of thing at finishing schools for ambassadors.'

Clare grinned at the thought.

'I spoke with mother today. She is expecting you on Friday, Christmas Eve. A room is being prepared for you. I'm going home earlier, probably on Wednesday, to help her with the arrangements. When you come, we shall have to be very chaste and proper. So we have only this weekend to be unchaste!'

I moved out the Algonquin on Friday morning feeling decidedly the worse for wear. The previous evening I had met with a half dozen of the set, and we wined and dined late into the night. . .and into the morning.

Off the record, I gave them an account of the reception held by Robert Lansing, The Secretary of State. Spicing it a little to make an amusing tale. Dwelling on how people carefully avoided each other, circulating the grand salon as though taking part in a slow-motion schottische.

I remember Heywood Broun, laughing, and saying it was an old German dance; and I grabbing the hand of Luigi, our waiter, and executing a few twirls to illustrate the story.

I also recall asking Dottie Rothschild if she had tied her beloved Edwin Parker down to a date. In her own distinctive manner, she came back with.

'I'm working on it, Dan. Mind you, I'm only marrying him to get a change of name.'

The cab dropped me off and I slowly mounted the stairs of Clare's apartment block. She had given me a key, and I let myself in. Leaving the suitcase in the hallway, I sat down on the couch for a brief rest.

I was awoken by a hand gently shaking my shoulder.

'Wake up sleepy head.'

She peered at me closely.

'God, you look awful. Are you unwell?'

'You could say that. I met up with the Algonquin set last night. They get together most Thursdays to round off the week. I don't drink much. Probably because I succumb more readily.'

I closed my eyes. 'Just leave me to die here.'

An hour later Clare woke me again.

'Drink this.'

A large black coffee was pushed into my unsteady hands. I sipped it slowly.

I was not up to expressing my devotion that night. . .but made up for my lack of libido over the next few days.

CHAPTER FORTY TWO

When the taxi pulled up at the house in Scarsdale, Clare ran down the drive and hugged me.

'I missed you!' she cried. 'Everything's ready. Do you think it will snow? If it does we could be stuck here for weeks.'

I looked skywards. I sincerely hoped not. I had to return to London immediately after the celebrations at her parents' place.

We walked up to the house. Mrs Johnson was standing at the door, smiling.

'Hello, Daniel.'

Her eyes scanned the heavens.

'Looks like you're bringing the snow with you.'

Normally, at Christmas time, my whole family gathers at the house in Worthing. Aunts, uncles, cousins, my siblings' partners and children. Everyone pitches in, and the festivities assume the manner of a convivial Italian party. I had let my parents know I would not be there. Unfortunately this was the second time in successive years. Suddenly, I missed the thought of the noise, the laughter, exchanging presents, bracing walks along the sea shore to clear one's head. For a brief moment I felt a pang of homesickness

'Penny for them,' said Clare. We were sitting in the orangery reading the newspapers.

'Just thinking about my folks at home. How they enjoy this time of year.'

'Tell me, how do you celebrate Christmas when you're at home in England?'

I smiled, and lent back in a comfortable rattan chair overlooking their tree-lined garden. For a moment I was transported. Everything was so vivid. The words came easily as I described the chaos, the unconventional meal times, the joy of all being together, the continuous laughter, and everyone who was capable pitching in with the chores.

'Sounds wonderful,' mused Clare. Then she brightened. 'Perhaps I might witness it next year.'

'I would like that very much.'

Her face took on a different cast.

'Actually, I've got something to tell you. I really hope you don't mind too much.'

The words came out in a rush between the silences.

'I'm sorry, darling, but I shall not be coming back with you when you return. I've squared it with my editor. Let me explain. Father cannot afford time away from his business at the moment, so mother has asked me to

145

accompany her to New Mexico for a few months, while she recuperates.

'We are going to visit her sister, Aunt Elizabeth, who is married to a Baptist minister. He is taking over a new church in Carlsbad. Weird name for a town in that state, isn't it? Apparently, they changed the name from Eddy to Carlsbad because the mineral waters there are like those of the European spa at Carlsbad in Bohemia. The waters should help her constitution. Do you mind? I'll rush straight over to England when we come back. The thing is. . . I couldn't say no. You do understand, don't you?'

She was wringing her hands uncertainly.

I realised there was little else she could do. I covered her hands with mine.

'Of course you must go. She'll welcome you by her side.'

You honestly don't mind?'

I shook my head.

She stared at me for a moment, then leaned sideways and kissed me hard. Then harder still.

It was ill-judged. Her father appeared in the doorway with several neighbours.

I drew back embarrassed. Clare, on the other hand, was quite unabashed.

'Hello, Audrey, Derek, David, Rosemary. How nice to see you.'

Over the next couple of days I was introduced to a bewildering number of people as the household ebbed and flowed with guests. Names were declared, light-hearted as well as earnest conversations were held with all manner of people. For seventy-two hours the Johnson household catered for a transient number of visitors.

On Tuesday morning, when I was packing, Clare slipped into my bedroom.

'Hold me tight, Daniel. Kiss me so that I'll remember it for the next couple of months.'

I dutifully obliged.

Fortunately, the likelihood of snow did not materialise.

The ship docked in Liverpool, which meant a six hour train journey. After the bright lights, warm fires and delightful company, the flat in Ebury Street was cold and uninviting.

I removed my shoes and dropped onto the bed. Covering myself with the eiderdown I fell fast asleep.

CHAPTER FORTY THREE

When everyone at the War Propaganda Bureau returned after the break, I was first into the office, just ahead of Charles Masterman.

'Well, well. . .nice to see you, Daniel. Did you get to Washington? Come into my office.'

We sat either side of his conference table

'An interesting tale, Charles. I not only went to Washington, I met the new Secretary of State, Robert Lansing.'

'Did you now. How did that come about?'

'I recounted the evening at the reception, with less levity than when told to the Algonquin set.

'I also had a long discussion with Malcolm MacKenzie, the embassy's resident intelligence officer. Very useful. I raised the question what would really encourage the United States to go to war? Several points came out of it. Firstly, there is enmity between Japan and America. Inflaming that situation, with Japan on the side of the Entente, could well lead to the US joining the opposition, the Central Powers.

'On the other hand, America feels vulnerable in the Caribbean, because of its economic need of the Panama Canal. So much so, with Haiti encouraging close ties with Germany, as you know America invaded the island state recently, and is now virtually running Haiti's affairs. We might well be able to stoke a few fires, and get the two countries squaring up. . .to our advantage.'

'Hmm. . .an entertaining idea, Daniel. It bears thought. Give me your suggestions how we might exploit the situation. Anything else?'

'There was one thing, nothing of consequence. I mentioned the Germans have this agent working for them in America. A journalist called William Bayard Hale. He speaks execrable German, which, from what I could overhear at Lansing's reception, is a cause of slight irritation at the German delegation in Washington. We might be able to exploit that in some way? Tell me, what's been happening here?'

'Quite a lot, actually. We've been mainly concerned with increasing military numbers. Even though conscription has now been introduced, we need to persuade eligible, young men that serving their country is for the greater good. Do you know, we've had to publish reprints of all the pamphlets written by Conan Doyle, Arnold Bennett, Rudyard Kipling and Chesterton, and produce quantities of posters with the message to would-be recruits its their duty to stand by the flag.

'The trouble is we are still taking a hammering on the Western Front, that's why we need more men. And we're pulling out of Helles, marking the end of the Gallipoli campaign. Just to put you in the picture, things have reached the point that I expect any day to hear that Portugal and Germany are at war. On the Eastern Front things aren't quite so bad now that the Russian soldiers are finally getting the weaponry they need.'

'What about the political situation in Russia? Is this fellow Lenin still stoking the fires from a distance?'

Masterman rummaged around the items on his desk, before pulling free a number of sheets of paper.

'Don't ask me how I got hold of these,' he said, waving them in his hand.

'This is the draft of a forthcoming booklet of his. The text is in French, so one of their agents must have acquired it, and had it translated. It's called, *Imperialism, the Highest Stage of Capitalism*, by Vladimir Ilyich Lenin. Take it, see what you think. The nub of it is generating financial profit from imperial colonialism is the ultimate stage of capitalism, sucking the life blood from the downtrodden. From what I've read, it's a synthesis of Karl Marx's economic theories propounded in *Das Kapital*. In Russia's present volatile state it could well fan the flames of unrest.'

'Any more reprisals against us? Or has that been sorted out?'

'I wouldn't say it has been sorted out, more petered out. That notion of yours to get around on motorcycles has worked well. I think we can now forget about Trojan horses trying to undermine our activities.'

'You sound very certain, Charles. I hope you're right.'

'Don't worry about it, Daniel. Tell me, how is the delectable Miss Johnson?'

CHAPTER FORTY FOUR

'I still can't understand why you haven't had time to visit them.'

The question hung in the air. She looked over her cup. 'After all, Clerkenwell is not so far from where you live.'

Whenever my mother becomes confrontational, Italian overtones play with her words. Arms begin to wave, and all the long-forgotten mannerisms appear.

I remember when she got angry with me as a teenager. The hands used to go to her hips, and she would adopt "Mediterranean mama" attitudes. There was a hint of it now as we sat by the fireside.

'Your Uncle Emilio wrote to me, you know. He told me to make sure you paid your aunt a visit. Families are important, Daniel. You must never forget that.'

My father was reading a newspaper. He peered over his glasses at me and grinned.

'He has been travelling a lot, Sofia. He seems to spend more time in America than in England. And I probably know the reason why. He is chasing after Clare Johnson. Am I right, Daniel?'

I nodded, and felt myself redden under his gaze.

'It looks like it's serious, Sofia,' said my father softly.

I stayed the weekend.

Early on Monday morning my father got his new motor car ready, and offered to run me to the railway station. As I climbed into the passenger seat of the fourteen horse power Humber, my mother again reminded me to make sure I visited my Aunt Rosa and her family.

'And don't you forget, Daniel!' were her parting words as the vehicle rolled down the drive.

CHAPTER FORTY FIVE

Once again they met in the Flying Angel Club in Victoria Dock Road. On this occasion the discussion was brief and to the point.

'We are to remove this man, Kindred. I am told to make it look like an accident in the street,' murmured Erik Müller, the acknowledged leader. Contact with the fatherland was made through Müller's cell. This time a fourth member had been co-opted.

'What do you mean, a road accident? 'asked Karl.

'He falls in front of a motor vehicle, or is trampled by a horse. Whatever, it is has to look like an accident, as we did with Brady and Beresford.'

Müller stared fixedly at the new recruit, Meik Fischer. Or as his passport and sailor's ticket declared, Michael Fisher.

'This will be your opportunity, Michael, to show us what you can do. Here is a photograph of Kindred. Follow him for a few days. Get to know his habits, his feeble disguises, and how frequently he changes his routes to and from the National Insurance Commission building. Pick your moment. As I say, just make sure it looks like an accident. If you think there are any problems, telephone me or Karl, we can advise you. Any questions?'

Fischer, a tall, heavily-built man, with synophrys, a fusion of the eyebrows, shook his head. Müller wondered briefly if he were up to the task. But to expose himself, Karl or Ernst too often would inevitably lead to trouble. The law of averages dictated that ultimately they would be seen, faces remembered.

CHAPTER FORTY SIX

That day, varying my journey according to instructions, I decided to travel by underground train and stroll from the station to St James' Walk.

Aunt Rosa, her husband Thomas and their five sons occupied two adjoining houses in the Walk. My aunt and uncle lived in one, and their five sons lived in the other. Although two of them were currently away, working in the coalmines in Wales. The other three continued to run the family coal merchant's business; and next to the houses, behind large green gates, was their coal yard, warehouse and stabling for the horses.

I knocked a little tentatively on the door which was opened exuberantly by Uncle Thomas.

'I saw you coming up the road, Daniel. Rosa!' he shouted. 'Guess who's here?'

My aunt's diminutive figure bustled along the passageway from the kitchen and pulled me down into an embrace against her ample bosom.

'Daniele, you're a bad boy! You have not been near us for ages. Come in! Come in! Thomas, tell the children we have a visitor.'

The three children, young men all over six feet tall, broad-shouldered with strapping physiques, exuded a faint air of aggression. In truth, they were docile, well-mannered and polite. They trooped into the parlour and each of them embraced me like a long-lost cousin. The back slapping, though delivered with affection, still smarted for a time afterwards.

Like me, they had been excused military service. Their coal business, essential for the warmth and well-being of their customers, was considered of national importance, and gave the brothers exemption from conscription.

At first, I was reticent about my work with War Propaganda Bureau. But as we sat there, reminiscing about the past, talking about the family both in Italy and England, so I gradually found myself telling of the work I did. Touching upon my travels to the Western Front, the forays to the United States, and even the attacks upon members of the Bureau.

'That sounds dangerous, Daniel,' remarked my uncle.

'Emilio wrote to me telling me about it, Daniele,' said my aunt, concern in her voice. 'You should take more care. What does your mother think? She must be worried for you.'

'I'll be all right. Anyway, I think the attacks upon the Bureau have petered out. The precautions we have taken seem to have done the trick.'

But I caught the glance she exchanged with my uncle.

'What are you working on at the moment, Daniel?' asked Robert, one of the sons.

'Trying to get the United States to commit troops to the Entente's side in the war. But the president is adamant the country will never join in the conflict.'

'That's because there are so many immigrants from Europe living there,' exclaimed my uncle. 'Although they are now American citizens, they still have strong ties with the families left behind in Germany and Austria. Like we do, Rosa, with your people in Italy. I've read they are quite vocal about the United States remaining neutral, staying out the war.'

I was surprised that Uncle Thomas was aware of the situation.

'That's part of the problem, Uncle. The other is the reluctance, as they see it, to get involved in a squabble three thousand miles away. It doesn't affect them. Why do battle in someones else's country? Whoever wins, it won't affect what happens to the United States.'

'What does my brother, Emilio, think, Daniele?' asked my Aunt Rosa.

'He is worried that the Italian army has not done as well as they had hoped. They surprised the Austrians with their offensive, hoping to move into the South Tyrol and recover Istria and the northern territories they lost a century ago. But the terrain has made life difficult. They are now involved in trench warfare similar to that in France and Belgium.'

I left in the late afternoon, carrying a brown paper bag with string handles. It contained a lasagne in a small cast iron dish. My aunt had prepared it especially for me. She believed I was far too thin and needed feeding up.

At Farringdon Street Underground Station I bought a ticket to Victoria, intending to change at Mark Lane and take a District Line train going west. Waiting for the train's arrival, I glanced at those around me, at the same time my hand closed around the Smith and Wesson revolver in my coat. It still felt clumsy, even though the barrel had been shortened to fit more easily into the pocket. Always remain alert even in the most innocuous of situations the Special Branch man had emphasised.

A crowd had started gathering on the platform for the train was overdue. Standing next to me was a woman with a baby in her arms and a toddler held fast by reins. I saw her grip on them tighten when a deep, rumbling sound grew louder and louder. I glanced down and saw the anxious look the little boy gave his mother. There was a rush of air as the electric train clattered into the station, its air brakes hissing and the steel wheels groaning as they found purchase on the rails. The little boy was clearly frightened as it squealed towards the end of the platform. As it neared us, his lip trembled and the teddy bear he was clutching fell from his hand.

I bent down to retrieve it. In that brief second I was aware of a dark shape passing over my head, and the horrified look of the mother as something fell screaming into the path of the oncoming train, which shuddered to a desperate halt. Abruptly, a piercing scream was cut short.

I stood up, still holding the toy bear not quite comprehending what had

152

happened. Until I peered into the woman's face,.. It was a mask of disbelief, panic, fear for her children. Realisation dawned in a rush.

I took her by the arm, picked up the little boy and led them to a bench. Suddenly aware that people were rushing past us away from the scene, while others in uniform struggled to get through the mêlée.

After we were questioned by the police, they organised a taxi to take us to our destinations. It stopped Chester Square, a short walk from where I lived in Ebury Street, and I alighted as well.

'The woman, Mrs Ethan, had said little during the journey, other than to repeat, "that poor man. . .that poor man," and hold tightly to her children. I paid the taxi while she walked to her front door. She fumbled a key from her handbag, and inserted it in the lock.

'Thank you, Mr Kindred.'

Not at all, Mrs Ethan. Is there anything more I can do?'

She shook her head.

I turned to walk away when she said. 'Perhaps I should have mentioned it to the police, Mr Kindred. That man had his hands out in front of him. On reflection, I don't think it was to save himself. I think he was going to push you in front of the train!'

I walked back to my flat, thinking about what she had said. It was when I pouring myself a stiff drink I realised the paper bag holding the lasagna was missing.

CHAPTER FORTY NINE

'They found a merchant seaman's ticket in his wallet,' said Masterman, replacing the telephone on its cradle. 'It gave his name as Michael Fisher. 'However, this is the interesting bit, when they checked with the Registrar General of Shipping and Seamen, no such person was listed by that name that matches their year and place of birth, their rank or rating, and so on. Even his list of official vessel numbers and signing-on dates appears to be a work of fiction.'

Charles' eyebrows flexed in a meaningful way.

'If the fellow isn't who he ought to be, Daniel, it could well have been a botched attempt on your life,' he said grimly.

'There was no need to replace the dish, Daniele,' said Aunt Rosa. I had felt obliged to do so for when I knelt by the toddler to pick up his teddy bear, the paper bag containing the lasagna had dropped to the platform beside me. The unknown sailor had trodden on it, taking it with him when he plunged to his death.

'How did it get broken?' asked my uncle. 'They're quite sturdy.'

'Someone knocked it out of my hand at the Underground Station.'

'What the man who committed suicide?' he asked guilelessly. 'I read about an incident at Farringdon Station in the newspaper. Would you believe, on a crowded platform a chap leapt in front of a train. Nasty business.'

He noticed the expression on my face. 'Come to think of it. . .it happened not long after you left here.'

He stroked his chin thoughtfully.

The boys trooped into the house for afternoon tea.

'Brian, what time did Daniel leave when he was here last. Four? Quarter past four? It couldn't have been much later.'

'About four,' said Brian, the eldest of their sons. 'Why do you want to know?'

Now Uncle Thomas was peering at me intently.

'Come and see the new lorry the boys have just bought, Daniel. They'll be able to speed up coal deliveries now they are motorised as well.'

I was taken into the yard to gaze at their acquisition – a green Thornycroft BT flatbed lorry with the family name painted on the sides.

'It's a magnificent machine, Uncle,' I said, praising the vehicle.

'Never mind that. I don't want your aunt worried. Tell me how you really came to break the dish. You were there when it happened weren't you? That's how it got broken. Did you try to save him? Was that it?'

'I took a deep breath. 'Quite the reverse. He was trying to kill me.'

I told them the whole story. The police did not know the truth of the matter, though the young woman with the two children had put two and two together.

CHAPTER FORTY EIGHT

They got together in a pub.

It was early evening, and there were few customers at the bar when they carried their drinks to a far table.

'So the job was bungled,' commented the leader of the trio. 'What on earth was he thinking, trying to get rid of him in such a public place?'

'Obviously, he wasn't up to the task,' remarked another, putting the beer glass down and wiping foam from his mouth.

'The question is what are we going to do about it?' added the third.

There was a brief silence until the leader spoke up.

'Well, he has been warned now, and will be very much on the alert. For the moment, I would suggest we take turns in following him, keep him under surveillance. Work out his routines. He must have some sort of pattern to his movements, even when he tries to vary them. Do you agree?'

The other two nodded their acquiescence.

CHAPTER FORTY NINE

'This is straight off the teleprinter, Daniel. You'd better read it.'
Masterman thrust it into my hand.

MARCH 9th - Mexican rebels crossed the border into New Mexico. They attacked the township of Columbus, razing it to the ground. Reports indicate twenty American citizens were killed. Other unconfirmed cross-border raids by Pancho Villa's rebels (Villistas) have taken place in recent months, and the United States' Government is mobilising a contingent of troops led by General John Pershing to deal with the insurgents. 'MESSAGE ENDS

'My God! Clare is down by the Mexican border with her mother! They're at Carlsbad, not far from Columbus!'
'I know. You told me. That's why I showed you the news agency message.'
I was not aware of pacing up and down in Charles' office. A host of thoughts cascaded through my mind. Over-riding all was the need to go to her immediately, yet aware that I was not readily able to fund such a trip.
'Look, Daniel, if you are concerned about the costs, take the material – the leaflets, pamphlets, the works by our tame authors, and the press releases – with you. They were destined to be sent in the diplomatic bag to the embassy. All you'll then need to do is pay your way from Washington D.C.'

'I followed him to Southampton, and watched as he boarded the *Mauretania* bound for New York. So, there's nothing more we can do until he returns. We 'll just have to keep a close eye on his place in Ebury Street.'

I managed to get a berth at the last minute. After the rush to organise the trip and have the propaganda material, printed in the American idiom, parcelled up, suddenly I could relax a little. More so because of the ship on which I was sailing. Unlike most transatlantic liners, the *Mauretania* has a top speed of twenty-six knots: more than capable of outrunning any German vessel.
Five days later we docked in New York At the terminal I ran to the nearest telephone and rang Scarsdale.
The same voice, the same intonation.
'The Johnson residence.'
'Mr Lyons, it's Daniel Kindred. Is Clare at home?'
'Mr Kindred! I'm sorry, sir, she is not. Miss Clare is in El Paso. Mr

Johnson went to collect them immediately we heard news of the raid on Columbus. But only Mrs Johnson came back with him. I'll call him to the telephone, sir.'

A moment later.

'Daniel, my boy, where are you?'

'I've just arrived at the liner terminal. When I heard of the rebel attack I came straight over.'

'Dammit, Daniel, she wouldn't come back with her mother and me. As Clare was on the spot, almost where it happened, she wrote a piece for the Herald. It was a scoop for the newspaper. As a consequence, they told her to stay put, get some interviews and some photographs of what's been done to Columbus. I spoke to the editor, a friend of mine, who said if she has been in the trenches in France she will be in much less danger in New Mexico. But I'm worried, Daniel. . .'

His voice tailed off. I was worried too.

'I'm catching the next train to EL Paso, Mr Johnson. I'll sort it out. I'll telephone you when I can.'

I stayed overnight at the Algonquin. No one came in that I knew. Just as well, for I had an early morning train to catch. The first leg was to Washington, where I delivered the propaganda material to Malcolm Mackenzie, the intelligence officer.

Three hours later I boarded a train for Chicago. A mind-numbing journey, all the more fretful because I wanted the train to race to its destination. I had reserved a coach seat, so at least I was able to rest and fall in and out of a restless sleep. We rattled and clanged into Chicago Union Station just before lunch the following day. In the afternoon yet another train carried me south-west towards El Paso, where we arrived in the early hours of the morning. I had been travelling overland for three days.

Mr Johnson had told me where Clare was boarding. Tired, travel-weary, and concerned, I hefted my carrying bag onto my shoulder and set out to walk the half mile to the Camino Real Hotel.

From what I could see in the half-light, El Paso was not nearly as basic as I had imagined. In fact, when I stood before it, the hotel was a modern many-storied building. In the lobby a sleepy receptionist said. 'Sorry, pal, no vacancies. The country's press has taken every last room.'

'Don't worry, Just give Miss Johnson's room a ring, please.'

He looked at me strangely.

'Miss Clare Johnson, right?'

'Correct.'

'Buddy, this is the middle of the night, you know. Are you sure you want to disturb her?'

'Just telephone her room, please. I'll take the receiver.'

He shrugged and used the telephone on the desk.

It was ringing when he passed it over,
'Michael, what time do you call this?' responded a sleepy voice.
Michael? Who the hell was Michael?
'It's not Michael. It's Daniel. I'm downstairs in the lobby.'

CHAPTER FIFTY

'Do you think I embarrassed him? Running through the lobby in my nightdress like that.'

We were in Clare's room, sitting on the bed, my arm around her shoulder.

'So tell me. . .who is Michael?'

'Michael? Oh, he is a reporter on the El Paso Morning Times. He was going to give me an early call, and we were going to Columbus with a photographer. He has been escorting me to places and meeting people the out-of-town journalists wouldn't know about. He saw the material I sent to the Herald, and wanted to help me with stories the others wouldn't be able to cover. You'll like him.'

I doubted it. I had feared Clare was not safe out in the wilderness of New Mexico; but perhaps the danger was from another quarter.

'Anyway, did you have business in Texas or New Mexico?'

'I was just passing, and thought I'd drop in and see you.'

She gazed into my eyes for a moment.

'You're kidding me. . .aren't you?'

'Of course I am. When the news reached me in London of the Mexican raid near to Carlsbad, I couldn't get here quick enough. I was really worried for you. Your father said you wouldn't come back with him, and he was concerned for your safety, too.'

'Well, as you may have seen, here in this corner of Texas, El Paso shed its frontier image about twenty years ago. Columbus, across the state line in New Mexico is, or was until ten days ago, still a one horse town. An easy target for the Villistas. Where mother and I were, in Carlsbad, that could have been raided, though that's a longer incursion into New Mexico. I doubt that Pancho Villa will try that now that the New Mexico National Guard has been rallied. General Pershing's troops will be here any day now. That's what all the other press boys are doing, waiting for the General to go into Mexico and capture Villa.'

'And when do you finish here?' I asked.

'Once I've got the interviews and photos I'm heading back to New York. I'll write up several stories, then, my darling, it's back to Europe.'

I was right. I did not take to Michael; and he was definitely put out by my presence. So much so, the next day I opted out of the trip back to Columbus. Instead, I went to the building housing the El Paso Morning Times.

Even in the deep south-west of America the allusion to the Times of London still opens doors. After a few minutes I was ushered into the office of James Black, the newspaper's founder and current editor.

160

'Well, sir, what can I do for such an august journal as yours, pray?'

'At the moment, Mr Black, this is merely a personal visit to El Paso. I just want to understand the facts behind the Mexican incursion into New Mexico. Are they trying to recoup lost lands?'

'No, sir, they're not. The raid on Columbus was to seize weaponry and supplies to re-equip Pancho Villa's forces. It was not a government-inspired attack, leastways not on this occasion. But, memories are still raw. Seventy years ago we Americans took Texas from them, as well as New Mexico and California. Even though we paid for the privilege, we also applied force of arms, and it still rankles. I think many down there might welcome the chance to reclaim lost territories.'

I spent a profitable hour with Mr Black before taking him to lunch. Over the dining table, his tongue loosened by wine, he became even more expansive about Mexican-American relations. It was after four o'clock before I returned to the Camino Real and rested in the room the receptionist had managed to find for me.

I was awakened by a tapping on the door.

'Daniel, are you in there?' came an urgent voice.

I opened the door and Clare walked swiftly past me.

'Where have you been? I was worried. Michael and I got back about three, and you were nowhere to be found. I've been up here several times, banging on the door.'

'I'm sorry, darling, I must have dozed off. I had a heavy lunch with Michael's boss and drank a little too much.'

'Michael's boss? Whatever for?'

'Just gathering background material about the situation.'

'You could have asked me! I could have told you what you wanted to know.'

Two red spots appeared on her cheeks.

'Of course you could. However, I wanted to understand if the raid on Columbus was the prelude to more incursions. To get the opinion of someone who lives on the border.'

'What do you think I've being doing interviewing people? '

'But you were getting residents' points of view. I wanted a more political review of the situation.'

'I've got that as well! Honestly, Daniel, all you had to do is ask. You've got a tongue in your head! Even if it is furred up with drink!' she added, and flounced out the room.

CHAPTER FIFTY ONE

The trouble was I did not want to reveal what I had in mind.

It would have been dismissed in a moment as a nonsensical idea. Too fanciful for words. Too tenuous to work, for all the elements to fall so precisely into place.

Over dinner that evening I apologised to Clare, who was equally dismayed at her harsh words.

'I was worried, Daniel. I didn't know what to think when I couldn't find you. I shouldn't have sounded off like that. Of course, you should see and speak to whomever you please.'

I reached out and took her hand.

'Do you know something, Miss Johnson? When we go back to England together I want you to marry me. Would you do me that honour? Shall I go down on one knee and issue a firm proposal?'

I didn't realise what I had said. It just came out. But many a true word spoken in jest, and in love. And I adored that young woman sitting opposite me. I wanted to be with her. . .always.

She hurriedly looked down. No engaging smile, no light in her eyes. Instead she removed her hand from mine, and gripped the edge of the table.

The silence was broken by words I shall never forget.

'I don't think I can be your wife, Daniel.'

She pushed away from the table and ran from the dining room. I spent a most miserable night alone in my room.

The next day we boarded the train for Chicago. En route I finally got a tearful explanation of why she could not marry me.

'You know my ambition has always been to become a recognised journalist for the New York Herald. They gave me a sort of role as the European correspondent, but it was really a probationary job, to see how I would do,' she sniffed.

'I was in Carlsbad when the Mexican rebels came across the border, and got myself a scoop. I beat all the other journalists to the story. The editor liked the angle I took so much, he offered me a permanent job. I received a wire when I got back to the hotel yesterday. That's what I wanted to tell you . . .but things kind of got in the way.'

She reached over the armrest. 'I do love you, Daniel, very much. But I would lose everything I've sought after if I went to England. You do see that, don't you darling?'

I nodded dumbly.

Thoughts flashed through my mind. Come to the United States, then we could marry. But that would mean giving up my job with the War Propaganda Bureau, and if I did, that would mean immediate conscription into the army anyway. We would still be an ocean apart.

CHAPTER FIFTY TWO

Ten days later I was back in London.

Charles asked me how the trip went, but I was non-committal. He sensed something was amiss, and did not refer to Clare or the situation on the Mexican/American border.

That is until we went to France.

I worked through the Summer of 1916, producing my share of propaganda material, discussing with the authors the themes for pamphlets they might care to write, and spending a great deal of time with John Buchan.

Buchan had been commissioned to write a *History Of The War*, and on a number of occasions he came into Wellington House to pick our brains. The magnum opus was to be serialised in twenty four instalments in the form of a magazine.

Given the pervading climate of the time and Buchan'sapproach to the task, the history was slanted generally towards what the government wished to be portrayed. Consequently his *History of the War* was historically inaccurate. While I admired the man very much, I could not accept his style of working.

'Don't worry, Daniel,' remarked Charles, 'only another week, then we are off to France and Belgium. Get your film man, Benett-Stamford, to come with us.'

A few days before we departed I wrote to Clare.

I mentioned I was off to the Western Front again with John, the film maker, although I had no idea what it was all about. It was one of Charles Masterman's forays, and he was keeping very quiet about why we were going.

We both wrote regularly to each other; but words of endearment were excluded. If we could not be together, why torture ourselves?

We arrived in Amiens, and were informed that the action would be taking place close to a village called, Flers–Courcelette. This was near Bapaume, twenty miles north-west of command headquarters.

On this occasion, we were ferried across country in an army lorry. In fact, there were at least a dozen lorries in the convoy, carrying soldiers and a clutch of officers.

'Presumably, the officers are attending, whatever this is, as observers,' I said to Charles, as we bumped along rutted roads. 'So are you going to give us a clue as to what we are doing here?'

'We, my friend, are going to witness and take moving pictures of a most remarkable event.' He grinned, and rubbed his hands together. 'An event that will swing the war in our favour.'

'I hope so,' I said dryly. 'When I first came out to the front line it was fifty miles nearer to Germany than it is now.'

'What's this thing called then, Charles?' asked Benett-Stamford.

'Things, John. There's more than one. They are called landships.'

'Thank you, Charles, for that tidbit of information. But John and I are none the wiser.' I added sourly.

'Don't worry, Daniel. You'll see them in a very short while.'

Two hours later we arrived on the outskirts of Flers–Courcelette. We walked the remaining six hundred yards to the supply trenches. John took charge of the camera, I carried the tripod and canisters of film.

'I would suggest you position yourself on that slight mound, John?' said Masterman, pointing behind us.

'A trifle exposed, don't you think?' I said.

'I doubt there'll be any enemy shooting once the plan goes into operation.'

I shrugged, and John and I took ourselves back to slightly higher ground.

Suddenly, one of the British officers blew several short blasts on a whistle which interrupted the sporadic gunfire being exchanged. This was followed by the sound of heavy engines bursting into life, which seemed to come from the direction of a standing of trees away to our left.

Then a host of rumbling noises erupted from the wood, and I had my initial glimpse of a most terrifying machine. The first of a number, which began forming a line, before lurching across uneven ground towards the enemy trenches.

'My God!' I cried. 'What are they?'

'I told you. . .landships,' shouted Charles above the din.

They were metal monsters on caterpillar tracks. Guns fixed on top and on the sides of their bodies. Whether they could shoot as the steel leviathans pitched and yawed across ploughed fields was of no immediate concern. To find one of these instruments of war bearing down on you would create unimaginable terror. Few would be prepared to remain at their posts. I was fearful of their might, and they were our machines.

Imperturbably, Benett-Stamford continued to turn the camera handle, whooping for joy as he captured the first use of landships in open conflict.

In the cold light of the next day, a more critical assessment was made of the landships' contribution. Obviously, having to traverse the heavily scarred terrain of the Somme battlefield, led to mechanical failings. Moreover, the landships were manned by crews who had had little training in their operation. Nonetheless, of the forty nine destined for battle, thirty two made it to the field of war. The effect on the enemy was pronounced; and we made

165

our way back to the French coast delighted to have taken the first moving images of the landships engaging and routing the German forces.

On the train from Dover to London we had a first class compartment to ourselves. We were still euphoric about the effect of the landships, and in high spirits at the thoughts of what we could make of the propaganda about the Entente's new weapon.

When Benett-Stamford left us for a visit to the end of the carriage, Charles idly remarked. 'Are we going to see the delectable Miss Johnson over here soon, Daniel? Or am I imagining that things between you are not going smoothly?'

Immediately the mood changed. From elation to dejection in a handful of words.

I stared out the window for some minutes before replying.

'No, Charles, she is not coming to England. She now has a permanent job with the New York Herald. Something she has been after for a long time.'

'I see.'

Another silence.

Then he said. 'Have you thought of working over there?'

I turned to look at him.

'Charles, you and I both know that if I left the Bureau I would be conscripted. Either way, Clare and I would not be together.'

'I suppose I was thinking that you might still work for the WPB, but spend more time in the United States. After all, we still desperately need them to join the Entente. These landships are all very well, but they won't win the war for us.'

'I can't see that making a lot of difference, Charles. I don't think I would like to be parted from her half the year, and neither would she. I didn't tell you, but I proposed to her when I was over there last. Clare wouldn't accept, and she wouldn't agree to living in sin if I spent six months of the year away from her back here.'

The door slid open and Benett-Stamford dropped into a seat.

'Did you know,' said Masterman, glancing across at John and myself. 'although "landship" was the term given by some Admiralty committee, it was considered too descriptive and might give away what it was all about. As a consequence, the committee cast around for an appropriate code term for the vehicles.

'The factory workers assembling them were told they were producing "mobile water tanks" for desert warfare in Mesopotamia. "Water Container" was considered as a name, but rejected when those offering advice and guidance realised they would become known as the WC Committee. Eventually the term "tank", as in water tank, was suggested, and that, my fellow travellers, is now the landship's official designation.'

CHAPTER FIFTY THREE

'He is back. We must start trailing him again.'

Their heads were bent low as they discussed how best to utilise their time and their resources.

'We'll take it in turn. I shall do the early morning, and wait outside Wellington House until lunchtime in case he leaves the building.'

He turned to one of the others. 'You take over at two o'clock. This is when he is most likely to be on the move, so keep a close watch on the entrance.'

He turned to the third man. 'That means you'll be doing the late shift, from seven until he retires. He leaves his flat two or three times a week, and gets back about eleven. I would say this is the period when he will be the most vulnerable. So keep a careful eye out. We'll keep this routine going for a week, then swap around. The person doing nights taking the afternoon watch. Is that OK with you two?

There were nods of agreement.

'Fortunately, we are not too busy at the moment, which is a good thing.'

He paused for a moment, before adding. 'Wherever we are, make sure we know where the nearest telephone is located.'

CHAPTER FIFTY FOUR

Among the correspondence was a letter bearing an American stamp.
I tried to leave it until last, but its presence got the better of me.

Dearest Daniel,

I hope Charles is not leading you into danger. I have the strongest feeling his enthusiasm could well over-ride the need for caution. Take the greatest care -, think twice before you follow him into any situation.

I seem to be doing well at the Herald. Favoritism is no longer a term I need concern myself about. The material I am producing appears regularly in the newspaper, and soon I'll be getting my own by-line. How about that!

Write soon,

Clare

I still missed her terribly. Even reading her brief note had my heart pounding. Why did the war have to come between us? I agonised frequently over this question. But, in reality, I knew it was the war that had first brought us together.

Charles put his head round my office door.

'Daniel, are you free next Tuesday evening? I want you to come with me to a meeting and dinner with the authors. Buchan has arranged it at Brooks's in St James' Street.'

'OK. What are we going to discuss?'

'I know for a fact that Buchan wants to massage the facts about our troop losses. Understandable in a way. He wants to hold on to public morale.'

'Well, you know my views about the *History Of The War* series. I've been helping him research and collate the material, which he uses very selectively. Frankly, as an historical work it's totally misleading.'

Charles humphed.

'He has the blessing of the War Office on this one. But you're right, it's a question of balance, and perhaps he has gone too far the other way.'

'I can go along with not showing photographs of dead British soldiers,' I said thoughtfully. 'But forbidding the disclosure of documents detailing our defeats must eventually become an albatross around our necks. Then who will believe anything we say.'

'I found out the other day,' said Charles, 'that if such classified information "slipped" into the hands of the public, it would be considered as treason. How barmy is that? The number of families receiving news of the loss of their fathers, husbands or sons, is mounting daily. That alone will give lie to massaged reports.'

'I don't want to make life difficult for you Charles, but if Buchan is advocating a full-scale whitewash of the facts, I shall feel compelled to say what I think.'

CHAPTER FIFTY FIVE

'Our quarry is on the move. He was collected by someone in a taxi. Fortunately, I was close enough to overhear the address they're going to. It's Brooks's Club in St James' Street. I also discovered there's a meeting of writers working for the Bureau taking place. As he is with someone, it might be better if the two of you join me. Come in our own transport and meet me on the corner of King Street and St James'.

We dined well and sat back to enjoy the port as it made its way around the long table. There were sixteen of us with John Buchan acting as host. I was talking to Rudyard Kipling when Buchan lightly tapped a wine glass for attention.

'Gentlemen, with your permission, I would like to return to the subject under discussion before we came to table. The essence of it was this. Are we the appropriate arbiters, should we be the ones to decide what the man and woman in the street read about the conflict now raging in continental Europe?

'Because we are privy to the confidences voiced in the War Office, in the Foreign Office, and even in Number Ten, you and I,' he scanned those sitting on both sides of the table, 'have a duty to perform. It's a delicate exercise. One that needs the utmost care in the choice of words, their impact, and the lasting effect they will have on our readers.

'As a consequence, I believe, strongly believe, that we tell the truth, but the very limited truth about our reversals in battle, the losses we sustain, and the harsh realities of warfare. Where men are pitted against men, both intent on ending each others' lives.

'To get the discussion moving along, let me set out my stall. I do not wish to mislead the public, merely to provide the level of information they can assimilate without prejudicing the moral fibre and morale of this country.'

Buchan spoke in a soft, Scots accent that was a pleasure to listen to. What is more, the tone, the cadence of his words, were persuasive. All those present were readily in sympathy with his views. Well, nearly all.

There was a mild chorus of "here, here", several diners gently banging the table in approval. I glanced at Masterman, who was carefully pouring port from an elegant decanter into his glass.

There was a brief silence, which I broke by loudly quoting, *'Quis custodiet ipsos custodes?'*

Buchan looked in my direction.

'I'm not sure I follow the meaning of that remark, Mr Kindred. Who guards the guards? What are you implying?'

'It's quite straightforward, Mr Buchan. Who gives us the right to alter facts to suit the circumstances. Who is it who would decide how far we in this room should go to hide unpalatable truths? In your view it is essential to disguise the grim realities of war, and only glorify the modest successes the Entente achieves. Are you aware that to date Britain alone has lost close to three-quarters of a million men? On the first day of the Battle of The Somme alone, we suffered close to sixty thousand casualties. Each had a family who mourned their deaths. Seven hundred and fifty thousand families, Mr Buchan, have been exposed to the full horror of war by their losses.'

I glanced at Masterman. He was staring fixedly at the table.

'When that figure doubles, which it will before this conflict ends, a lot more people will know the truth. At that point, honeyed words that minimise our setbacks, that gloss over the pain and suffering of our troops, that paint a totally unrealistic picture will be derided and scorned. Our credibility will be shot, anything we say will be discounted as mere wind, empty puffery.'

In the end no decision was reached. The debate struggled to find common ground. The only area of agreement was to hold back any film or photography that would upset those who had lost loved ones in battle, and jeopardise recruitment and conscription.

Buchan caught up with me as we were making our way down the stairs.

He put his hand on my shoulder. 'I don't agree with your sentiments, Daniel. But I cannot deny they were nicely argued.'

He nodded to Masterman.

As we passed through the entrance door and stood on the pavement waiting for a taxi, Charles said. 'There are times when I'm with you, Daniel, that I fervently wish the ground would open up and swallow me. That, or to be whisked away from it all when you get on your high horse.'

At that very moment his wish came true.

CHAPTER FIFTY SIX

It happened so suddenly there was little time to shout or retaliate.

A motor car squealed to a halt in front of the club.

Three men appeared out of the shadows and literally bundled Masterman and I into the back seats. As I heaved myself upright, something struck me a glancing blow to the head. Momentarily stunned I fell back and hit the side my head against the door handle. As a pall of darkness enveloped me, my abiding memory was of Masterman toppling forward between the front seats.

I came to leaning against a damp wall. I could not see. Then slowly I realised I was blindfolded. I went to raise a hand to my face, to find my arms were bound behind my back, and the rope knotted tightly to ties around my legs. Unable to move all I could do was listen to faint sounds.

I could hear heavy breathing, and stretching out my legs touched a body. I presumed it was Charles lying at my feet. No doubt, similarly constrained, and still unconscious. I prodded him as gently as I could. After a few minutes he emitted a low groan.

'Where are we?' he croaked.

'Search me. I'm blindfolded, are you?

'Yes. . .and I've got hellish cramp.'

I could feel him trying to flex his arms and legs.

'God, this is painful.'

'Try to sit up and wriggle over here.'

He eventually managed to right himself and shuffle backwards to lean against the wall beside me.

When his breathing quietened after his exertions, he remarked, almost casually. 'Do you know, young Daniel, I think we are in the shit.'

'That was my conclusion, Charles. They couldn't shoot us in the dark outside Brooks's, in case they missed. So we were abducted and, no doubt, will be dispatched come the moment.'

Neither of us mentioned the fate of Bob Brady or Monty Beresford.

We sat side-by-side, alone with our thoughts. I wanted desperately to hold Clare in my arms. I could think of nothing else. To tell her how much I loved her. If only the circumstances had been different.

'I shall miss my wife and family,' he said in a low voice. 'I've just realised how much I've taken them for granted. Work has absorbed all my attention. What a fool thing to have done.'

It was a heart-felt comment. I could not let it pass without an opinion.

'I suppose you have devoted a lot of your time to the Bureau. But look at it this way. It was for your children to enjoy a secure future. Freedom to live their lives as they want, not ruled by the dictates of others.'

'Do I detect honeyed words?'

'No, simply the truth as I see it. No, as it really is.'

We fell silent.

'Do you know,' I said aloud, breaking the stillness. 'When I was in America a few weeks back, down on the Mexican border, I had an idea how we just might bring the USA into the war. It was far-fetched, fanciful even. . . but somehow it might have worked.'

Charles grunted. 'Well, I doubt we'll ever know.'

Another lengthy pause in the conversation.

'What exactly was this momentous idea, Daniel. I'm tied-up, but not tied up at the moment, so you've got all the time you want to tell me.'

I passed the next hour explaining the notion I had had. As I laid out my thoughts, so to me, they seemed all the more extreme.

'And that's about it. Congress and the House of Representatives vote to join forces with Britain and its allies, and President Wilson has to go along with their decision. Now you can shoot down the whole idea.'

But the opportunity was denied him.

The sound of a creaking door being pushed roughly to one side was followed by urgent footsteps. Hands reached out and pulled us roughly to our feet.

I felt the knot of my blindfold being untied.

I dimly perceived our captors. . .and yet, as my eyes grew accustomed to what little light there was, I could not allow myself to believe that before me was the smiling face of Brian, my cousin.

'What on earth are you doing here?' I shouted, as pent up emotions got the better of me. 'Who are all these people?'

'I'll tell you after we get you untied and out of here.'

Brian, with his two brothers, Edward and Leo, got Charles and I into the cab of their lorry. We were taken to Aunt Rosa's house in St James' Walk.

Charles remarked dryly.'We were snatched from St James, then rescued and delivered to St James.'

We hobbled into the parlour, still suffering from the long hours of being trussed up. I did not appreciate the extent to which loss of circulation and cramping of the muscles could play havoc with one's movements.

Drinking warm tea, gradually stretching our limbs helped to restore our well-being. Then, I was insistent on learning how the family had brought about our release.

Uncle Thomas explained.

'We've been worried for you, Daniel, ever since the attack at the underground station. Brian said there was nothing for it, we would have to follow you whenever you were away from your place of work. He devised a schedule, and the three boys took it in turn to keep a close eye on your whereabouts. It threw us a bit when you went off to America. But when you came back they resumed their surveillance.'

He sipped his cup of tea.

Leo took up the story. 'Tonight I was outside your flat and overheard you say Brooks's Club. I got there by bus and telephoned for Brian and Edward to join me in the lorry. Perhaps it was intuition, luck or some sixth sense, I'm not sure. However, according to the reception clerk, your dinner was going to run late. And with two of you together, two birds with one stone, it just seemed the right ingredients for something to happen.'

'And it did,' declared Edward. 'When you were shoved into the car and it sped down Piccadilly, we followed it in the lorry. They were unsuspecting. Who would use a lorry to tail another vehicle? Would you believe they drove into our territory, to a yard off York Road, behind King's Cross Station.'

'At that point,' came in Brian, 'I telephoned the police, who put me onto some people called Special Branch. We were keen to go in and sort out your kidnappers, but were strongly advised to wait until this Special Branch arrived in force. When they did we joined in the fray. Apparently, there were about a half dozen people in the building, and guess what?'

'They were members of a German spy ring,' said Masterman.

'How did you know that?'

CHAPTER FIFTY SEVEN

I felt my heart lurch in my chest when I glimpsed the Manhattan skyline.

I was standing on the foredeck. It was raining, the wind was howling and it was cold. I did not feel a thing, other than a deep sense of joy and a certain contentment.

Charles and I had had several meaningful discussions since our abduction. There was no disguising the fact that if my cousins had not maintained their vigil, had not taken steps to keep me safe, the Bureau would have lost two more employees.

Moreover, the heartfelt comments made by Charles about his family, my desire to draw Clare into my arms, would never have had the chance of being fulfilled.

Even now I exulted in the fact that Charles had given me that opportunity. But it came with strings. The wild idea I had expressed to him, when held captive in the back streets of King's Cross, was to be put into action.

The trouble was I could not truly foresee how it might all come together. There were any number of imponderables. It was a risky venture.

But so was my expedition to win back Clare.

I had not forewarned her I was coming. I loved her deeply; however, though it was only months since we had parted, she may have acquired another admirer. She was an attractive young woman. One who would catch the eye of numerous would-be suitors.

I booked into the Algonquin, and stayed well clear of the bar.

If there were any of the set winding down after a day's work, it could have had consequences. I wanted a clear head for what I was going to do the next morning.

After breakfast, I could not eat more than a slice of toast with some black coffee, I walked the half mile down Sixth Avenue to the Herald. The closer I got, the more nervous I became. When the distinctive building came in sight, my hands were damp, my collar suddenly a size too small.

I walked up the stairs to the first floor, through swing doors, past an unmanned reception area and into the newsroom. It was a vast cavern of a place. Full of desks, telephones ringing, typewriters clacking and the over-riding cacophony of people shouting, and occasional laughter, All taking place in a pall of cigarette smoke. The Times' newsroom was never like this.

I peered through the haze. Scanning faces, looking intently for the one person who mattered. There she was. I recognised the hair, hanging over her features like an auburn theatre curtain. She was speaking into the telephone.

Periodically she would sweep her hand through the curtain as she made an emphatic point in the conversation.

'Can I help you, buddy?' came a voice at my elbow.

No thanks, I can see who I want.'

I strode down an aisle between desks.

'Now wait a minute, you can't. . .'

'Stop him someone!' A voice called out.

The room went suddenly silent. There was an interloper.

I was thirty feet away when she put down the receiver and looked up.

Her hand went to mouth, her eyes misted. She rose unsteadily from her seat, then ran full tilt into my arms and burst into tears.

'God! I must look the most awful sight.'

We were in an interview room with windows overlooking the newsroom. Everyone had walked past, stared openly, and grinned at the two of us.

'I'm sorry if I've created a problem with your colleagues out there,' I said, holding tightly onto her hand.

Clare shrugged, then smiled. 'How long are you here for? No, I don't want to know. You're here, that's all that matters.'

There was a peremptory knock at the door and a man in his fifties walked into the room. 'Clare, you've posted your copy for tomorrow's edition, so why don't you take Mr. . .Mr?'

'Daniel Kindred, sir,' I said rising from the chair.

'Pleased to meet you Mr Kindred. You've created quite a stir coming in here and waylaying our Miss Johnson. So you two run along, and I'll see you tomorrow, Clare.'

We left hurriedly, Clare with her head down. Outside she took me to a nearby coffee shop.

'Right, what are you doing here?'

'It's a long story.'

'It seems I've got all afternoon.'

'OK, but not here. Let's find somewhere to walk.'

We took the elevated train up 6th Avenue to 58th Street, and strolled through Central Park. Crossing the Gapstow Bridge at the north-east end of The Pond, we found a bench at the water's edge and sat down.

'OK, now tell me.'

I explained everything. The kidnapping, our rescue and our surprise rescuers, Charles's lament in captivity, and the overwhelming realisation of how just how much she meant to me. I also told her of the idea I had to encourage America to enter the war, to which Charles Masterman had given his blessing.

'The trouble is, has Charles allowed me to put the scheme into practice because he thinks I could bring it off, or because my family saved him from being executed?'

Clare took hold of my hand.

'Daniel, I'm sorry to say it, but it's probably the latter. It's payback for giving him another chance to appreciate just how much his family means to him.'

Hmm, probably. But that's why I'm here, and I'm going to give it a damn good try.'

'Good for you, darling.'

She leaned into me. I put my arm around her shoulder. In a quiet voice she asked. 'Is that why you've shaved off your beard?'

I did catch up with the Algonquin set. At least five of them, which made for a less intoxicating evening. Clare had gone up to Boston on an assignment for two days, which allowed me to catch up with my journalistic friends.

'Well, well, look who's just walked in,' grinned Ruth Hale.

'Well I'll be damned!' exclaimed Heywood Broun.

Alexander Woollcott, nodded and raised his glass. 'Welcome back, Dan. So, what you are having to drink?'

'Just a small gin and tonic, please.'

Heywood raised a finger to the barman.

'By the way, have you met Kaufman?' he said over his shoulder.

He turned and called out. 'George, Beatrice, come over here. Come and meet a very good friend of ours.'

When handed my glass, Heywood, by way of introduction, declared. 'George is engaged to Beatrice and is a budding playwright. At the moment he is doing stage reviews for the New York Times.'

As we shook hands, he went on. 'As you can tell, Daniel is a Brit. But we don't hold that against him. He works for the London Times, and occasionally graces us with his presence.'

When the opportunity arose I had a word with Alexander.

'How are you, my friend?' he asked. 'Still up to mischief?'

I grinned, and perched on a bar stall beside him.

'Alexander, I want to give you something.'

I took from my pocket photographs of the tanks when they first appeared at Flers–Courcelette.

'These are the British tanks in operation during the first few days of the Somme offensive.'

Woollcott studied them intently.

'I saw a copy of the Philadelphia Ledger which showed what they thought was your secret weapon on their 19th September front page. These look nothing like it. Can I use these photos?'

Yes, of course. I wanted to repay the kindness you showed when you organised the film show at the Strand theatre.'

'Can you give me a little more detail?'

'Yes. You see, I was there when they arrived on the battlefield.'

His eyebrows rose. 'Were you now? The ideal guy to give me the full story.'

'Just one thing, Alex, I have to tell you that I am about to pass on the photos to a Herald correspondent.'

'What, to the irrepressible Miss Johnson? Is she your *belle copine*?'

'Sort of, Alexander.'

We sat next to each other at the dinner table and he surreptitiously made notes. As we were coming to the end of the meal, I said casually. 'By the way, do you know of a fellow called William Bayard Hale?'

'Yes. . .yes I do. Our paper has featured him in its columns a number of times. Why? Do you think his association with our president and the Germans is significant? If you like I can get you copies of what the NYT has written about him.'

A bundle of past editions of the New York Times arrived the next day. I took them with me when I went to Clare's apartment.

I had not realised how late it was until I heard a key turn in the lock and Clare appeared. She stood in the doorway, hands on hips.

'When you're at home with a newspaper, do you always discard each sheet once it's read? Just look at this place. There are torn pages everywhere.'

'Sorry, darling, I'll collect them up. I've been doing background research on William Bayard Hale.'

While I put the unwanted pages in one pile, and those with useful information in another, I told her about my evening with the Algonquin set and Alexander Woollcott.

I went to my bag and produced a raft of photographs and a several pages of typewritten notes. The journalist's instinct took over. Clare took the materal to the window and studied the pictures and typewritten document.

'Wow, can I use this stuff for a piece in the Herald?'

'That's why I've given it to you. Though, as you appreciate, Woollcott has the photographs as well. Mind you, he didn't get the write-up. I did that for you to save time. Time you can now spend with me.'

She came across the room and jumped into my lap.

'I always knew you'd come in useful some day!'

CHAPTER FIFTY EIGHT

I learned a great deal about William Bayard Hale.

I read and stored for reference the cuttings from the Times, and paid several visits to the New York Public Library on Fifth Avenue at 42nd Street. The *Beaux-Arts* landmark building houses outstanding research collections in the humanities and social sciences.

It appeared Hale was in his late forties, and an active journalist still writing for Cosmopolitan, and also Current Literature and World magazines. Moreover, at one stage he had been the Paris correspondent for the New York Times. What intrigued me more was that on leaving university, he studied and was ordained an Episcopalian priest. Hale was a preacher in Massachusetts until he became involved in politics.

In a great deal of the material there were strong suggestions that he was a major influence in the election of the President, Woodrow Wilson, in 1912. As a paid agent he spoke out forcibly for Germany against Britain, opposing the supply of munitions to the Entente. His book, *American Rights and British Pretensions on the Seas,* published in 1915, was a condemnation of the British blockade of the Atlantic. He alleged it hindered the country's trade with Europe. It was clearly intended to stir American resentment at what Hale depicted as Britain's high-handed attitude.

It was obvious he carried quite a bit of journalistic muscle. How to turn it to advantage was uppermost in my thoughts. I had to get inside his mind. To do that I needed to get to know the man.

I went to the British Embassy in Washington and had a lengthy discussion with Malcolm Mackenzie. I told him of the plan, sanctioned by Charles Masterman, to gain his views of its feasibility.

Somewhat to my surprise, he was all for it.

'If it came off, Daniel, it would be a master stroke. How can I help?'

'There may be occasions when I need to use your wire service, or items requested that would best come in the diplomatic bag. That sort of thing, Malcolm.'

He nodded. 'No problem. Here is my direct telephone number.'

Then he asked. 'What name will you be using? I'd better make a note of that.'

I took the passport from an inner pocket, and handed it to him.

'What do you think?'

He studied the document. '*Schweizerische Eidgenossenschaft Reise-Pass.*

'Hmm, Swiss Confederation passport, issued in the border town of Schaffhausen in 1910. So you are masquerading as Ulrich Vonlathen, that's a good Swiss-German name. What about your local accent? Have you mastered that?'

'I think so. I've been studying the local dialect, though most will speak *Hochdeutsch* over here.'

'Yes they will. Well, Ueli, that's the diminutive you'll have to get used to, I wish you every success.'

CHAPTER FIFTY NINE

Clare invited me to spend the weekend at her parents' place in Scarsdale.

We arrived on Friday evening, and Lyons escorted me to the room I now almost regarded as my own. It overlooked the rear of the house, and from the wide terrace there was an expanse of lawn and an array of various species of trees leading down to a distant stream.

I had finished unpacking when Clare knocked on the door.

'Ah, preserving appearances,' I grinned. 'Normally, you burst into any room without warning, most often when I'm in the shower.'

'Different house rules. I like mummy and daddy to think I lead an unblemished, respectable life. That I don't entertain a certain man I could mention after hours.'

'They don't suspect anything?'

'They probably do. But I'm not saying, and they won't ask.'

We walked down the winding staircase with her holding my arm.

It was after dinner, Clare and her mother had wandered out to the terrace and her father and I were alone in the drawing room.

'Something to drink, Daniel?'

'Not for me, Mr Johnson, thank you. That wine during the meal was excellent.'

'Would you like another glass? It's a Californian red from a winery of a friend of mine. They really are making great strides out there, capitalising on the failure of the European wine industry a few years back.'

'Please. I'd enjoy a little more of that.'

He busied himself opening the bottle and filling two glasses. When he came over to place mine on an adjacent side table, he said.

'Forgive me, Daniel, if you think my question is impertinent. Naturally, I'm interested in Clare's companions, but when I ask her what exactly you do, she never seems to give a straight answer. I know at the moment you are working for one of your government agencies, but can you tell me a little more about what you do?'

This is tricky. How far do I go in revealing my hand? Or do I perpetuate the smoke screen?

'At the moment Mr Johnson, as you've been told, I am on secondment to a British government department which fosters closer ties with countries whom we regard as allies. My role. . .'

Clare's father interrupted me.

'What, trade development, creating sound business relationships?'

'Well, not. . .'

'I'm all for that, I can tell you. My company is involved in munitions, and we are selling a great deal of our output to Great Britain. I must admit being a neutral in this conflict has allowed us to sell to all the warring countries. That is, until your naval blockade put a stop to our European trade. Still, I can't grumble, we are doing well on the business with you people.'

He looked reflectively into his glass.

'The problem we are now finding are senseless acts of sabotage. The culprits, when they're caught, are usually migrant Americans objecting to the production of weapons. But to my way of thinking, those masterminding the break-ins, the damage to plant and the fires, are German. We have heavy security, but I reckon many of the incidents are caused by insiders. We employ a lot of migrant workers in our factories in New Jersey. Many have German and Austrian roots, so sympathise with the Central Powers.'

He held the glass to his lips, and stared at it reflectively.

'But it's more widespread than that. This William Hale fellow has a lot to answer for, inciting discontent because you people are blocking trade routes and hampering business. Have you read what he wrote about loss of trade? Bloody man, and to think he is a member of my club.'

'Oh, which one is that?'

'The Union Club, on the northeast corner of Fifth Avenue and 51st Street. He hangs around with another journalist, fellow called Crowninshield, Frank Crowninshield, a well-known socialite and editor of Vanity Fair magazine.'

Clare and her mother came through French windows into the room and the conversation moved to other topics, away from my activities. Mr Johnson had made assumptions about me. Perhaps I was wrong allowing him to gain the wrong impression. One day I'll put him right. However, inadvertently, I had gained a valuable lead to how I might engage with William Bayard Hale.

Back in the city I spent Thursday evening with the Algonquin set.

In particular I wanted to discuss the Vanity Fair editor with Dorothy Rothschild, soon to be Parker. Her waspish humour was at its best as she talked about the changes and new features he was introducing to the magazine.

'Do you know I was writing about the prom season recently, and finished with the line, "If all the girls who attended the Yale prom were laid end to end, I wouldn't be a bit surprised."

'He sent his assistant down with the instruction to remove it. I said no. She came back later and said Mr Crowninshield wants to see me in his office. So I said to her straight. Tell him I'm too fucking busy - or vice versa.'

Significantly, I learned that he took long lunches at his club on Tuesdays and Fridays, meeting up with his cronies.

I spent the following Tuesday lunchtime watching the Union Club from the steps of Saint Patrick's Cathedral on the opposite corner. I saw

Crowninshield arrive, followed shortly by Bayard Hale. They came out about two hours later and strolled down Fifth Avenue.

It was the same routine on Friday.

On Sunday morning Clare and I were reading the newspapers when her telephone rang.

'It's my father,' she mouthed.

I looked over after several minutes and she was staring unsighted into the distance.

'That's awful,' she murmured. 'Was anyone hurt?'

When the call ended she immediately dialled another number.

'My editor,' she said.

'Have you heard?' were her opening words. Then she added. 'Apparently there's been a huge explosion on Black Tom Island. . .It's the one next to the Statue of Liberty. . .That's right. . .I'm told it's a major munitions depot. About two million pounds of ammunition was stored in freight cars, and another hundred thousand pounds of TNT was on a barge tied up there, waiting to be exported. . .How many hurt? . .Well as I understand about ten people. . .No, I don't know who was responsible, but it's thought most likely German saboteurs. . .Sure I'll go, if I can get close enough to the place. Apparently, the whole area has been cordoned off.' She replaced the receiver.

'Did you hear what has happened?'

I nodded.

'I have to go. Will you come with me?'

'Of course.'

We could not get within two miles of the island, which I discovered was more a land-filled promontory accessed by road.

We had met with a photographer, who suggested we got ourselves a boat, and he knew where to hire one. It turned out to be a small motorboat fitted with a cabin. At first it seemed ideal, until we plunged into the wake of other larger craft. Then we pitched, rolled and were awash with flying spray.

Passing the Statue of Liberty it was clear it had suffered damage from the explosion. We managed to manoeuvre ourselves close enough to Black Tom Island, and for a few pictures to be taken by a very wet photographer. Suddenly, a police launch appeared and we were stridently told through a megaphone to clear the area.

Back at the Herald building, Clare spent a great deal of time on the telephone to her father. His company had had a large consignment of arms in a warehouse on the island, and had been kept informed of the event.

The explosion had been the equivalent of an earthquake measuring five point five on the Richter scale, and had been felt as far away as Philadelphia.

Windows were broken up to twenty five miles away, including thousands in lower Manhattan. It was now understood seven people had been killed in the explosion, and many had suffered injury from flying glass.

Clare's editorial and several photographs were destined for the Herald's front page the following day.

CHAPTER SIXTY

In any plan luck undoubtedly plays a key role in its execution.

Clare had wanted me to accompany her, and help where I could; and I asked the same of her.

She was to act as look-out and signaller. Meanwhile I wrote an article in German about the Black Tom catastrophe with a very obvious bias. This was stored in a large envelope with one side split.

I then identified the shop in Fifth Avenue and bought a large selection of flags, paper hats and fireworks, requesting they store them until I could collect all the items later in the week.

All was in readiness.

When they left the Union Club together, Clare told the taxi driver to turn down Fifth Avenue and stop in two hundred yards. He had been well paid for his time, and was more than happy to do her bidding.

When it drew into the kerb she waved to me and I entered the shop. Collecting my many parcels I lodged the split envelope on the top, and stood by the door. The next thirty seconds would determine the entire future of what I had in mind. This manoeuvre was critical.

I stared intently at Clare as the seconds ticked down. For a moment pedestrians blocked my view, but her hand was still raised. I could even see it trembling. Then it dropped, and I pushed blindly through the door – straight into their paths.

I genuinely hurt my hip in the tumble, and it was not a charade when I cried out in pain. Crowninshield also went down, and Hale staggered as we collided with each other. My packages and boxes went flying, as did the envelope with the manuscript.

I called out. *'Scheiße! Armleuchter! Schauen Sie jetzt, was Sie getan haben!'*

Hale, picking up the sheets of paper, replied in poor German. *'Es tut mir leid, dass wir Sie nicht sahen!'*

So he did not see me and is apologising. All the better.

Clare came from the cab. 'I saw what happened. Are you badly hurt? Can I do anything?'

She started to help me to my feet.

'Thank you, madam. I shall be all right.' I said in English. 'I have the feeling I was equally at fault.'

Hale was suddenly absorbed reading the title page of the article.

'Are you some sort of writer?' he asked.

'I am a journalist, sir,' I replied brushing myself down.

'Where is this intended? Are you sending this to a publication in Germany?'

I started to gather the fallen parcels. 'Why do you ask?'

'This is not the sort of material that would be acceptable to American newspapers, that's why.'

'If you must know, it has been written for newspapers in Baden-Württemberg.'

'Why do you want to know, William?' asked Crowninshield.

'Let us just say the tone of this piece could be misconstrued. If I have understood what is written, the headline proclaims, "Weapons destined for Great Britain go up in smoke".'

Hale stared at me several times as he read it.

'It goes on, "Many thousands of tonnes of weapons and explosives, about to be used against us in the war, were detonated in the heart of New York. An impressive display, which not only did considerable damage to the city, but also to the hearts and minds of those who would support the Triple Entente. It is measures such as this which will force this war to an early conclusion, with the Central Powers bringing peace to Europe and beyond".'

'What are you going to do about it, William?'

'Absolutely nothing, Frank. . .absolutely nothing. And I hope this young man will accept that this slight contretemps was a mishap in which neither side was to blame. I bid you good-day, sir. . .madam.'

He was going to walk away. The plan had failed.

They resumed their stroll down Fifth Avenue.

However, Bayard Hale had gone no more than ten yards, when he turned and beckoned me.

'Take my card and telephone me when you have a moment.'

I walked back to Clare and grinned.

'The bait has been taken, my love.'

I walked over to the cab. The driver had a bemused look on his face, having witnessed all that had happened.

'Have you got any children?' I asked.

'Three. . .why?'

'Would they like some paper hats and fireworks?'

CHAPTER SIXTY ONE

The cable to Masterman had similar wording with a minor addition.
"BAIT TAKEN. NOW FOR STAGE TWO. DK"
I allowed several days to pass before phoning Hale.
'Yes?'
'Mr Hale?'
'Who wants him?'
'We bumped into each other on Fifth Avenue.'
'Ah, it's you. I'm glad you've phoned. I was wondering if you might. Come and see me at my office on Fifth Avenue. I want to discuss something with you.'
He gave me the address and we agreed to meet the following morning.

He led the way into a sumptuous office with a good view of the New York Public Library. Ironic to think that a short while ago I was in that very building researching the man now proffering a chair.
'First things first. Tell me your name and where you're from.'
No small talk from Mr Hale. He got straight to the point.
'My name is Ulrich Vonlathen. Friends call me Ueli. I am a freelance journalist working for newspapers and journals in Southern Germany and in the Swiss canton of Schaffhausen, where I was born.'
'So you're Swiss national.'
I nodded.
'What sort of German do you speak?'
'Pardon?'
'You know. Do you speak with a Swiss accent, your local dialect, or what?'
'Mr Hale, I speak with a local accent when it's necessary in the dialect of my canton. At other times, of course, in *Hochdeutsch.*'
He nodded thoughtfully. 'Where did you learn English?'
'I left home when I was eighteen and went to live with an aunt in England. I attended a minor university and studied journalism.'
'Where?'
'Bristol University. After I graduated I came to the United States.'
Once more he nodded. Then murmured. 'You know, don't you, I could have had you arrested for writing that stuff you had on you when we, as you say, bumped into each other. That was subversive material. You could be detained indefinitely in this country for such an inflammatory editorial. Lucky for you I picked it up and not someone else. Just imagine, you could be facing ten years in the slammer for what you wrote.'

He leaned forward.

'You realise I could still have you put away.'

The man was talking nonsense, but I assumed a slightly obsequious air.

'Why would you want to do that? The United States is a neutral country, it wouldn't do that to me.'

'Believe me, Vonlathen, this country does not welcome foreigners who applaud when its buildings, businesses and people are damaged. For all I know you could have been one of them who fired Black Tom Island.'

'Of course I wasn't!'

He ignored my protest.

'So let me make you a little proposition. You work for me, writing the sort of stuff I tell you to write, speaking to the people I tell you to speak to, and I keep my mouth shut. What d'you say?'

'No.'

'I don't think you quite understand, Vonlathen. You don't have a choice. But I'll sweeten it by paying you the going rate of thirty dollars a week, plus expenses.'

I kept quiet for several minutes, ostensibly thinking it over.

'Well?'

'OK. . .I guess.'

'There's just one thing. One of my clients is the German Legation in Washington. They'll need to check you out.'

We stood up, and Hale stretched out his hand. I shook it.

'By the way, Ulrich, what were you doing the other day with all those flags, paper hats and fireworks?'

'Some friends of mine and I were going to celebrate a belated Swiss National Day. Back home in Schaffhausen it's a wonderful occasion. Everyone goes up to the Rhine Falls above the town which is illuminated. There is an amazing fireworks display, and we drink wine until daybreak. I miss the happy days we enjoyed in my youth, and still celebrate the occasion wherever I am, though perhaps not always on the day.'

'Right. I shall expect you here on Monday morning at nine o'clock sharp, OK?'

'Read these briefing notes. They are in German, and as you've probably gathered my grasp of German isn't good enough to pick up the nuances, the subtleties of the language. Take your time, I want your thoughts on how you would get to grips with what they're seeking.'

He passed over a document with *Zentralstelle für Auslandsdienst,* Central Office for Foreign Services, prominent on the cover.

I spent the rest of the day and the following morning reading and thinking how to achieve their aims.

After lunch I strolled into Bayard Hale's office.

'Got time for a discussion?'

'Give me a few minutes, Ulrich. I want to speak to a real estate company. I've seen some offices on Broadway that might suit.'

In this instance my suggestions to Hale had to be close to what the Legation believed were workable recommendations. Enough to be seen to work in their favour. Well, almost.

OK, Ulrich, let's hear what you've got to say!'

From what I had gleaned about William Bayard Hale, he was an excellent writer, had a first-class, logical brain that allowed him to assess facts and manage people, and was able to convey his ideas lucidly and with conviction. But I doubted he had the abilities to be a propagandist. I was about to find out.

'As I see it, Mr Hale, while the key objective is to win the hearts and minds of the American people, to make them sympathetic to their cause. . .'

'Our cause, Ulrich,' interrupted Hale. 'Don't forget that. They like us to think we are an extension of the embassy, and embrace the same ideals.'

'OK, if that's the case we are missing something fundamental to our cause. Our propaganda in this country is hamstrung by our inability to understand the American people.'

He smiled sourly. 'OK, for the moment their cause, and that's where we come in.'

I nodded.

'So tell me my young friend, what we have to do.'

'As I was saying, the propaganda in America suffers from a misunderstanding of the American character. The Germans believe the average American citizen will not be swayed by rhetoric or sentiment. To reach them effectively, we need to provide facts. They prefer logical argument to indirect messages. Material should be written in a manner which is almost legally precise, so that Americans can make their own judgement about the German side of the conflict.

'Well, nothing could be further from the truth. A tug at the emotions will win more followers than information about steel output in the Ruhr.'

'Wait a minute, you have read their briefing document, I presume? What they want is key here. Whether I agree with you or not, Berlin has decided the propaganda message. I don't think we should, or even could, alter that.'

'Well, I believe we should introduce a few marginal adjustments. At least top and tail the facts with more eye-catching material.'

'Hmm. . .perhaps.'

'The second area we need to address is the approach. German propaganda has almost always been reactive. Too much energy is spent defending Germany against the Entente's charges of crimes against persons - civilian and military - and cultural buildings and monuments. The German military leadership should deal head on with the invasion of Belgium and unrestricted submarine warfare, and the sinking of the Lusitania. Explain the rationale behind such acts.

189

'We should also make good use of those writers and authors in the United States with similar views to ourselves. People like the Irish-American author Frank Harris, the German-American Frank Koester, and Professor Edwin J. Clapp of New York University. Moreover, we should utilise the peace movements to our advantage. They could well be effective in keeping America out of the war.'

I could tell by the gleam in Hale's eyes I was striking the right notes.

'There's much, much more we could do to improve relations between Germany and the United States. The points I've raised are for our immediate attention.'

'Other than changing the message, I like your thinking, Ulrich. I want you to write down what you've just told me, and all the other proposals you have in mind. In fact, do a complete presentation document for me to take to Washington. How long will that take you?'

'At least three days if you want a thorough appraisal of the direction the propaganda should go, the steps to achieve their goals and a costing of all the elements, Mr Hale.'

'Hmm, leave out the last part, the finances. We'll do that as a separate item once the main programme is agreed.'

Suddenly, he rubbed his hands together just like Masterman. 'Well done, Ulrich. This could work well to our advantage.'

CHAPTER SIXTY TWO

I showed Clare a copy of the document I had prepared for Hale.

'This is good stuff, Daniel. Could he have prepared such a document? Was he testing you, do you think?'

'I don't think so. Frankly, it has a few deliberately, misguided proposals, but Hale seemed genuinely pleased to take it with him and present to Count Johann Heinrich von Bernstorff, the German ambassador, and to his intelligence people.'

'Was it in English like this, or in German?'

'Both. Hale's German is not that good.'

He returned two days later.

'Ulrich, come in here!'

I dutifully walked into his office.

'I have to tell you they liked the ideas we put in the document, and are more than happy for us to act on all the proposals. It seems von Bernstorff has quite a tidy slush fund, so costs are not important. In fact, my remit has been extended. They want to target the black minorities, the Jews and the resident American-Germans with our propaganda material.'

'How do we do that?'

'I don't know. You work it out. That's what you're paid for.'

'OK, but I may have to employ someone to do the research.'

'No problem. Let's just get this show on the road.'

In the end I did not have to resort to outside help. I managed to acquire the help of The German-American Alliance. By 1914, it had over two million members in branches in over forty states. It was especially well-represented in St. Louis, Chicago, Milwaukee and Cincinnati.

Equally, the six thousand strong Lutheran congregations in America were prepared to pass on bulletins issued by the German Press Bureau and Information Service. However, the tone of these bulletins was teutonic: in short, dogmatic and righteous, which did not endear those unsympathetic to the German cause.

After several weeks in Hale's employ the master /servant attitude I had first encountered slowly changed. It was clear I was making a significant contribution: regularly penning press material justifying the German *putsch* into Belgium to stabilise a country riven by general strikes; and the antipathy of the Flemish and the Walloons towards each other. It needed an authority to bring order and peace to the region. It was a pity France thought otherwise, and had conceived it as a barbarous act bordering on annexation. I ignored the taking of sides as a result of the Balkan crisis. I wrote the material with a

191

wry smile, thinking of my reaction to John Buchan's preparedness to alter the facts.

Clare became my go-between with Mackenzie, the British Embassy intelligence officer. It was she who alerted me to his visit to New York, and who arranged for our meeting on a ferryboat up the North River.

A cool breeze was blowing as we passed Chelsea Piers, and few were outside watching the shoreline.

'So you are in the pay of the Germans, Daniel, or should I say, Ueli,' grinned Malcolm, as he and I strolled around the short, forward deck.

'Yes, I suppose you could call me a double agent. It seems to be working out all right, though the people in the embassy still have my passport. They're still doing a search.'

Perhaps he noticed the uncertainty in my voice.

'You've no need to worry on that score. The Directorate of Military Intelligence, Section 6, the people I work for, has assured me that everything will stand up to scrutiny. Ulrich Vonlathen was born in Schaffhausen in 1886, and left when he was eighteen. He really did make his way to England, but there the trail ends. That will be enough to satisfy any mid-level enquiry.'

'What do you mean mid-level?'

'If you were thought a subversive, they would peer under every conceivable stone. But they don't, so they won't.'

'Right. . .but if they did?'

'You, my friend, would be well and truly in the mire,' he said in his soft Edinburgh accent. 'But let's not dwell on that. Tell me what's happening on your front. Clare passed that copy of the proposals on to me, by the way.'

A sudden gust almost took his hat from his head.

'I should be more wary,' he said ruefully. 'The last time I lost a hat that way was on the Potomac. The wind whisked it away. As I was on business, I claimed for a replacement on my expenses. Do you know, the finance manager rejected the claim. So the next month I did my expenses I attached a note saying, the hat is in there somewhere, see if you can spot it.'

His slightly whimsical manner eased my disquiet.

'I've been in touch with a number of groups who will disseminate the propaganda. Here is the list of them willing to circulate pamphlets, postcards and photographs.'

I slipped him an envelope.

'I also have meetings lined up next week with a number of pro-German authors and people of influence. My intention is to get them to write material outlining how peace-loving and benevolent the Germans are. I am also writing material for the newspapers extolling teutonic virtues. Another aspect of the programme is to encourage some of these peace movements to parade and rally against America joining in the conflict. I'll pass on the dates via Clare, so that they can be broken up before they start.'

'Good. I've got a few morsels for you. You know that medal that was struck in Germany commemorating the sinking of the *Lusitania*. I've now got a parcel of British copies, complete with the correct date. I'm going to circulate them to people of influence, who would react badly to receiving such an item.'

I grinned at the thought.

'The other thing I wanted to mention, Malcolm, is the fact that the New York Evening Mail is actually owned by the German Government. I've only just found out. Do you think you could discreetly bring about public disclosure?'

'Most certainly. And I know exactly how it should be done.'

'Have you seen this?'

I looked up from the spread of Sunday newspapers. It was mid-morning, we were due to visit Clare's parents for lunch, so it was a hurried scan of all the broadsheets.

'No, what is it?' I murmured, looking across to Clare sitting on the couch.

She read a bit more.

'Well, I'm damned! I didn't know that.'

She passed over a page of The New York Times.

It was all there, just as I had hoped.

"It is reported that Edward Rumely, vice president, secretary and publisher of the New York Evening Mail, was arrested late yesterday afternoon by agents of the government and charged with perjury. The charge grew out of a statement filed with A. Mitchell Palmer, the Alien Property Custodian, in which Rumely asserted that The Evening Mail was an American-owned newspaper.

The Government is in possession of evidence which shows that instead of being American-owned, the paper is, in fact, the property of the Imperial German Government, which on June 1, 1915, paid Rumely, through Walter Lyons, of the former Wall Street house of Renskorf, Lyons & Co., the sum of $735,000, which effectively transferred control of the newspaper to the Kaiser."

Alexander Woollcott had done a neat job.

CHAPTER SIXTY THREE

I learned about it from Clare's father.

'Of all things, it was lying there on the table when Gordon Bennett and I were about to take a brandy after an enjoyable lunch,' he muttered. 'How the devil it got into the club I don't know. I called the steward immediately and had it removed. The infernal cheek of some people!'

'You say it was called *The Fatherland*?'

'As blatant as that. In fact, there was even a supplementary headline which read, "Fair Play for Germany and Austria-Hungary." I must admit to having mixed feelings about our neutrality. It would suit me of course, as a munitions producer, if we did join the conflict. But in my heart I cannot condone American forces being sent into a war not of our making, not even on our own soil, and consigning them to die fighting for someone else's cause.'

Clare squeezed my hand. I picked up the signal and made no comment.

On the way back to the city I asked if she had ever heard of *The Fatherland*.

'No, it must be one of those closet magazines that exist just for expatriates and the homesick.'

If that were the case, I thought, perhaps I could tap into it in some way. Eventually I obtained a copy of the journal from a barber's shop in the German enclave of Yorkville, on the Upper East Side. It comprised thirty six pages of text and a few advertisements with a dominant illustration on its front cover. In this instance it declared "The Great Anglo-American Conspiracy Exposed", and depicted a young Aryan couple leading others towards, seemingly, a better future. Good, rousing stuff. The articles were well written, and by some notable people.

I showed it to Hale. 'What do you think of this, William?'

By now we were on Christian name terms.

'I've heard of it, but never actually seen a copy.'

He flicked through the magazine.

'Hmm, interesting material. The presentation is a bit melodramatic, but it could be useful. What are you going to do about it, Ulrich?'

'Meet the editor. Get him to take some of our stuff and go and see some of the contributors.'

'Right, I'll leave it to you then. I'm off to the Union Club.'

I found the address, and rather than telephone decided to go in person. I headed west on 37th Street towards the heart of the garment district.

I found the magazine's offices occupying two floors at the top of a building that had seen better days. I estimated there must have been about twenty people scurrying up and down the narrow flight of stairs between the offices. When I asked to see the editor and gave my name, Ulrich Vonlathen, I was shown to an attic room where a fellow about my age dressed in a well-worn, brown suit was seated at a desk.

He rose to greet me, saying brusquely. 'Yes, what do you want? I'm very busy at the moment, can't it wait?'

'I'll come back when it's more appropriate,' I replied shortly.

'No, wait, sorry. I was caught up with something I was writing.'

He held out a hand. 'George Sylvester Viereck. You are?'

'Ulrich Vonlathen.'

Sit down, Herr Vonlathen,' he said in German, moving some papers from the one other chair.

'Look, I'm sorry to interrupt you,' I began. 'As I do not work so very far away, it seemed easier to come round rather than telephone.'

He ran his fingers through a mop of untidy hair.

'We produce a weekly magazine, Herr Vonlathen, so it's always frenetic here. But that can wait for a moment. What can I do for you?'

'I work for William Bayard Hale, who handles the propaganda for the German Embassy over here.'

'I've met him, though briefly, at the embassy in Washington. The ambassador had the idea of forming some sort of cabinet to address the indifferent publicity they were getting. He invited me along with Franz von Papen. But it didn't get very far. Von Papen was declared *persona no grata,* and shipped back home. So you now look after the propaganda, do you? And presumably, you have come to enlist my help. Well, as you might have realised from our magazine, *The Fatherland,* that is our raison d'être. What have you in mind?

I removed several articles I had written from a briefcase and put them on the desk. Viereck picked up each one and read the opening paragraphs.

'These are good. . .very good. I'd most certainly like to feature them in the magazine over the next few weeks, if you agree?'

'Of course. I was hoping you might find them useful.'

Then an idea appeared to strike me.

'You say you know the ambassador?'

'Well, I've met him and had a brief discussion. As I said he was thinking of creating this *Propaganda Kabinett,* but it came to nothing when von Papen was sent back.'

'Supposing, if I could arrange it, you featured an interview with von Bernstorff in *The Fatherland?* What would you say to that?'

'I would say, great! And we'd put his portrait, with a suitable caption, on the magazine's front cover.'

Now I had a name I sent a wire message to MacKenzie asking if he could provide some background information on George Sylvester Viereck. When

Hale got back to the office I told him of my meeting with the editor of *The Fatherland*, and his request to interview the ambassador in Washington.

'When does he want to do the interview?'

'As soon as possible.'

'Well it can't be in the next few weeks. I'm going down to Florida for a break. It's all arranged. Tell this fellow, Viereck, it will have to wait.'

'I don't think it can wait. As I understand it, Viereck has a free front cover coming up and wants to fill the slot now. It would be a pity to lose such an opportunity, for it to go to someone else. Also, you should know that Viereck is a personal friend of Von Bernstorff. We can't afford for him to discover we've ignored such a request.'

'Damnation! Well, you'll have take him down to Washington yourself. You can retrieve your passport at the same time. Don't be too lavish on the expenses, mind.'

'OK. I'll arrange it for next week.'

For the first time, I telephoned the German Embassy. Until now contact had been solely Bayard Hale's domain. The ambassador's aide-de-camp checked von Bernstorff's diary and confirmed that next Wednesday, at four o'clock precisely, would be convenient. I quickly telephoned Viereck and finalised the arrangement.

Among the mail that arrived at Clare's apartment was a bulky, nondescript envelope. Nor was there a sender's name or address shown on the back. When opened, she discovered several fullscap pages to which a note was attached.

Dear Ueli,

This is as much as I have been able to dig up on your friend.

Normally, once you've read such notes I would expect you to eat them. But in this instance, you can just burn them!

All the best, Mac

'What friend? Who is Mac talking about?'

'The editor of *The Fatherland* magazine, George Sylvester Viereck.'

I studied the information sheets. I presumed they were prepared in the normal way intelligence officers submit such documents. It was not a casual summary, more an official report.

Below the Foreign and Commonwealth Office heading of the rampant lion and unicorn either side the crown, was presented.

SUBJECT :   George Sylvester Viereck
                    (popularly known as "Sylvester")

PLACE/DATE OF BIRTH: Munich, December 31st, 1884
PARENTS :   Louis and Laura Viereck
EMIGRATION :   United States of America, 1895

CITIZEN :	American
EDUCATION :	College of The City of New York
CAREER :	Poet, writer, lecturer and propagandist
PUBLISHED WORKS :	(1904) *Gedichte*
	(1907) *Nineveh and Other Poems*
	(1907) *The House of the Vampire*
	(1910) *Confessions of a Barbarian*
	(1912) *The Candle and the Flame*
MAIN PURSUITS :	Editor of "The Fatherland" and "The International"
STATUS :	Married, Margaret Edith Hein, 1911

RANDOM NOTES : In 1910, with the assistance of ex-President Theodore Roosevelt, Viereck founded the journal *Rundschau zweier Welten* and began promoting cultural exchange between the United States and Germany. While *Rundschau zweier Welten* enjoyed little success, it did pave the way for the launch of Viereck's weekly magazine *The Fatherland* during the early months of World War I. A publication which would serve as a vital platform for Viereck's pro-German political convictions.

The Fatherland took upon itself the task of exposing the malfeasance of the Allied countries, of revealing the prejudices and distortions of the American press, and of rallying German-Americans in their own defence. Its bias was strictly pro-German, and did much to advocate America's position of neutrality in the Great War. George Sylvester Viereck soon found himself romanced by German propagandists working in America, including Heinrich Albert himself. By 1915, however, U.S. secret service agents has compiled significant evidence of Germany's propaganda efforts in America, and Viereck has found himself under investigation by the Justice Department. While no formal charges have been laid, Viereck was ousted from several literary societies, and run out of town by the occasional mob of angry "patriot-vigilantes".

SUMMARY : A pro-German idealist, prepared to go out on a limb for his beliefs. A capricious temperament, though an intriguing poet. He has many radical friends; and has recently acquired the writing skills of Aleister Crowley for *The Fatherland*. Crowley is an English occultist, ceremonial magician, poet, and mountaineer, and responsible for founding the religion of *Thelema*.

These people are on the edge of logic and reason. Watch yourself!

I pushed the sheets of paper in her direction.
'Read MacKenzie's report, Clare, you may find it interesting.'

We boarded a late morning train at Penn Station.
Immediately we were seated Viereck took a book of poems from his

197

carrying bag and began reading. Not a word was uttered the entire four hour journey. When the train eased into Washiongton's Union Station, he jumped to his feet, stowed away the book, and turned to me.

'What about something to eat. I'm famished.'

But we did not have time for a leisurely meal. Instead, we had a sandwich and coffee at Swings on the corner of 17th & G Street, before taking a cab to the German Embassy just west of Thomas Circle at 1435-41 Massachusetts Avenue.

It was the first time I had seen the building. It had all the appearance of an old, rambling mansion. Not the type of building I would have associated with the clean-cut, functional teutonic style epitomised by Walter Gropius.

We confirmed our appointment with the ambassador at the reception desk, and were led to a waiting room off the lobby. A dismal room offering little cheer.

Five minutes passed when the door was briskly opened and a fellow I had seen before strode in.

'Good afternoon.' He stared in my direction. 'Herr Vonlathen, my name is. . .'

An image of the evening organised by the Secretary of State, Robert Lansing, flashed through my mind. The man standing in front of me was Heinrich Albert, the resident intelligence officer.

'Albert, the embassy security officer.'

He was holding my passport in one hand and tapping it with a finger of the other.

'Herr Vonlathen, something doesn't seem quite right. Can I ask you a few questions?'

'Of course.'

I looked up at him steadily, but my heart was pumping. Surely he must hear it.

'Your passport tells me you have been back to Switzerland on two occasions since the war between our country and the Triple Entente began. But the immigration stamps are not clear. How did you make the journey? How did you travel to and from Europe?'

The stamps had been deliberately smudged, but not enough that an expert could not determine the European port of entry.

'I travelled by the *USS Rijndam* of the *Nederlandsche-Amerikaansche Stoomvaart Mastschappij*, the Holland American Line, on all four crossings. The ship docked at Rotterdam.'

'And from there, how did you get to Switzerland?'

I shrugged. 'There are various routes, but in the past I've taken a train to Cologne, and. . .'

'What were the stops along the way?'

'Arnhem and Nijmegen, where we crossed into Germany. Why do you ask?'

He ignored my question.

From Cologne where did you go? Basle or Zurich?

'Zurich.'

'How long did it take?'

'About six hours.'

Albert nodded, and continued tapping my passport. Viereck was looking at him in puzzlement.

'At Zurich where did you go?'

'I took the train to Schaffhausen.'

'Via Bulach?'

'No the line doesn't go that way. It goes via Thayngen, stopping at Winterthur, and on to Schaffhausen. It takes about an hour.'

'So, why did you go back to Scaffhausen. To see your parents?'

'My parents are dead. It was more to enjoy the National Day at the Rhine Falls, From a child I have always been attracted to the festival.'

He handed me my passport.

'Mr Hale told me you went back occasionally for the Swiss National Day celebrations. Welcome to the German Embassy, Herr Vonlathen.'

'It's a draughty old place. Do you know it has seventy rooms and thirteen bathrooms. Theodor von Holleben, the ambassador here in ninety three, decided on the building, then was promptly recalled. We've been looking for new premises ever since.'

Whereas Albert and I had conversed in English, Count Johann von Bernstorff, the ambassador, spoke in German. He was in an expansive mood. Seated on a chair in front of the ornate marble fireplace, his legs crossed, he carried an aura of authority behind a suave façade. Of medium height, his narrow features were adorned with a wide, handsome moustache.

Viereck and I occupied a large settee. As the ambassador was chatting, the editor of *The Fatherland* was searching his carrying bag for pencil and paper.

When he was ready, Viereck launched straight into the interview.

'I already have the main caption for the front page below your picture. It will declare, "Americans Be On Your Guard".'

Von Bernstorff's eyebrows rose.

'Why should they be on their guard, Herr Viereck?'

'I'm not talking about the work done for you by Heinrich Friedrich Albert or Captain Franz von Rintelen, Ambassador, I mean the American public should be on their guard against the false, misleading propaganda being circulated by the British.'

'What do you know of these men, Herr Viereck? Albert is my commercial attaché, and Ritolen has replaced von Papen on my staff. They are merely undertaking work consistent with their declared roles. Nothing more.'

Viereck shrugged.

'Of course, Ambassador. So I shall begin by asking you what led to your appointment here in the United States? I want to build a picture for our readers of the man they will see on the front cover.'

Von Bernstorff had been ruffled by Viereck's remark about people in the embassy. I would have to find out more.

'Well, Herr Viereck, you could say I was destined to take on the ambassadorship here in America, for my career path was always in a westerly direction. I was a counsellor in London up to 1906, and whilst my family disagreed with the Bismarck's policies I was always in favour of them, particularly to found the German Reich without Austria.'

I sat beside Viereck while he fleshed out von Bernstorff's personality, moved on to his politics, and then his views on the war. How Germany was being vilified as the instigator of the conflict, and how an utterly misleading picture was being projected across the forty eight states.

Viereck was about to question the ambassador's approach to countering the enemy's propaganda, when the door opened and Heinrich Albert burst in, walked quickly over to von Bernstorff, and whispered in his ear.

'Excuse me, gentlemen. I must attend to something,' the ambassador declared, and hurried from the room.

'Some act of sabotage has probably gone adrift,' muttered Viereck.

A few minutes later von Bernstorff returned.

'Sorry for the interruption. I have just learned that the attempt to replace our submarine cable between Borkum and Tenerife has failed.'

He caught Viereck's questioning glance.

'Herr Viereck, we have a research station there which is, or rather, was a relay point for our transatlanitic messages. The run of cable to the Spanish island was cut by the British navy eighteen months ago. So we shall have to continue using the cables belonging to neutral countries.'

'Which countries do you use, Ambassador?'

The question had been on my mind, and I had voiced it without thinking. The ambassador glanced at me. 'Sweden, of course. Holland, and when time is not pressing, messages are taken by courier to mainland Spain and onwards to the Canary Islands. You were asking me, Herr Viereck, how we counter the propaganda issued by our enemies. Well, as you are no doubt aware, we use William Bayard Hale and his associates to do that for us.'

He nodded in my direction.

'Herr Hale produced a most excellent document on the steps he would take on our behalf, and we fully concurred with the proposals.'

'Which were?'

Von Bernstorff went to his desk and picked up a copy of the document.

'It's all in here. Though, I am sure Herr Vonlathen can tell you of its contents, which, of course, are not for publication in your article, you understand.'

Viereck suddenly lurched to his feet. 'Excuse me, Ambassador, I must use the facilities.'

He strode out the room.

'An interesting character is he not, Herr Vonlathen? His magazine is much enjoyed, I understand, by German-Americans with strong feelings for the Fatherland.'

'I believe the circulation is around a hundred thousand copies. Probably four times that number get to read it. Yes, Your Excellency, a very useful medium.'

'But don't you think a little melodramatic? Not enough facts, much of its content is rant and hyperbole.'

'True, Ambassador, but that's what gets to the public. That's what influences opinion.'

The ambassador stared at me for a moment.

'What are you telling me, Herr Vonlathen? That our propaganda should be as inconsequential as the scribblings of Herr Viereck? That you disagree with the programme?'

'Not with the programme, Count von Bernstorff, but the message. Actually, I believe that the material we send out should be a mix of factual reporting and more colourful rhetoric. In fact, if I could, I would give greater emphasis to exaggeration. Not excessive, but I would certainly embroider the detail. I'm not talking about general thundering or preaching a gospel of hate. Someone once told me, effective propaganda should influence individuals, while leading them to behave as though they had decided their own responses. It comes down to the manipulation of collective attitudes. Whether Viereck knows it or not, his inflammatory journal probably turns more hearts, and then minds, in that order, than what is disseminated at present.'

The ambassador looked thoughtful. Before he could comment, I added. 'When William was briefed on what the delegation wanted, they gave him guidelines issued by Berlin, and dismissed anything he suggested as unworkable in this country. But people act differently over here. Bayard Hale told me in unequivocal terms that whatever ideas he had, he was told not to deviate from the dogma. As a consequence, Herr Hale produced a glossy document. But it is no more than a reflection of what he was told to do – not necessarily what he could achieve. In effect, we are little more than a conduit to the media. What we produce is strictly in accordance with the clearcut views expressed by your communications team.'

The ambassador was still frowning at what I had said when Viereck returned. He picked up where he had left off and continued asking questions and noting the answers for another hour.

'Thank you, Ambassador,' said Viereck as we were preparing to leave. 'I shall send you a copy of the article before we publish, just to make sure we are in agreement. I think I will add another line to the illustration of you on the cover, "Count Johann Heinrich von Bernstorff, who successfully holds the hardest job in the United States".'

We shook hands and were edging towards the door when von Bernstorff said. 'Presumably you will be staying over in Washington at this late hour?'

'I thought we might run late,'I remarked, glancing at my watch. 'So I booked rooms for us at the Willard. We'll catch an early train back to New York tomorrow morning.'

We agreed to meet at seven o'clock in the lobby and dine in the hotel restaurant. I had just come out the shower when the telephone rang.

'Herr Vonlathen?'

'Yes.'

'Von Bernstorff here. Look, could you spare me a little time this evening? I'd like to continue the discussion we had this afternoon.'

'Naturally, Ambassador. However, I have committed to dining with Viereck. Could I come to the embassy afterwards?'

'Of course. Any time. I don't usually retire until well past midnight.'

'He was checking you out, wasn't he?'

'Albert? He was just doing his job.'

He's not security, you know. He's their top intelligenceofficer. Still, you obviously passed the examination. So how do you think it went, the interview?'

I looked up from the plate.

'Well, I thought. You asked all the right questions. Whether you got the answers you expected is for you to decide. But I believe von Bernstorff was quite forthcoming. I shall be interested to see the finished result.'

Viereck waved a fork in my direction.

'I said I'd send the text to him for approval. I'll send it to you too, if you like?'

'Please. We can then tailor our press items so they're in line with what you're going to publish.'

'Right.'

There was silence for a time while we ate.

'Do you know much about Heinrich Albert?' asked Viereck. 'I've met him a few times. He is responsible for the espionage and sabotage operations in the United States. He also arranges forged passports and documents for German-Americans who want to return to fight for the German armed forces. But he is merely a tool of the delegation. Our respected Imperial German Ambassador is the mastermind behind most of the incidents calculated to obstruct arms shipments to our enemies. For example, the mission to destroy the Welland Canal which circumvents Niagara Falls. A good idea, unfortunately, it was a dismal failure. But the recent Black Tom explosion wasn't. That was a success, thank goodness. No, von Bernstorff is certainly no saint.'

'More wine, Sylvester?'

'Hmm, thank you.'

He tipped his glass forward as I poured from the bottle.

I called over the wine waiter and asked for another.

'So who is this fellow, Rintelen?'

'Captain Franz Dagobert Johannes von Rintelen, my friend, was a German Naval Intelligence officer until he was seconded to the embassy. He operates on a Swiss passport like you. I mean, whereas you are Swiss, he masquerades as Swiss. When in the field he assumes the name of his brother-in-law, Emil Gasche. Being a naval man, Black Tom was probably his handiwork.'

I poured more wine into his glass.

'How do you know all this, Sylvester?'

'It's my job to know, Ueli. Anyway, you forget I was close to becoming a member of the *Propaganda Kabinett* at one time, before von Papen got the push.'

He was slurring his words, and leaning heavily on the table. It would not be long before I would have to help him to his room.

'Does your magazine make much money, Sylvester?'

'Why? Do you want to invest in it?' He giggled. 'It makes enough. Enough to pay all the staff with a bit left over for me.'

Suddenly, he stood up and dropped his napkin on the table.

'I think. . .I think I should go to my room.'

He leaned on me as we made our weaving way from the dining room, and was hanging on me when we got to the lift. I almost had to carry him to along the corridor. Taking the key from his pocket, I opened the door and after several attempts managed to heave him onto the bed.

Then I left for the embassy.

CHAPTER SIXTY FOUR

'A nightcap, Herr Vonlathen? Or would you prefer coffee?'

We were in the ambassador's private rooms. On my arrival, his aide-de-camp had opened the main door and escorted me up several flights of stairs to von Bernstorff''s sanctuary. We were in a large, comfortable room, though slightly too cluttered for my tastes. The soft lighting falling upon furnishings redolent of a bygone age.

We sat on opposite settees either side of an ornate fireplace.

'Coffee, would be most welcome, sir.'

He leaned sideways and tugged a bell pull. A moment later the fellow who had ushered me in appeared at the door.

'Some coffee if you please, Gottfried.'

The door closed silently.

'I was perturbed by your remarks this afternoon, Herr Vonlathen,' the ambassador said flatly. 'They suggested to me that we had appointed the wrong man for the job. In that moment I was quite prepared to dismiss Bayard Hale, and whoever worked with him on our propaganda.'

He stretched out an arm and took a pipe from a rack on a side table. Taking tobacco from a pouch, with a practised hand he swiftly filled the bowl, tamped it down, and lit up. When to his satisfaction, he removed the pipe from his mouth and pointed it at me to emphasise his words.

'But I am also aware the people in my communications department follow instructions from Berlin. They have little room to deviate from given policy. Such dictates apply wherever we have an embassy, to ensure a common face is projected to the world. Now, in most circumstances that is appropriate.'

There was a lengthy pause.

A cloud of smoke briefly enveloped the man opposite when the pipe was returned to his mouth and he drew on it reflectively.

'Then I considered more carefully what you had said,' von Bernstorff continued. 'And I came to the conclusion that whilst we follow the current strategy, as outlined in Herr Hale's document, we should adopt a complementary approach along the lines you suggested.

'Let us retain the format of Herr Hale writing articles about the shortcomings of the British, the French and the Russians. They have merit, ansd they satisfy our masters in Berlin. But at the same time. . .'

There was a discreet knock at the door and the ambassador's ADC arrived with the coffee.

Intriguing, I thought, What was he going to say?

'Thank you, Gottfried. I shan't need you any more tonight. I would suggest you retire.'

The fellow bowed and left the room.

'Now what was I saying? . . .black or white, Herr Vonlathen? Are yes. . keep the programme others are happy with, yet operate another which is more. . .how shall I put it? More suited to appeal to the man in the street.'

'I'm not sure Herr Hale has that turn of mind to write such material, Ambassador.'

This was the watershed. By isolating my employer, would it all collapse around me? Would they employ someone else to do the work?

'Herr Vonlathen, I would not want him to. I am a sufficient judge of people to determine that you could perform such a task. I shall go further. I think that in the future you should be our main contact. I am aware that Hale speaks our language poorly, and has no understanding of the German psyche.'

Von Bernstorff used the German word, *Seele,* which meant both psyche and soul - even Jung had difficulty defining what he meant by psyche and by soul.

'I must discuss this with William first, Your Excellency. After all, I am his employee.'

'I don't think so, Herr Vonlathen. It's Ulrich, isn't it? So Ulrich, I shall write to him telling him of my decision. I assure you, he will accept the arrangement. The letter will be waiting for him when he returns from Florida. I shall expect you to take on the role shortly thereafter. Is that understood?'

As expected, the knock came at three o'clock in the morning.

It was a muffled tap on the door. When I opened it Malcolm MacKenzie stepped smartly past me into the room, and dropped into a chair.

'So, how did it go?' he asked in a whisper.

Suddenly, I couldn't help it, a huge smile spread across my face.

'I've done it, Malcolm. I've bloody done it! The first part of the plan I spoke about is working better than I ever thought it might!'

'So tell me what is going to happen.'

'Bayard Hales will continue to write his essays on such things as the unlawful use of a naval blockade, and so on, and I will write the racy, eye-catching stuff for the masses. But the best bit, my friend, the icing on the cake . . .von Bernstorff wants me to be the liaison between the Hale setup and the embassy. I shall be inside the very walls of the delegation, pouring a little something inflammatory on troubled waters. What about that?'

'Brilliant! Though you know what that means?'

I shook my head.

'It means you will be subject to much greater scrutiny than you have been until now. OK, you passed as a Swiss National, but what about New York?'

'What do you mean?'

'I believe you have a close relationship with Miss Johnson?'

'You know I do.'

'Ueli, if they were to discover the fact she is a reporter on the Herald, which is strongly pro-Great Britain, and her father supplies munitions to the British. . .well you would very quickly become *persona non grata* with those wonderful people on Massachusetts Avenue.'

CHAPTER SIXTY FIVE

It was a tearful departure from Clare's apartment.

I had explained the point made by MacKenzie, that it would only be for a short while, a few months at the most. Moreover, we could meet together, every two or three weeks at some place out of the city. Nevertheless, when the time came to go she clung tightly to me.

I had found a rooming house on the south side of Washington Square Park. When I got into a cab and told the driver where I wanted to go, he replied. "Are you sure? That's Tramps' Retreat." Apparently, while to the north it opened onto Fifth Avenue, the opposite side had a less genteel quality.

I had not been aware of the numbers of homeless people circulating the Park until I alighted. We came to a halt outside the Judson Hotel. I entered the lobby and spoke with a large, no-nonsense female behind the desk, who booked me in for a couple of weeks. It was cheap, and I soon realised why. A bed, chair, miniscule chest of drawers and a mirror comprised its amenities. A stained, threadbare carpet covered much of the floor, which did little to raise the chill air of discomfort. I quickly came to the decision I would not remain long in these surroundings.

After unpacking I strolled across the park and took a trolley up Fifth Avenue from 8th to 41st Street, arriving at William Bayard Hale's offices. I rewrote several press releases – one about top quality engineering, for which Germany had a world-wide reputation, and the other on the German fashion trade. A new monochrome look had emerged during times of war, perhaps unfamiliar to young women in comfortable circumstances. Women dropped the cumbersome underskirts from their tunic-and-skirt ensembles, simplifying dress and shortening skirts in one step. I was able to liven it up with a few provocative sentences, and refer to how women were now tackling jobs once thought the province of men. There was a kindred spirit abroad that drove them to secure a meaningful future for their loved ones.

"Kindred spirit", that was what was needed.

Two days later my employer walked through the door.

'Ulrich, get in here!'

I walked into his office to see Hale waving a letter. I could make out the German embassy letterheading.

'OK, what's been going on behind my back. Are you trying to steal my business, or what? Godammit, Ulrich you've really done it this time. I thought we had a good thing going here. No one does that to me. Pack your things and clear out!'

I leaned against the door post.

'OK. I leave, and do you know what. You'll lose the German account. They might give it to me, but I doubt it. I'll tell you why. They are looking for a mix of factual material – that's you – and the billboard, emotive stuff I can produce. The ambassador now recognises that the dictates from Berlin are stifling their propaganda. He wants to appeal to the hearts of the American people instead of purely to their minds. Together, we are a winning combination. Apart, they'll look for someone else to do their work.'

His eyes narrowed.

'You ought to be thanking me instead of canning me. You were going to lose a great deal of money if I hadn't stepped in and told the ambassador we could produce material that hit home with the masses. So, do you want to reconsider, or do you still want me to leave?'

'Hmm. . .perhaps I was a little hasty. You'd better tell me the whole story.'

I took a chair and gave a full account of what had transpired on the visit to Washington with Viereck. I also explained the reason the embassy had suggested I be their contact was because they preferred to discuss matters in German. Hale, himself, had admitted his mastery of the language was poor.

All the while Hale sat at his desk, his hands steepled, fingers under his chin.

'Right. You are no longer an ex-employee. Moreover, to confirm your re-employement I shall take you to lunch.'

We dined at the Union Club. Throughout the meal I sincerely hoped I would not encounter Clare's father.

I had been to the German Embassy. Once more the appointment had been made for late afternoon. However, on this occasion it was I who had suggested the time.

Viereck had sent a copy of what he had written, giving what he thought was full justice to the ambassador's views. As a courtesy, he had also provided me with a copy. On the train down to Washington I went over the article like a sub-editor. Amplifying certain comments, deleting others, improving the syntax, tightening the whole article to make it a more pleasing read. Importantly, one that could ignite pro-German sentiments.

'Herr Vonlathen, come in, come in. Some refreshment perhaps after your train journey? I was going to have some wine, would you care to join me?'

'Thank you, Your Excellency, I would.'

The ambassador went to the side table, poured the wine and handed me a glass.

'What do you think? A friend of mine has a vineyard in Hochheim, on the right bank of the Main in the Rheingau region. He really produces the most excellent Rieslings. This is my favourite.'

'I am an instant convert.' I stared intently at the wine in the glass. 'This really is remarkable.'

'I'm pleased you like it. Now, my friend, to business. I've gone over what the editor of *The Fatherland* has sent me. Frankly, Herr Vonlathen, I was not impressed. Now what do I do about it? I can't release it as it is.'

'I have also read it, sir, and came to the same conclusions. If you'll allow me, I'll show you what I have done.'

Fifteen minutes later.

'That's excellent, Ulrich. You've changed the emphasis and in many instances the context. . .and it works beautifully. Let us go with this re-write. Will you tell him, or shall I?

'If you send back this document as your corrections, Viereck won't argue. He will readily accept the changes. On the other hand, if I send the revision to him, there will be lengthy discussion, every line in the piece subjected to fierce debate.'

He nodded. 'So be it. By the way, the communications people have some posters for you. They've just arrived from the *Zentralstelle für Auslandsdiens,* our beloved Central Office for Foreign Services. Tell me what you think of them, though I may already know the answer. They're on the table.'

We took our wine to view the posters, which were spread across the expanse of the tabletop.

'Well?'

I studied them carefully before I answered him.

'While British posters rely heavily on artistic flourishes and effective slogans, these are much more matter-of-fact. Frankly, these war posters are nothing more than large, illustrated graphs detailing the resources of Germany compared with other nations. Take this poster for example. It contrasts Germany's combined national income with Great Britain's. It features a smiling, well-fed German citizen holding a much larger wallet than the sour-faced, emaciated Briton. So what? How could this really incite you to fight for a future under German rule. Then take this one. Access to Germany blocked by British ships is the caption. The picture is one depicting mothers and children starving in the streets for lack of food. Showing a well-fed citizen in one, and hungry families in another makes a mockery of all this material. It's expatriate national pride, not food or money, that one needs to tap into.'

All the time I was speaking, von Bernstorff was nodding his head slowly in agreement.

'Well, take them anyway. Show them to Herr Hale as examples of what should not be produced. By the way, have you met our communications team? It might be worthwhile. Get to know them, and when I'm not in residence, you can liaise with them.'

'A good idea, sir.'

The bell pull was tugged with a flourish.

'Gottfried, send up Martha and Wilhelm. Herr Vonlathen wishes to meet them.'

He bowed. 'Your Excellency.'

Moments later the pair were ushered into the room.

'Allow me to introduce you to Martha Drucker and Wilhelm Bergmann. Martha, Wilhelm, this is Ulrich Vonlathen. He looks after our propaganda, along with Bayard Hale.'

We shook hands.

'I understand,' I began, 'that the *Zentralstelle für Auslandsdiens* sends a great deal of material over to the United States. Can you tell me what you do with it? How is it distributed?'

Martha glanced in the ambassador's direction.

'Until recently, Herr Vonlathen, we used to send it to our people, who are committed expatriates in many of the German/American societies. Now we have instructions from His Excellency to show him all that arrives from Berlin. He then decides where it should go.'

'Don't be shy, Martha. I can tell you, Ulrich, a lot of it is now burnt.'

After they had left the room, the ambassador and I chatted for another half hour, before I took a cab to the Willard.

The knock came on the hour at three.

I had not been able to sleep, and rolled off the bed to answer to door.

He came quickly into the room, and we silently shook hands.

'How are you, Ueli, bearing up?'

'Actually, Malcolm, I'm quite enjoying it. The alias seems to come naturally. Leastways, I think so. There have been no suspicious looks, or searching questions.'

'Good. Well, I've got several messages. Here's the first, an envelope smelling vaguely of perfume.' He grinned. 'I wonder who that's from? The second is a wire from your Bureau, from Charles Masterman.'

I unfolded the wire from Charles, which was in simple code.

WELL DONE. I KNEW YOU COULD DO IT.
NOW TO DRIP POISON IN THEIR WORDS. ALL
FUNCTIONING SMOOTHLY HERE. THOUGH
SOME CONCERN ABOUT ALEX BREWER. NO
REPORTS VIA OUR DUTCH CONTACTS.CM

'Good news, bad news?'

'A little worrying. One of our people, the chap responsible for the German desk, went under the wire and we've lost contact. He was on a scouting mission in Berlin. But he is a resourceful chap, I'm sure he'll bob up somewhere. Now can you wait a few minutes while I read the rest of my mail, and write replies?'

CHAPTER SIXTY SIX

The front cover of *The Fatherland* was devoted entirely to Count Johann Heinrich von Bernstorff's image. The magazine had not used a photograph but a drawing of the ambassador giving him a more pugnacious look. But it worked. He stared from the cover, demanding the reader took note of what he said.

I phoned Viereck.

'Good morning, Sylvester. I thought I'd telephone to add my congratualtions on the piece by the ambassador, and the front cover. It certainly is arresting.'

'Talking of arresting, Ueli, I had the police round here yesterday muttering about traitorous material. They can't do anything of course, I'm an American citizen. Supposedly, I can say and write what I like. I wonder how long that will hold true?

'Anway, I'm pleased to tell you the count himself has already spoken to me. It was congratulations all round. I told him his adjustments to the piece made quite an improvement. We were virtually slapping each other on the back.'

I showed William a copy of *The Fatherland*.

'Striking, but a bit immoderate, don't you think? I'm not sure I like such prose taken to excess.'

Each to his own, I thought.

For the next few months I worked on my side of the account, and Hale did what he did best. Fairly dry, penetrating articles that reached out to politicians, academics, and intellectuals. I concentrated on the masses. Those whose voices would be heard by their sheer number.

I went down to Washington regularly to report on progress; to react to any changes of opinion within the delegation; and to learn of any mishaps, ill-judgement, or significant errors in the workings of the embassy. Sometimes, I would be called to see the ambassador. Most of the time I liaised with Martha and Wilhelm. Equally, there were occasions when Heirich Albert and Franz von Rintelen joined the discussion. Albert's supposed role was to monitor expenditure. It was all very amicable, and the measure of how much their guard was down was when both hinted they were involved or were aware of acts of sabotage.

They derided one of their operatives, the naval attaché, Karl Boy-Ed. The son of a Turkish sailor and a well-known German novelist, Boy-Ed was a flashy, suave epicure well known to many among the New York elite. They also made fun of Wolf von Igel, von Papen's successor.

I learned that von Igel worked out of von Papen's former office on the 25th floor of a building at 60 Wall Street, and was busy on yet another terrorist plot.

The information was duly passed to Mackenzie.

American investigators raided the premises two weeks later and discovered several suitcases of documents that revealed the culprits of a number of incidents set to undermine the country's munitions industry.

A month later a name came up at an embassy meeting. Martha was scathing in her remarks about an agent named Werner Horn. It would appear some months earlier Horn had placed the dynamite on the Vanceboro bridge – a major rail crossing between America and Canada.

'Would you believe,' said Martha, 'this fellow set the charge on the Canadian side of the span, then ran back to the American side to evade arrest as a spy in a belligerent nation. What is more, he changed into his German army uniform in order to claim to the neutral Americans he was a soldier not a spy. He is still in hiding in New York, in an apartment on East 85th Street. *Dummkopf!*'

Mackenzie was apprised of Herr Horn's whereabouts in the early hours of the next morning.

It was during one of the visits to the German delegation I learned of Heinrich Albert's visit to New York. Alarm bells rang. Why would he travel to the Big Apple? Had there been too much of a coincidence that after I departed the embassy, acts of sabotage were discovered, operatives taken into custody?

Perhaps Albert was checking me out a little more thoroughly. If he dug too deeply I could be in serious trouble. Could I afford to take that chance?

In the early hours, after letters were exchanged and I had written replies to Clare and Masterman, I explained my possible predicament to Malcolm.

He listened intently, then calmly replied. 'Hmm, as you say, can we afford to take that chance?'

'I may be imagining things, but he has been cool to me in recent times. I must admit I feel vulnerable.'

'OK, leave it to me. I'm friendly with Bill Flynn, the director of the Bureau of Investigation. I'll get him to come up with something, and leave a discreet message at the Judson. After all, it's in everyone's interest.'

The telephone rang.

'Ueli, it's Sylvester. I thought I should just mention, Heinrich Albert took me to lunch today. Guess who was the topic of conversation?'

I could readily guess.

'No, who?'

'You! He mixed the questioning up of course. Referring to other things, idle gossip, you know. But it was obvious he was digging around, trying to find out more about you. So, old buddy, you're under the microscope. Have you done something to upset him?'

'Not to my knowledge.'

'It's probably nothing. But just to let you know he's coming back tomorrow, ostensibly to speak with Aleister Crowley. I hope he doesn't come here too often. It'll give *The Fatherland* a bad name.'

He was still laughing at his own joke when he rang off.

Was I being too sensitive? Was Albert chasing me down? Critically, had he broadcast his suspicions to others? The more I thought about it, perhaps unguarded comments in my presence had resulted too soon in action taken by the police, special agents, and the Bureau of Investigation.

Heinrich was no fool. If a more reasonable interval of time had been allowed to pass, conceiveably there might have been less cause for suspicion. Now I had the strongest feeling I was under Albert's searching gaze, and he was dissecting my background piece by piece in an attempt to discover the real me. If he did, I would lose my hard-won intimacy at the embassy; worse, it could cost me my life.

I had communicated to Clare, in a note passed via Mackenzie, that I was going to book a weekend for us up the coast. We would take a New Haven Line train from Penn Station to Stamford, Connecticut.

Although I roomed at the Judson, I still used the restaurant and bar at the Algonquin. I also made use of the concierge, and stopped at his desk after a pleasant lunch with Alexander Woollcott of The Times.

'Robert, could you do me a favour? I want to make a booking for this coming weekend at the Shippan House Hotel at Shippan Point.'

'Certainly, Mr Kindred. A single or double room?'

He asked the question without a flicker of an eyelid, nor a twitch of the mouth.

Discretion at its highest.

Unconsciously, I leaned forward and said in a low voice. 'A double.'

'No problem, sir. I was thinking, to make the weekend even more memorable, why don't you go by steamboat? There's a special craft called the *Shippan* which sails from Pier Fifteen up the East River. It's a most pleasant journey, so I'm told.'

Excellent, could you book that for me as well, Robert?'

Of course, sir,' he said with a smile.

I came out the hotel on 44th Street and turned left towards the junction with Fifth Avenue. I had almost reached the corner when two people I knew well crossed the intersection. They were in deep conversation. One was William Bayard Hale, the other, Heinrich Albert.

I could only guess the pair had lunched at the Union Club, and Hale was being interrogated by the German intelligence officer. The subject, Ulrich Vonlathen.

I crossed the road, ran along East 43th Street, down Madison Avenue and through the back door of the building housing Hale's office. I wanted to be at my desk when they showed up. But minutes later only William came through the door.

Was it my imagination, was Hale just a little cool towards me? Nothing was said when I showed him a short story I had written for inclusion in *The Popular Magazine*. It was a light, frothy piece dwelling on a detachment of German soldiers consorting with Belgian villagers and handing out food parcels.

'Who's this for?'

'Street and Smith's *Popular Magazine*. I'm also doing something similar for Frank Munsey's *Argosy*. Do you know how well-liked these sorts of magazines are? They sell in their thousands, and are widely bought by all classes. The cover prices are only ten or fifteen cents a copy.'

'Hmm. . .OK. I shan't bother to read it. This sort of thing doesn't appeal to me at all.'

'You should, it's a great medium. *All Stories Weekly* is another I'm going to write something for.'

'Hmm.'

I went to the Judson that night my mind in a whirl.

Perhaps it was paranoia. The trouble was I had no one to whom I could talk. Phoning Clare was out of the question. I did not want her involved, for any harm to come her way. So, I had a miserable meal at a diner the other side of the square, and a sleepless night worrying about possible exposure.

This uncertainty lasted several days, without a word from MacKenzie.

CHAPTER SIXTY SEVEN

'This is wonderful, Daniel! Aren't you clever to think of taking a boat to the hotel.'

I grinned, and mentally thanked Robert, the concierge.

'So how is it all going? How is your friend, the ambassador?'

'Do you know, I've heard all sorts of tales about him. That he is the ruthless mastermind behind any number of bombing incidents, assassinations, and abductions. Yet I like the man. I really can't believe he cold-bloodedly organises such acts of sabotage. But, reports strongly suggest he is responsible.'

'How friendly is he?'

'How do you mean?'

'Come into my parlour said the spider to the fly type of friendship. Is he about to pounce?'

I laughed. 'No I don't think so, except. . .'

'She gave me an anxious glance. 'Except what, Daniel?'

'Well, I have the strongest feeling his chief intelligence officer is doing more than just a routine check on me. He is in New York at the moment, speaking with people who know me. I mean as Ulrich Vonlathen, not as Daniel Kindred. The façade should be foolproof, but you can never tell. If he discovers my true identity the embassy doors would slam shut so fast . .'

'Or you could meet reprisals. Come into my parlour type. Oh, Daniel, you do walk a very thin tightrope. Give it up now. You don't need to do this.'

She held tightly to my arm.

The bright sunshine of a few moments ago had suddenly been hidden by clouds. Just like Clare's usually sunny disposition.

We walked into the breakfast room and were shown to a table overlooking the beach. The dismay of the previous afternoon now replaced with ready smiles.

In the late morning we decided to take a stroll along the beach round Westcott Cove towards the golf club at Halloween Park. Taking lunch there if it were open to non-members.

In the clubhouse we headed for the reception desk. The Sunday newspapers had been delivered, and while I was waiting for someone to appear, I casually glanced at the headlines, then scanned the rest of the cover.

And there it was. A small news item at the foot of the page.

I gasped when I read it, and Clare came scurrying to my side.

215

'What is it? What's wrong?'
'Read that!'
She did so, aloud.

"Around midday yesterday Bureau of Investigation agents arrested a forty five year old man from Berlin, Germany. He is named as Heinrich Albert.

It is alleged that Mr Albert established a cover firm called the Bridgeport Projectile Company to purchase and destroy munitions that would otherwise be destined for the Allied Forces.

He was exposed as a possible spy when he left his briefcase, which contained sensitive documents, on a New York trolley. The case was picked up by one of BOI Director William Flynn's counter-intelligence officers.

The papers are said to have documented Albert's expenditure of $27 million to build a spy network in the United States, and for financing dock strikes, attacks on shipping, and bombing munitions plants.

Mr Albert was under surveillance initially because of his association with George Sylvester Viereck, the editor of The Fatherland, a pro-German publication."

She turned to me, a look of amazement on her face.
'Phew, that's a stroke of luck.'
I did not mention my conversation with Mackenzie. He had clearly come good, though if he had let me know I might have slept a little more easily.

'Martha at the embassy telephoned. I said you'd call her back.'
I had just returned from my lunch break.
'Thanks, William.'
I went into my office and shut the door.
She answered on the first ring. 'Martha Drucker.'
'Martha, it's Ulrich Vonlathen. You called me.'
'Yes, Ueli. The ambassador asked me if you could come to the embassy. There's something he wants to discuss with you. I know you were expected next week, but he said it's quite urgent.'
'Of course, Martha. I'll get an early train tomorrow and be with you about lunchtime.'
'He was rather hoping you could come today, Ueli.'
'Oh.' Suddenly, my stomach started to flutter. 'Well if it is that important I'll get a train within the hour.'
'Thank you, Ueli. Shall I tell him you'll be here around six this evening?'

I found it difficult to think logically. Throughout the four hour train journey my mind was a jumble of disconnected thoughts – with fear of being exposed as a British agent uppermost. I suppose that was what I was. A spy who preyed on unguarded remarks to hammer home another nail in the Germanic coffin.

But I did not really see myself in that role.

Did I not help the teutonic cause? I knew for a certainty the material I wrote had a powerful effect on readers, encouraging them to have a defiant voice, especially among many German/Americans.

On the other hand, I also hindered. For every item of propaganda that was issued, another was written causing Americans to wince, become angry, even antagonistic at Germany's disregard for their feelings.

For example, I re-ignited the outcry by circulating an anonymous fact sheet about the Dernberg speech made the day after the sinking of the *Lusitania*. In the speech, Dr. Bernhard Dernburg, former German Colonial Secretary, and regarded as the Kaiser's official mouthpiece in the United States, justified the firing of the fatal torpedo. According to Dernberg, the liner was "a man of war, carrying contraband and munitions, and therefore, a legitimate target."

What was telling, I also revealed in the circular, William Bayard Hale had written the speech. Biting the hand that fed me?

The raised voices were sufficient prompt for Hale to leave New York for a while. I later discovered that he had made a brief visit to Germany representing The Hearst Newspaper Group.

Another little tidbit, floated on the journalistic breeze, pointed the finger at Franz von Rintelen, naming him as the man behind the Black Tom episode. Moreover, von Rintelen had worked with a chemist, Dr. Scheele, to develop time-delayed incendiary devices known as pencil bombs. These were placed in the holds of American merchant ships, causing fires in the holds, thus encouraging crews to jettison munitions cargoes. They had had considerable success in this form of sabotage, and I named a number of merchant ships that had suffered this fate.

As a consequence, I felt the counter-propaganda offset the advances I made on behalf of the delegation. Perhaps, even chalking up a marginally higher score. Needless to say, the New York Times and the Herald had been in the forefront of pointing wagging fingers.

When the cab pulled up outside the embassy, I drew a deep breath. What sort of reception would I receive? This is it, I thought, make or break.

The main door opened and I was escorted up the winding staircase by Gottfried, the ambassador's ADC. Never given to small talk or idle comment, I was unable to gauge any feelings towards me.

We marched along the corridor to the tall, double doors. He gave a brief knock, and opening one side, stood back to let me pass.

CHAPTER SIXTY EIGHT

'Come in, come in, Ulrich. Thank you for coming so promptly.'

He drew me to a chair beside the ornate hearth.

'Something to drink? A dry sherry perhaps?'

'Please.'

He moved to a cabinet and selected a bottle.

'This is a fino. Is that all right?'

'Yes, thank you, Your Excellency.'

He handed me the glass and took the chair opposite.

'This is slightly awkward,' von Bernstorff began. 'You are probably aware Herr Albert has been detained by the American authorities. He was in New York for a specific reason.'

Now my heart was pounding. I scanned the room preparing for a quick exit.

The ambassador stared at me. 'He was there to check the current attitude of the major American newspapers and journals towards our country. I know Herr Hale and yourself have been doing a good job on both fronts, but you must appreciate I needed a third party assessment of what is actually being achieved. There has been criticism of us in the press lately, and I wanted to determine if we were gaining or losing acceptance of our efforts in Europe.

'As I said, it's no reflection on you, you understand. You do the best you can. Unfortunately, Heinrich bungled the task. Instead of undertaking a discreet mission on my behalf, he has now got himself into serious trouble. I don't believe for a moment he left his briefcase on a tram. That's a fabrication, a set-up by the Bureau of Investigation. But the newspapers are painting an unbelievable tale, that he was involved in sabotage. Ah, you've finished your sherry. Another glass?'

Unknowingly, almost with relief, I had drunk it straight down.

'Please, Ambassador.'

He rose, took my empty glass and went to the cabinet. Over his shoulder he continued the conversation.

'So that leaves me in a bit of a predicament. You see, I was going back to Berlin to submit my six-monthly report on our activities. Now, whereas I can be a little creative in highlighting our achievements, my masters will have been apprised of Albert's so-called misdemeanours. They will have seen the newspaper headlines and be concerned the tide of opinion is, at present, flowing against us.'

He had hardly touched his sherry, but he now raised the glass to his lips.

'So we have to do something of note, something that will hopefully correct the situation. . .and I thought of you.'

He took another sip.

'My idea is that we feature the Foreign Secretary of the German Empire, Herr Zimmermann, in an article like the one you re-wrote for me in *The Fatherland*. But this time in a leading newspaper. What do you think?'

'Good idea. It could do much to redress the balance.'

'That's what I thought.'

He placed his glass on a side table, then rubbed his hands together.

'So, I shall expect you to come with me to Berlin in two weeks time. I'd like you to interview Minister Zimmermann and write the article. Don't worry, we can be there and back in time for Christmas, Ulrich. Unless, of course, you want to spend it with relatives in Schaffhausen.'

CHAPTER SIXTY NINE

'Let him go? After all the trouble I've been to!'

'Not straight away. Say in about three weeks time. I can't think they'll be able to hold him much longer anyway.'

Malcolm was sitting in his usual chair.

'Hmm. . .I'm not certain I'm going to say anything to Bill Flynn. You're probably right, they won't be able to keep him more than a month at the outside. Then Albert will be declared *persona non grata* and shipped back to Germany. I'm just pleased you weren't subjected to intense scrutiny. We could only create a superficial background. It would not have taken too much ferreting around before things started to unravel.'

'Now you tell me. So what happens when I go to Berlin? Will I be exposed then, when I've no way out?'

'Listen, Ueli, if the embassy vouch for you, you'll be OK. . .I should imagine.'

'Should imagine?'

'I'm just pulling your leg, laddie. You'll have no worries.'

Somehow I didn't feel comforted.

That weekend I told Clare of the proposed trip.

We were staying at the Clifton Hotel, on the Canadian side of Niagara Falls. From our room, a half mile away, we could see the river come to an abrupt halt where the water cascaded into the basin below.

We had spent the morning at the Falls, deafened by the thunderous roar, feeling the water and mist on your face as we stood beside the torrent. It was a truly, amazing experience.

Over lunch I told her all that had happened. Albert was not investigating me, he was in New York to determine Germany's standing with the press and public. This was for von Bernstorff's report in Berlin in a few weeks time.

Malcolm MacKenzie had engineered Albert being taken into custody with the BOI. He knew William Flynn the director, and they had picked him up. The problem now was Heinrich's arrest had sparked off a wave of discontent against the Germans To counter the adverse criticism, von Bernstorff wanted to produce a major newspaper feature on the views and aims of Arthur Zimmermann, their Foreign Affairs Minister.

'I suppose that's a possible way out of the mess they've created,' Clare remarked. Then added. 'Or should I say, the mess you seem to have created.'

'The thing is, Clare. . .the thing is, von Bernstorff wants me to write it.'

'That's not a problem, is it?'

'I'm not sure. The ambassador wants me to go to Berlin and interview Zimmermann.'

'What! No way! You're not to go anywhere near Germany! It could all be a trick to get you over there. I might not see you again. Tell them you can't go, Daniel! Tell them you can't go!'

'It's not as easy as that. I've told von Bernstorff, and even told MacKenzie I would.'

She stared at me, furious, deeply upset.

She said in a low voice. ' Don't you see the potential danger you would be in? It would be a foolhardy thing to do.'

She put her hands on her hips. 'Daniel, if you go, don't look for me when, or if, you come back. Now I'm going back to New York, with or without you!'

CHAPTER SEVENTY

I tried constantly to reach Clare. I telephoned the newspaper, the apartment, her parents' home. All without success. Eventually, I wrote a letter declaring my love, but also stating there are occasions when one just has to follow a path wherever it might lead. This was true for her as well. A prime example being her insistence on staying close to the border in New Mexico, regardless of the danger of further raids by Mexican insurgents. I included details of when I would be back in New York, and sincerely hoped she would let me see her.

There was no reply.

Von Bernstorff, accompanied by the taciturn Gottfried, were waiting for me at Pier Forty at the North River Terminal. We were sailing on the *Nieuw Amsterdam,* one of the newer ships of the Holland/America Line.

Our destination was Rotterdam, and from there by train across Holland to Cologne, where we would take another to Berlin.

It was an uneventful crossing, largely perhaps because the owners had painted the ship's name on both sides in huge letters. Hopefully, U-boat captains sailing the Atlantic would learn of its neutrality before closing within range of its torpedoes.

We travelled first-class, which was a new experience. Interestingly, Gottfried, always the ambassador's close companion, never appeared at the dining table. Presumably, he ate either in his cabin or in another restaurant. I never did find out.

Away from the confines of the embassy, von Bernstorff was an affable, almost gregarious. Gone were the pretensions of office. In fact, he remarked upon it one evening when we were at dinner.

I asked him what he might do next, after his stint in Washington.

'Hang around the Foreign Office until I receive a new posting, I suppose.'

'You've no idea where that will be?'

'No idea at all. Though it won't be in some god-forsaken place, some distant outpost in Africa. I've done all that. In the diplomatic service you start on the outside of a ring, and gradually work your way towards the centre. America and Northern Europe is the gold in the bulleye. As long as I don't make a blunder or fall from grace, I should get another top posting. That is if ths damned war goes the way we want. If we lose, I suppose it could be anywhere,' he said wistfully.

I find that wine, not spirits, leads me into asking questions that, sensibly, I should steer clear of.

'Do you enjoy being acknowledged as "Your Excellency"?'

He shrugged.

'I did at first. But then you come to realise it doesn't mean anything. It's the office people are acknowledging, not the incumbent. When, as you say, my stint comes to an end, I revert to plain Johann von Bernstorff. All the pretensions are whisked away.'

'I suppose in your case though, it reverts merely to Count von Bernstorff.'

He smiled. 'Yes, I suppose it does.'

Six days later we docked in Southampton.

It was a brief call of eight hours in the British port. Predictably, German nationals and those associated in the war with Germany were not allowed to disembark.

The following day we arrived in Rotterdam, took a taxi to the station and boarded the train for Cologne. It was an uncomfortable journey, crowded and slow. We stopped for some time at Nijmegen, before eventually crossing the border.

When our passports were checked the guards clicked their heels and bowed when confronting von Bermstorff. Being in his company the formalities for Gottfried and myself were immediately eased.

At Cologne there was another delay.

'I understand, Gottfried,' said the ambassador, 'that since the war started they have dispensed with almost all *Schnellzüge* in Germany. There are no more express trains. Instead there is a new classification, the *Eilzüge*, fast-stopping trains. Whatever that means.'

The train finally got under way. This leg of the journey was more agreeable and certainly more comfortable. I even fell asleep. Five hours later I was awakened by Gottfried shaking my arm.

'Wake up Herr Vonlathen, we have arrived in Berlin.'

A taxi took us to the Hotel Esplanade on the Potsdamer Platz, one of the German capital's most luxurious and celebrated hotels. Its richly ornamented sandstone façade was of the Belle Epoque; and the interior's palatial design redolent of both the Baroque and Rococo eras. It beat the Judson on the south side of Washington Park by a country mile.

At dinner, once again Gottfried was absent. Though, on this occasion, I learned from the ambassador that Berlin was his home town, and he was visiting family.

We sat in opulent surroundings while two waiters met our every need. Perhaps they were over-attentive, for they rarely left us long enough to hold a private conversation.

It was when they hurried away to serve the main course that von Bernstorff leaned forward and said. 'It is all arranged, we shall have a preliminary meeting with the minister first thing in the morning. He will not keep you long, just sufficient for introductions to be made and for you to pass over the list of questions you wish to put to him. He likes to be fully briefed before any interview, you understand.'

I had not prepared a list. I work in an impromptu fashion, switching back and forth with my questions, until the gems roll off the tongue of the interviewee.

'Right,' I replied, digesting the remark. 'I'll have to prepare something. I hadn't realised he worked in that manner. By the way, can I ask you a question?'

He drank from a glass.

'What do you have in mind?'

'Am I paying for my room here, or the Ministry of Foreign Affairs? If I'm paying I'll check out now. I couldn't afford the prices they are likely to charge.'

He laughed loudly, disturbing the chapel-like silence observed by other diners.

'Have no worries on that score. The government has an arrangement at the hotel, and the people here bill the respective ministries direct.'

'In that case I'll have a large breakfast in my room before stepping into the fray. What time is the first meeting?'

'You may have to forego your pampered breakfast. We meet Minister Zimmermann at eight o'clock. I hope you brought a warm coat with you, the forecast is for snow tomorrow morning. The first of the season.'

I managed to eat a roll and drink two cups of coffee before meeting the ambassador and his aide-de-camp in the lobby.

'Good morning, Ulrich. I think we shall walk to The Ministry of Foreign Affairs. It's not very far, no more that a kilometre. The ministry building is on Wilhelmstrasse, next door to the Reich Chancellery.'

It was cold. Fortunately, contrary to the forecast, it had not snowed.

Fifteen minutes later we walked up the main steps of number seventy-six, Wilhelmstrasse, and through double doors, both opened by military-uniformed security guards allowing a dignified entry.

A uniformed officer stepped forward to greet us.

'Good morning, Count von Bernstorff. You and your colleagues are expected.'

'Good morning, Oberstleutnant, you are then aware we are seeing the minister at eight o'clock.'

'He is already waiting for you in his salon, Your Excellency.'

I felt physically sick. My head was pounding, my heart thumping. Any minute now the lieutenant-colonel will recognose me, and the game will be well and truly up. All those months of working to gain access to the embassy in Washington; writing endless articles and pamphlets; cultivating friendships and alliances – all for nothing. In the next thirty seconds I shall be named as a

British propagandist, even as a spy, whose name, real name, is Daniel Kindred – not Ulrich Vonlathen.

'Would you and your people care to sign in, Ambassador?'

The army officer led the the way to a reception desk, and taking up the visitors' book, held out a pen for the ambassador. He placed his signature on the open page, and handed the pen to Gottfried. I looked over his shoulder to see him write, Gottfried Schultz.

The it was my turn.

Below the ADC's name I penned an untidy signature.

The lieutenant-colonel looked at me intently. 'I am afraid. . .'

My heart sank. This is it. . .curtains.

'I am afraid, sir, it is a little indistinct. May I make a note of your name.'

I croaked. 'Vonlathen. . .Ulrich Vonlathen.'

Not the bat of an eyelid.

'Perhaps, lieutenant-colonel, you will escort us to the minister's office?'

'Naturally, Your Excellency. This way if you please.'

As we mounted the wide, marble staircase, von Bernstorff asked.

'Tell me, lieutenant-colonel, what is your name?'

'Brauer, Your Excellency. Oberstleutnant Alex Brauer of the Eighth Army commanded by General Friedrich von Prittwitz.'

'On the Eastern Front, eh? Up against Samsonov's Second Army. I see you acquitted yourself well, from the row of medals. Is that a "wounded in battle" decoration? Is that why you are back in Germany?'

'Yes, Your Excellency. For the moment I have been posted here on light duties. But soon I hope to rejoin my compatriots.'

'Well done, soldier. Well done.'

I could not believe my ears, or what I saw before me.

This was Alex Brewer, who operated the German/Austria desk at Wellington House. When he disappeared, the uncomfortable conclusion was he had been assassinated by the same people who had murdered Bob Brady and Monty Beresford. But here he was. In the heart of the German capital, a lieutenant-colonel in one of their crack regiments.

So he, Brewer, was the spy in our camp. The enemy agent who had been feeding information to his people in London, enabling them to pick us off at will.

Why hadn't he exposed me? Or was he letting me stew? Waiting to be ushered into Zimmermann's office before declaring me the viper in their nest.

CHAPTER SEVENTY ONE

He knocked on the door. When he heard the curt response, "Come!", Brauer turned the handle and stood to one side, allowing us to pass into the minister's office.

Zimmermann came round his desk to greet us.

'Gentlemen, let us make ourselves comfortable.'

He led us to a number of well-padded chairs gathered around a coffee table. He looked over his shoulder.

'Danke, Oberstleutnant, können Sie gehen.'

Brauer bowed and left the room. Not a word had been said.

The ambassador turned to his ADC.

'I don't think I shall need you for the moment, Gottfried.'

'Johann, it is good to see you again,' opened Zimmermann, shaking von Bernstorff's hand. He turned towards me. So you are Herr Vonlathen?'

'Minister, I am pleased to meet you.' I stepped forward and shook his hand.

'Is it too hot in here for you, Herr Vonlathen. I do have the heating up high.'

'No, no, Minister. I'm flushed having just come in from the cold.'

He nodded. 'Well, if you are sure? As the ambassador perhaps explained, he and I will spend the morning in discussion. This afternoon, you and I will meet. You will interview me for an article in one of the American newspapers. I am already aware of the reason, and the need to redress the situation in the United States. So, you have a list of the questions you wish to ask me?'

'I have always found, Minister, that the best interviews, those that lead to informative, well-presented articles, are the result of relaxed conversations. If I gave you a list you would give me neat, political answers. Nothing would show of your character, your passions, your appreciation of what life offers. So, no, not a list as such.'

A frown creased his forehead.

I took from a pocket an envelope and handed it to him.

We were a silent trio as he opened it, took out and unfolded a sheet of paper.

He stared intently at it for a moment, then burst out laughing, before passing it to von Bernstorff. Who read it aloud.

'Interview. Part One - You will ask me any questions you wish.
Part Two – I will ask you questions. You can tell me if they are
not relevant, too intrusive, or can only be answered after several
glasses of schnapps.'

Von Bernstorff smiled and handed it back.

'We shall do exactly as you suggest, Herr Vonlathen, 'declared Zimmermann agreeably. 'In fact, I look forward to our conversation. Shall we say two o'clock?'

'Thank you, Minister.'

I rose from the chair, and with a slight bow to each of them made for the door. Outside the lieutenant-colonel was waiting. With a click of the heels he said. 'I shall escort you to the door, Herr Vonlathen.'

As we walked down the stairs he muttered. 'We must talk, you and I. There is a bar in the Potsdamer Strasse called *The Victoria.* Meet me there at six this evening.'

Promptly at two o'clock Minister Zimmermann came forward to greet me.

No waiting around in draughty, dreary Victorian corridors, as one does in London when calling upon ministers of the crown. In Whitehall, importance of position was often measured by how long visitors were kept waiting.

'Herr Vonlathen, come, sit over here,'

We moved to the more comfortable chairs.

He took my sheet of paper from his pocket.

'We shall follow your script, to see where it leads us. I want to assess how right or otherwise, you are.'

From a carrying bag I took out pen and pad.

'I may know the answers to your questions, but I would like to make a note of what you ask.'

'Good. Now to begin. Where exactly were you born?'

On my guard, I replied. 'In the cantonal hospital in Schaffhausen.'

'And the street where you lived?'

'Otterngutstrasse. Apparently, when I was due my mother walked the two kilometres to the hospital for exercise.'

'And your school?'

'At quite a young age I attended the International School in Schaffhausen.'

He smiled. 'I don't know if the answers are correct or not. When asked, Oberstleutnant Brauer told me. "We always check their *bona fides,* Minister. To establish if they are the person they say they are". I've done that. Let us move on. My first real question to you is this. Is the embassy in Washington doing the job I want it to do?'

'What you are really saying, Minister, is should I have complete faith in their activities? Well, I'll not obfuscate, hide behind weasly words. I'll tell you precisely as I see it. The ambassador, Count von Bernstorff, treads a difficult path. He has the *Zentralstelle für Auslandsdienst* sitting on his shoulder, and while their dictates are suited to the minds of those in the Fatherland, they don't work in other countries, most certainly not in the United States.

'As a consequence, he has asked that we run a dual programme. Carry out the wishes of the Central Office for Foreign Services, but also introduce a campaign to win the hearts and minds of the American public. Not just the committed German expatriates with close ties to this country, but the nation as a whole.

'By and large we are succeeding. However, when Heinrich Albert, and others such as von Rintelen, make gross errors of judgement, it rebounds on our efforts. For every step forward, there are too many occasions when we suffer two steps backwards.

'I accept they should counter the munition shipments to the Entente, but they should also employ sufficient skill to remain undetected.'

Zimmermann nodded, and asked another question.

'How do we evade the British blockade of the Atlantic?'

'An interesting question, Minister. I'm sure you've considered all the ways to broach the British Navy's *cordon sanitaire*. But as I said, I shall endeavour to answer everything you put to me. So here's my response.

'If food supply is a priority at the present time, I would resurrect another company similar to Albert's Bridgeport Projectile Company, but call it something quite innocuous. I would then enter the food market as a charity helping the distressed in Africa. I would charter Danish ships, and when loaded, despatch the vessels to Iceland to pick up supplies of dried fish.

'There are discreet quays in Reykjavik where you could load everything off the Danish ships onto Icelandic ships. The Danish ships would then head south towards Africa. Any suspicions by the Entente would appear to be groundless. Meanwhile, the Icelandic ships, belonging to a neutral country, would cross the Atlantic and dock in Copenhagen. A comparatively short distance from Schleswig-Holstein and Hamburg. A simple decoy technique.'

Zimmermann grinned broadly. 'No, Herr Vonlathen, we haven't considered that one.'

I did not mention that for the past few weeks I had been thinking about any number of aspects that might arise in our discussion. The blockade was just one of them; and I had had a possible solution ready.

'Herr Vonlathen, Admiral von Holtzendorff, who is head of the General Staff of the navy, is proposing to Chancellor von Bethmann Hollweg, that we sanction unrestricted submarine warfare in the Atlantic. His belief is that the ferocity of such a tactic might just keep America out of the war if the results were spectacular and shocking enough. How would you answer that?'

'He would be making a tactical error, Minister. I accept that ships flying the flag of neutral countries are carrying supplies destined for Great Britain. Moreover, the blockade is holding because the German surface fleet is not strong enough to defeat the Royal Navy. But unrestricted submarine warfare would be the utmost folly.

'Firstly, all that we have been doing to portray Germany as a compassionate nation, whose forces have been used primarily to defend its boundaries, and to bring about a more united Europe, would be reversed in an instant. Far from keeping the country neutral, allowing unrestricted warfare at sea, taking out ships of all stripe, the United States would be clamouring to join the Entente.'

Although I was keen to see America come into the war, I could not countenance indiscriminate sinking by U-boats.

He spent some minutes digesting my reply.

'Hmm. . .that is also my opinion. I must do my best to deflect the Admiral and the Chancellor from sanctioning such a step.'

He moved on to the subject of Ireland.

'How much of a diversion from the conflict would it cause the British if we supported the Irish in their demands for Home Rule?'

'I thought you had already done so following the Easter Uprising.'

'We did. In fact, we supplied two shipments. The first was twenty thousand rifles and four million rounds of ammunition. Unfortunately, they went down with the vessel. However, we did send more weapons, mostly captured Russian rifles. I'm thinking of doing something on a much bigger scale. Arming the rebels with all manner of weaponry and ammunition and letting them create havoc. Would that work, do you think? Would it divert attention away from the Western Front?'

How do I answer this one, I thought.

'The Irish to whom you are referring, Minister, are not your ordinary Republicans. The people you would be helping are the dissidents. They get, as Germany does in the United States, highly emotional support from emigrants. But that's largely vocal coupled with ample supplies of cash. There's a lot of noise, a lot of propaganda, but if you analyse it, I'm afraid the support just isn't there.

'What you have to take into account are the numbers. Even if you armed every dissident Republican who would support Germany, there would still not be sufficient to make a serious stand against their old enemy and – this is important –it would be against the general will of the Irish people. The majority of those who are eligible have signed on to fight for Great Britain.'

There were numerous questions such as this.

In effect Herr Zimmermann was using me as a sounding board for his own thoughts.

Suddenly, it was gone five o'clock, and we had not even touched upon Part Two. A knock on the door heralded the arrival of von Bernstorff. He stood in the doorway. I glimpsed Brauer standing at his shoulder

'Arthur, I thought I'd remind you that Pietersen is here.'

'Of course. I am sorry Herr Vonlathen, for the moment we must bring our conversation to a close. I am aware we have not got as far as you would have wished, but do you have enough to create the material you require?'

'Unfortunately, Minister, the second session is more important than the first. Can you fit me into your schedule at any time tomorrow?'

He went to his desk and opened a diary.

'It would appear I have no spare time for the next two days. I could make it Friday at ten o'clock. Would that suit?

'We are returning to the United States on Thursday, Minister,' I murmured.

'You mentioned your relatives in Schaffhausen, Ulrich,' murmured the ambassador. 'Surely, this would be an opportunity to visit them? If I recall, the last time you returned to your home town was three years ago.'

How the devil did he know that? I could only presume Albert had told him when he checked my passport all those months ago.

'I would miss the ship at Rotterdam.'

'Not really a problem. There's a Dutch ship sailing for the States every three or four days. A booking could easily be made on another sailing,' said von Bernstorff urbanely.

'That's settled then,' declared the minister. 'Ten o'clock on Friday morning.'

He was sitting at a banquette in the rear of the bar where the lighting was subdued.

I did not see him at first. In my mind I was searching for a military uniform. On this occasion he was smartly dressed in a grey suit.

'Good evening, Daniel. Do you know, I didn't immediately recognise you today. I had forgotten how you looked without a beard. So you are Ulrich Vonlathen from Schaffhausen? Well, well. Are you going to tell me how you came to walk into the Foreign Affairs building with the German Ambassador to the United States? The last time we spoke was in Wellington House.'

I am not sure what my feelings towards Alex Brewer were. Here was an enemy agent, one who had betrayed the people I worked with to murder squads. Yet, he had not unmasked me to the authorities. If he had I would undoubtedly have been shot as a spy.

'I have not changed sides, if that's what you're thinking,' I said shortly.

'So you are on a mission,' he murmured. 'The same as me.'

'What mission could that be? You are a German, and an officer in the German army. Your mission was over when you left England, *Oberstleutnant Alex Brauer!*'

'Let me correct you. I am *Polkovnik Alexei Pivovar.* In English, Colonel Alex Brewer of the Imperial Russian Army. *Pivovar* is Russian for brewer. Did you think, if I were German, you would have made it past the front door today. I would have denounced you in a flash, my friend.'

'A Russian spy? Well I'm damned. Did you have any connection with German agents in England?'

'Are you seriously suggesting I betrayed our comrades, Brady and Beresford?'

He looked intently into my face.

'You are aren't you? Let me tell you, I was placed in Wellington House just as an observer. Good God! We're allies in this war! All I did was evaluate the work being done so that we could copy it in Moscow. That's all.'

I drank long and deep from my glass of beer.

'What on earth are you doing here, in Berlin? How did you get here?'

'When I left the Bureau, it was easy to slip back across Europe into Russia. There, I was given a new mission. To discover when this radical, Lenin, might be inserted into the country and start stirring up trouble.

'The place to begin was the Foreign Affairs Ministry in Berlin. To learn what I could and discover Lenin's whereabouts. Crossing into enemy lines was straightforward, as was the disguise. We have the most excellent forgers in Moscow.

'I learned that, at the moment, Lenin is being held by the Germans somewhere in the Swiss canton of Zurich. The trouble is we don't exactly know where. They intend to insert him into Russia, where he can do untold damage. My task, on behalf of the Imperial Army and the Tsar, our commander-in-chief, is to learn what they're up to. Hopefully, to snuff out the threat.

'If he gets a toehold in my country there will be anarchy and revolution, which is what Germany is seeking. Then, we would no longer be a fighting force. The Eastern Front would simply collapse.'

I was silent, looking into my glass. From what I had gathered Alex's country was about to implode; and Russsia in turmoil would reduce the Triple Entente to two - Great Britain and France. Getting the United States involved in the conflict was suddenly even more vital.

'So tell me,' said Brewer casually, drinking from his glass. 'What are your plans for the next couple of days? Visiting your so-called relatives in Schaffhausen? I was listening at the door when Zimmermann arranged your meeting for Friday.'

'It's a bloody nuisance. Now I shall have to go through the pretense of taking a train ride south to Zurich then on to Schaffhausen.'

'I see. In that case you may be able to help me.'

CHAPTER SEVENTY TWO

'It would seem the Foreign Secretary of The Imperial German Empire was much impressed yesterday,' remarked von Bernstorff over the breakfast table.

'I wonder what gave him cause to say that?'

'Come on, Daniel. I'm told you gave him straight, no-nonsense answers even to some difficult questions. He was particularly impressed by your grasp of the politics and military ramifications of this damnable war. He also said you proffered some worthwhile advice.'

I shrugged, and tried to change the subject.

'More observations, sir. So what time are you off?'

'At eleven o'clock we make our way to the railway station. I understand that on Friday it's your turn to put questions to him. Is that right?'

Yes, it's my turn.'

'A word of caution, Ulrich. Be very careful.'

In fact, I was at the *hautbahnhof* long before the ambassador and Gottfried, his ADC. I was going in the opposite direction on a ten hour train journey to Zurich.

The compartment was occupied by two other men. Both elderly: both with the appearance of having drunk themselves to a standstill. Not that they were boisterous. Neither said a word. They fell asleep to a chorus of snoring, grunting and belching. After three hours, as if an unknown hand had shaken each by the shoulder, they awoke as we pulled into Weimar. With curt nods, they sidled into the corridor, slid the door shut, and descended the train.

It was quiet thereafter, allowing me to wonder why I had agreed to make this twenty hour round trip in an attempt to discover the whereabouts of the secretive Mr Lenin.

'Brewer, Brauer, or Pivovar, was persuasive. Not that I would have made the trip on honeyed words alone. The reason I finally agreed to sit for an eternity on a train was because the Entente did not want revolution if it led to a weakening of the Eastern Front. If that happened, Germany would send thousands of their troops to the Western Front, which was already under considerable strain.

How I was possibly going to locate the insurgent in just twenty four hours was a mind-numbing puzzle. I forced myself to think in his shoes. A radical living somewhere in a canton of Zurich which covered two thousand square kilometres was the proverbial needle in the haystack. It was unlikely he was living in a remote village, so I thought about the towns. There were three or four including Zurich where he might be in hiding.

I went back and forth over his background. A bourgeosie revolutionary who considered his pen and his voice as tools to ignite the masses. He was always writing manifestos, pamphlets and treatises. Perhaps he would need access to reference books. In particular to libraries. They would be my starting point, and I would first check those in Zurich, the canton's capital.

It was eight o'clock in the evening when the train finally pulled into Zurich's main station. I felt unbelievably weary. It was all I could do to keep my eyes open.

I spoke with a taxidriver who took me to the Rössli Hotel, which was an old townhouse on the Rössligasse, close to the banks of the Limmat. It was a small, charming residence not far from the town centre. Ideal too, for the university, which was situated in Rämistrasse, no more than three hundred metres away.

After breakfast the next morning I walked out the hotel into a blizzard. Mounds of snow already lined the pavement edge, and I was suddenly worried my train back to Berlin might be delayed. Trudging through the swirling gusts that blew ice particles into my face, I turned into Rämistrasse and counted down the numbers. However, it was not difficult to find. Number seventy one turned out to be one of several large, brownstone buildings housing, I was proudly informed, the cream of Swiss academia.

I was further informed the university library was not to be found there. It was located on Strickhofstrasse, about four kilometres north, at the very end of Rämistrasse.

I turned up the collar of my coat and jammed a hat on my head before braving the blizzard. As luck would have it, a taxi was dropping a passenger right outside. I ran down the steps and jumped in the open door before the previous occupant had even paid his fare.

'Strickhofstrasse thirty–five, please.'

Perhaps it was a premonition, or simply the thought of being stranded and having to walk back.

'Driver, will you wait for me for two or three minutes?'

'The meter will keep on running. It's up to you how long you take.'

It did not even take one minute. The library was not only closed, its services were not available to non-students.

'Damn! Tell me driver, is there a main library open to the public?'

'Of course, the biggest and best in Switzerland. It's on Zähringerplatz.'

When we pulled up outside the library, very similar in style to the university building, I realised that I had done a complete circle of Zurich. The Rössli Hotel was only four hundred metres down the road.

The city's skyline was dominated by the spire of the church next to the library. I found out it is called the *Predigerkirche*, the Preacher's Church, and the library occupied the site of what was once the monks' cloisters.

I paid the taxi driver and mounted the steps. If Lenin were not a regular visitor to the central library, that was it. The weather was closing in, there would be little chance of going on to Baden or Winterthur, and traipsing around Zurich would be a lost cause.

In the library I made my way to the reception desk.

'Good morning, I'm looking for a friend of mine who has moved to Zurich. I was told he comes frequently to the library, and I wondered if he were here this morning?'

Beneath a greying head of hair tied in a bun, and heavy-framed, glasses, the woman had a kindly smile.

'We have many visitors to the library, mein herr. However, if your friend uses the reference section, his name would be listed in our registered users' file. What is he called?'

'Lenin. . .Vladimir Lenin.'

'He is a Russian gentleman, is he?'

'Yes, sorry, I should have mentioned. . .'

She rose from her seat and went to a filing cabinet, where she spent some moments studying a file.

She dropped it back into the drawer, closed it with a practised hip, and turned towards me.'I'm sorry. We don't appear to have anyone by that name using our services.'

That was it then. A boring, uncomfortable ride back to Berlin – with nothing achieved.

'Well, thank you for checking. It was most kind of you.'

I had gone several paces in the direction of the exit, when she said. 'We do have one Russian gentleman upstairs in the reference section. But his name is Ulyanov.'

I halted in my tracks and smiled back at the librarian.

'No, that's not the man I'm looking for.'

But it was.

I went into a coffee shop across the Zähringerplatz, and took a table by the window. Being wintertime, the trees were bare and this afforded me a clear view of the library entrance. It was my man alright. Ulyanov was his family name. He had changed it to Lenin some years ago when on the run from the Russian secret police.

After two hours and four cups of coffee, suspicious glances prompted me to leave. I strolled up and down, sheltered in doorways, and stood hunched on the leeward side of the trees until chilled to the bone. There was nothing for it. I would have to go into the library and seek him out.

As I neared the steps, Vladimir Ilyich Lenin pushed through the door, adjusted his fur hat, put on gloves and made his way along the platz. Ten steps behind him came two men, whose mien identified them immediately as bodyguards.

234

However, their role as guardians was merely token. I could only think that waiting interminably for their mark had dulled awareness of their surroundings. They were oblivious to the fact I was quite openly trailing them some twenty metres back.

We walked southwards through the old town. When the trio in front of me turned into an uninviting, narrow street, a front door opened and a woman appeared. She kissed Lenin's cheek, drew him into an unprepossessing little house, and firmly closed the door. Without so much as a backward glance, the guards walked on to an adjacent dwelling and went inside.

I had all the information I required. The woman was Lenin's wife, Nadia Krupskaya; and they were living at number fourteen, Spiegelgasse, close to a sausage factory.

I passed him a note as we mounted the stairs, and it disappeared quickly into a pocket. Lieutenant-Colonel Brauer nodded his gratitude as he opened the door.

'Herr Vonlathen, Minister.'

Zimmermann was already seated in one of the comfortable chairs by the fire, which was burning well in the ornamented grate.

'Would you care for some coffee?'

'Please.'

'Could you tell my secretary for me, Brauer?'

'Of course, Minister.'

I sat down in a chair opposite the minister and once more took a pen and pad from my bag.

'Where do you want to start, Herr Vonlathen?'

'What I want to discover, Minister, is the catalyst, the prompt, that got you into politics. I don't mean something like it was my destiny, or I wanted to help the unfortunate enjoy a better life. I want to know when you made the decision to become a career politician. So, that's my first question.'

'You're right, I could give a trite answer. But the rules of this engagement are set, so I'll tell you. I graduated in law, and worked as a junior in a law firm in Leipzig while I studied for my doctorate. After which I moved to Berlin. I wanted to be at the centre of things, where it was all happening. A friend told me he was seeking a position in the diplomatic service, and as jobs were scarce, I too applied. I got taken on in the consular section.

'I had several posts in the far-East, before being called to the Foreign Office, where I've been ever since. You could say luck paid a huge part in my career, and frankly, I did not see it as providing a service to others, but in creating an opportunity to earn a very good salary. I am afraid there was no hint of altruism at all in my choice of employment.'

'How refreshing, sir, to come upon reality in an answer.'

'Having said that, Herr Vonlathen, I should point out that the position of Foreign Affairs Minister carries any number of responsibilities, and you need compassion and understanding to do the job effectively. With due modesty, I think I ably carry out my duties in the correct way.'

'I was going to say, Minister, that the many attributes you have suit well the demands of the role. That's how I shall write it.'

A nod of the head indicated he was satisfied with my interpretation of his openess. We moved on through his life and how it had shaped the man. How events such as being the third member of the decision-making group alongside Kaiser Wilhelm II and Chancellor Theobald von Bethmann Hollweg, to support Austria-Hungary into what sparked off the beginning of the conflict. My questions touched upon his opinion of the execution of Edith Cavell, his declared support for Roger Casement, and the military incursions into various parts of Africa. In this instance I was thinking of the Portugese and their eventful declaration of war due largely to Germany attempting to wrest territories from them by force.

In every respect he was prepared to reveal his innermost thoughts. Although the enemy, I warmed to the man. He sat there, at times examining his own point-of-view almost for the first time. When his replies suggested some degree of personal exposure, he would twirl his luxuriant moustache. There were occasions when he was every inch the voice of government, and at others, the uncertain penitent of faulty decisions.

I moved on to the Eastern Front. But in a circuitous way.

'If Vladimir Ilyich Lenin were to return to Russia, disorder and insurrection might follow. There's little doubt the Tsarist regime would topple. In fact, the country would be rent asunder. If that were to happen, the German army could probably march through the country to Vladivostock without a shot being fired.

'If that comes about, would you use the forces currently fighting on the Eastern Front to secure German possessions seized by the Japanese in the Pacific and East Asia?'

'I doubt that we could, Herr Vonlathen, for two reasons. The Japanese Navy is their most potent force. You must remember, it is the third largest in the world after the British and American Navies. As a consequence, it is a law unto itself. In the far-east the Imperial Navy, not the government, decides how best to deploy its ships, which territories to annex.

'The German Navy is not nearly as large. Moreover, the majority of its ships are deployed in the Atlantic and inshore waters of Europe. Regrettably, we'll just have to suffer our territorial losses in the distant east. Even if we had the manpower, we would not have the means to transport them. I'll let you into a secret. We have even tried to negotiate with the Japanese, but talks have always broken down.'

'Another question, Minister. What would be your reaction if America chose to join the Entente? Too many blatant errors of judgement continue to be made by those carrying out subversive tactics in the United States.'

'I am aware of that Herr Vonlathen,' replied the minister shortly.

'Frankly, I walk a tightrope. We need to keep America neutral, out of the conflict. Yet, we cannot afford to let munitions from that country reach the Entente forces in Europe. If the withdrawal of Russia from the war came about, then the extra troops you referred to would be used to strengthen our position on the Western Front. If it came to it, I am confident we could then withstand America's presence in the war. But I am hopeful they will stay neutral, and with a greater concentration of troops in Belgium and France our victory would be assured.'

'Seemingly, Minister, this is all predicated on a political coup in Russia. How will you ensure that this takes place?

'I am not at liberty to discuss that, Herr Vonlathen.'

'I understand , Minister.'

Only too well, I thought.

'So, it would appear, Minister, that timing is all. There is unrest in Russia, and growing by the day. But before the catalyst to revolution can be unleashed, it has to reach a certain temperature. When it does, given the right ingredients, the Russian hierarchy, government, and the army will crumble, falling like a pack of cards. The Eastern Front would simply dissolve, opposition melting away. But that has to happen before America were to become involved. Otherwise the balance of power could so easily swing the other way.'

'You put it most succinctly, Herr Vonlathen.'

Suddenly, I knew what my next words would be. I conceived a damascene moment of the utmost clarity.

'You mentioned the Irish uprising earlier, Minister, and your idea that by providing them with firearms, the British would react if hostilities broke out on their own doorstep. A domestic issue, which involved a lot of blood being spilt, would be more of a priority than waging war in a foreign land.'

Yes, but it didn't happen, unfortunately.'

'Well, supposing you could bring about a similar event in America. They might be so pre-occupied with their own internal problems, joining the battle in Europe would be furthest from their minds. That way they would retain their neutrality.'

He stared at me with a look implying he was sitting next to someone suffering a brain seizure.

'Are you suggesting we provoke another civil war between the US states?' he muttered in an uncertain voice.

'Let me explain myself. Earlier this year I happened to be in New Mexico. I was witness to a raid by Mexicans on the border town of Columbus. A group of insurgents, led by a man called Pancho Villa, literally destroyed the town, and killed twenty American citizens.'

'Yes, I know, Herr Vonlathen. At one stage we provided Villa with armaments. The reason for this and other cross-border raids was largely due to America withdrawing supplies of weaponry and financial support.'

It was my turn to be surprised.

'But, Minister, do you know how President Woodrow Wilson reacted?'

He shook his head.

'He sent five thousand troops under the command of General Pershing. He and his force are still roaming Mexico searching for Villa.'

'A little over the top, I would suggest. But what is your point, Herr Vonlathen?'

'Just imagine, Minister, how the United States would react if Mexico made an armed, concerted effort to reclaim all the lands lost in the war seventy years ago. That war was disastrous for Mexico. In addition to the loss of Texas, it was forced to sign away nearly half its national territory. California, New Mexico, Nevada, Utah and parts of several other US states.'

Herr Zimmermann was now listening to me intently.

'What are you saying, Herr Vonlathen?' he said in a low voice.

'Just consider, sir, what a heavily-financed, well-equipped military offensive would achieve. The Mexican President, Venustiano Carranza, is having a torrid time, as do most of their presidents. This would be grasped by him as a means of diverting the hearts and minds of the Mexican people into a common cause.

'Thousands of American soldiers would be despatched to the south-western states. The result, major warfare on American soil, and all thoughts of allegiance to the Triple Entente would disappear.'

The Foreign Secretary of The Imperial German Empire was like a rabbit caught in the headlamps. Arthur Zimmermann was lost to the world as his mind engaged the possibility of check-mating America's involvement in the conflict. Finally, he snapped out of his reverie.

'A most interesting notion, Herr Vonlathen. Most interesting. I would have to discuss the matter with my colleagues. Logistics of such an enterprise, costs, and so on. Then we would need to discover the attitude towards such a proposal with Carranza. Still, that's my concern, not yours. Do you have any more questions for me?'

CHAPTER SEVENTY THREE

I saw Arthur Zimmermann one more time before I departed.

I was collected from the hotel by Brauer who said little, presumably in case the car driver overheard.

As we walked up the stairs he muttered. 'I thank you for the information, Daniel. Give my best wishes to Charles Masterman when you see him.'

I was ushered into the minister's room.

'Herr Vonlathen, I wanted to thank you personally for the various discussions we had. They were most enlightening. Can I now presume you have enough material for a newspaper article?'

'Unquestionnably, Minister. I shall also send you a copy of the suggested text before itgoes to the newspaper.'

'Excellent. Now, I have something I would like to present to you.'

He nodded to his aide-de-camp, who was standing next to Lieutenant-Colonel Brauer. The fellow stepped forward and handed the foreign secretary a box.

'This is presented with our gratitude and best wishes.'

As he handed it to me he opened the lid so I could see its contents.

It was a medal commemorating the sinking of the *Lusitania.*

At Rotterdam I boarded the steamship, *Rotterdam IV.* Another relatively new ship of the Holland/America Line.

On this occasion its first port of call was Southampton, where we stopped to take on passengers and refuel the coal bunkers. I used my British passport to get off the ship, and made my way into the centre of the city to find an hotel. I shut the folding door of a telephone booth, and phoned Charles Masterman. The call was brief.

'Well, well, Mr Daniel Kindred. Where are you?'

'In Southampton until six o'clock. Then I sail for the States. Look Charles, I've a lot to report, can you come down? If you can, let's met in the station bar at two thirty.'

It was another uneventful crossing, presumably thanks again to the name of the liner painted large of both sides. It gave me plenty of time to go over what I had relayed to Masterman. On reflection, it was all a bit tenuous. Now, in the cold light of an Atlantic day, I could not possibly see how it might work out.

Six day later we docked at Pier Forty and I took a taxi to the Judson. It waited while I collected my things, then drove me to the Algonquin.

Throughout the voyage I had been thinking of Clare. How she would react if I phoned her. I decided to go to the New York Herald and meet her when she left the building. That way she wouldn't be able to slam down the telephone, cut me off before I told her how much I loved her.

I was there early and waited outside in the cold. At least it was not as bitter, nor snowing, unlike my earlier experience outside Zurich's National Library.

When the Herald's offices emptied there was no sign of her.

As the last of the newspaper's staff walked out the door I stopped a fellow I recognised. He was one of the copy-editors.

'Is Clare Johnson working late?' I asked.

He seemed to recall vaguely that he had seen me before.

'She hasn't been in this past week. I believe she's unwell. The last I heard Clare was being nursed at her parents' home.'

I ran as fast as I could to Penn Station.

Frustratingly, I had to wait thirty minutes for a train.

As the train journeyed north I was urging it on whenever it stopped at a station. It took an interminable length of time to reach Scarsdale.

I dashed out into the forecourt and grabbed a taxi.

When it pulled up outside the Johnson's house, I ran up the drive and hammered on the door.

Lights came on, I could see a form approaching through the opaque glass. Several chains were loosened, and Lyons, the Johnsons' man, peered round the door. He said nothing, just continued staring at me.

'Who is it, Lyons?' came Mr Johnson's voice. Suddenly the door was wrenched open and Clare's father appeared on the doorstep.

'Good God! We thought you were dead!'

'Who is it, dear?' called Mrs Johnson.

I pushed past them into the hallway as Clare's mother walked through from the sitting room. She paled and slumped onto a convenient chair.

'We thought you were dead,' she said in a whisper.

'Where's Clare? Is she all right? I was told she was ill. I must see her.'

'She's upstairs in her room. Please don't just appear,' pleaded her mother. 'She is still in shock. Let me break the news.'

I was perplexed. Why did everyone think I was dead. As we climbed the stairs Mrs Johnson explained. 'I know you've been abroad, Clare told us. But when she went to meet the ship on which you were supposed to return, and you weren't on board, she feared the worst.'

She knocked on the door, glanced at me, then slipped into the room.

I waited anxiously outside, wondering what was being said. I heard a muffled cry, and the patter of running feet. Suddenly the door burst open and Clare flew at me, not in joy but in rage. She was pounding my chest, crying, and unheard of in this genteel household, swearing at me like a New York cab driver.

The blows were landed in rhythm to the colourful language. I did not feel their pain, but perhaps to quieten the blasphemy coming roundly from her lips, I kissed them, then drew her to me in a tight embrace.

'My God, Clare, I've never heard such profanities. I suppose it's mixing with all those newspaper people.'

I looked over Clare's shoulder at her mother's shocked features.

'Is everything all right?' called Mr Johnson.

'It will be in a minute when Clare puts on some decent clothes. Come downstairs, Daniel, while she dresses herself.'

Clare pulled away. Staring into my eyes, she leaned forward and kissed me. Then delivered a mighty slap to my cheek.

'Don't ever do that to me again!' she shouted, and flounced back into her bedroom slamming the door.

Seconds later it opened and once more she rushed into my arms.

The red weals were still on vivid display when she came into the room.

'Oh, Daniel, I'm sorry. Not for doing it, but leaving the evidence.'

She sat next to me on a couch and took my hand.

'What happened, Daniel, did you miss your sailing?' asked her father.

I felt my hand squeezed.

'Yes, one of those things. I had to go back to England, and missed my return reservation.'

Well, half a lie, we had called in at the British port.

'Couldn't you have let Clare know you'd missed the boat, Daniel? asked her mother. 'She thought all kinds of dreadful things had happened.'

I glanced at her daughter. 'Yes, I should have done. I'm so sorry.'

Later, when we were walking in the garden, I told her the reason for my delayed return. In fact, I recounted the whole story, from the moment I embarked to my meeting with Charles Masterman at Southampton railway station.

'Good Lord, Daniel, that must have been an awful moment. To come face to face with someone you'd worked with in the Bureau in London, and he was about to shop you.'

'My first thought was Alex Brewer was a German spy, and had passed on information to others of his kind hiding in the shadows. But he wasn't. He was a Russian spy, working for one of our allies.'

'Do you think this minister, Zimmermann, will do something about helping Mexico reclaim its original territories?'

'I honestly don't know. He had a gleam in his eye, but it may be my wishful thinking. I asked Masterman to keep a watchful eye on any communications sent by Berlin to Mexico City, but that's all I could do. We'll just have to wait and see. I also suggested he set up a surveillance team to monitor Lenin's whereabouts, so we know when he's on the move. By the way, do you think the Herald would be interested in running this piece I'm doing on Zimmerman?'

'I honestly couldn't say. Is there any hurry? At the moment there's not a great deal of sympathy for your German friends. Why don't you wait until things improve?'

'You're probably right. Anyway, I haven't even written it yet. Then it goes to Zimmermann for approval. If, of course, the newspaper chooses to amend, alter, or adjust what's written, that's their prerogative. I'll mention that in the explanantory letter sent with the article.'

I grinned at her. 'And it will change quite markedly. As you know, my original aim was to ensnare the ambassador. For him to state Germany's intentions, ignoring this country's sensibilities. The piece in *The Fatherland* was to pave the way, to lull him into sharing confidences. Now we have bigger fish to fry. I shall have the Minister for Foreign Affairs making injudicious remarks that will most certainly anger the American public. The article just might tip the balance. Especially, if it were rumoured that Germany supported Mexico in reclaiming their lost lands.'

There was a brief silence.

'Oh, I almost forgot. Can we go back to the house, I want to show you something.'

I went upstairs and retrieved my carrying bag

'Let me show you the present Arthur Zimmermann, the Foreign Minister, gave me.'

I opened the lid of a box. Removing the medal she studied it intently.

'My God! How utterly tasteless! Fancy striking this to commemorate a disaster.'

Clare turned it over. 'There's something wrong, surely? They've given the wrong date. The *Lusitania* was sunk on 7th May. Not 5th May as inscribed here!'

I removed another more delicate box from the bag, and pressed it into her hand.

'A small gift for you.'

Clare opened it: a diamond necklace lay on a silk lining.

'Oh, Daniel, it's beautiful. Help me put it on.'

She held it to her neck while I fixed the clasp. Then she went across the room to a large, ornate mirror, and stood there admiring the necklace from various angles.

'It's absolutely beautiful. Daniel, thank you.'

Clare came swiftly to my side and kissed me. At first in pleasure for the gift, then more amorously, then more ardently. We stayed locked in each others' arms, until she said.

'I was going to say I couldn't possibly accept such an extravagant gift. But now I believe I can.'

'So what prompted the change of heart?'

Clare stepped back and holding my hands, murmured.

'You asked me once if I would marry you. At the time I said no, my career came first. But when I went to meet you from the ship, and you weren't on it, I imagined the worst. I realised then all that I had lost,' she gave a weak smile. 'Or thought I had lost. So this time I am not waiting for you to ask again. You might not. So. . .I am proposing to you. Daniel Kindred. Will you marry me, please?'

Tears came to my eyes. For a moment I could not speak. Then in a voice I could hardly recognise, croaked. 'Yes! Yes! Yes!'

Her parents came hesitantly into the room.

'Is everything all right? I heard shouting,' said her father anxiously.

Clare grinned at her mother.

'So you did ask him, Clare,' said her mother urbanely.'Was that a yes I heard him holler?'

We were sitting companionably in front of a warm fire drinking champagne. Her mother had thoughtfully instructed Lyons to put some on ice.

'I'm not sure I can get used to a woman proposing to a man,' muttered Clare's father. 'It doesn't seem right, somehow.'

'I should have asked your permission first, sir,' I remarked. 'But the initiative was taken from me.'

'Never mind the niceties,' declared my mother-in-law to be. 'It's about time you two got together. You are lost without each other.'

CHAPTER SEVENTY FOUR

'You're back then. How did it go?'

William Bayard Hale, surprisingly, seemed pleased to see me. He even took me to lunch. There was an all too-obvious ulterior motive; and it was when we were on the main course the questioning began.

I gave him an edited account of what transpired. In a number of instances, marginally adjusting the course of events to suit my own imterests.

'So you had two sessions with the Foreign Minister. Is he happy with the work we're doing for them?'

'Hard to tell, William. I think he would have been if the likes of all those bungling saboteurs didn't undermine what we are trying to achieve. I know Zimmermann attacked von Bernstorff about the incompetence his people are showing at the moment. That probably was the cause of the ambassador's irritation with us.'

'What do you mean irritation? Surely, we are fulfilling the brief he gave us. What about that piece in *The Fatherland*? You can't get much better propaganda for the cause than that.'

'That's what I said. He replied, "Those readers are already committed to our ideals. They are Germans first and Americans second. I want all Americans to acknowledge what we are doing. That must be your goal."

'This was in front of Zimmermann. He went on. `This article you are producing for the minister. I want it in the top, national newspaper in the United States. And if you can't do it, Herr Hale must. Otherwise I shall move the account.`

The fork was held aloft, suspended in mid-air, as Hale considered the supposed ultimatum.

'My God! What shall we do, Daniel? I can't afford to lose their business. I've just signed a lease for offices on Broadway.'

'I'm sure one of us will be able to place the article, William. Don't worry, we've got a month or more to come up with a newspaper who'll run with it. In the meantime, I'll write the piece and send it to Zimmermann for approval.'

It took me longer than I expected. But, at last it was finished, and I showed it to William.

'Hmm. . .the minister comes over quite well. I like the way you initially created the suggestion of a series of negative attitudes, then cancelled each one out by Zimmermann giving a measured explanation. It adds to his standing, and to Germany's aims for a "combined Europe". Is that a euphemism for expansion of the *Reich?*'

'Probably,' I smiled. 'If you are happy I'll take it to Washington on my next visit. The ambassador can forward it in the diplomatic bag.'

'Ulrich my friend, come, sit by the fire. These rooms are so damnably cold. The sooner we find somewhere else the better. Hopefully, a building with central heating. So, I understand your discussion with the minister went well. What did you do beforehand? Did you get to see your relatives?'

'I went to Zurich and visited members of the family living there. I also had the chance to do some Christmas shopping. Do you know, Your Excellency, I was convinced I saw that Russian. . .what's his name? Yes, Vladimir Lenin when I was walking through the Zähringerplatz. I can't think it was him. But this chap was the spitting image.'

Von Bernstorff changed the subject.

'So, now you have written the article. Good, very good. May I read it before it goes to Berlin?'

'Of course, Your Excellency.'

For the next twenty minutes I sat enjoying the warmth of the fire whle he read the typescript.

He removed his glasses, and tapped his knee with them.

'I think it is extremely well-written, as I have come to expect of you. However, I am not sure that drawing emphasis to some subjects is the right approach. Even though the minister answers all the points extremely well.'

'I understand the comment. But how would one lead into a topic if the circumstances were not voiced. Don't forget, Ambassador, Germany is on the back foot here. There is a lot of negative opinion in the press about your country's questionable activities, not just in Europe, but here, in the United States as well. An anodyne piece offered to the press would simply be thrown in the wastepaper basket. It also has to contain elements of controversy to ignite readers' interest and to ensure there's less chance of it being heavily sub-edited.'

'Hmm. . .I suppose you're right. OK, It will go in this week's bag. I'll write the covering note and explain that meeting the contentious issues head on will limit sub-editing. Thank you, Ulrich. Can I tell him which newspaper the article will appear in?'

'It has yet to be confirmed, Your Excellency, but at the moment the New York Herald is showing keen interest. It will be presented in the form of an interview conducted by the newspaper's special correspondent.'

He nodded, then said.

'Right. Well, we'd better call in Martha and Wilhelm. Clear up any outstanding matters.'

He came at the usual time of three in the morning.

'We are moving towards the endgame, Malcolm. The article is on its way to Germany, and I have a meeting with the editor of the New York Herald in a few days time. I now know his views, he supports the Entente in the conflict.'

'Courtesy of the delightful Miss Johnson, no doubt.'

I nodded.

'It's a delicate manoeuvre, but I think I'll be able to swing it. If all goes according to plan, taking the Christmas break into account, the best day for the Zimmermann article to be published would be Saturday, 20th January, when people take their time reading a paper. Hopefully, 1917 will be a better year than this one.'

'That's the amended version, isn't it?'

'That's right. But they won't know that until the newspaper arrives on the embassy doormat.'

'Have you got a copy for me?'

'Yes, and that of the article being sent to Berlin.'

He glanced at the text destined for the Herald.

'Ouch! Did the Foreign Minister say that?'

'Well, not in so many words. But the sub-editor was tight on space, and something had to give.'

'It's certainly a devious plan. I didn't think you'd ever pull it off. But it looks like it just might work, Ueli. . .or should I now start calling you Daniel?'

'Not for the moment. Give it another couple of months. I wonder if Zimmermann ever swallowed the bait of supporting Mexico in a border war. Now that would have put *"Die Katze im Taubenschlag"*.

'Meaning?'

'The cat amidst the dovecote, same meaning in any language.'

'Actually, Masterman sent me a wire,' Mackenzie said. 'I forgot to mention it. He informed the codebreakers in Room 40 at the Admiralty to to intercept any cable messages coming from Germany. That was a couple of weeks ago. He feels it's unlikely anything intended for the Mexicans will now come through.'

I was disappointed. When the idea came to me, and I had mentioned it to Zimmermann, his reaction had almost convinced me he would act upon the proposal.

With the German embassy winding down several weeks before Christmas, in a rare moment of benevolence, Hale suggested I also leave early. There was a proviso. "Be back no later than January 4th, and ready to work harder in 1917."

That evening I asked Clare if she would like to come to England with me and spend Christmas with my parents.

'As far as William is concerned I'm going to celebrate in the Florida sunshine, so I won't be in contact if anything comes up.'

'There's a problem, Daniel, you won't have a tan. I'll have to use some of my make-up on you. But, yes, that would be wonderful. Will your brother and sister be there? I'm dying to meet them all.'

By the sheerest good fortune I managed to obtain a cancellation on the ship, *Nieuw Amsterdam*. I'd sailed on her before, though, this time we would be disembarking at Southampton.

There were three changes of trains before the engine laboured into Worthing Station, and vented steam as though on the point of expiry. I saw my father waving as we walked the length of the platform, a porter wheeling a trolley with our luggage followed us through the ticket barrier.

I have rarely seen such a show of affection, hugs and a handshake for me, kisses for Clare. As we drove along the seafront my father chatted away almost without pausing for breath.

As we pulled into the drive, the front door opened and my mother, my siblings and their partners and children poured out to meet Clare and I. She was suddenly engulfed by chattering women, all talking at once.

I glanced at my father, who shrugged and said as he removed the cases.

'I have never understood how they can hold so many different conversations at the same time, yet take in what each is saying, and give multiple answers. It's as much as I can do to comprehend one.'

'Don't try to reason it out, Daniel,' grinned my brother. 'It's one of the secrets of the universe.'

Slowly we made our way into the house, across the hall and into the drawing room.

It was an hour later, when we were drinking tea that my father asked. 'So, what have you been doing in America all this time, Daniel?'

I looked at Clare, who smiled. 'He has been in Germany for a while advising their Foreign Minister.'

My father roared with laughter. 'She has a ready wit, your Clare, Daniel.'

'Actually, I've been writing press material for a small company run by a fellow called William Bayard Hale in New York, dad. Not very enthralling. Far more significant is the fact Clare has consented to be my wife.'

The reaction took me aback. Squeals of excitement, cheering and shouting, followed by uncomfortable back-slapping. I did not realise that six grown people could make that much noise. I glimpsed Clare being hugged time and time again.

'Richard, this calls for champagne,' declared my mother. 'Can you get some from the cellar?'

After three or four bottles had been poured into glasses and consumed, and everyone was sprawled in deep armchairs and settees, my sister, Paula, asked casually. 'So. . .when and where did he propose to you, Clare?'

Clare was leaning against me. We looked at each other.

'I asked her when we met up in El Paso at the beginning of the year. Have you heard of the Mexican, Pancho Villa? He raided a town in New Mexico, across the America border. I was worried for her safety and went down there to rescue her. Only she didn't want rescuing, she wanted a story. She refused me.'

'Oh, so you must have proposed again. When did you do that?'

Before I could answer Clare said. 'He didn't. I proposed to him. He was away on a business trip, and expected back on a certain date. But he didn't arrive.'

She turned her face towards me, the semblance of a tear in her eye.

'I thought he was dead.'

The room went silent. No chinking of glasses, no hushed tones. In that moment only the tick of the clock could be heard.

'A week later he came to my parents' home where I was staying. I was a wreck. When he appeared I knew I could never go through life without him.'

My mother spoke with a catch in her voice.

'I'm delighted you are marrying him, Clare. He needs a woman like you.'

My sister and sister-in-law came over and pulled her into a fierce embrace.

It was an emotional moment. My father blew hard into a handkerchief. I found I was breathing deeply to avoid being overcome.

It was a remarkable few days.

On several occasions I borrowed my father's two-seater and took Clare on a tour of the South Downs'villages, along the coast towards Eastbourne and beyond, and to my old school, Lancing College.

She loved the countryside, and was overwhelmed by the college.

I had stopped the car on the approach road, and the mediaeval-style buildings looked magnificent set against the tree-lined slopes of the South Downs.

'You were a pupil here? Wow! What a fabulous place!'

We toured the buildings. She was entranced. The chapel took her breath away.

'How old is this?'

'To be exact. . .six years.'

'You're kidding me.'

Clare was gazing all around her.

'Well, it was started forty odd years ago and finished in 1911.'

She turned to me, a gleam in her eye.

'Let's get married here, in this chapel. And then we can send our children to the school.'

I grinned at her. 'Then they'll have to be all boys. It's not a mixed school.'

'Oh! Well never mind, we'll have all boys.'

It was an outstanding Christmas.

The whole family came together again on the day. The women prepared the meals, and we men did the clearing and washing–up. I noticed that Clare was frequently in a huddle with my mother and either my sister or sister-in-law.

It was when we were having afternoon tea a few days later that my father came into the room and whispered in Clare's ear. Whereupon, she smiled and kissed him on the cheek. Then she rose to her feet.

'Listen up everybody, I've an announcement to make. Daniel and I are getting married sooner than I thought. In fact, even he doesn't know how soon. But my father-in-law to be has called in a massive favour from the bursar at Lancing College, and we are getting married in the chapel on 7th April, in just three months time.'

This time the congratulations were a little more subdued. Clare came over, sat on my lap and kissed me.

'I hope it was a welcome surprise, darling.'

'So who is running the show now?'

I was in Charles Masterman's office at Wellington House. I was calling in on the Bureau before returning to the States.

'Do you remember that conversation we had when we were tied up and left for dead? I realised just how much more I should have given to my family, and that important ingredient was time. Well, I'm doing that now. I no longer work all the hours God gave us, I've handed the reins over to John Buchan.'

'I didn't think you saw eye-to-eye.'

Charles shrugged. 'I'm not sure we do, but that's the situation. By the way, next month we officially become The Department of Information. When you return you'll be still be responsible for propaganda in the United States, Portugal and Spain, while I shall be looking after books, pamphlets, photographs and war art.'

'Good for you, Charles. I think you have done them proud, and now your family will see much more of you. I'm glad.'

He came from his desk and we clasped each other in manly embrace before shaking hands.

We arrived back in New York on 3rd January, and immediately headed for Scarsdale.

'Something is up, I can tell by the look on your faces,' said Clare's mother without preamble.

'We. . .I, have set the place and date for the wedding,' Clare said, half apologetically. 'I hope it doesn't bother you, but it's in England, in the quaintest chapel you've ever seen. Please say you're not cross.'

''Of course not, Clare. I'm happy for you and so will your father be. But that doesn't leave a lot of time for the preparations. I'll get started on the lists straight away.'

'Mother is a great list maker, Daniel. She draws up lists of the lists she wants to make. Obviously, you'll want to liaise with Daniel's mother. So I wondered if you and daddy might like to go over to England in March, so you can sort things out?'

'That sounds a good idea.'

Just then Mr Johnson arrived home.

'I've just been told when and where the wedding will be, dear. It's in England, in a chapel.'

Clare's father took it all in his stride.

'No problem. Have you done your lists yet, Jean?'

'For goodness sake! It's not that bad. Anyway, Daniel's parents have invited us over before the event. So that we can compare lists.'

William Bayard Hale was in a scratchy mood.

'Where the Germans are concerned, there are still several items outstanding, and I've promised the editor of this new business magazine that's coming out, "Forbes: Devoted to Doers and Doings", that he can have the article on industry in the Ruhr Valley by next week. And another thing, someone called Martha Drucker from the embassy phoned. Could you go and see them before the weekend?'

'I'll go tomorrow. Zimmermann has probably sent back the article for the New York Herald. I hope there aren't too many alterations and he wants to see the corrected version. The newspaper should have it in their hands by the eighteenth of the month at the latest.'

'When's it due to appear?'

'Saturday 20th January.'

'Plenty of time. Still you'd better get down there and smooth the way.'

Martha came to reception to greet me.

'I hear you had a good trip before Christmas. How are things in Berlin? A little depressed still?'

'In truth, Martha, things aren't too good. People are going hungry, there isn't enough food in the shops, even if you can afford to buy it. This British blockade is beginning to tell.'

She led the way up the stairs, along the corridor to the ambassador's room.

She tapped lightly on the door and pushed it open.

'Herr Vonlathen, Ambassador.'

'Ulrich, how nice to see you. Martha, could you organise some coffee? Then come and join us.'

We moved to the comfortable chairs.

'So, Ulrich, I am pleased to say that there are very few changes to your article about the Foreign Secretary. In fact, he thinks it's a nicely balanced piece, and answers the points most non-Germans would want justified. Let me me get it.'

Von Bernstorff went to his desk and returned with a file. He peered at it for a moment, then said. 'Zimmermann thinks that perhaps it should also be published in *The Fatherland*. What do you think?'

'I shall have to adjust the tone and rhetoric to suit Viereck's particular style. But there's no reason why not.'

'Good, good. I'll let him know. Here's the amended text.'

I glanced quickly at it.

'Not too many changes. So we can keep to the publishing date of 20th January?'

'No reason why not.'

Martha and the coffee arrived and we discussed the items and events currently in the pipeline. Now and then I looked across at the ambassador. It was evident something was on his mind.

We had finished, Martha had left the room, and I was stowing away material in my carrying bag, when von Bernstorff said. 'Tell me, Ulrich, when you were with the Foreign Secretary did he mention submarine warfare?'

I fixed the second strap.

'Yes he did, Ambassador. He asked me, in the first session, what my thoughts were about unrestricted submarine warfare, and would it deter America from joining the conflict? I replied quite the opposite. It would most likely encourage America to go to war. I had the feeling he felt the same.'

'It's not just the Kaiser who now favours it, but Erich Ludendorff as well. Those are heavy odds. A pity they don't take notice of what we say.'

'Is there nothing one can do?'

'My friend, when you have Kaiser Wilhelm, von Ludendorff, and some of the top admirals advocating indiscriminate attacks on tankers and merchant ships of every nation except those of the Central Powers, it's an uphill battle. The Foreign Secretary has a tough fight on his hands. But there we are. So, when do we meet again?'

'Twelve days time, on 16th January.'

'I presume it's in my diary. Thank you, Ulrich, we shall see you then.'

CHAPTER SEVENTY FIVE

My first priority - after being proposed to, then being advised the ceremony was just weeks away – was to buy both an engagement ring and a wedding ring.

My knowledge of what might be desirable was limited. I had a fair idea of Clare's likes and dislikes in clothes, furniture, and décor, but little idea of what a girl with clearcut views on most things would enjoy on her finger the rest of her married life.

The person I could ask, whom I thought might be the nearest in temperament and style, was Dorothy Rothschild. Neither Clare nor I had got used to spending all our nights together. Each of us suffered the hang-up of a firm, Christian upbringing. So when a sense of propriety frequently prevailed, by unstated consent, I would take myself off to my room at the Algonquin Hotel.

It suited me that Thursday evening. I kissed Clare a chaste goodnight and took a cab to 44Th Street. A merry group of them were, predictably, clustered round the bar.

'Dan, my very good friend, we haven't seen you for a while. Where have you been? In a foggy, damp London?'

'No, Heywood, taking tea in Berlin with the German Foreign Secretary.'

'That's a good one. Do you hear that everyone? I like that. He's been having tea with the Germans in Berlin. What you should have said, Dan,' Heywwod added, 'is coffee with the Kaiser. A hint of alliteration makes it trip more easily off the tongue. Anyway, what are you having to drink? '

We were ushered into the Pergola Room where we dined and enjoyed some excellent wine. It was at the end of the meal, people were circulating, dropping into chairs to chat with one another, that I took the opportunity to sit next to Dorothy.

'Hello, Daniel. You know, one of these days I'm going to find out what you really do for The Times when you're over here. I'll bet it something secretive, and certainly not for your newspaper.'

I grinned. 'Perhaps one day soon I'll tell you the full story. But for now I need your urgent help. I got proposed to by a beautiful lady a few weeks ago, and the wedding is taking place in a couple of months time... '

Dorothy interrupted. 'Got her pregnant did you? What is it, a shotgun wedding?'

'No, though I wouldn't have minded if it were. The thing is, I want to buy an engagement ring and a wedding ring, and I'm not sure what she would like. Her name is Clare, she's a bit like you really, and that's why I'm asking a favour. Will you come shopping with me?'

She grinned, and leaning forward kissed me on the cheek.

'I'd be delighted. I wish Mr Parker were as quick off the mark. Sure, we love each other, but I get the feeling he's tight with his money. It's like ducking for apples – change one letter, and you've got the story of my life. So when do you want to go?'

'Tomorrow?'

I took my fiancée to dinner at Delmonico's.

Over coffee, I took her hand.

'Now I'm going to reverse the proposal. Will you, Clare Adelaide Johnson, take me as your husband? At this point, accept that I am on one knee and am hoping earnestly you'll do me that great honour .'

'Darling, of course I will. Anyway, it's a bit too late now to back out, even if I wanted to. Mother has filled the sitting room with lists. She couldn't possibly change them.'

I drew from my pocket a small square box.

As I moved it across the table in Clare's direction, I lifted the lid.

The moment of truth.

A sharp intake of breath told me nothing. But then she lifted the ring from its ornate box and stared at it intently.

'Oh my. . .oh my'

'What does that signify?'

She put me out of my uncertainty.

'This is the most gorgeous ring I have ever seen.'

She slipped it onto her finger, rose from the chair, and openly embraced and kissed me in the middle of the crowded restaurant.

Then she waved the third finger of her left hand for all to see.

Whereupon there was a round of applause and cheering.

My face was the colour of my wine.

CHAPTER SEVENTY SIX

On 16th January I caught the "early bird" train non-stop to Washington.

Wilhelm Bergmann, Martha's co-worker in the Communications Department, was in the reception area and escorted me up the stairs.

'You are here early, Herr Vonlathen. But that is good, after you have spoken with the ambassador, there are some thoughts Martha and I have had which we wish to discuss with you.'

'Delighted, Herr Bergmann. Although I should like to take a mid-afternoon train back to New York.'

'Oh, the ideas we have won't take long. We could discuss them over lunch if that suits you?'

'Let's do that.'

He knocked lightly on the door, which was wrenched open by Gottfried Schultz, the ambassador's aide-de-camp.

The ambassador was at his desk talking on the telephone.

'Thank you, Bergmann, you may go. Please enter, Herr Vonlathen.'

Gottfried quickly shut the door.

Strange. My impression was that we were going to discuss the propaganda programme and the results of our efforts these past weeks.

'Sit over here, please.'

The ADC drew me to a settee. I could not hear the muted conversation, but the ambassador was clearly agitated, frequently tapping a sheet of paper that lay on the desktop in front of him.

After a few minutes he slammed down the receiver, and sat motionless in deep thought.

Finally, and wearily, he rose from his seat and walked over to a chair opposite.

'We are done for, Ulrich. I was speaking with our security concerning a message I sent to Zimmermann. They have just decrypted his reply. It was read to me over the telephone. It said, "You will do as instructed, there is no other course of action."'

Von Bernstorff's head dropped forward. He stared unseeingly at the carpet.

Eventually, he muttered. 'I cannot tell you what I must do. But it could be the end of all we have been desperately trying to achieve. In the circumstances, I must ask you to leave. Someone, on my behalf, will be in touch with you and Herr Hale.'

Gottfried led me down the stairs, opened the main door and ushered me out. I walked along Massachusetts Avenue towards the Hahnemann Memorial and Scott Circle in a daze.

This is where I usually find a cab.

This time it was a private car.

A hooter sounded, and looking round saw Malcolm Mackenzie feverishly beckoning me through the windshield.

I got in.

'What the hell are you doing here? Do you realise you've probably broken my cover! That was a damned fool thing to do!'

'Not another word. Not until we're back at the embassy!'

Sir Cecil Spring-Rice came forward to greet me.

'Good, you found him.'

'I waited as close as I could to the embassy.'

I turned towards the intelligence officer.

'There had better be a good explanation for all this.'

'There is. . .oh, there is, my boy,' chuckled the ambassador. 'Show him, Malcolm.'

He drew two slips of paper from the folder he was carrying.

The first was a cable sent by the Commonwealth and Foreign Office and addressed to the ambassador.

For the most urgent attention of
His Excellency, Sir Cecil Spring-Rice,
British Ambassador to the United States

Dear Sir Cecil,

I am sending a copy of a decrypted message sent this day to the German Ambassador in Washington.

Naturally, we must be sure this is an official command. As a consequence, until its source is confirmed, I ask that you tell only those whom you believe should be aware of these changed circumstances.

My kind regards,

Jeremy Leigh-Singleton

16th January 1917

I set aside the covering note, and with a sense of foreboding, read the decoded message from Arthur Zimmermann, Foreign Secretary for Foreign Affairs.

```
                                TELEGRAM RECEIVED.
       ..CELED
       ..tor 1-8-58
   ....rton, State Dept.          FROM  2nd from London # 5747.
By Muck 9 Eckhoff Auttwurt
 Date Oct. 22/57

         "We intend to begin on the first of February
    unrestricted submarine warfare. We shall endeavor
    in spite of this to keep the United States of
    America neutral. In the event of this not succeed-
    ing, we make Mexico a proposal of alliance on the
    following basis: make war together, make peace
    together, generous financial support and an under-
    standing on our part that Mexico is to reconquer
    the lost territory in Texas, New Mexico, and
    Arizona. The settlement in detail is left to you.
    You will inform the President of the above most
    secretly as soon as the outbreak of war with the
    United States of America is certain and add the
    suggestion that he should, on his own initiative,
    invite
    ~~~~~ Japan to immediate adherence and at the same
    time mediate between Japan and ourselves. Please
    call the President's attention to the fact that
    the ruthless employment of our submarines now
    offers the prospect of compelling England in a
    few months to make peace." Signed, ZIMMERMANN.
```

'My God! He really has done it! He knows what the outcome of unrestricted submarine warfare will be, and he has used my suggestion to offset potential conflict by allying Germany to Mexico's cause! Well I'm damned!'

I turned swiftly to Mackenzie.

'How on earth did you get hold of this? Von Bernstorff was in a mighty flap only an hour ago. How could our people in London find out what they're up to? They couldn't possibly monitor every cable being sent across the Atlantic. Surely, German cables to the States go via the lines in neutral countries, like Sweden or Denmark. In fact, the American cable is linked to Copenhagen.'

Mackenzie glanced at the ambassador.

'You might as well tell him, Malcolm.'

'Ueli. . .Daniel, I mentioned we cut the German cable, which went via Tenerife. Messages were boosted on the island for the Atlantic crossing. Would you believe, though many may have forgotten, everything now goes through a relay station at Porthcurno, near Land's End.

'As I understand, Zimmermann's message was delivered to the US Embassy in Berlin, and then transmitted by diplomatic cable to Copenhagen for onward transmission over transatlantic line to Washington. . .after passing through the booster station in Cornwall.'

'Well, I'm damned!'

'Our naval intelligence people in Room 40 already had German cipher documents, including the diplomatic cipher 13040 and naval cipher 0075. The rest was a piece of cake. What I'm telling you is very hush-hush, of course. The Americans don't know we read their cables.'

'So, when do you tell them?'

'That's the problem,' interjected the ambassador. 'While disclosure of the cable would obviously swing U.S. public opinion against Germany, the people in Room 40 are reluctant to release it. Not only would it expose the fact that we can break German codes, but that Britain is eavesdropping on U.S. transmissions. We've got to come up with some plausible answers as to how we got hold of it, and that it's genuine, not a fake that we British are responsible for.'

'So what happens now?'

The question was directed to both of them.

'We wait,' replied Malcolm. 'There's not a lot we can do at the moment.'

'The cable went to von Bernstorff for onward transmission to Ambassador von Eckardt in Mexico City,' explained Spring-Rice. 'I wonder if von Bernstorff will send it or suppress it?'

'He'll send it,' I murmured.

'How can you be so sure?' queried Malcolm.

'I was in his office when his security people read over the reply to a cable he sent back to Zimmermann. He repeated it to me, though I didn't understand its significance at the time. He said the cable stated, "You will do as instructed, there is no other course of action".'

'Then what if Mexico agrees?' asked the ambassador. 'The result could be just what Germany wants – tieing up American forces when we need them in Europe.'

'It won't happen, Your Excellency,' I murmured.

'How do you know it won't?' asked Mackenzie fiercely.

'For the three very good reasons, explained to me when I was in El Paso last year. Just after that hothead, Pancho Villa, raided the town of Columbus, I spent some time in the border towns of New Mexico and Texas. I spoke at great length with James Black, the owner and editor of the El Paso Morning Times. Someone who has his finger on the political pulse of his Mexican neighbours.

'He told me the President of Mexico would never sanction a full-scale war against the United States because militarily the US is far stronger in its ability to wage war. Secondly, other foreign relations are at stake. If Mexico were to go to war to reclaim its lost territories, it would strain the accords with a number of South American countries. Economically, it would be a foolhardy move, and Brazil would certainly declare war on Germany.

'The other point to bear in mind is the so-called financial support being offered. This would be used to buy munitions, and where else could they get them from but the United States. It's the only sizeable arms manufacturer in the Americas. That's why I put the notion to Zimmermann. It could never possibly work.'

'I see,' muttered the ambassador. 'Well he's now got himself a tiger by the tail. This telegram, when it is made known to the Americans, will lead to all sorts of repercussions.'

'Well I hope the people in this mythical Room 40 come up with some answers soon, 'I remarked. 'German submarines are going to sink everything they see in their periscopes in a few weeks time.'

CHAPTER SEVENTY SEVEN

William's face was that of a condemned man.

I had intimated that, for some significant reason of which I was unaware, the German delegation in Washington had appeared occupied and fearful for their future. They had not wanted to discuss anything to do with propaganda. In fact, I was very quickly shown the door.

'They are not going to cancel our work for them, are they?' he asked anxiously. 'They can't do that, we've got a signed contract.'

Little use to anyone if the country is at war with our client, I thought.

'And then I read the telegram, Clare. I couldn't believe it. It's dynamite. When it becomes public the lid will come off.'

'So, why isn't it public now?'

'Good question. The answer is the cryptographers back home don't want to reveal they are reading German cables. At the moment the British are privy to many of their transmissions. If that became common knowledge,we'd lose even that slight advantage.'

'Hmm. . .how did William Hale react? I take it you gave him some indication his role as the mouthpiece for the Germans is likely to come to an abrupt end.'

'He looked as though his world was about to implode.'

'I don't like him very much, but you can't help feeling sorry for him.'

'You'd be surprised how much money our Mr Hale has made out of them. He has more than enough to keep him in brandy and cigars.'

I continued to go into Hale's office, but we did very little. It was as though the German Embassy had ceased to function. Whenever I phoned and asked for Martha, Wilhelm, or even the ambassador, I was advised they were not available. Whoever it was operating the switchboard added that when they were able they would be in contact. They never were.

With the lid about to blow, I withdrew the article scheduled to appear in th Herald. It was no longer necessary.

This situation lasted for a further two weeks.

On 3rd February 1917, the American grain ship *Housatonic* was sunk by a U-Boat. That same day, the United States severed diplomatic ties with Germany, and their embassy in Washington was closed.

Virtually every newspaper carried the story, including photographs of Count Johann Heinrich von Bernstorff and his staff leaving the building on Massachusetts Avenue.

'German ships are now prohibited from docking in this country, presumably, they'll take one that sails into Rotterdam,' commented Clare.

'That's if they can all get on a Holland/America liner. People are finding it difficult to get berths on passenger ships now ordinary steamships are potential targets for the U-Boats.'

I had spent the night in the Algonquin, and the following morning was getting ready to go into the office, when the telephone rang. It was William Hale.

'Are you coming in today, Ulrich?'

There was a tremor in his voice, I suspected he was now counting the cost of lost business. It was a daunting prospect for him.

'Yes, in about twenty minutes, William. I guess there's little more I can do, so I was going to gather up my personal belongings.'

'Good. . .good. . .I'll see you then.'

Again that odd quaver.

Although a cold February day, at least it was bright with only a faint breeze. I walked the three blocks down 5th Avenue, and just past the public library turned into the building housing William Hale's workplace. I judged he would not be making much use of the rented rooms on Broadway now.

Up five flights of stairs and in through the half-glazed main door.

'Ulrich, is that you? Can you come in here?' Hale called.

'Right,'

I removed my overcoat and scarf and hung them on the hat stand.

Then strolled across to William's room.

The door was open.

Two steps in and I could see Hale sitting woodenly at his desk, staring fixedly over my shoulder.

The door slammed shut.

As I turned, a female voice said. 'Good morning Ulrich. Or, should I call you Daniel?'

Martha Drucker had been hiding behind the door with Franz von Rintelen.

I glanced back at Hale, who had a puzzled look on his face.

'You didn't know his real name, Herr Hale? Let me enlighten you. It is Daniel Kindred. All the time he was working for you, you were harbouring a British spy.'

I looked at the couple, weighing them up. They would not represent too much of an obstacle to my escape.

Von Rintelen smiled. He had read my thoughts. Slowly he took a nine millimetre German service pistol from his coat pocket.

'A deterrent against foohardy moves, my friend.'

Martha walked over to me and slapped my face hard. Then she did the same to the other cheek. My head was rocked back from the force of the blows.

'At first I thought you were a traitor. I saw you get into a car with diplomatic plates, and checks showed it belonged to the British Embassy fleet. Franz here, found out what Heinrich Albert should have discovered long ago, that you were Daniel Kindred. The same Daniel Kindred that works for the War Propaganda Bureau in London.'

Martha Drucker was pacing up and down in front of me, gradually stoking the fires of rage.

'You used us, Kindred! You played us for gullible idiots! What I cannot reconcile is what you got out of it. Everything you wrote was good, better than fucking good, it did much for the cause. So, tell me, what was it that spurred you on? What did you tell your masters?'

She halted in front of me.

'Eh? What was it?'

'I was waiting for the odd tidbit of information. It never came.'

'Too right it didn't come. So why persist?'

'Ever hopeful, I guess.'

'Bullshit, Kindred.'

She kneed me hard on the thigh. It would have been more damaging if I had not turned slightly sideways. I didn't mention I was biding my time, and when the moment came, publish damning and irrefutable evidence the ambassador was masterminding lethal acts of sabotage. But it had gone one step higher. Instead I had ensnared their Secretary of Foreign Affairs.

'Do you know, Franz and I genuinely believed the telegram, supposedly sent by Minister Zimmermann, was a fake. And that you, Kindred, were behind it. Only someone who knew the system, the workings of the embassy, spent time in the ministry in Berlin, could have concocted such a thing.'

She started pacing the carpet again.

'We came to New York to kill you. Do you know that? We thought you were to blame for all that has happened. It was by the merest chance we went to bid farwell to Count von Bernstorff. As he was about to board, and we were shaking hands, he revealed that Zimmermann had confessed he sent the cable. That the Foreign Secretary was responsible for the disaster.'

Hale was sitting at his desk in a trance-like state.

'But we still came to exact justice, Mr Kindred,' Martha declared in English.

Von Rintelen stepped forward and aimed the pistol.

'If you shoot me, you'll also have to shoot Mr Hale.'

'True. So this is what I'm going to do.'

He suddenly raised the gun to head height, and swung it with all his force against my temple.

The pain was overwhelming. I was losing consciousness and falling to the ground, when Martha Drucker started kicking me.

CHAPTER SEVENTY EIGHT

Clare insisted on pushed me in a wheelchair to the entrance, even though I protested I was quite capable of walking.

Mr Johnson and Lyons were waiting by the car and they both helped me into the back seat. Clare placed a blanket around my legs, and took the seat beside me.

She held onto my hand while recounting the story told her by William Hale. Once my attackers had gone and he had come out of his stupor, Hale had called an ambulance, which rushed me up 5th Avenue to the Mount Sinai Hospital. The amount of blood spilled had masked the extent of my injuries, which after being cleaned away, were fortunately minor.

When I regained consciousness, my head was in bandages, and so too were my ribs. I had a splitting headache and severe pains in the chest. But I was alive.

Before leaving Hale had telephoned Clare at the Herald for me. An hour later she arrived at the same time as her father and Lyons to take me back to her parents' home in Scarsdale.

I was helped up the stairs to a bedroom. Lying on the bed, I received my instructions.

'Stay there, don't move, until I come to collect you for dinner in a couple of hours!'

Then she came over, gently kissed me, and said in a low, tearful voice.

'Oh, Daniel, I was so worried when told you were in hospital.'

'It could have been worse, darling. If Martha Drucker and this fellow von Rintelen had thought for a moment I had anything to do with Zimmermann's telegram, they would have shot me.'

A few days later I had unbandaged my head and ribs. It felt more comfortable without the bindings. I still moved carefully, but I was as anxious as Clare to return to the city.

It was thought a train journey might be uncomfortable, and so Lyons drove both of us to Clare's apartment.

The telephone was ringing when she opened the door. Clare moved swiftly to answer it.

'Hello. . .Oh, hello, Malcolm. . . Yes he's here, he is coming to the phone. Bear with him, it will take a moment.'

When I reached her side, she whispered. 'Malcolm MacKenzie.'

'Malcolm, good morning.'

'I've been ringing around for the past couple of days trying to locate you. I was told by a contact in the Bureau of Investigation that von Rintelen was in

New York, trying to dig up information about one Ulrich Vonlathen.

'He got chapter and verse, Malcolm.'

'What do you mean?'

He uncovered the fact there is no Vonlathen, and paid me a visit. I wound up in hospital.'

'Oh, I'm sorry, laddie,' he murmured in his soft Scottish burr. 'Are you all right now?'

'Let's say I'm on the mend.'

'Well, you've got an excellent wee nurse to look after you. I suppose when you are able, you'll be returning to England. Before you do, can you pay us a visit in Washington?'

'Of course, Malcolm. I'll let you know when we are coming. I'll bring my wee nurse with me.'

I did not mention the reason why suspicion had fallen on me. Martha Drucker had seen him pick me up in an embassy car that fateful day in January.

I went back to Hale's office to find a "To Rent" notice on the door. When I tried to telephone his home, the line had been disconnected.

Further enquiries came to nothing. William Bayard Hale had vanished.

Malcolm Mackenzie came to greet us.

He noticed the deep cut on the side of my head.

'Is that a memorial to von Rintelen's visit?'

'The more obvious one, yes. Though, by the time we get married it should have faded away.'

He shook my hand and kissed Clare's cheek.

'Let me lead the way.'

We mounted the familiar winding staircase and headed towards the ambassador's room. Though this time he threw open both sides of the double doors.

'Surprise!' 'Surprise!' was shouted by everyone I had got to know in Washington over recent months.

The ambassador come forward. 'Daniel, good to see you. And this must be the highly-regarded Clare I have heard so much about.'

He pressed glasses of champagne into our hands.

All the embassy staff, as well as Samuel Insull and Sergei Mitzkof, were there. I introduced them all to my fiancée as we circulated and chatted to people who had become firm friends.

Insull had come all the way from Chicago. Mitzkov had come a mere five hundred yards.

When Samuel clapped eyes on Clare, he said. 'I know you, Miss Johnson. You interviewed me some months ago for an item in the New York Herald.'

'That's right, Mr Insull. I didn't think you would remember.'

263

'I rarely forget a face, and never one as pretty as yours.'

He drew her to one side.

Mitzkov nudged me.

'Sam has always had an eye for the ladies.'

He glanced at my head. 'The fruits of war?'

'You could say that, Sergei.'

'By the way, Daniel, or should I call you Ueli? My colleague, Alexei Pivovar sends his regards. It was unfortunate that the person, whose Zurich address you gave Alexei, was given other accommodation two days before a visit was made. Apparently, his wife, the activist Nadya Krupskaya, had been complaining ceaselessly about their living conditions until the authorities succumbed, and they were moved. To where we have yet to discover.'

'From what I can gather, Sergei, things are hotting up back home.'

'You are right, my friend, time is running out for us.'

Clare took my arm, and the conversation turned to other topics.

CHAPTER SEVENTY NINE

Clare and I, together with her parents, sailed from Pier Forty at the North River Terminal in Mid-March.

My underlying concern - neither of us had properly discussed where we would set up home. The subject had come up on a number of occasions, yet there had never been meaningful debate. It was still left hanging in the air.

I had little doubt I could get a job in the United States; but the closer we got to England's shores, the more the ties of home encircled me.

Before its onward journey to Holland the *Rotterdam IV* liner called in at Southampton. My father was there to welcome us with the Humber. We drove to the house in Worthing, and my mother came out to greet us as we pulled into the drive.

I have always been struck by the way women size up one another. Whereas men deliberate and a friendship gradually unfolds, women either take to a person, or dismiss them on sight.

Fortunately, in this instance, they were bosom friends in seconds. My mother and Clare's mother had an immediate rapport, and carried on a seamless conversation as they walked away towards the garden. We were forgotten.

I unloaded our cases and took them into the house.

My father offered Mr Johnson something to drink, and they sat companionably in the drawing room watching their wives wander around the flower beds, shrubberies and among the trees that lined the boundary.

When they came back to the house, Clare's mother said. 'George, Sofia knows so much about gardening, and she has some wonderful plants and flowers, I asked her to come over to Scarsdale and advise us.'

My father grinned, and poured another drink for Mr Johnson.

'All I do, George, is dig holes and light bonfires. We do have a fellow who comes two or three times a week to help in the garden. Like me, he takes orders from Sofia.'

'John,' said my mother. 'I've asked Julia to stay with us, rather than a hotel in the town. There's plenty of room, and it will give us more time to finalise the wedding.'

Clare and I exchanged glances.

We were up against two formidable women. From henceforth the details would be removed from our hands and taken firmly into those of our two mothers.

George and John, my father grew to like and understand each other. They played golf together, went off to inspect the shops, and visit local pubs. They went in the two-seater my father had held onto, so there was no room for any other passengers. Not that our mothers complained. They were too busy fine tuning the arrangements.

The invitations had gone out to friends and relatives on both sides of the Atlantic long ago. Although a few close family members from the States were coming to the event, others were invited to attend a ceremony in Scarsdale in a couple of months time.

I was sitting in the sun room one morning when Clare's father dropped into a seat beside me.

After a brief word about the weather, was the sun going to hold, he said forthrightly. 'We haven't really talked about this. So tell me, Daniel, how are you two going to provide for each other? When you have children, how are you going to support a family?'

'You make a good point, Mr Johnson. Clare and I haven't even decided where we are going to live. Here, or in America.'

He nodded. 'I'm aware of that. Clare told me. She's been hesitant to bring up the subject with you. She thinks you want to work in America, and probably as a journalist. Is there much money in the newspaper business?'

'I can't think there's a lot, frankly Mr Johnson.'

'Well, you could always come and work for my company.'

'Making munitions? I don't think so, sir.'

'I guess I can understand that. Clare wouldn't work for the company either. So. . .are you set on working in America?'

'Frankly, anywhere Clare wants to live, as long as I'm by her side, I'll be happy.'

'You wouldn't miss working in America?'

I wondered where he got that notion. Given the choice, it would always be England. But only if Clare were there.

'I don't think so.'

'Right. Let's talk about this later, Daniel.'

He wandered off leaving me with my thoughts.

I went for a solitary walk along the beach. I enjoy people's company, but there are moments when I have to be on my own. I was heading back towards the house when my father's car stopped on the roadside.

He got out and joined me. We stared at the sea lapping the shore, the smudges of smoke on the distant horizon, the mournful cry of gulls as they wheeled overhead.

'I don't think I could ever leave this place, you know. Your brother feels the same. But you've always had itchy feet, haven't you?'

'I don't know dad. Once upon a time I couldn't wait to see over the next hill, round the next bend. But in recent years I have had one or two experiences that have altered my perception of life.'

What, meeting Clare?'

'That as well. No I'm talking about life-threatening moments when you long suddenly for what you've passed up. What you realise were your happiest times. Like this for instance. Walking along a stretch of sand with a gentle breeze in your face. There are other places in the world that are similar, but nothing truly like an English beach, even in winter.'

He didn't say anything for a while.

'Clare has intimated that you want to go and work in the United States. I'm sure you'd do just fine over there.'

'I don't think when the war is over I want to work for a big newspaper anymore. I was talking with Clare's father yesterday, and I said I wanted to stay in journalism. I still do, but not at someone else's bidding. Do you know I've come to realise what I enjoyed best. Working on the West Sussex Gazette. Doing all the jobs that were necessary, from teaboy to chief reporter. Those years were really something.'

He got back in the car and drove home.

I walked back wondering why such a random thought had popped into my mind.

CHAPTER EIGHTY

I went back to work at the Bureau in London – or as it was now called, The Department of Information. Clare spent half her time in Worthing and the other in London, staying with me in the flat in Ebury Street.

April approached and I asked for leave from John Buchan, who headed up the department with the rank of lieutenant-colonel.

'How long for?'

'Two weeks at the most. Several days to get organised for the wedding, and ten days afterwards.We'll have a brief honeymoon, and I'll be back on 16TH April.'

'Well, if you must. We haven't seen a lot of you these past months, so I expect you to buckle down to some hard work.'

'You haven't seen me because I've been working in America and Berlin. If you're not satisfied with my work, then fire me.'

I think my nervousness was beginning to show.

When I went back to Worthing that Friday evening I sat on the train contemplating the chance remark I had made to my father. It had come to me out of the blue. Or had it? Perhaps, it had been there, hidden, waiting for the moment to invade my thoughts.

On Sunday morning, in addition to the national newspapers I scanned the pages of the West Sussex Gazette. One particular notice intrigued me. It was tucked away on the back pages, among the classified advertisements.

The following Monday Clare and I travelled to London. She was meeting friends, and doing yet more shopping for the wedding. I did much of what was expected of me under Buchan's critical gaze, and kissed goodbye to Clare when she boarded the Wednesaday evening train from Victoria.

Thee next day I worked hard to finish a piece for Alexander Woollcott at the New York Times, and left the building at nine o'clock.

In the early hours of Friday morning I caught the first train to Brighton, had breakfast in the station buffet and strolled down to the Central Auction Rooms in Robert Street. I bought a catalogue and took a position to one side of the main room where I could see most of the likely bidders.

I still found it hard to state with any clear reasoning what had prompted me to miss a day's work - no doubt inciting Mr Buchan's ire – to attend an auction. The notion I latched onto was what the cost might be to buy all the requisite parts of a business to which, and I now freely admitted to myself, I was irresistibly drawn.

The auction room filled. Soon, most of the seats were occupied and people began to fill the spaces along each side of the hall. The items had obviously attracted a great deal of interest, and it was not long before my view of the rostrum narrowed with the press of numbers.

As a clock struck eleven, the auctioneer climbed the small dais and surveyed the crowd.

'Good morning, everybody, my name is Edwin Tully, and I am in charge of today's proceedings. The sale comprises the machinery, furniture, and all the many items used in publishing the newspaper, The Surrey Mirror.

'Sadly, this journal has now ceased trading, and it is my job today to dispose of the company's remaining effects. All the goods listed in the catalogue were available for viewing at the original premises in Reigate. However, the owner, having recently moved to Brighton, wishes the sale to take place in his new place of residence. Therefore, I shall commence the auction by offering item one, a Platen Printing Press with a rate of four thousand impression an hour. Who'll start me at. . .'

A voice boomed out close to the front on the left hand side of the hall.

'I don't wish to spoil the day's enjoyment, Mr Tully, but I came here to buy a newspaper printing company. I don't want to spend my time bidding for each piece that comes under the hammer. If you are willing, my business partner and I are prepared to buy the whole catalogueof items at their reserve prices, plus ten per cent. I can't say fairer than that.'

I could not believe my ears.

The gentleman who had just bid for the lot was my future father-in-law. His American accent had bounced off the walls, and even though I could not see him, his was a very individual voice.

There was a great deal of murmuring while the auctioneer leaned down from the dais to take instructions. Presumably from the owner.

A minute passed. . .then two.

Abruptly, the auctioneer rose to his feet, banged the gavel once, and declared. 'The entire catalogue is sold to that gentleman!'

With obvious dissatisfaction, the many potential buyers and those expecting an interesting spectacle, gradually drifted out the auction room. As it cleared, I was able to make my way to a desk beside the dais.

Mr Johnson, my father, and Clare were completely unaware of my presence, until I tapped her on the shoulder.

She was still like a startled rabbit caught in a car's headlamps.

'Daniel,' she murmured. 'What are you doing here?'

'More to the point what are you doing here with these two?

Both fathers turned slowly round.

We sat in the dining room of The Old Ship Hotel having lunch.

Clare was still clutching at my hand, uncertain, still wondering if our parents had gone too far. My initial reaction had been that such decisions were to be made jointly, not unilaterally.

'However, when asked to explain why I had attended the auction, try as I might to say casually, I was purely interested in seeing the prices the various items might fetch, Clare remarked it was the same thing. I had not conferred about attending the auction either.

'Perhaps it was my fault, Daniel,' murmured my father. 'I just happened to mention to George how you yearned for the time you spent at the Gazette. He said, in a conversation you had with each other, that you would go anywhere Clare wanted to be. And she wants to be here, in Sussex.

'George and I just thought that if you were going to live together down here, then why not run a newspaper. We bought it jointly as a surprise wedding present. It was called the Surrey Mirror. Why not rename it The Sussex Mirror, and set it up in Worthing? Peter is buying yet another store, and the warehouse we're using will soon be too small. You could rent that.'

I grinned at the three of them.

'Amazing. I would like to remain here, in this part of England. I always have.'

Clare kissed my cheek. 'I know you are only saying that to please me darling. I understand perfectly.'

Who was I to disabuse her.

CHAPTER EIGHTY ONE

The wedding was a triumph for two determined, list-making females.

Everyone, from the officiating bishop to the fellow employed in the car park performed under the sternest gazes.

It was like a well-rehearsed play in the West End. Everyone knew their part and dared not walk into the furniture.

The whole thing was orchestrated from the front pews, in the college grounds where the photographs were taken, and from the reception top table with a series of pursed lips and fierce nods.

When the moment came for my speech, the cue was a raised eyebrow.

However, I was enjoying myself; and judging by the radiant look on her face, so was Clare. What added to that feeling was, on the previous day, 6th April 1917, the America president had declared war on Germany. He did so with the full backing of the Senate and The House of Representatives. I had fulfilled my task.

I sat down to applause, and leaning sideways kissed the bride on her cheek. We had come a long way together. From the muddy fields of Ypres to the realisation that, in the not too distant future, she and I would be producing our own newspaper.

As I looked around at the many guests, the sounds of laughter, the buzz of conversation, all slowly diminished. For a moment I was immersed in the deepest introspection.

It was not really a lie told to Arthur Zimmermann. Events, though unlikely, could have played out as I suggested to him. It sounded plausible. It sounded inviting. It came back to a lesson I had learned from a journalist called George Creel. Creel had been heavily involved in President Wilson's re-election campaign. At the time we were talking about the mechanics of persuasion, and the merits of propaganda.

I always remember his comment.

"Propaganda is most compelling when the person, or people, you are trying to influence, believe that a particular course of action is their own idea."

On 29th March, 1917, Zimmermann had given a public speech in which he admitted the telegram was genuine. He alone had conceived the idea.

In that moment I realised I had had enough of half-truths, innuendo and blatant misrepresentation. Soon, in a corner of Sussex, I would be able to paint life afresh. Not in honeyed words, but in prose that was meaningful, which expressed the truth, in all its shades.

No longer would I need to lie for this land.

Author's Notes

The idea for the novel came from a signature I found in a book bought at a hospital fête. Its title, "A Short History Of The Great War", was written by A.F. Pollard. Inside on the fly leaf was a signature: "C. Masterman".

Who was Masterman? With no great expectations I typed the name into the computer, to discover that Charles Masterman set up the War Propaganda Bureau during the First World War.

I researched the Bureau, and gradually thoughts of a novel about its activities took shape.

Charles Masterman used journalists skilfully to write much of the Bureau's material. he also relied upon celebrated authors of the day to pen leaflets, pamphlets and telling short stories.

The Great War has been labelled the first modern propaganda war, or "the first press agents' war." This was particularly true in the United States, which, as a major industrial power, was a rich prize for propagandists on both sides of the conflict. Whichever alliance secured the country as an ally, would gain serious advantage.

In the early years, President Woodrow Wilson was adamant the United States would stay clear of the fray. With a growing ethnic bias towards Eastern Europe, though naturalised, there were many of the population who held dear to their roots. Thus, neutrality appeared the best option. It ensured the status quo, that an internecine struggle within America itself would not flare up.

However, Germany was always on the back foot. Most often it was defending the Triple Entente's charges of crimes against persons - both civilian and military. The sinking of the Lusitania, the execution of Nurse Cavell rocked the beliefs of all American citizens. These incidents, coupled with bungled, subversive acts in America - the Black Tom Island Explosion was one of many – began colouring people's views.

The German military leadership gave their propagandists much to defend. The final straw was the Zimmermann telegram advocating unrestricted submarine warfare, and financial support for Mexico if the country were to wage war to reclaim lost territories.

One weapon that Germany held up its sleeve was undermining the resistance on the Eastern Front. Achieving this meant it could boost troop numbers in the west. Their ace in the hole was the radical, Vladimir Ilych Lenin. He had been tucked away in Switzerland awaiting the moment he could foment unrest in Russia, and bring about the collapse of the country's military machine.

On 9th April 1917, three days after the Declaration of War by America,

Vladimir Lenin and Nadya Krupskaya, his wife, together with a number of fellow exiles, boarded a train that took them from Bern to Gottmadingen, just short of the official German crossing at Singen.

From there they travelled in a sealed carriage on a special train accompanied by two German army officers and ten million dollars worth of gold. A gift provided by the German government. Its primary use - to incite revolution.

The train travelled through Germany, and a ferry took them to Sweden. From Stockholm they boarded another train to Petrograd, Russia's capital. Formerly, St. Petersburg, it was renamed in 1914 to rid the city of its germanic-sounding name.

The rest we know is history.

Most of the characters in the novel were real, and all the events took place in the time frame, 1914 – 1918. Moreover, they perform their roles in the story as they did during the war.

Also, at this time, the casual get-togethers of journalists, poets, theatre critics and stage producers, developed into the more formalised Algonquin Round Table. Dorothy Rothschild married Edwin Parker in 1917, and became the *grande dame* of the set which had their own dining room at the hotel.

William Bayard Hale was undone more by thoughts of a healthy bank balance than lack of patriotism. The government's decision to take arms against the Central Powers cast him into the spotlight; and he attracted growing resentment for his services to the German cause. Eventually, Hale was ostracised by his colleagues, acquaintances and friends, and was forced to spend his days abroad.

Room 40, also known as 40 O.B. (Old Building), was a section in the Admiralty most identified with cryptoanalysis work during the First World War. The good fortune for the British was to get hold of the SKM code books from the captured German ship, *Magdeburg.* These were supplemented later by the VB cipher books taken from another wreck. This essential information gave British codebreakers access to enemy orders being relayed to their navy.

The other critical factor was the transatlantic cable system. From whatever European country cable messages were dispatched, they passed through the Cornish relay unit which boosted their onward transmission. Another portal available to Room 40.

The Zimmermann telegram was written in Code 0075, a fairly simple substitution process that the British had already partially broken. It did not take long to fill in the gaps; and four months later the naïve German Secretary of State for Foreign Affairs fell upon his sword and resigned.

It was strongly rumoured that the German Embassy in Washington D.C. was a hive of subversives, who attempted all manner of terrorist acts to counter the export of munitions to the Entente. Of those whose success rate was seemingly higher than his associates, Franz von Rintelen, a naval intelligence officer, managed to evade capture for some months after America joined the conflict.

However, he was eventually brought to justice by following orders in a telegram, ostensibly sent by the German Admiralty. It remains unconfirmed that it originated from Room 40. He was told to report back to Berlin. As a consequence, he sailed on 3rd August 1917, on the neutral Holland-America liner, *Noordam*.

However, once in territorial water when it docked briefly at Southampton, von Rintelen was taken into custody. At first, he protested his innocence so convincingly, both the Swiss Minister in London and Scotland Yard were persuaded of his innocence. That is, until the head of Room 40, Admiral W. R. "Blinker" Hall, stoutly declared him to be a German spy and saboteur. Von Rintelen confessed, and was imprisoned in Britain for twenty-one months, before being interned in Atlanta, Georgia for three more years.

Patrick Gooch